The Hollow

The Hollow

Jessica Verday

SIMON PULSE

NEW YORK   LONDON   TORONTO   SYDNEY

᭦

SIMON PULSE
An imprint of Simon & Schuster Children's Publishing Division
1230 Avenue of the Americas, New York, NY 10020
First Simon Pulse hardcover edition September 2009
Copyright © 2009 by Jessica Miller
All rights reserved, including the right of reproduction in whole or in part in any form.
SIMON PULSE and colophon are registered trademarks of Simon & Schuster, Inc.
For information about special discounts for bulk purchases,
please contact Simon & Schuster Special Sales at 1-866-506-1949
or business@simonandschuster.com.
The Simon & Schuster Speakers Bureau can bring authors to your live event. For more information or to book an event contact the Simon & Schuster Speakers Bureau at 1-866-248-3049 or visit our website at www.simonspeakers.com.
Designed by Paul Weil
The text of this book was set in Caslon.
Manufactured in the United States of America
2 4 6 8 10 9 7 5 3 1
Library of Congress Cataloging-in-Publication Data
Verday, Jessica.
The Hollow / Jessica Verday. — 1st Simon Pulse hardcover ed.
p. cm.
Summary: High school junior Abbey struggles with the loss of her best friend, Kristen, who vanished on a legendary bridge, but her grief is eased by Caspian, an attractive and mysterious stranger she meets in the Sleepy Hollow cemetery.
ISBN 978-1-4169-7893-0 (hardcover)
[1. Grief—Fiction. 2. Ghosts—Fiction. 3. Supernatural—Fiction. 4. High schools—Fiction. 5. Schools—Fiction. 6. Irving, Washington, 1783–1859. Legend of Sleepy Hollow—Fiction. 7. Sleepy Hollow (N.Y.)—Fiction.] I. Title.
PZ7.V5828Hol 2009
[Fic]—dc22
2008042817
ISBN 978-1-4169-8541-9 (eBook)

To Lee—Here's to many more Feliz Navidads, Tainted Loves, and Cocaine Blues, babe. From the moment I looked down and saw those black boots, I've never looked back. And if I had to do it all over again, I would. Thank you for being my brainstorming partner, idea generator, beta reader, critique partner, personal cheerleader, awesome assistant, and best friend.

PREFACE

They said she killed herself. Everyone was saying it.

What started out as a rumor, quietly whispered among small gatherings of polite people, quickly grew into something that was openly discussed in large gatherings of impolite people. I was so sick of hearing them talk about it.

They questioned me. Over and over again, trying to find out if I knew what had happened. But my answers didn't change. Yet it never failed—someone else would ask, as if one day my reply would suddenly be different.

I didn't know, but I should have . . . and I've been haunted ever since.

Chapter One

LAST WORDS

From the listless repose of the place, and the peculiar character of its inhabitants . . . this sequestered glen has long been known by the name of Sleepy Hollow.
—"The Legend of Sleepy Hollow" by Washington Irving

It was funny. At a time like this, wasn't I supposed to be thinking serious thoughts of eternity, and the afterlife, and all that? As I glanced around me at the small groups of people huddled around the room, it seemed like that's what *they* were all thinking about. Each somber face reflected their pious thoughts, but all *I* could think about was the hair-dyeing incident.

It was funny.

I guess I should have been thinking about all the things I wanted to say. All the things I couldn't say. And all the things I'd never get the chance to say. But I didn't. It wasn't like any of this was *really* happening anyway. She's only been missing since June 9. Sixty-eight days. That's not long enough for her to be . . . dead.

You can't have a viewing of the body if there is no body. And someone can't really be gone from your life forever if there is no viewing. It all works itself out. This was only an act. Just motions we were going through.

I stared at the closed casket a bit longer, and then shuffled off to the side as someone came up right behind me. The message was silent, but it was still there. *You've had your turn. Now move on.*

I moved on.

Closer and closer to the wall I pressed myself, trying to blend in. A moldy, stale smell wafted around me, and I recognized the cloying odor of flowers past their prime. Like the room itself had absorbed years of their stench. Putting one hand behind my back, I reached out to touch the yellowed lily-of-the-valley-patterned wallpaper. It was rough and bumpy under my fingertip, and covered every square inch of a room that looked like it hadn't been updated since 1973. It was awful.

The room started filling up, and I shuffled to the left. Here, the pea-soup-colored shag carpet was completely worn through in several spots. Faded pictures of shepherds guarding their sheep decorated each wall, but they were all slightly water stained, and hung with gaudy gold wire. I was amazed at the overall tackiness.

Why on *earth* would someone pick a room like this to gather a large group of people into? It had to be the ugliest room I had ever seen. A bingo hall would have been more appropriate.

But every time I thought about slipping out of the room and away from all these people, Mom would catch my eye and give me a look. That sorry-honey-but-it-won't-be-much-longer-I-promise look. Which meant that it would, indeed, be much longer.

Especially since Mom and Dad seemed more than happy to spend a full twenty minutes talking to every person who entered the room. So I stared at the ugly wallpaper . . . and that nasty carpet . . . and those gaudy pictures. . . .

I had to get out. I gave Mom the signal, or at least what I hoped passed for some sort of signal, that I was escaping for a walk. She didn't respond, but since she was halfway across the room, it wasn't like she could do anything to stop me.

The nearest doorway took me to a hallway that ended in a large foyer at the front of the funeral home. The foyer was old and dusty, and decorated with hideous fake flowers and fake wood paneling that covered the bottom half of each wall. Someone had apparently thought that it would be a good idea to continue the flower theme out here and had pasted a green ivy border, which was just as awful as the lily of the valley wallpaper, directly above the paneling.

It was *not* a good look.

Then I saw a bench. The coat rack next to it was full, but the bench was empty. And all mine.

Suddenly I didn't mind that ugly wood paneling, or the even uglier ivy border. It looked quiet over there on that bench, and I sat down to contemplate how nice it was that someone had been thoughtful enough to put it here just for me.

But my thoughts were interrupted when three people came out of the viewing room and started walking toward me. Since the bench and the coat rack were positioned right next to the outside doors, I desperately hoped that they were leaving. I wasn't in the mood to force a smile and make small talk with people I didn't want to be around.

They were all dressed in black, their "viewing finest," I'm sure. Miss Horvack, a substitute teacher, was on the right, and I noticed Mrs. Kelley, the town historian, on the left. I didn't recognize the woman in the middle. Sleepy Hollow might be a small town, but that doesn't mean I know *everyone* who lives here.

Their loud whispers disturbed the air, and I tried very hard not to listen to what they were saying, but I quickly gave up when something interesting caught my attention. I edged closer down the bench to listen in.

"—trying to throw eggs at cars from the bathroom windows. Eleven and nine they were. Eleven and nine!" Miss Horvack's gravelly voice broke through as she spoke louder and louder.

"Mmm-hmm," someone murmured.

"Thank goodness I was there to stop them. After ten minutes I just opened up the door and hollered in that they had used up the bathroom time limit and that they needed to make their way out of there. Good thing I did too," she huffed, her voice getting more excited. "Wouldn't you know it; they came scrambling out with the eggs sticking out of their pockets. I was flabbergasted. Flabbergasted, I tell you!"

Mrs. Kelley spoke up now. "The parents just don't care anymore. That's the real shame of it. Kids these days need to learn some manners."

"Children of all ages have no respect. No respect for their parents and no respect for their elders. None at all. That's what happened with that Kristen girl, I bet." I listened closer as the woman I didn't recognize joined in. "She had no respect for her family. I heard she was doing all sorts of drugs, just like her brother."

The outraged gasps of the two other ladies merged with my quiet snort of disbelief. Kristen would never do drugs. This woman obviously had her facts *very* wrong.

"It probably *was* drug related," Miss Horvack agreed. "These kids today are all doing the drugs. Everything's about the drugs."

Mrs. Kelley voiced her strong agreement about "the drugs."

"And what does it all boil down to?" The third woman paused, and then took over the conversation again. "No respect, just like I said. They have no respect for anything. Her poor parents."

Miss Horvack and Mrs. Kelley quickly agreed, each stating several more reasons for the obvious downfall of society's youth.

I couldn't believe what I was hearing. Who *were* these people to spread rumors about Kristen like this? Everyone in Sleepy Hollow knew that Kristen's family had never gotten over the loss of their only son to a drug overdose eight years ago. If there was one thing that Kristen would *not* have gotten involved in, it was "the drugs."

Curling my hands into fists, I felt each fingernail dig sharply into my palms, and I tried to control my anger. But I couldn't take it anymore. These women were *wrong*, and they needed to know it. I jumped up to interrupt them, but then I saw Mom peeking out of the doorway from the viewing room. She saw me too, and raised one eyebrow. "There you are, Abigail."

I knew that look. And that eyebrow.

I stared Mrs. Kelley and Miss Horvack directly in the eye as I stomped past them, to prove that I'd heard what they'd said, and to let them know that it had pissed me off royally. They pretended not to notice.

When I re-entered the lily room, I went to stand up front with Dad. He put his arm around my shoulder, and it was nice to feel the support. The conversation that I had overheard ran through my head, playing out over and over again. I wanted to confront those women and set the record straight. To tell them what I thought of people who would talk about Kristen like that, and how inappropriate it was. Ultimately, though, I just wanted to let them know how very, very wrong they were.

Instead I just stood there and stared blankly at the casket.

Kristen's school picture from last year had been placed next to it, and I concentrated very hard on that picture, trying to tune out everyone else around me. Her mom had asked me if she could use a picture of us wearing big goofy hats and big goofy grins. But I hadn't been able to answer her. I just didn't know what to say when she'd asked, so I guess she'd taken that as a no.

Looking at that plain school picture, I suddenly wished that I had said yes. There should be a picture of us up there, even if this *was* just an act. I should have been able to give Kristen that much, at least. Everyone here deserved to see the *real* Kristen, not just some stiff, posed side of her.

The people around me started to bow their heads and close their eyes, and I realized that Reverend Prescott was closing the evening with a prayer. It didn't take very long, and when he was finished, I followed Mom and Dad across the room for our final rounds.

Kristen's parents were very emotional, so we rushed through a quick good-bye with them. I was actually a little relieved, because the last thing I wanted to do was blurt out something terribly inappropriate, like how I was going to miss the lasagna her mom used to make for me.

Reverend Prescott was next, along with whomever else we happened to pass on our way out. It ended up taking us twenty-five minutes to make it out of that room, and I had never been so happy to see the hallway.

The trio was still there, only now they had attracted a slightly larger crowd. They didn't even bother to stop talking while we squeezed by them, and their words drifted over me.

"Poor thing."

"So sad, having to bury an empty casket."

"They'll probably never find the body."

"If she was depressed, then it was obviously a suicide."

I turned and gave Mrs. Kelley and Miss Horvack another look as I passed, only this time I added a glare to it. Pushing my way through the heavy exit door, I stepped outside with Mom and Dad and tried to let the cool night air calm my raging temper. The doors echoed loudly as they closed solidly behind us.

The gossipers never even noticed.

I lay awake in bed that night, staring at the ceiling, until the first few fingers of dawn were stretching into my room. I tried to force myself to get some sleep, but it didn't last for very long, and neither did the sunshine. It turned cloudy and overcast by midmorning.

The funeral was supposed to be at four thirty, but after lunch I couldn't handle being indoors anymore so I grabbed a light raincoat and told Mom I was going for a walk. She was in the middle of discussing press releases and funeral write-ups with Dad, so she just waved a hand in my general direction. I was out the door before she had a chance to ask where I was headed, grateful that she wasn't going to make me sit down and discuss my "feelings" with her, or something.

Not really knowing where to go, I started walking slowly up the hill that led away from the house. A chilly breeze blew by, and I stopped for a minute to shrug on the yellow coat, stuffing a hand deep inside each pocket.

I watched as the ground moved beneath me with every step I took, and it wasn't long before I found myself at the only cemetery in the entire town of Sleepy Hollow. It stretched for miles, and Kristen and I had come here practically every day. It was *our* cemetery.

Slipping through the large iron gates that guarded the main entrance, my feet automatically found the well-worn pathways that we had walked so often. I took my time wandering past the grassy hills, weaving around trees and bushes, and stopped every now and then to look around. There was always something interesting to see each time I came here.

Whether it was a freshly tended grave site, or a toy positioned on top of a tombstone, it always varied. But every once in a while something strange and unusual would appear. Something that made you wonder why that particular item had been left, and what the story behind it was.

Today it was a chair.

An old-fashioned chair made out of wrought iron with a slatted wooden seat rested right next to a freshly sown grave. The chair was waiting, as if to seat someone so that they could talk to whoever had been so recently placed inside the earth. It was both disturbing and beautiful at the same time.

Debating briefly, I took a quick look around to make sure that I was still alone. I didn't want to bother any grieving family members that might be nearby. Then I strayed off the path and walked up to the chair, being careful to step around the loose soil.

"Can I sit here for a moment?" I asked the fresh grave. "I promise to move if the rightful owner of this chair shows up."

A limb from a nearby cherry tree swayed up and down, so I took that as a yes. Carefully brushing off the seat, I sat down.

Vast grounds surrounded me on all sides, punctuated with small bursts of color. Several large trees had started to change shades, and each one was a bright, bold contrast to the muted softer colors of the cherry trees scattered among them. The graveyard would be absolutely stunning when fall actually arrived and all of the leaves turned.

"This is a beautiful spot," I said quietly, speaking to the dirt beside me. "I know you haven't been here very long, but I think you'll like it. A giant maple tree sits behind us, and the shade reaches all the way down to the bottom of the hill. Some of the leaves are starting to change now, and it's breathtaking." I had spent so much time visiting this cemetery that it didn't feel strange at all to be talking to a grave.

"I have a friend who's going to be buried here later today," I continued on. "Not right here in this part, but down near the Old Dutch Church section. I hope they have a tree down there for her. She would like a tree. Wherever she is. . . ."

The wind picked up, and I fell silent. It howled around me, making an eerie moaning sound. More sad than scary, it was like the wind was mourning for my loss. And even though this whole thing was just one big fake moment in time, I definitely felt a loss. In some ways, I think that knowing she really *was* dead would almost be easier to understand. In some ways, that would be easier to deal with.

Something shiny suddenly caught my eye. I leaned forward to get a better look.

It was a small bulldozer moving steadily along one of the paths down below. After a couple of minutes chugging, it rolled to a stop by an erected awning. Several people were standing around, and two of them were holding shovels. In the back of my mind somewhere, I knew what they were going to do. I also knew that I probably shouldn't watch them do it.

But I couldn't turn away.

In rapt attention I watched as they began the slow process of digging a grave. The bulldozer raised and lowered its arm several times, each turn coming back up with a pile of gleaming dark dirt. Then the workers pushed their shovels down into the hole. I assumed they were packing in the sides and removing any stray dirt.

Over and over this happened, and still I watched them. I should have felt something. Anger . . . disgust . . . sadness. But I didn't feel any of those things. Instead I was hypnotized.

When it had finished its chore, the bulldozer chugged back up along the path. The men threw their shovels to the ground and moved on to set up a wide metal piping system around the

 15

edges of the empty hole. Once that was complete, the workers moved the awning and several white chairs into place beside the grave, and then loaded the shovels and themselves into a truck and drove away.

It was amazing to see the complete conversion of an empty piece of land to an available burial site. And a little hard to understand how easily it could all be done.

The wind moaned again, and several raindrops fell onto my head. I had completely lost track of time, and I probably needed to get back home to get dressed for the service. Out of the corner of my eye I saw a dark shadow move, but when I faced the direction that I thought it had gone, there was nothing there.

Turning back to the grave next to me, I raised my voice slightly to be heard over the pitch of the wind. "Thanks for the company." I stood up from the chair and gave a farewell salute before carefully stepping onto the path. I glanced one more time over my shoulder, but the shadow was gone.

That was when the sky opened up.

Huge raindrops fell hard, each one splattering on impact. I tucked my hands back inside my raincoat so that at least one part of me would stay dry. Even if it was only a small part.

The pathway along the graveyard turned slick with water and mud, and it splashed along the bottom of my jeans and shoes as I walked. Unfortunately, I was still pretty far from where I'd entered, and even farther from my house. I had nothing but a long, wet, miserable walk home to look forward to.

Chapter Two

THE FUNERAL

There are peculiar quavers still to be heard in that church . . . which are said to be legitimately descended from the nose of Ichabod Crane.

—"The Legend of Sleepy Hollow"

I barely had enough time to dry off and change into a black dress before I had to leave to go back to the cemetery.

The funeral service was held inside the Old Dutch Church, and every single wooden pew was filled. The remaining space was standing room only. The whole town had shown up.

While the sharp tapping of rain on the stained-glass windows beat like a drum in the background, the reverend droned steadily on and on. The way he spoke of Kristen made her sound less like the best friend I had known so well and more like a stranger whom I'd never met. It was odd and disconcerting.

A faint burning smell clung to the room, a familiar scent introduced by the large boiler furnace being turned on in response to the gray, chilly weather outside. I shifted uncomfortably on the hard pew, and found my eyes wandering over to the large painting that was hanging above the reverend's head. It was a depiction of the scene made famous by Washington Irving, showing a frightened Ichabod Crane looking over one shoulder while a dark and menacing headless rider rose up behind him.

I had asked Reverend Prescott once why the painting was hung in the church, and he took great pleasure in telling me his rather lengthy view on the virtues of keeping our eyes ahead to the Lord when the devil rides up behind to offer temptation. By the time he had finished, I was sorry I had ever asked that question.

Suddenly the reverend stopped talking and everyone around me started getting up. It was time for the final procession.

People filed out of the church one by one, huddling under umbrellas and trying to stay dry beneath the safety of the over-hanging eaves for as long as possible. But it was a useless act, and they were soon driven to accept wet defeat.

I followed as my parents joined the solemn crowd moving slowly toward the grave site. Although most of them tried to walk carefully along the treacherous pathways, each step they took yielded a heel or toe that quickly got stuck in the mud. It would be a soggy and bedraggled gathering arriving at Kristen's grave today.

Skirting around the main path, I walked apart from the others. I took a grassier lane that wasn't quite as muddy, but the rain streamed down my face since I hadn't brought an umbrella with me. It felt like déjà vu from earlier. Once again, I was caught out in the rain.

When I reached the grave site, I was lucky to find a small patch of unoccupied awning, and I stood under it, silently waiting. The pallbearers carried the casket over to the burial ground and then loaded it onto the metal lowering frame. Mom tried to catch my eye, while people walked up to the grave to give their final respects and say a few words.

She kept making a small jerking motion with her head, urging me to go up and say something, but I just shook my head back at her. I couldn't get up there and face these people. Not now, not like this. This was all fake, but I couldn't very well stand up there and say that.

More people went up. Many reached out to touch the casket, and one boy laid a single flower on top. It surprised me when he stepped in front of the crowd and stated simply that he would miss the chance to get to know Kristen better. His brown curly hair was a mess, and his matching brown eyes were red-rimmed and watery. He looked like he was ready to start bawling at any second. I stared at him as he shuffled along. I knew he went to school with us, and his name was Brad, or Brett, but other than that, I didn't know anything about him.

So why did it sound like he really *would* miss Kristen?

I recognized a couple of other people from school too, *cheerleaders*, who went on and on about what fond memories they had of Kristen. How she'd been such a good person . . . they would miss her *so* much . . . blah, blah, blah. Such useless words. They didn't *really* know Kristen. For them it was all about how much attention *they* would receive.

And then it was over.

With one final flower tossed, tear shed, and good-bye said, the service ended and it was time to leave. An empty casket placed into the cold, hard ground was supposed to symbolize my best friend's life.

It felt vastly inappropriate.

~ ~ ~

The crowd left quickly, braving the mud puddles to venture back to their cars. They had done their part. Now it was time to move on.

I stayed where I was until the last of them had gone. Mom and Dad were walking with Reverend Prescott back to the church, and hopefully they understood that I wanted some time to myself. To sort things out.

Taking a step closer, I concentrated on the casket. Everything had been turned upside down these last couple of months. I didn't know which way was up anymore, and all of a sudden I didn't have anyone to ask. It made my head hurt, and I felt like I would never be able to untangle all my thoughts.

But most of all it made my heart hurt. Inside my chest a giant vise grip had squeezed hold and was slowly crushing everything that worked in there. One day I would have nothing but a black hole inside of me.

A short burst of light abruptly caught me in the eye, and I looked up, temporarily pulled away from my misery.

The sun was peeking out from under a cloud, valiantly trying to make its way through the rain. A shaft of light hit the side of the casket and changed it from an ordinary, dull shade into a starburst. Every shiny fleck of paint was momentarily illuminated, showing the true color of the casket to be a vibrant blood red, and I smiled. *Red was our favorite color.*

Then the sun disappeared.

I reached out and touched the casket lid. It was cold. So cold that I immediately snatched my hand away. It almost felt like it had burned me.

I just stood there. I couldn't bring myself to say anything . . . not out loud, at least. But a thousand thoughts raged inside my head, while a thousand feelings raged inside my heart.

The weather mimicked my emotions. A fierce wind rattled by, howling in outrage. The edges of the plastic awning flapped angrily against the aluminum poles holding it up and made a horrible ringing sound. Even the rain pounded harder, lashing out its bitterness.

And that was when I felt someone watching me.

I looked out over the rows of tombstones, memorial plates, mausoleums, and crypts. Past trees and bushes. There, standing next to a huge mausoleum built into the side of a hill, was a boy.

He was dressed in a black suit, with a white shirt and a black tie, and his hair was so pale that it almost looked white. His hands were clasped in front of him, and I saw he didn't have a raincoat or an umbrella. The rain had completely soaked him through. I couldn't see what color his eyes were, he was too far away for that, but he looked right at me, and his gaze held mine.

Who is he? Does he know Kristen? Or is he here for someone else?

The wind continued to howl around me, and the rain pounded on the scant shelter overhead. Whoever he was, he was crazy to be standing out there. Before I could even think it through, I found myself taking a couple of steps out from underneath the awning.

I should go talk to him, I thought. *Find out if he's here for Kristen. Find out why he's staring at me. Tell him he's nuts for getting soaked out here.*

But the wind drove me back. The fierceness of it was so sudden that I staggered backward and had to grasp on to the nearest awning pole for support. The rain didn't relent either, and it streamed down my face, leaving the same type of tracks that tears would have.

Head held high, grasping on to that pole for all I was worth, I stared back at the stranger. Daring him to come closer. Demanding that he not look at me with pity in his eyes.

The wind ruffled the edges of his clothing and blew his hair into his face, but he stood where he was. Then he bowed his head slightly.

Something told me that he meant it as a sign of respect, so I nodded back. Then I turned to take one last look at the casket behind me. Meeting him would have to wait. Today I had different things to think about.

The rain started letting up a little as I walked farther away from the grave site. I spotted my parents talking to Reverend Prescott on the stone steps of the church, and I definitely didn't want to get caught up in any of that. I moved quickly to the car as I took my cell phone out of my jacket pocket and dialed Mom's number.

She reached into her purse and glanced at her phone before taking a small step away from the reverend. "Abbey?" she answered distractedly.

"I'm just going to walk home from here, okay, Mom?" Even at a distance I could tell she didn't like that idea. A look was forming on her face.

"I think you should come with us to the Maxwells', Abbey. They went through a lot of trouble to arrange a gathering, and since Kristen was your friend, it's only appropriate that you be there."

"Mom," I sighed. "I'm really not in the mood to be around a whole bunch of people right now. I just want to be left alone."

"You should come, Abigail." The use of my proper name was *not* a good sign. Not at all. "You can have all the time you need to yourself afterward."

"But, Mom—"

"It's being catered, Abigail!" The sudden click of her phone being shut made my mind up for me. My mother *lived* for catered events, and obviously that meant I had to as well.

"Fine, whatever, Mom," I grumbled to myself as I trudged over to the church steps. I waited impatiently for them to hurry up and finish their conversation with the reverend. They took their time, of course.

After an agonizing ten minutes of small talk, they finally said their good-byes to the reverend and we left the cemetery.

It was a short drive over to the Maxwells' house, but there were already cars lined up around the block when we got there. Dad dropped Mom and me off at the front door, while he went to go find a parking spot. Mom only took three steps inside the house before she was stopped by someone. I heard her laughter drifting behind me as I kept moving past the hordes of milling people and headed straight for the kitchen.

I found Kristen's mom in there. She had her back turned, and both arms were buried in a sink full of detergent suds. As I stepped closer, I could see there were only two mugs and a couple of plates in the sink. Hardly enough to worry about washing when you had a house full of guests.

Then I saw her shoulders shaking. I didn't want to interrupt her grief, so I quietly made my way back out to the hallway.

A beverage table had been set up nearby, and I grabbed a clean mug to pour some hot water into. Dropping in an herbal tea bag, I waited for a minute, and then stirred in a little milk and sugar. The warmth of the mug felt comforting in my grip as I picked it up and sipped slowly, blocking out everything and everyone around me.

But my moment of peace was shattered when someone abruptly bumped into my shoulder, causing me to grasp the cup tightly.

"S-sorry," the person stuttered.

I turned with a scowl on my face and saw curly brown hair in front of me.

"That's okay," I said. "Don't worry about it, Brad."

He picked up a mug too, and then struggled with opening a tea bag. "Actually, it's, uh, Ben. I'm in your class at school."

Right. "Okay then, see you around." I was *so* not in the mood for conversation right now. All I wanted was to be alone.

I contemplated going up to Kristen's room but decided against it. It didn't really feel right, for some reason, being in her room without her there. So I chose the basement instead. There was a faint, musty odor, which I breathed in as soon as I started walking down the stairs. Upstairs had felt like a stranger's house with all the extra people around, but down here, it was just like I remembered. I was relieved to step into familiar surroundings once again.

A battered desk lamp sitting on an old coffee table had been left on, and it cast a weak yellow glow, leaving most of the room cloaked in darkness. This room had always felt so safe and warm to me in the past that the dark didn't bother me at all. I walked over to an old rocking chair sitting partially in the shadows, and I settled in, balancing my cup of tea. Leaning my head back, I closed my eyes as I slowly rocked back and forth and thought about old memories.

"It looks terrible, Abbey! I'm never coming out again."

Her voice drifted out to me from the crack at the bottom of the bathroom door. I thought I heard a sniffle, and then came the unmistakable sound of nose blowing.

"Come on, Kristen. Open the door," I pleaded. "Let me see what it looks like. It can't be that bad. Just open up."

"Oh, it's bad. Very, very bad. I should probably shave my head. Do you know how much wigs cost? Or maybe I could get full extensions put in."

"You are not going to shave your head, Kristen," I replied loudly. "And do you know how expensive extensions are? If it's really that terrible, we'll just dye it another color. That's an easy fix."

"What about hats?" she countered. "Would it look weird if I wore a different hat every day?"

Even though she couldn't see it, I shook my head at her and was just about to use the if-you-won't-come-out-then-I'm-coming-in tactic when the lock clicked and the door slowly opened inward.

I took three steps inside and tried very hard not to let the shock show on my face. "What did you . . . do?"

"I don't know!" she wailed, holding up a badly colored piece of hair. "I was just so tired of having a flaming red bush on top of my head! I thought black dye would help tone it down a little. I know it looks terrible."

She was close to tears again.

"Hey, Kris, it's not that bad. Let me see it for a minute." Stepping close, I inspected her still-wet hair. The black dye had covered up all the red in certain spots, but in others it had completely missed.

"Why don't you dry it, and then we'll see if it looks any different," I suggested.

"Okay." She sighed sadly and grabbed the blow-dryer from a cabinet under the sink.

"Why didn't you wait for me?" I yelled over the blower noise when she turned it on high. "I would have helped you."

"I don't know!" she yelled back. "I guess I wanted it to be a surprise. Let you see it when it was all done, you know? Well, done right, of course."

"You're crazy." I made a circular motion with my hand by my head and grinned. She laughed, and I sat on the edge of the tub while I waited for her to finish. Ten minutes later her hair was completely dry, and looking more streaked than spotted.

I stood up. "Now let's take a look at this again."

She grabbed a brush and ran it through her hair, parting it to the side like she always wore it.

"See?" I said, rearranging, fluffing, and then patting down a couple of stray pieces. "If you wear it this way, it looks good. Like you totally meant to do it."

"Really?" She turned from side to side in front of the mirror. "Do you really *think* it looks okay? You would tell me if it didn't, right?"

"Of course I'd tell you, Kristen, that's what friends are for. Honestly, though, it looks good this way. Almost like you dyed it black and added a couple of red highlights."

She took another glance at the mirror. "I don't know, Abbey." Her eyes were worried.

"It looks good." I reassured her. "Really."

Then inspiration hit.

"Hey, what if I put red highlights in my hair? We'll tell everyone that we had our hair done together. What do you think?"

Her eyes lit up. "That's a great idea. Thanks, Abbey. We can go get the stuff now, and then I'll do your hair after dinner."

"Sounds like a plan." I grabbed a small washcloth from the towel rack next to her and started wiping off stray hair dye splatters on the sink. "Mom and Dad have a meeting at the Horseman's Haunt tonight anyway, so it'll be an empty house for me."

Her smile was a mile wide. "I'll go tell Mom that you're staying for dinner." She started to walk out of the bathroom but stopped short and turned back with a sheepish look on her face. "Would you put the blow-dryer away for me?"

I nodded, and smiled to myself as I heard her yell down to her mom that she wanted lasagna and garlic bread for dinner.

My favorite meal.

Yeah, that's what friends are for.

It was a soft sound that made my eyes fly open and my head snap forward. I scanned the room, certain that I'd heard footsteps.

I almost missed him.

Even though he was sitting a couple feet away from me, his black suit blended in completely with the shadows. Only his hair gave him away. The white-blond color glowed in the dark room. It was the boy from the cemetery.

I felt him looking at me, and I swear my heart started beating faster. I didn't know what to do, what to say . . . but I had to ask him *something*. I spoke quietly, trying to calm my racing pulse. "Did you know Kristen?"

I waited for his answer. The space of two heartbeats went by . . . and then another. My question hung in the room between us.

There was no reply.

I raised my voice slightly, in case he hadn't heard me. "So, um, how did you know Kristen Maxwell?" I shifted in my chair, and the squeak it made echoed through the room. I took a small sip of tea to distract myself.

"Sorry, did you say something to me?" He spoke so softly that at first I wasn't sure if I had imagined his response.

I was taken aback by the question. *Did he really not hear me at all?*

"I wanted to know if you knew Kristen." I grew bolder with each word. "I saw you at the funeral today and was just wondering how you knew her."

"You were wondering how I knew Kristen," he repeated, still speaking softly, almost to himself. Then his voice grew louder, and he leaned toward me. "I've seen her . . . around."

But *I'd* never met him before. Was he some type of secret admirer or something? I tried to examine him closer, but he was still hidden by the shadows. His voice sounded older. Maybe he had been a friend of her brother's?

"Did you know Thomas?"

"Thomas?" He sounded puzzled. "No, I don't know any Thomas."

"Kristen's brother?" I prompted, waiting for his reply.

"No, I didn't know she had a brother." His voice was louder

now. Like he was getting closer, but I hadn't seen him move at all. *That* made me slightly nervous. Here I was alone with a stranger who had come to Kristen's house and down to her basement, yet he didn't really seem to know her, or her family. It was all very strange.

I covered up my nervousness with a small laugh. "Oh, okay. Well, I'm going to go upstairs to see if they need any help cleaning up." I abandoned my tea at the foot of the rocking chair and stood up, heading for the stairs. I made it up four steps before I realized that the stranger had followed me. I turned.

He stood at the bottom of the staircase, obscured in darkness. "You don't have to be afraid of me, Abbey. I'm actually here because of you."

"How do you know my name?" I gripped at the stair railing. My question came out in a squeak. "Who are you? What do you mean you're here because of me?"

"Don't worry, Abbey. I'm a friend." He leaned forward, placing himself in a pocket of light so that I could see him clearly.

Shock hit me first. Followed by a feeling of . . . something else. He was *gorgeous*. A total hottie.

I almost laughed at myself for thinking that at a time like this.

His hair was the first thing I noticed, up close this time. The pale color was unusual but it had a sharp streak of jet-black that angled across his forehead. His eyebrows were dark too, and he had a very straight nose and full lips. But his eyes were what really struck me. They were such a clear, shocking green that I felt a shiver dance along my spine as he gazed at me. His eyes were stunning. And they looked kind.

"You're Kristen's best friend, right?" His voice held a soothing, calm quality now, and he looked up at me with such interest that I felt some of my nervousness vanish. "Tell me about her."

I looked away for a moment, flattered that he was paying me any attention, and then angry at myself that I even cared. My eyes fell on the corner of the room where Kristen and I had spent so much time together, and I started talking about it to distract myself from my turbulent emotions.

"Do you see that corner over there, by the bookcase?" I leaned over the railing to point, and he nodded. "When we were little, Kristen and I used to come down here on rainy days. Her mom would take a couple of sheets and string them up around the bookcase to make a tent. Then we'd grab some books and a flashlight and go sit inside, and read stories to each other. Her

35

mom always brought us cucumber and peanut butter sandwiches with all the crusts cut off while we were in there."

I laughed at the memory. "We went through a real cucumber and peanut butter phase. I have no idea why."

Then I found myself confessing even more. "It was almost like Kristen had this secret place in her basement that we could go to whenever it rained. I used to call it my magic rain castle, and I thought it was the coolest thing ever." My cheeks reddened from the story and how much I had revealed. "I don't know why I told you that. It's pretty silly, huh?"

He had an amused look on his face. "I don't think it's silly. Every kid should have a place like that to play in. I wish I would have had one of those. It sounds like fun."

"Thanks," I said, smiling back at him. "That was a good memory. I needed that." The silence in the stairwell grew, and I became aware of how loud and fast my breathing sounded. I concentrated on regulating it, trying to breathe more normally.

He spoke quietly, and I had to lean forward to catch his words. "If you ever decide to build your magic rain castle again, Abbey, let me know. I'll have to stop by for a visit."

My breath caught on those words, and my heart skipped a

beat at the implication behind them. I didn't know what to say, so I didn't say anything at all. My mind raced frantically, thinking about all the questions I had for him.

The jarring ring of my cell phone interrupted us. I glanced down at the screen and grimaced when I saw who it was. "Sorry, but I have to go take this. It's my mom."

I walked up to the top of the stairs and answered the phone. "Uh, hi, what do you want—I mean, what's up, Mom?" I glanced over my shoulder. I could still see his bright green eyes. He was staring intently at me, so my response to my mother was a bit distracted. "Yeah, um . . . okay."

Her voice echoed loudly through the phone, and I looked away. "I'm almost ready too. I was down in the basement. . . . Yes, I know. Of course I'll tell the Maxwells good-bye. I'll see you in five minutes."

I looked back over my shoulder and mouthed the word "Sorry" as I stepped out the basement door. He nodded and disappeared into the shadows below while I headed to the kitchen to find Kristen's mom.

She was still there, now drying dishes, and I hesitantly crept closer. She appeared calmer, and glanced over her shoulder when she heard me coming. "Abbey, hi." Her voice was soft, and her eyes were slightly reddened, but her smile was encouraging.

Reaching out for a hug, I remembered belatedly that I had left my cup downstairs in the basement. She didn't say anything while she hugged me back, but I didn't need to hear the words. I knew what she was feeling.

"Do you want me to stay and help you clean up?" I asked.

She shook her head. "No, don't worry about it, honey. I'll take care of everything. It'll give me something to do." Her voice broke slightly on the last sentence, but I pretended not to notice.

"You'll call us if you need anything, right? Anything at all."

"Sure, sweetie." She tried to give me a brave smile, but it didn't work. "Tell your parents good-bye for me."

"Okay," I replied. "I will. Take care of yourself." She nodded, and I squeezed her hand once before I left the kitchen.

Mom was waiting for me out in the hallway.

"I'll be right back, and then I'm ready to go," I told her. At a nod of agreement, I turned around and headed back toward the basement. I had one more good-bye to say.

But when I got down there, he was gone.

"Hello?" I called out, walking over to the rocking chair to pick up my cup. I felt stupid for not asking him what his name was. I flipped on a nearby switch, and the room was instantly flooded with eight bulbs of sixty-watt fluorescent lighting.

It only confirmed what I already knew. He wasn't there. I wasn't going to get the chance to say good-bye, or find out his name. I didn't even know if I'd ever see him again.

Flipping the light switch one more time on my way back out, I paused for a moment in the dark. "Thank you," I whispered over my shoulder to the empty room.

Chapter Three

NIGHTMARES AND HALLUCINATIONS

They are given to all kinds of marvellous beliefs; are subject to trances and visions; and frequently see strange sights, and hear music and voices in the air.

—"The Legend of Sleepy Hollow"

I didn't get very much sleep over the next several days. School was starting in two weeks, but that was the least of my worries. Ever since the day of the funeral I'd been having nightmares. I couldn't remember any of them, but they were always there, at the corner of my mind and on the very edge of my consciousness.

Then it started getting worse.

I'd wake up suddenly, my body drenched in sweat, while my eyes frantically searched the darkened corners of my room. I usually saw the shape of a person. Like someone was in the room with me.

If I concentrated, and strained my eyes hard enough, the shape would disappear. I knew it was nothing more than shadows on the wall, but each night, for those brief couple of seconds, my heart pounded in sheer terror.

More than once I found myself calling out Kristen's name. Asking, pleading, with her to be there. Knowing in my head that she wasn't, but hoping in my heart that somehow she was. I thought I was going crazy.

After the fourth night in a row of nightmares and hallucinations, I think I really did start to go a little crazy. I struggled to stay up at night, sleeping only when morning came. I didn't feel rested at all, but at least it kept the nightmares at bay.

Keeping myself occupied all night, though, was a whole different set of problems.

I tried reading first. I found a book that I hadn't started yet, and it was interesting enough to hold my attention through the first night. But that afternoon I was too tired to go get any new books, and that was a problem when midnight came around again.

Flipping through some old magazines killed time the second night, but it didn't work quite as well, and I kept nodding off. Morning took a long time to arrive when my body was demanding that I sleep.

It was the next night that I ended up calling Kristen.

After checking my e-mail, including every old account I'd ever set up, I had only managed to kill about an hour. There were several new shopping websites to browse, but they didn't really hold my attention either. What I was really missing was Kristen's buddy icon signaling that she was online too. We almost always signed on within minutes of each other. It was strange, not seeing her screen name pop up automatically.

With a heavy sigh I hit the sign off button and watched as the screen shut down in front of me.

Spinning slowly back and forth on my chair, I scanned the top of my desk. Several piles of paper were stacked in one corner, and a couple of CDs were propped up by a small jewelry box. My cell phone was plugged into an adapter on the printer stand, blinking a red light at me, signaling that it was fully charged. I picked up the phone and automatically hit the number one to speed-dial Kristen. It wasn't until the voice mail message started playing that I realized what an idiot I was.

The sound of her voice was so normal, and familiar, so . . . real. I had called her cell phone almost every day before she'd disappeared, and never given it a second thought. Short messages, long messages, funny messages, even angry messages . . . I had left them all. Such a small, insignificant thing to do, but now I realized how important each one of those messages had really been.

A loud beep on the other end got my attention. I didn't know if I should say anything. Holding my breath for a second, I paused, and then spoke in a rush of jumbled words and thoughts. "Hi, Kristen, it's me. I don't know . . . I don't know what to say, or even why I'm doing this. It's not like . . . This is . . . stupid. . . . I'm sorry."

I hung up the phone, feeling frustrated and angry at myself for calling. It wasn't like she was going to call me back. Wherever she was, her cell phone wasn't with her. She'd left it at home with a dead battery the night she disappeared.

Grabbing a blank piece of paper from my desk, I started doodling. Small pictures, bizarre designs, crazy symbols . . . anything that came to mind. I scribbled these things over and over again, until I had to grab a fresh sheet. Then I started writing down my thoughts. About everything and about nothing.

By dawn I had filled eight sheets of paper with random words. It was an exhausting process, but now that it was morning, I fell into a deep sleep.

~ ~ ~

I slept through breakfast again, and really felt like skipping lunch, too, but Mom gave me a strange look as I stumbled into the kitchen.

"Are you feeling okay, Abbey?" she asked, putting a hand to my forehead.

"Yeah, I'm okay," I admitted, sitting down at the table. "I've had a hard time getting to sleep lately."

Carrying over two bottles of water, she sat down next to me and slid one over. I stared at my hands resting on the tabletop, not paying attention to anything else. *I really should go back to bed. I'm exhausted.*

"Do you think you're not sleeping well because of the funeral?" Mom's sudden question startled me.

"That probably has something to do with it." The conversation from the funeral home sprang to mind, and I heard those women talking about Kristen again. "Or it could have something to do with the fact that some people in this town don't have any common decency, or good manners."

She frowned. "What do you mean?"

"I mean that this town is so freaking small, all it takes is one person to start an untrue rumor, and before you know it, it's become the absolute truth." Frustration filled my voice. "You *know* what I'm talking about, Mom, and you know it's not right. I heard some people saying that Kristen either killed herself or was into drugs. They shouldn't be spreading rumors like that. It's not fair to her family, and it's not fair to her."

Patting my arm, she put on her sympathetic tone. "I know how you feel, Abbey. But there's not much we can do. People talk. It will die down eventually."

"You *don't* understand, and you *don't* know how I feel," I snapped. "Or you would do something to stop the ones who talk about Kristen behind her back. Use your position on the town council. Do something about *them*."

"I can't control what the people in town think, Abigail. You know that." She stood up and walked over to the dishwasher. "Just ignore them; it will all blow over soon."

I couldn't believe that she was telling me to just ignore them. I was supposed to stand by and let people talk about my friend? No way.

"Well, *I* can do something about it, Mom." I felt anger taking over now. I was furious. "I can stand up for my best friend. Even if you're not willing to."

Stalking out of the kitchen, I left the water behind, and pounded my way upstairs to my bedroom. I slammed the door shut to let her know that I meant what I'd said. She would probably yell at me later for doing that, but I didn't care.

I only meant to close my eyes for a minute or two when I lay down on my bed, but I must have fallen asleep, because the next thing I knew, Mom was leaning over me and calling my name.

Struggling to a sitting position, I yawned loudly and rubbed my eyes. "Tired . . . just taking a nap. . . . Why did you wake me up?" I mumbled.

"How would you like to go to that new herb store with me?" she said.

"The one up by the cabin?" I asked groggily. "But it's an hour away. Do you really want to go there?"

"Sure, why not?" She shrugged. "I have a couple of papers to drop off at Mayor Archer's house along the way, but other than that, I'm up for it if you are."

I was too tired to argue about whether or not this was a trip for me, or Mayor Archer, so I let that one go. At least she was trying.

"Okay." I forced a smile. "Let's go."

We headed down to the car, and I grabbed some grapes to eat on my way out. Skipping breakfast and lunch so often was finally catching up with me. It didn't take me long to finish them off, and I popped the last one into my mouth before climbing into the passenger side and buckling my seat belt.

Mom got into the car too and put the key in the ignition but didn't turn it on. I tensed, waiting to see if a lecture on how I should control my anger was coming my way.

"Abbey . . . ," she started. Clearing her throat once, she tried again. "If you ever need to talk about Kristen . . . or anything else, well . . . I wanted to let you know that you can always come to me. If I can't help, we can find you a professional to talk to." Her blue eyes were full of concern, showing the tiny wrinkles around them.

"Thanks, Mom." I smiled weakly. "I'll let you know if I need something." I must have looked as close to the edge as I felt, if Mom was talking about me seeing a professional.

My response seemed to satisfy her, and she smiled back at me, looking relieved that her part was over. She started up the car, and we headed toward the Archer residence. Ten minutes later we arrived at their front door and Mom promised she'd be out in five minutes. As her door slammed shut, I grabbed a pen and small notebook from the glove box, knowing that I'd be in for a wait. Mom's "five minutes" were usually more like twenty.

I started making a list of all the things that I hoped to find at this new store, and was completely lost in thought when Mom's door opened again. "Sorry that took so long," she said, climbing into her seat and adjusting the rearview mirror. "I had to go over a couple of things with the mayor."

"Not a problem," I responded, still occupied with my list. I added tester vials and bergamot oil to the page. I was running low on both of those. We got back on the main road again, and I put the notebook down as soon as I felt myself begin to get sleepy. I knew I wasn't going to last long.

The sound of a door opening startled me, and I woke up with a jerk. Looking over at Mom, I smiled sheepishly. "Sorry I fell asleep. I guess I was still pretty tired."

"Don't worry about it," she said. "We're here."

I craned my neck to take everything in as I climbed out of the car.

A large green metal sign with a glossy finish greeted us, proclaiming the name of the store to be A Thyme and Reason, and I fell in love with it instantly.

The shop itself looked like it had once lived a past life as a grand old turn-of-the-century house, complete with gingerbread trim, floor-to-ceiling windows, and a gabled roof. The outside was painted in several varying shades of green and magenta that complemented each other wonderfully, and I knew that this was the type of store I wanted to own one day.

As we stepped inside, I saw that it was even better than I had hoped for.

Not only did the store have plenty of herbs available, but there were jar and bottle sections, vials and sample kits, and packaging supplies of every kind. They also carried almost every type of perfume oil known to mankind.

I was in heaven. I could have happily spent weeks here. They had almost everything on my list.

After browsing for about forty-five minutes, I figured that I was probably treading close to Mom's patience limit, so I started narrowing down my choices. I picked up several sample-size tester vials, a couple of large amber bottles, and a new set of glass droppers.

Mom finally caught up with me in front of the oil section.

"What's the bergamot oil for?" she asked, watching me choose which size bottle I wanted.

"You know that autumn harvest perfume I made for you last year? I want to make that one again this year, but with a more earthy tone to it." I debated between ginger and cranberry essential oil as I answered her.

"I absolutely *loved* that perfume!" she said. "Can you make me one for winter this year too? Something with a Christmasy smell to it?"

"Sure," I replied, adding peppermint, vanilla, and balsam oils to my collection. Then I grabbed small bottles of both the ginger and the cranberry and added those to my pile as well. The last thing I picked up, before tearing myself away from the shelf, was a huge bottle of jojoba oil.

Now I had everything I needed.

"I'm finally ready to go," I said, staggering under the weight of my selections as I led the way up to the front of the store.

"This place is absolutely gorgeous," I told the lady standing behind the register, once I'd made it there. "The owners did a great job decorating it, and the supplies are amazing!"

She laughed. "Well, thank you. I decorated it myself, and I appreciate the kind compliments."

"Do you have a website that I can order some more stuff from?" I asked eagerly. "I usually get my supplies from a shop by my house, but they're really tiny and they don't have even half of what you have here."

She laughed again and nodded, handing me a business card with the store name and website address boldly printed on it. I tucked it safely into my back pocket as she started ringing up my items. Mom surprised me by paying for my rather hefty bill without telling me to put anything back, and also picked up a classical music CD for herself.

I grinned from ear to ear as we waved good-bye to the store owner and headed outside. "Thanks for taking me here, Mom," I said, piling the bags into the car. "It was fun."

She just smiled at me, and we climbed into our seats. We didn't really talk on the way home, but she put on the CD she'd picked up at the register, and it filled the silence nicely. It was a calm and quiet ride back, and I actually managed to stay awake.

Later that night, surrounded by my recent purchases, I was eager to finally get back into my work. Since Kristen's abrupt disappearance, I'd lost all of my passion for making perfume. My heart just wasn't in it, so I'd given up completely. But tonight it was different. I felt centered again, for the first time in a long time. I was ready to tackle a new project.

I didn't have any worries about staying awake as I readied my work space. Every time I made a new perfume, it required steady concentration and copious amounts of note taking throughout the entire process, so I knew it would keep me busy. Midnight came and went, and I barely even noticed. By five a.m. I was surprised that it was already time for me to try to get some sleep.

I slept soundly, and actually woke up feeling eager and excited later that afternoon. Creating new perfumes was a tricky business. It involved several rounds of testing different oil combinations, looking for reactions, checking notes, comparing samples, writing down new notes, and then starting the whole process all over again with each new scent choice.

And I loved every minute of it.

There were a million and one possible scent combinations, and it was up to me to find the ones that complemented each other. Sometimes it was difficult, but it was never, ever boring. And the best thing about the whole process was that each night seemed to fly by. They didn't drag on anymore, threatening me with shadows and dreams.

I started working a little earlier each night, and sleeping a little less during the day. After perfecting the formula for Mom's autumn harvest perfume, and creating a brand-new winter scent, I decided to do something different. Something that filled me with fear, and more than a little trepidation, but something I knew I had to do.

I was going to make a perfume for Kristen.

She had asked me several times before to make one specifically for her, but I'd always hesitated. It was a challenging thing to do, creating scents for people that not only smelled good but also mixed well with their body chemistry. Since Kristen was my best friend, I always felt extra pressure to make sure her signature scent would fit her perfectly. I never wanted to disappoint her in any way. But this time I decided to give it a try.

It ended up being much harder than I had ever thought it would be.

I couldn't find scents that blended well, and after several hours of laboring on it, I gave in. Standing up from my worktable, I walked around the room to stretch my legs. A headache was starting to pound between my eyes, and I rubbed my temples with my fingertips. There was no way I could keep working with strong scents while I had a headache. I wouldn't be able to concentrate.

Grabbing several pillows from the foot of my bed, I carried them over to the window seat and piled them up high. Hopefully, if I just rested my eyes for a while, the headache would go away . . . hopefully.

I settled into my nest of pillows and rested my cheek against the window pane. It was cool and helped to ease the pounding in my head a little. I sighed at the temporary relief. This spot was pretty comfortable. *I could stay like this for hours.*

When I opened my eyes again, the world outside had gone suspiciously orange. Then I realized it was sunrise. I had slept through the night without any nightmares.

Over the next couple of days I slowly readjusted my sleeping schedule. I didn't fall asleep until after midnight, but at least I wasn't sleeping during the day anymore. Which was a very good thing, because school started on Monday.

Chapter Four

FIRST DAYS

❧✿❧

His school-house was a low building of one large room, rudely constructed of logs; the windows partly glazed, and partly patched with leaves of old copy-books.

—"The Legend of Sleepy Hollow"

It wasn't until I'd made it four blocks away from home on Monday morning that I realized I was going in the wrong direction. I stopped short, coming to an abrupt halt in the middle of the sidewalk. There wouldn't be a daily stop at Kristen's house to pick her up. Not this year . . . and not next year. Those wouldn't happen ever again.

A small ache started throbbing in the vicinity of my heart, and it made my chest hurt. I rubbed at it while I turned in the direction of the high school and began walking slowly toward it. Alone. I took several gulping breaths of air to try to make the sensation go away, but it wouldn't. I kept feeling like I was forgetting something the whole time I walked.

I was still occupied with my thoughts when I came to the metal doors that marked the entrance of the school, and passed through them to the main hallway. A large hand-lettered sign taped to the wall on my left directed all incoming traffic to the gymnasium for an assembly.

Following the sounds of new sneakers squeaking loudly on the recently polished wooden floors, I shuffled along with the growing crowd, merely one more student in a very long line. As I pushed my way through the swinging red doors, I could see that several rows of metal bleachers had already been set up and were quickly being filled. Forcibly reminding myself that no one would be saving me a seat this year, I headed to the back of the room and chose a spot next to the section generally reserved for teachers.

Principal Meeker stood awkwardly at a podium set up in the front of the gymnasium, and he cleared his throat loudly several times while waiting for the squeaking and shuffling noises to die down. He was wearing a seventies-style brown paisley shirt that did *not* flatter his portly frame in *any* way and, unfortunately, already bore the faint marking of a sweat patch under each arm.

It was totally gross.

When the noise finally settled to a dull roar, Principal Meeker clapped his hands together once and began to speak. "Welcome back, students and faculty. I trust that everyone had a beneficial and educational summer vacation?" Two caterpillar-esque eyebrows rose expectantly above his thick black glasses and he paused. After a moment of awkward silence he adjusted his glasses and resumed speaking.

"Before I go over some general rules for the upcoming school year, I wanted to address a recent tragedy that has greatly affected our school and community. As most of you already know, over the summer vacation Kristen Maxwell was involved in a . . . er . . . fatal drowning . . . accident."

I could hear shifting in the seats as suddenly hundreds of heads seemed to turn and glance in my direction. Hollow High only had about four hundred students, and at that moment it felt like every single one of them was staring at me.

My eyes locked onto the floor. I concentrated hard on the toe of my shoe so I wouldn't have to see them all looking at me. *How much longer is he going to talk about this?*

"In light of this terrible event, we will have extra grief counselors on hand for anyone who needs help sorting through their grief." The heads shifted away, and I was no longer the main topic of interest. "They will be available both before and after the lunch period in the guidance counselor's office for this entire week. Please don't hesitate to stop in and see one of them if you feel like you need to talk to someone about this."

He looked out at us and the eyebrows rose again. "Just remember, folks, this is not a get-out-of-class-free card. The counselors are only to be used by those who legitimately need them."

Then he proceeded to share a few of his memories about Kristen and opened up the floor for anyone else who might want to do the same. Several teachers stood up and said all the usual false sentiments. Things people say when they don't really know the person but feel obligated to praise them in some way. It all ran together in one never ending blur.

Every once in a while someone would glance back in my direction and give me the look, clearly wondering when I would stand up and speak. I was *really* starting to get tired of that look. Of other people trying to decide for me what I should or shouldn't do.

Finally three sobbing, sniffling, teary-eyed girls stood up and slowly made their way to the front of the room. They were, of course, the most perfectly dressed, perfectly made-up, perfectly coordinated people in the entire school. A murmur of excitement rippled through the crowd.

Everyone knew who these girls were.

And *I* knew that not a single one of them had ever bothered to say anything to Kristen, or me, since we'd started middle school together.

The tallest one, and clearly the leader of the pack, Shana Williams, spoke first. "We just wanted to say that we can't believe such an awful thing has happened. To lose one of our fellow students at such a young age is just so . . . so . . . tragic." She sniffed daintily and flipped her perfect golden hair with one hand.

I rolled my eyes. These girls didn't care about Kristen. All they cared about was the attention they were getting.

"The varsity cheerleading team has decided to dedicate this season to the memory of Kristen Markell," Aubra Stanton spoke up from the middle of the group. She was the only brunette of the bunch. "We will do our best to make sure her memory lives on through all of us."

I snorted loudly when I heard this, causing several teachers to look at me with sympathy. They probably thought I was "sorting through my grief" or something.

The shorter blonde, Erika Something, took her turn. "She was just such a good person, you know? I can't believe she's really gone." She promptly burst into delicate sobs, being very careful not to smear her pristine makeup, while the other two girls hugged her.

I almost gagged.

First, they couldn't even get Kristen's last name right, and then they had the audacity to stand up there and act like they'd been best friends with her their whole lives? *What total bullshit.* They didn't care about Kristen. They hadn't even *known* Kristen.

The sound of my boots hitting the wooden floor echoed loudly through the room as I stood up and made my way out of the gymnasium. I let the doors slam shut behind me and didn't bother to look back, choosing instead to head for the nearest bathroom stall to hide out in until the bell for first period rang.

It was going to be a *very* long school year.

The morning crawled by, and while everyone else around me struggled to get back into the habit of listening to teachers and taking notes again, I struggled not to think about Kristen. There wasn't even an empty seat waiting for her. Like nobody expected her to come back.

When the bell finally rang signaling the end of history and the beginning of lunch, I slid out the door and hurried to the cafeteria. I desperately needed a break. But it wasn't any easier in there, and I automatically scanned the crowd for Kristen's face as I walked to our usual spot. A couple of people smiled at me when they passed by, but I couldn't smile back. I didn't want their pity. Or their forced company.

After an excruciating twenty minutes spent picking at my food, I left the cafeteria before the main rush hit the hallways. Heading for my locker, I was grateful that Kristen's locker hadn't been assigned to anyone else yet, since it was directly next to mine. As long as it stayed empty, I wouldn't have to put up with someone new trying to take over her space.

I jumped when the second bell rang, and then I grabbed my book bag, startled into action. Slamming my locker door shut, I rushed to my next class.

The afternoon dragged on even slower than the morning, and every second was agonizing. I was relieved to find that my last class of the day was only a short study hall. A study hall, I quickly learned, that juniors and seniors were allowed to skip for the second half of the school year.

That was the highlight of my whole day.

But even that brief moment of happiness faded, and five minutes later I was ready to go. The eighteen minutes I had left until freedom felt more like eighteen hours.

Since I wasn't going to actually study or anything, and no one was sitting next to me, I propped my books up to hide my head behind and closed my eyes. For a while I just sat there. Thinking about the day so far, and dreading the rest of the school year. *Maybe I should talk to Mom about homeschool. . . .*

It was the loud buzzing of the bell and someone bumping into my desk that jarred me awake. Wiping some drool off my mouth with one hand, I glanced around to see if anyone else had noticed. Fortunately, there wasn't anyone left *to* notice. I was the only one still here. Grabbing the books in front of me, I shoved them into my book bag and headed for the door.

One day down, eight hundred million more to go.

I took the long way home, mulling over the painful hours I'd just spent in school. It had not been a pleasant experience, and the last thing on earth I wanted to do was repeat today over again. That homeschool idea was starting to sound better and better.

As soon as I reached the back door and walked into the kitchen, Mom's voice greeted me.

"So how did your first day go? The principal called."

All thoughts of homeschooling instantly left my brain, and I was frozen into place. A million different scenarios ran through my mind while that statement sank in. *What did the principal call about? Am I in trouble for storming out of the assembly? Or for taking a nap in study hall? How should I play this out?*

I tested the waters slowly, shrugging nonchalantly. "It was fine. Principal Meeker held an assembly and mentioned Kristen . . ."

Glancing out of the corner of my eye, I saw that Mom was working on some paperwork at the table, and I sighed with relief. That was *always* a good sign. It meant she was thinking about something more important than me.

"That's what he called about." She didn't even look over at me, but shuffled some papers around. "He was letting all the parents know about the extra grief counselors available at the high school. I hope you'll set a good example for the other students, Abigail."

I had no idea what she meant by that. "Sure, Mom." *Whatever.*

"I'm going upstairs to start on homework now. Call me when dinner's ready?"

"Okay," she replied distractedly, and I took the opportunity to make a quick escape up to my room.

Throwing my book bag onto the bed, I shut the door behind me and paced around the room, feeling caged-in and restless. I didn't know what to do with myself. I *should* be with Kristen right now. Walking through the cemetery or hanging out at the bridge. Talking about the first day back at school and who had worn what. Sharing notes while commiserating about how unfair it was for teachers to assign homework the first night . . . any of those things.

This didn't feel right. I wasn't used to being so alone.

Desperate to hear her voice, to fool myself into thinking that everything was normal again, I picked up my phone and called her number. I was greeted by a cold automated the-number-you-have-dialed-is-no-longer-in-service message. I couldn't even hear her recorded voice anymore.

Collapsing onto my bed, I was bombarded with images from the day. It was confusing, and overwhelming, and I couldn't hold back my tears anymore.

I could still hear Principal Meeker announcing Kristen's death in front of the whole school. I could see the unused locker next to mine, where she should have been keeping her things. To call her phone and not have her answer it . . .

Sliding down to the floor, I curled myself up into a little ball and rocked back and forth; trying to will away the hurt and emptiness, to shove it back down to that dark place inside so I wouldn't feel it anymore. A vise grip had grabbed hold of my heart and was squeezing all the life right out of me.

I couldn't handle this type of pain. It was too big. Too raw. Too much.

When Mom called me down for dinner, I told her that I didn't feel well and was going to bed early. It wasn't a total lie, since my chest hurt and I felt sick to my stomach. But I had no intention of going to bed. Instead I finished up all of my homework and started working on Kristen's perfume. It was a long and exhausting night, and I didn't sleep at all.

The next day I had a hard time concentrating on my classes at school and ended up falling asleep in study hall again.

But I knew it didn't matter. No one cared what I did anyway.

~ ~ ~

On Friday afternoon I hauled ass after the last bell rang and practically ran from the classroom, but slowed down once I left the building. On one hand I was *extremely* happy that I would have a two-day break from that miserable soul-sucking hellhole of a place called school, but on the other hand it wasn't like I was going to have all kinds of fun being alone at home.

I plodded toward the house but at the last minute changed direction. Maybe I didn't have to spend *all* of my time at home.

Knocking twice when I came to the Maxwells' door, I stood awkwardly on their front porch. Usually I would have just followed Kristen right in, but things were . . . different now. So I waited.

Kristen's mom opened the door, and a wide smile split her face when she saw it was me. "Abbey, come on in. You don't have to knock. I thought it was the mailman."

I grinned back and stepped into the familiar hallway, trying very hard not to think about the last time I had been here.

"Hey, Mrs. M., I just wanted to stop in and say hi. With school starting and all this week, I've been kind of . . . busy," I finished lamely.

Well, something like that. Sad, overwhelmed, upset, hurt. Busy? Same difference.

She waved me into the living room and sat down on a small baby blue couch while I chose a nearby pink and green flowered armchair.

"So how's junior year going so far?" she asked me, leaning forward slightly. "They say that junior year is when you get all of the hard work out of the way so you can enjoy your senior year."

I forced a fake laugh. "I don't doubt it. Lots of hard work this year, that's true. It's going to be a tough one."

"It sure is," she said softly, folding her hands together and resting them in her lap. "I know Kristen—" Her voice broke on the name, but she kept speaking. "Well, she was really looking forward to this year. She couldn't wait for prom, and to start looking at colleges."

Leaning closer to her, I patted one arm. "I know she was, Mrs. M. I know." I tried to think of something else to talk about. This was not going very well.

"She should be here, Abbey, with you." Her sudden exclamation echoed my thoughts from earlier in the week. "Starting school. Doing homework. Making plans for the weekend. Not . . . this." She looked around the room helplessly. "Now it's just an empty house."

"What if she's still out there?" I asked her, just as suddenly. "Why did you give up so soon?" I knew I shouldn't say those things, but I couldn't stop myself. The filter between my brain and my mouth had spontaneously erupted.

She looked at me sadly. "You know she's not out there, Abbey. You know what they found." She couldn't say it, but I knew what she was talking about.

"The cops should have done more," I said angrily. "I've seen how these things work on *Law and Order*. They don't give up so easily, and they bring in other agencies. What about the FBI? Why weren't they called in? They would have done something. Just because she's missing doesn't mean she's dead."

"It's not like this is the first time it's happened," she refuted. "When that old man fell in last year, his body didn't wash up for six months."

"I know. It's just . . ." I sighed and shook my head.

"Since there was no ransom note, no evidence of a kidnap—"

"What about the blood?" I interrupted. "It could have meant someone hurt her."

This time it was her turn to shake her head. "The police know what they're doing, Abbey. They said the small amount of . . .

blood . . . on that rock was consistent with someone hitting their head and falling in. You *know* that already."

"Yeah, well, I still think they should be looking harder. Like the cops on TV."

"Life's not a television show." She sighed wearily before standing up from the couch. "Do you want some ice cream? I think I need some double mint fudge right about now." I nodded, and she left the room momentarily, before returning with a large carton and two spoons.

We passed the tub of ice cream back and forth several times before she spoke again.

"I didn't want to give up on her, Abbey," she said plainly. "But we needed some type of closure. With Thomas it was different. This time we just needed to have some type of an end to it all. Do you understand that?"

I didn't understand. But I *did* wish with all my heart that the sadness could go away for her as easily as that ice cream did.

Chapter Five

CHOICES

❦

Over a deep black part of the stream, not far from the church, was formerly thrown a
wooden bridge. . . . This was one of the favorite haunts of the Headless Horseman. . . .

—"The Legend of Sleepy Hollow"

The following Tuesday, after another rough day at school, I had a pretty strong feeling that if I went straight home, I'd end up on my bedroom floor again, rocking back and forth. Which was not a pleasant prospect. I discarded that idea and started walking, unsure of where I was headed but knowing that I had to keep going.

When I came to a fork in the road, I paused, thinking over my options. Something tugged at me and told me which direction to take. Five steps later the two huge wrought iron gates that marked the entrance of the Sleepy Hollow Cemetery greeted me.

I inhaled deeply, took one step back, two steps forward . . . and sealed my fate.

I never thought that something as simple as walking could be so difficult, but that first step was big. And so hard to take. Every tentative move I made felt earth-shattering as I remembered the last time I had been in this cemetery . . . the reason for it . . .

It was not a good memory.

Concentrating on putting one foot in front of the other, I trudged slowly along the path. I knew where I had to go; there was someone I needed to talk to.

Tombstones of all shapes and sizes greeted me along the way. Multigenerational family plots were tucked behind narrow crooked fences that served as separators. Flimsy barriers erected between the living and the dead.

Mausoleums and crypts, with faded names that I knew by heart, rose majestically from the earth. Their outsides, although ravaged by the effects of time, still provided a safe place for the bodies that rested inside, and I nodded my head as a sign of respect to those once graceful homes of the departed.

And then I passed the chair.

It was still here, resting beside its grave. A fine covering of grass now grew along the surface of the grave, and fresh flowers surrounded the edges of the plot. I waved hello before quickly moving on.

The trees around me were bursting with the vivid colors of autumn. It was absolutely beautiful, and I stopped momentarily to take it all in. I realized then how much I had truly missed visiting this place. It was my home. My sanctuary.

When I finally came to the end of the path, I turned left and stepped around another huge mausoleum carved into the side of a hill. A giant slate door guarded the entrance, but my destination was the next spot over . . . Washington Irving's tomb.

After following the narrow stone steps that led the way up to a little iron gate, I gently pushed the gate open and crossed over into the Irving family plot. I knew this spot better than any other. Kristen and I had stopped by here almost every day.

When we were younger, we'd played make-believe among the tombstones and spent hours speculating about the legendary scribe who had made our small town so famous. We'd dreamed of the mythical figures buried down below in the Old Dutch section and had scared each other silly with ghost stories involving the Headless Horseman. And on more than one occasion we had spilled our secrets to a storyteller who had been gone for so long yet still fascinated us with his words.

I couldn't think of a more perfect way to have spent my childhood.

Suddenly the forgotten memory of a fourth-grade school project popped into my head, and I smiled to myself. It felt like it had been a lifetime since Kristen and I had painstakingly copied down each name on the tombstones in the Irving plot (gravestone rubbings weren't allowed) and used information from old newspapers at the library to design an elaborate family tree. We'd also put together a "family newsletter" detailing highlights and favorites from each person's life.

It was an A++ for both of us on that one.

Kristen had been so proud of that extra "+" the teacher had given us. It was all she could talk about for days. I shook my head, and the memory disappeared, relegated once again to the back of my mind. It really *had* been a lifetime ago. *Hers*.

Wandering slowly among the tombstones, I took my time to read the dates and words inscribed upon them, saying hello to each family member as I passed by. I stopped near the huge oak tree that stood in the middle of the plot and ran my fingers over the carved initials etched into it. So many letters. So many different stories.

But I didn't linger long, and when I reached Washington Irving's stone, I glanced down at the familiar sight of offerings left behind by his adoring fans. Stacks of pennies, dimes, quarters, and even foreign currency were piled high around his tombstone. People had been doing it forever—or at least for as long as I had lived here—and I still couldn't figure out the logic behind it.

There were also a couple scraps of paper tucked under several small rocks sitting next to the grave. Messages, no doubt, written to the famous author.

In a town that celebrated and revered "The Legend of Sleepy Hollow," it was impossible *not* to learn about Washington Irving. His works were required reading in the school curriculum as part of the town's history, and students were encouraged in English class each year to write letters to him.

Kristen and I had written to him several times. A lot of kids liked the extra element of danger that went along with delivering a letter to the dead on Halloween night. We had done that, too.

But to me, "The Legend" had always been . . . more. More than just a school assignment, or a town obsession. More than just some topic to talk about with my best friend. It meant more than any of those things. I don't know what the connection is, or why I even have it, but I think it's always been there.

For my part now, I plucked a single wild violet from a cluster of flowers growing next to the oak tree to leave as my token.

"Good day to you, Mr. Irving." I spoke quietly as I bent down to place the flower beside a stack of coins. I straightened, and then hesitated, not sure how to start. "I'm sorry I haven't visited in a while. Some things have . . . changed."

I couldn't think too much about what I was going to say, or how to say it, so I tried to let the words come naturally. "Kristen hasn't been by to visit you either. She won't be . . . coming back. At all. There was an accident."

The words sounded hollow and foreign to my ears.

"There are a lot of rumors going around, but none of them are true." I spoke quickly now, to get it all out. "They say she drowned in the Crane River, but they still haven't recovered her body. A funeral was held a couple of weeks ago. They buried an empty casket." My voice cracked on the last sentence, and I paused to take a minute. "That . . . that's pretty much it."

I wasn't expecting any type of reply, and obviously I didn't get one. A light breeze picked up, and for a second I swear I caught the sound of two little girls laughing. I listened more closely, but it disappeared. There was no one there. I traced the lettering on the tombstone as I whispered sadly, "Yeah, she won't be coming back."

A soft crunching noise distracted me, and I turned to see an old man with gray hair scooping up the scattered leaves that had fallen over the small plot. I had no idea how long he had been there, or what he'd overheard, but he was surprisingly graceful as he moved around the bulky tombstones.

After making five or six piles, he pulled out a small bristled brush from his back pocket and proceeded to wipe off the top of each grave. He didn't say anything to me, or even act as though he knew I was there. I gave it another minute and then walked over to him when he dropped to one knee and started pulling at stray weeds running along the edge of the wrought iron fence.

"I can help you with that if you want," I offered.

He gazed up at me with large brown eyes that had deep wrinkles in the corners. He looked surprised that I wanted to help. "I thank you for your offer, and gladly accept," he said softly.

I looked at him quizzically. *Is he serious?* Most of the old people I knew didn't talk that way. Then he smiled, and his eyes glowed with mischief. I could tell that he knew exactly what I was thinking.

Blushing, I dropped to my knees and started yanking weeds wildly, heedless of the grass stains my jeans would probably suffer. We worked side by side in silence for a couple of minutes, and then he sat straight up. Something was in his hand, and he held it out to me.

"Look, we have a prize here."

I stared hard at the green leaf resting in his scarred and lined palm. "Poison ivy?" I guessed.

He smiled and shook his head. "No, something better." Then he tore the leaf in two, popped part of it into his mouth, and began chewing.

I watched him like he was a crazy person. If he started convulsing, or foaming, I would be ready to run for help at a second's notice.

"It's mint," he said, laughing at my expression and holding out the other half of the leaf to me. I cautiously took the outstretched offering, still watching him like a hawk. Holding it up to my nose, I sniffed deeply, and was surprised by the sharp aroma.

"You're right." I sniffed again, smelling the familiar scent a little more with each inhalation. "I've never seen it growing wild before. I'm used to finding it in a bottle."

He looked surprised, but pleased. "How wonderful! It has so many uses."

I nodded. "I use peppermint essential oil and mix it with other oils to create perfumes." It was strange, to blurt out something as personal as that to a virtual stranger, but I kind of felt proud that he was pleased I knew what it was.

He smiled enthusiastically and bent back to his task. "That's a very creative way to use it."

When he fell silent, I looked over at him, really seeing for the first time this stranger I was working with. He wore dusty blue overalls that had obviously been patched several times, and a matching short sleeve button-down shirt. His black boots were old and scuffed, but they had a comfortable, worn look to them. His gray hair blew gently in the wind, and he looked like he would be a nice grandfather.

"I'm Abbey, by the way," I said. "It's actually Abigail, but I like Abbey better."

"My name is Nikolas," he replied. "It is a pleasure to meet you, Abbey."

I started working on the weeds again, and it didn't take long for both of us to make our way around the fence. Once that was finished, we hauled over the clumps of weeds and added them to the piles of leaves. I wasn't sure what to do next. "So, um, are you a family friend or something?" I asked awkwardly.

"I guess you could say that," Nikolas answered.

"You know they have a caretaker for the cemetery that's supposed to do this sort of thing, right? His name is John."

I had met John several times before, and while he was very good at his job, he wasn't very friendly. But then I guess it takes a certain type of personality to be able to work alone with only the dead as company every day. Definitely not a job for a people person.

Nikolas pulled out a black garbage bag from another pocket and quickly stuffed it with the weeds and leaves before I even had the chance to offer my help.

"Old habits die hard," he said while tying a knot at the top of the bag. "I'm something of a caretaker myself." He smiled at me, and the corners of his eyes crinkled again. "Thank you for your help today, Abbey, and try to remember the good memories. They will help the sad ones."

I watched him closely as he lifted the bag over one shoulder and went down the narrow stairs, taking the path that led to the other side of the cemetery. So he'd obviously heard what I'd said. And yet it didn't bother me. That was weird.

Standing still for a moment longer, I knew that my time here wasn't over yet. I waved a silent good-bye to the Irving family, pushed my way back through the gate, and started toward the Old Dutch Church.

Dread filled the pit of my stomach as the stone structure loomed ahead, large and imposing. To my right was the Washington Irving Bridge, where Kristen had fallen into the river. To my left was Kristen's burial spot.

I looked in both directions, at a loss as to what choice to make. Again I felt that tug. It was an unseen prompt steering me toward my destination, telling me which way to go. So I listened to it. I chose the bridge.

The Washington Irving Bridge was a never ending project that was *still* under construction. While it was supposed to help bring in more tourists by re-creating the famous covered bridge that Ichabod Crane had been chased over in "The Legend," all it'd done so far was create traffic jams. And tourists don't like traffic.

So *that* plan had been a big fat bust.

With the delays from the investigation of Kristen's accident, and the winter months coming quickly, a temporary hold had been placed on the project. The way things were going, it would probably be another three years before the bridge was actually finished.

I walked slowly down to the river's edge and paused there. The water rushed by, swirling and bubbling, hypnotic in its frantic cadence. The sudden burst of a squirrel chattering in a tree next to me startled me, and I kept moving. Toward the bridge. Toward our spot.

Long before the town had decided to rebuild the bridge, Kristen and I had been meeting at the Crane River, named after the gangly love-struck schoolteacher who was scared off by the Horseman in Washington Irving's tale. A leftover platform from part of the old bridge sat directly above one of the newer concrete supporting towers, and it made a fantastic seat. The wooden beams made a bench of sorts, and your feet could swing out over the open water. There wasn't any railing in front to hold you in place, or catch you if you fell, but it was like you were literally sitting on top of the river.

The construction work they had done recently made the platform a little harder to get to, but I was still able to reach it. I climbed up the tower and wedged myself in, looking out over the water. The sun was warm on my face, but I was cold inside. Had it really happened here, at this place? Would I never get another chance to sit up under this bridge and talk with Kristen again? It all seemed so surreal. This wasn't how my life was supposed to go. It wasn't fair.

A car rumbled overhead, and I felt the vibrations all the way down to my toes, but I ignored it. Instead I thought about last year, how our first day after school had been spent at this bridge. . . .

"You'll never guess who asked me if you were taking French this year," I teased Kristen.

Her brown eyes grew wide. "Who?"

"Oh, it might *have been Trey Hunter." I ruined my feigned composure with a large grin. "He asked me where you normally sat, and if anyone special sits next to you."*

My smile grew larger when I saw her eyes light up at the news. "He

even thanked me very nicely after I told him. I think he likes you."

She blushed and looked away. Then her smile faded a bit, and she shook her head. "He probably just wants to ask me if I'll switch seats with him or something. I don't think he actually wants to sit by me."

"You don't know that, Kris."

"Yes, I do, Abbey. I just . . . do." She shrugged. When she turned to face me again, sad Kristen had disappeared and happy Kristen was back in her place.

"I have to show you this new shirt I got," she said excitedly. "It's a deep burgundy, with corset lacing up the front. But you have to let me wear it at least once before you borrow it, okay? Because I know you'll totally try to steal it from me."

Our laughter bounced over the water and came echoing back to us. . . .

Something caught at the edge of my vision and I lost that sound of laughter, snapping back to reality with a sharp jolt. I turned my head slowly, following a shadow until I could clearly see what it was. A small piece of yellow crime scene tape fluttered along the shallow edge of the water below, tangled up in part of a tree branch.

It was a cruel reminder of what else had happened here.

I stared at the tape, watching it surge in the water and then flap against the tree. It didn't belong here. It didn't belong anywhere, but *especially* not somewhere that meant a lot to me.

Climbing down from my seat was easy. I had done it a thousand times before, and it didn't take long for my feet to hit solid ground again.

Actually removing the piece of tape was not as easy.

I tried, at first, to reach into the river and simply pull it free from the tree, but it was firmly attached to that branch. Then I grabbed a stick with a sharp, jagged edge and tried to use that to unhook it. But I was too far away. No matter how hard I wiggled it, the tape still hung on. So I tried leaning out farther over the water.

That just resulted in making the stick I held too long. The closer I got, the less it wanted to hook on to that piece of tape. I thought about breaking the stick, but then it might end up too short. I was going to have to come up with some sort of different solution, though. The stick idea wasn't working out.

Surveying my surroundings, I saw a large rock that looked like it just might be able to give me the assistance that I needed.

It was close enough to the tree that if I stood on it, I could break my stick and try to reach the tape from there.

The only downside was that the rock was in the water. If I *really* wanted that piece of tape, I was going to have to get wet. I looked around again, double-checking my options. There *weren't* any other options. It was this or nothing.

Backing up along the river's edge until I found the driest and least muddy spot, I took off my boots. Then came my socks. I tucked them inside the boots and rolled my jean legs up to my knees. The water looked pretty high out there, and I didn't want to get any more of me wet than was absolutely necessary.

The first step in sent a shiver running through me. Although it barely covered my toes, that water was *cold*. I waded in a little deeper, gritting my teeth as the cold crept up my ankles. Letting my body get used to the temperature for only a moment longer, I plunged forward, trying not to poke myself with the stick that I was dragging behind.

Three more steps and I made it to the rock.

I climbed on carefully, trying to balance with my stick in one hand. Once I had both feet firmly planted, I lifted the stick up and broke off a small piece from the end to shorten it a bit. Then

I aimed it in the direction of the crime scene tape. The tape slid off the tree and down onto the stick. I grabbed for it and held it in my hand. Fingering the cold, wet, crinkly texture, I read the words POLICE LINE: DO NOT CROSS over and over again, thinking about the reason it had been placed here.

And then my foot slipped.

The sudden loss of balance surprised me, and left me struggling wildly to recover my footing. I couldn't fall in. No matter what happened, I couldn't fall in. That couldn't happen to me, too. I dropped the stick, and the tape, and leaned slightly to my left.

A couple of jerky wobbles later, and one brief windmilling motion of my arms, and I was able to regain my balance. I watched as the yellow tape floated down the river, riding along the current until it was out of sight. Now that it was gone, the landscape looked normal again.

Stepping very carefully off the rock, I slowly made my way back to shore. The water didn't feel as cold now, but it swirled around my ankles in a tugging motion. It was a precarious feeling, like I could be swept off my feet and carried away at any second.

As I got closer to the river's edge, I paid close attention to the shoreline. Any number of nasty surprises might be hidden along there. Things I didn't want sticking between my toes.

Then the sun reflected on something shiny and half hidden in the mud.

Fearing that it might be a piece of glass, I bent down for a closer look. All I could see were my bare toes. The clear surface of the water revealed the deep blood red that I had painted the toenails. And I remembered another shade of red, the color of Kristen's casket.

Giving a wide berth to whatever that shiny thing was, I stepped out of the water and onto dry land. As I walked toward my shoes and socks, my head was full of thoughts about that day in the cemetery.

"For a moment there I thought you were going to fall in."

I grabbed for my boots and looked wildly around me. Under the bridge, to my left, was a boy. A dramatic black streak stood out in his blond hair. I took a couple of steps toward him, being careful to watch the ground since I was still barefoot, and then looked him straight in the eye.

"Never," I scoffed. "I was in complete control the entire time."

He stared back at me and his voice was soft. "Clearly."

My tongue tied, and I wished I had something clever to say.

He just watched me with a small smile on his face, and I couldn't stop staring at his eyes. They were so vivid. I'd never seen a shade of green quite like that before. One corner of his mouth twitched up higher.

Is he laughing at me?

I heard a dull thud and realized that I had dropped one of my boots. I stared dumbly down at it until my brain kicked into gear.

Blushing, and feeling like ten kinds of idiots, I quickly dropped the other one beside it and sank to the ground. My feet were dry enough to put my shoes back on now, but I brushed off some imaginary dirt before slipping on my socks. I paid close attention to each foot, stalling for time. He didn't go away. And he didn't say anything.

After taking an *extraordinary* amount of time relacing each boot, and carefully rearranging the bottoms of my jeans, I dusted my hands off and stood up. He was still standing there, with his hands in his pockets.

"What's your name?" I asked.

"Caspian."

He didn't offer anything else.

It was starting to get dark now, and I knew I had to get home soon, but there was something I had to ask him. Something I needed to know.

"That day, at Kristen's house . . . what did you mean when you said you were there because of me?" I held my breath, waiting for him to answer.

I heard each word distinctly when he spoke. "I know how much Kristen meant to you, Abbey."

"You don't even know me. I don't know you. Why—?"

His shoulders rose and fell as he ran a hand through his hair, and he looked shy all of a sudden. "I don't know. I thought that maybe if I was there, it would help you . . . somehow. I just wanted to be there for you."

Those words took my breath away. "Thank you," I said softly. "It did."

I hated to break the moment, but I knew I was running out of time. "I have to go. I need to get home . . . dinner . . ." I couldn't look him directly in the eye. The words he had just said still hung between us. They were huge and powerful words.

"Yeah, me too."

A streetlight above the bridge kicked on automatically as

the daylight continued to fade around us. It cast a slight glow downward, leaving half of Caspian's face revealed while the other half was hidden by the darkness.

"So, it was, um, nice to meet you, Caspian, and . . . I guess I'll see you around sometime," I said nervously. *Is this the right way to say good-bye?*

"How are you going to get home?" he asked me.

"I go through the cemetery," I replied. "There's enough room to squeeze between the two main gates on the one side. Or sometimes I cut around the bridge. It takes longer, but it leads me directly to the main road, and I live right off of that."

"Will you do that, Abbey? Go around the bridge and take the main road?" He looked very serious.

"Yeah, I can," I said, although I was fuzzy on the logic behind his question.

"There could be a crazy person in there just waiting for someone to come walking by. I don't want you to get hurt," he said sheepishly.

Oh. *That* was his logic? I had been through the cemetery at night dozens of times before. While it was kind of creepy, and I'd usually had Kristen with me, nothing had ever happened.

But I kept that fact to myself.

"Okay." I smiled at him. "Thanks for thinking of me. See you later." I turned to walk away, trying to hide my megawatt grin before he could see it. He didn't want me to get hurt? *Wow*. Just *wow*. I might actually be close to a swoon here.

"What about Saturday, Abbey? Are you free Saturday morning? Will you meet me here?" His voice broke through my giddy thoughts.

I turned back. There was no amount of overdue homework or room cleaning duties that would stop me from answering that one. "I'm free." I tried to sound vague and nonchalant about it. "I can meet you here."

"Good. Saturday, then." The light shone off half of his face, and he was smiling. "Night, Abbey. Sweet dreams."

My stomach dipped.

"Good night . . . Caspian," I whispered. I don't know if I remembered to smile back or not. I was too busy telling myself not to trip over my own feet as I turned toward the main road.

Yeah, I was *definitely* going to have sweet dreams tonight.

Chapter Six

GREAT EXPECTATIONS

❧❀❧

I profess not to know how women's hearts are wooed and won. To me they have always been matters of riddle and admiration.

—"The Legend of Sleepy Hollow"

The next couple of days flew by, but I had a hard time sleeping again on Friday night. Only this time it wasn't nightmares or sad memories keeping me awake. It was excitement. I paced nervously around my room while my brain kicked into overdrive.

What should I wear?

What should I say?

What if he thinks I'm a total dork?

What if he stands me up?

When the clock on the nightstand started creeping close to three a.m., I forced myself to go lie down in bed and think sleepy thoughts. But that didn't work either, and I ended up staring at the ceiling. Glancing over at the clock again, I realized that I had only ... Crap. I didn't know how many hours I had left to get some sleep. Caspian never said what time he wanted to meet. Now my brain kicked into super overdrive, worrying about that.

Was nine o'clock too early? I'd have to get up before eight to be ready on time. Maybe ten or ten fifteen was better. Then I wouldn't seem so desperate. I could casually stroll into the cemetery and totally act like I hadn't given it a second thought. *Yeah, that's definitely the way to go.* Desperate was *so* not good.

Satisfied with my decision, I closed my eyes and thought back to the bridge for the hundredth time. Reliving every word he'd said, every gesture he'd made, I examined the memory from every angle. I didn't want to overlook any tiny detail or subtle nuance that had been there.

I don't want you to get hurt.

I couldn't stop a huge smile from spreading over my face as I heard those words in my head again. When I finally *was* able to fall asleep, I dreamt of piercing green eyes and haunting dark figures half hidden in the shadows.

They were sweet dreams, indeed.

~ ~ ~

Saturday morning came *way* too quickly. I stared groggily at the beeping clock, wondering why it was going off at the ungodly hour of nine, when it suddenly dawned on me what I was supposed to be doing today . . . and who I was supposed to be doing it with.

I jumped out of bed and ran over to the connecting shower. Humming softly, I lathered up my hair in vanilla-scented shampoo and then rinsed off with pink grapefruit shower gel. They both smelled delicious and perked me up even more.

My excitement waned, though, as I started to towel-dry my hair. I desperately tried to tame my wild curls into perfectly defined spirals, but they vehemently disagreed with me on that one. It was a battle I quickly lost.

Begrudgingly I settled for twisting up several sections and piling it all in a loose bun on top of my head. If I shook it out in about thirty minutes, then hopefully it would be sort of wavy.

Wavy hair is making a comeback, I tried to convince my mirrored reflection. *It's called "soft and romantic." You'll be a trendsetter.* But I didn't really want to set any trends. I just wanted to have sexy hair. With a heavy sigh, I went to go get dressed.

Of course my wardrobe turned out to be a complete crisis too.

The cargo pants I had thought about wearing were *not* very flattering once I actually had them on. If my butt was really as big as it looked in those pants, then I needed to do some squats, or lunges, or something, ASAP.

Panicking, I dug wildly through my closet for something else to wear, and the bed was soon covered in several heaps of hastily discarded clothing. I finally went with my these-always-make-my-butt-look-cute jeans and a long black wraparound sweater. I topped it all off with a red and black plaid fedora hat. After looking myself over exactly twenty-three times in the mirror, I felt pretty confident that my outfit was as good as it was going to get.

Some eyeliner, eye shadow, and a couple dabs of concealer were next, and I was almost done. I swirled some blush over my cheekbones and chose a lipstick in a shade called Daredevil. After carefully applying the lipstick, I cast another critical eye at myself. "What do you think, Kristen?" I said softly to the mirror. "Do I look okay?"

But the mirror didn't answer me, so I turned away to finish getting ready.

My hair was the last step, and I held my breath while I shook out the bun and tousled a couple of pieces. More than once in my life I had wished for perfectly straight blond-as-can-be hair instead of the black curly locks I was stuck with. But today I didn't wish that. Today my hair was soft and sexy.

After putting on my hat at just the right angle, I rearranged a couple of loose tendrils so they framed my face. It was turning out to be a good hair day after all.

I pulled a ten-dollar bill from my wallet and stuck it into my back pocket before grabbing my cell phone to check the clock one last time: 9:54. Perfect timing. It would take me about twenty minutes to get to the river. Punctual, but not desperate.

I hurried out of the room and clambered down the stairs to the kitchen. A note from Mom on the fridge said that she and Dad would be in meetings all day long and that I should pick up dinner later. Even more perfect. No parents asking annoying questions made my day a whole lot better.

There was a twenty-dollar bill under a magnet next to the note, and I could practically *feel* the rightness of the day as I scooped it up. I ate a granola bar and grabbed a cup of orange juice. Then I checked to make sure I had my house key before locking the door on my way out.

It was time to go to the river.

~ ~ ~

I tried not to walk too quickly, pacing myself to arrive just before ten thirty. I didn't know if Caspian had meant for me to meet him at the bridge or not, but that's where I was headed.

Skipping the cemetery, I stuck to the main road. My heart was beating faster, and butterflies were starting to swim in my stomach. I could see the bridge now. I scanned the river's edge but didn't see him. My heart sank. He wasn't here.

Yet, I tried to console myself. *He just isn't here* yet. He had said he would meet me, so there wasn't any reason to think that he wouldn't.

Maybe he decided against it, a little voice nagged in the back of my head. Or maybe he had already left. He probably had other things to do instead of waiting by a river all morning long. Doubt filled my mind, and my steps slowed. *Am I too late? Should I go back home?*

I checked the clock on my phone again: 10:27. Should I wait? For how long?

Uncertainty prodded me to climb down the embankment. I couldn't see under the bridge, and I clung to some small shred of hope that he might be waiting for me there. Stepping carefully around tree limbs and loose rocks, I made my way down. As I descended lower and the underside of the bridge became more visible, I spotted someone sitting on the ground reading a book. His hair gave him away.

My stomach somersaulted. . . . He was here.

He looked up when he heard me getting closer. His smile was beautiful.

"Hey, Abbey." He closed the book and stood up.

My answering smile was so wide, it felt like my face would split in two. "Hi, Caspian."

He lifted his other hand and held out a slightly wilted violet to me. "Sorry it's all . . . rumpled. I picked it for you earlier. They grow all over the place here."

I could feel the surprise taking over my entire face as my jaw dropped slightly. I was stunned. I didn't know what to do. He was bringing me *flowers*?

Okay, so technically it wasn't like a dozen roses or anything, but it was still oh-my-God amazing.

I grasped the flower's stem. Right above where his thumb rested. In some other alternate universe, where I was cool and completely not shy, I saw myself sliding my hand down to rest on his, all confident and sexy-like.

 98

But that was *so* not me in this universe, and with a soft sigh I deliberately made sure that there was at least an inch of space between us.

"Thank you," I replied. "It's . . . beautiful. Absolutely beautiful, Caspian." He grinned at me again, and my heart melted into a puddle at my feet. *Yes*, I wanted to tell him, *you have just made every single romantic fantasy I've ever had come true*. But since Coward is my middle name, I kept my thoughts to myself.

I grew even shyer when his gaze wandered over me. Frantically hoping that my hair still looked as good as it had in my room, I tried to discreetly run my tongue over my teeth in case I had any lipstick smudges on them. "I wasn't sure what time to get here. You never mentioned it." I let my gaze do a bit of wandering too, and noticed that he was dressed in black jeans and a black long sleeve shirt. It suited him, made him look dark and mysterious. And sexy. Very, *very* sexy.

Was I drooling? Good Lord, I hoped not.

He shrugged. "I'm just glad you could make it. Whenever you got here was good enough for me. Did you have sweet dreams?"

I shrugged back, praying a telltale blush wouldn't betray me.

"Yeah, sure, I guess I did. I don't really remember my dreams."

Liar, liar, pants on fire.

"You didn't go through the cemetery, did you?" He looked concerned.

"No. I went along the main road."

"Good," he said softly. "Good."

I glanced down at the book he was holding. I couldn't read the title. "How long have you been here?"

"Since seven. I didn't want you to think I was standing you up."

"Since seven? Seven *a.m.*?" I felt both my eyebrows rise up into my forehead.

"Yeah." He ducked his head shyly and changed the subject. "So, do a lot of people normally come by here?"

"Not really. It's pretty sheltered under the bridge."

He turned and made a slight leading gesture in front of him with his book. "After you, then."

I led the way under the bridge, holding tightly to my flower, and the wind picked up on the water, blowing a cool breeze over us. I caught the slight fragrance of my vanilla shampoo wafting on the wind, and I was glad that I had picked something warm to wear.

We both sat down somewhat awkwardly, with a foot of space

between us. I wanted to get closer but wasn't sure how to pull it off smoothly. Settling for "readjusting" my legs, I managed to lessen the space by an inch or two.

He didn't seem to notice at all.

I looked out at the river as I spoke. "So, what book were you reading before I got here?" Not exactly the most exciting of topics, but at least it was conversation.

"*Great Expectations.* I've already read it once before, but I'm sort of going back to pick up on all the things I missed. There are a lot of details."

I knew that one.

"Poor Pip and Estella," I sighed. "To be so unhappy for so many years? It kind of seemed cruel to keep bringing them together when they were younger since they could never be together in the end."

"Cruelness was the only reason why they knew each other at all, though," he pointed out. "Miss Havisham manufactured it that way to teach Estella to break hearts."

"I know," I agreed. "But don't you think true love should fix all? I don't know, maybe it's just the romantic in me . . ." I trailed off, realizing that the conversation was heading toward true love and happily-ever-afters. I didn't want to scare him off already.

"So did you think that the ending was believable?" I steered the conversation back to safer territory. "I really went back and forth on that one. Half of the time I thought it was pure genius, but the other half of the time I thought it was all too unbelievable. Like Dickens just picked the most unlikely twist and made the story work around that."

"I never thought about it that way, Abbey. I always pictured it as Dickens's way of portraying how a single moment can affect our lives so profoundly."

The intense look on his face made me burst out in laughter. I couldn't believe how much fun I was having talking about a book that had been mandatory reading material for school.

"I really didn't want to read it at first. It was assigned to us in eighth grade," I admitted. "Every day we were forced to read a chapter out loud to the whole class. It was sooo boring! And after we got to the part about the mysterious benefactor, this know-it-all kid told everyone who it was. I didn't believe him, so I took the book home that night and finished it. I was completely shocked when it turned out he was right."

"Oh, man." Caspian shook his head in disbelief. "What

an idiot. But you must be a fast reader to have finished in one night."

"Well . . . I *guess* I am. I can usually finish a book in a day or two. In all fairness, though, I had to stay up most of the night and then finish the last chapter right before school the next morning."

"That's still pretty impressive."

His flattery charmed me. *Am I good at anything else I could tell him about?* I could make killer French toast . . . and crepes . . . and I know the names of all the vice presidents. No, no, too much about me. I didn't want him to think I had an ego the size of Manhattan.

"What about you?" I asked. "You must like reading too. I haven't met very many guys who would reread a book like *Great Expectations*, or *any* book for that matter, and then willingly discuss it. You're not secretly recording this conversation for a college term paper, are you?"

He grinned. "No, I just decided to read some of the classics. Enrich myself in literature. Expand my brain. I don't know . . ." He looked away. "I'm not a fast reader, so it kills a lot of time for me."

"Do you have a lot of time to kill? Aren't you in college or something?" I cringed when I heard my questions out loud. "Sorry. You don't have to answer that."

"No, it's okay. I don't mind," he said. "I'm not going to college right now. I took some time off to . . . think about my options."

I didn't know what else to say, and we lapsed into silence. I racked my brain, trying to think of something else to talk about that didn't make me sound (a) boring or (b) stalkerish. So far I was drawing a blank. Then I thought about the cemetery behind us as inspiration.

"Have you lived in Sleepy Hollow long?" I asked him.

Ah, well, I never claimed to be the best conversationalist in the world.

"Actually, I'm from White Plains. I moved there about two and a half years ago, with my dad."

"Where did you move from?" I persisted.

"We moved from West Virginia. My dad got a job as the manager for an auto body shop. He's going to eventually take it over when the owner retires. New York offered better money than West Virginia, so we moved." He shifted the book he held from one hand to the other. "I transferred to the White Plains high school halfway through March and graduated the year before last. You go to Hollow High, right?"

"Yup." I gave a halfhearted sigh. "I'm a junior. I can't wait till graduation."

He was quiet for a moment, and then spoke again. "What about you, Abbey? Have you lived here long?"

"Born and bred. Mom and Dad grew up here, went to school together here, and got married here. The whole nine yards. I've never lived anywhere else."

"Wow." He laughed. "I bet you can't wait for college, then, to get out of this town."

I smiled at him. "Yeah, right? Actually, other than moving out of my parents' house, of course, I wouldn't mind staying here. Beautiful parks, scenery, this cemetery . . . and some of the best pizza I've ever tasted."

He laughed again, louder this time. It was a very nice laugh. "I agree with you on that one. New York definitely knows how to make good pizza."

We smiled shyly at each other.

"I want to start a business downtown," I blurted out. "I already have the store picked out for it and everything. It needs some work, but it has a beautiful bay window."

"Really?" He sounded surprised. "What type of business?"

Suddenly I grew hesitant at the question. I'd already said too much. I couldn't believe I had just told him that. Kristen was the only other person I'd ever talked to about it.

"I'm not really sure yet," I mumbled, looking away.

"No? No ideas at all?" he prodded gently. "I find it hard to believe that someone who already has the location picked out for her business doesn't have *any* ideas for what type of business to actually run there."

"Okay, okay," I groaned. "Yes, I have some ideas."

He cocked his head to one side, waiting patiently for me to finish.

I sighed. *Since I've already come this far . . .*

"I make perfumes, and I've thought about having a place where people can come and get their own scent custom made for them. I've also dabbled a bit in making soap and shampoo, although my last creation was a disaster and it will take a while before I get the formulas correct." The words came spilling out of me in a rush. "Basically I just want to have a little handmade bath and body shop, and call it Abbey's Hollow . . . in honor of Washington Irving." I peeked over at him, silently willing him not to say how stupid it all sounded. I wasn't up for rejection.

To his credit he didn't even look bored. "I like it."

"You do?" I asked him, a tiny bit shocked. "But what about the name? Do you think it's corny?"

"No. I don't think it's corny at all."

I gave him a tell-me-the-truth look.

"Seriously," he replied with a straight face. He leaned in a little closer to me, and his eyes held mine. "I really do like the idea, Abbey. I think it's great. And the name is the best part."

I didn't even think twice about telling him more. "I have a business plan started for it," I confessed. "But Mom and Dad are pushing me to go to some prestigious university. All I really want to do is take a couple of local business classes, and maybe apprentice with someone who runs their own herb shop. Or go to Paris and see what I can learn there." I shrugged halfheartedly. "I don't want to waste my life in school for something I have no interest in, you know?"

Another thought intruded, and I frowned. "Of course, all of my plans could end up going nowhere. Kristen was going to . . ." My voice caught, and I broke off. Looking down at the limp violet in my hand, I played with the stem and concentrated hard on not crying. "Kristen was going to help me with the shop. She had the most amazing ideas for the perfume labels and . . ."

A tear leaked out of the corner of my eye and I hastily wiped it away, trying not to smudge my makeup.

"It's okay, Abbey," Caspian said softly. "Don't cry. I think it's a good idea to open your shop. You'll be making Kristen happy by continuing on with your dream."

"Do you think so?" I asked, trying vainly to keep the quiver out of my voice.

He nodded gravely and then deftly turned the conversation back to my parents. "What if you compromise with them?" he suggested. "If you tell your mom and dad what your ideas are now, then maybe they won't waste their time planning a different future for you. You never know. It's worth a shot."

What he said made an incredible amount of sense. The simplicity of it made me feel stupid for not thinking of it myself. "Thanks for the advice, Caspian. I never would have thought of such an obvious answer. It was right there in front of me the whole time."

"You're welcome," he said. "Sometimes all it takes is looking at the problem from a different angle. You can always ask my advice, Abbey. I'll try to help whenever I can."

Was I hearing more behind that statement than he actually meant? I couldn't tell.

I cleared my throat. Time to move on to happier things so I didn't drag the whole day down with my sniffling and crying. "Do you want to see something? There's a tiny waterfall on the other side of the bridge. We'll have to walk a little bit to reach it. It's sort of hidden." If he noticed my sudden change of topic, he didn't mention it.

"Okay." He put his book on the ground. "I guess I'll leave this here for now and come back for it."

"No one will run off with it," I reassured him with a grin before standing up. Carefully tucking the flower into my jean pocket, I tried to brush off the back of my sweater to remove any stray rocks or dirt that might be clinging on. I did *not* want to find out later that I had been parading around with pieces of nature all over my ass.

Caspian stood too and once again motioned for me to lead the way. Turning, I led him out from underneath the opposite side of the bridge and we settled into silence as we walked along the riverbank.

"Have you . . . read anything by Edgar Allan Poe?" I ventured. I had to keep him talking. He would think I was a freak if I just stayed silent the whole time. "I loved his story 'The Tell-tale Heart.' Talk about creepy."

"I'll have to check that one out," he said. "I've heard of 'The Raven,' but not that one."

"'The Pit and the Pendulum' is another good one. Look for that one too," I said. *Am I actually getting better at this small talk thing?* Maybe it was because he was so easy to talk to. And he loved books. Could he be any more perfect?

"I guess living in the town of Sleepy Hollow means that you've read the story by Washington Irving, then, right?" He stooped to pick up a small handful of tiny pebbles, rattling them around gently as he spoke.

"Are you kidding me? They teach it in first grade at the elementary school. This town *idolizes* Mr. Irving. His other stories were good, but nothing can top 'The Legend of Sleepy Hollow.'"

"I think it's cool that his house is near here. Talk about truly loving the town you live in."

I nodded my agreement. "He's buried here too. On a hillside in the Irving family plot." I paused to turn back and point in the general direction of the cemetery. "I stop by there a lot. I'll have to show it to you sometime."

"It's a date," he said softly, catching my eye.

"Okay. It's a date," I repeated back to him. The butterflies started swimming around in my stomach again, and I felt my cheeks start to burn. I ducked under a low-hanging tree branch, holding on to my hat with one hand while also trying to slow my racing heart.

Inhale and exhale. Think calm, cool thoughts. What he'd said was no big deal. It wasn't even an official I'll-pick-you-up-and-we'll-go-to-dinner date. I was simply going to show him an old tombstone. No big deal.

So then why did I feel like hyperventilating?

He interrupted my mini freak-out session. "I actually have a little confession to make. Wanna hear it?"

I was cool. I was calm. I could answer him now. I shrugged. *Um, YES!* "Sure. What is it?" I was really getting good at this whole not-acting-too-eager thing.

"I haven't read the story yet," he said.

My brain must not have been functioning properly. That's the only excuse I have. "What story?" I asked dumbly.

He laughed. "You know, the story we've been talking about? 'The Legend of Sleepy Hollow'?"

I came to a dead stop and turned to face him. "Wait. What? *Seriously?* You've never read 'The Legend of Sleepy Hollow'? Good

God, don't let the natives hear you say that. You'll be tied up and roasted for non-book-reading historical duty or something."

He winked at me, and I could almost hear the grin in his voice as he leaned forward and whispered conspiratorially, "I'll have to count on you, then, Abbey, to fill the gaps in my education before any of them find out. Think you're up to it?"

My cheeks burned fire, but I managed to keep my voice normal. "I *guess* I can . . . but let's wait until we get more comfortable."

Hearing my words, and immediately realizing all the wrong ways that they could be taken, I jerked back around and pitched forward. I was a freak. A complete and total *freak of nature.*

We reached a split in the path, and I led us to the left. Squeezing between two large boulders, I motioned for Caspian to follow me as I tried to erase my words from just seconds ago. "Like I said, it's a tiny waterfall, but I still think it's pretty neat." We stepped all the way through, and a panoramic view spread before us.

Dozens of rocks had been spread out like giant stepping stones, and water rushed and pooled and trickled from one stone to the next. It ended with a free fall into a basin that was less than two feet deep.

I moved closer and settled onto a smooth, flat rock that offered the driest surface. It was wide enough for two, but to my instant regret Caspian perched on a hollowed-out tree trunk beside me. He tossed his handful of pebbles into the river and they made loud plunking noises before sinking to the bottom.

Then he angled his body so that he was facing me. "So, about this legend . . ."

A large smile crossed my face and I forgot all about my embarrassment from before. This was *my* story. I knew it backward and forward, and I couldn't *wait* to tell the tale.

"It starts with this gangly schoolteacher named Ichabod Crane, who also happens to be the choirmaster, town gossip, and general all-around errand boy. After teaching his classes during the day, he went from house to house to gossip and tell ghost stories at night. One of the favored stories of the time was about a Hessian soldier who had lost his head and was rumored to haunt the bridge and cemetery by the church. He was named the Headless Horseman."

I watched to see if he was getting bored or restless yet, but Caspian's eyes were focused solely on me. His eyes were gorgeous, and I had to fight not to get lost in them. It took me a second to pick up where I'd left off.

"So Ichabod Crane is happy teaching his little school and

being the gossip bringer, until one day he sees Katrina Van Tassel—daughter of Baltus Van Tassel—and falls madly in love with her. Of course, *I* think he probably fell in love with all the land, animals, and obvious wealth that Baltus displayed, but either way, he was bound and determined to have her."

I lowered my voice and gave it an ominous tone. "What Ichabod quickly realized, though, was that Katrina was a flirt and already had several suitors. The most popular one being Brom Bones. Brom was basically everything that Ichabod wasn't. Strong, well built, boisterous, and full of himself. A very manly man."

Caspian snorted, and I gave him a quick half smile.

"When Ichabod starts trying to court Katrina, Brom plays practical jokes on him. Terrorizing Ichabod's students, ransacking his schoolhouse, making fun of his singing voice . . . that type of thing. Then it all comes down to a big harvest celebration that the Van Tassels throw one evening. Ichabod is invited, and tries to finally win Katrina's hand. But something goes wrong, and Katrina turns him down. Brokenhearted, Ichabod leaves the party on his old, lame, borrowed horse, to wander home through the dark.

"You have to know where it goes from here, right?" I interrupted myself and asked Caspian.

He grinned. "Keep going. This is getting good."

I shifted my weight to one side and readjusted my legs. "Okay, then. . . . So as Ichabod is wandering home, every little noise is scaring him half to death because all he can think about are all the ghost stories he's been told. When *suddenly* he hears a horse following him. Closer and closer it gets. The hoofbeats echo around him, louder and louder. And then . . . he sees it. The Headless Horseman—riding a huge black horse and carrying his head on the saddle—is coming straight for him! Ichabod urges his horse on, but the Horseman is just too close, and Ichabod sees him rear back and throw the head directly at him!" I paused to take a breath, and shifted again.

"And then the next morning Ichabod Crane is declared missing, a shattered pumpkin is found beside his lonely horse, and Brom Bones marries Katrina Van Tassel shortly afterward, laughing all the way to the altar."

Caspian looked at me in disbelief. "That's it?"

"Pretty much," I said. "Of course it's much more entertaining when you read the actual story, instead of just listening to the abbreviated version, but that's it."

"So it was Brom Bones all along. There never was any Headless

Horseman or menacing rider. Just someone who pulled a nasty trick on a gullible person."

"Well, I wouldn't say that there's not a ghostly horseman. There are always stories floating around about him; Washington Irving didn't just make that up. But I don't think that it was the Headless Horseman who pulled that stunt. I think it was Brom. Jealous, pitiful Brom, trying to make sure he got his way. And he did."

Then Caspian smiled, a brief you-amuse-me smile, and shook his head. I raised an eyebrow.

"What?" I demanded.

"Funny mental picture, that's all," he said.

I waited for him to elaborate, but he didn't feel like sharing.

"You know it's rude to keep a girl waiting," I teased.

He smiled again. "My sincerest apologies. I don't want to show off my bad manners. That can wait for next time."

I nodded for him to continue.

"I was picturing *you* being chased by a Headless Horseman and then stopping to tell him off. It was funny."

"I don't think I'd do that." I shook my head. "The Horseman is one person I don't want to meet."

"Because he's a ghost?"

I shrugged. "Yeah, I guess. Wouldn't he frighten you?"

"Never," he scoffed. "I'm a manly man."

I couldn't hold in my snort of laughter. "Right, of course."

"It doesn't matter, though. I won't be seeing him anytime soon. I don't believe in ghosts." Caspian stretched out his legs, and disappointment hit me again that he hadn't sat down next to me. "The only thing I don't understand about the whole story is why the town idolizes Washington Irving so much."

I was appalled. "We idolize Washington Irving because he was an amazing storyteller, for one thing. He breathed life and imagination into literature. Taking bits and pieces of real people, and real places, and blending them into this beautiful American folktale that's lasted a hell of a lot longer than he did. When you live in the Hollow, you can't help but want to celebrate that. Or at least that's how I've always felt."

I stared down at my feet once I realized what a tirade I had gone on. Great, now he would think I was a raving lunatic. *Way to make an impression, Abbey. A nut job impression.*

Instead, he did the weirdest thing ever. He started clapping. "Bravo, Abbey. Have you thought about running for office?"

I made a face at him. "Sorry about that. Too much? My parents are on the town council, and sometimes I go to the meetings and really get into all this town pride stuff. I'm not like a fanatic or anything. It's just that some of the stuff they say makes a lot of sense." I shrugged. "You know, as a future business owner here and all . . ."

He smiled at me again. "You should never apologize for anything you believe in, Abbey. I meant what I said. You would make one hell of a politician."

"Uh-uh." I shook my head. "There is no *way* I would ever become a politician. I'm terrified of crowds. Ter-ri-fied. And the speeches? If I couldn't even say three lines in our fourth-grade school play because I was so nervous I threw up everywhere . . . well, something tells me that the public wouldn't appreciate cleaning vomit out of their clothes every time I had to give a speech." I giggled so hard at that mental picture that I actually had to wipe tears away.

Then I realized that I probably looked like a laughing hyena and tried very hard to compose myself. No need for more embarrassment. Luckily, Caspian was laughing too.

"Not all the town council meetings are interesting, though," I pointed out, glad to be talking about something different. "In fact, most of them are pretty boring. Whenever the conversation turns to zoning laws, lawn watering limits, or speed bump enforcement issues, my eyes start to cross. Then I just slip out and go wander through some of the other rooms. All the meetings are held in the museum, so I kind of get to take my own private tour."

"What type of stuff do they have in there?" he asked, leaning closer. "Like old artifacts, or newspapers, or what?"

I tried to picture the museum displays accurately in my mind. "They have pretty much everything, from things that were found— pieces of pottery, old canning jars, used musket balls, spinning wheels—to entire outfits that were worn in Washington Irving's era. One of the displays is dedicated solely to the genealogy of Sleepy Hollow. Who was born here, what families married into each other, and how their children's lives were interconnected. There are a lot of family Bibles and old newspaper clippings in that display."

I wasn't sure if that was what he'd meant about artifacts and newspapers. "If you mean actual newspapers from the town, though, all those are kept in the library's archive room."

We sat talking about everything and nothing for another hour, occasionally lapsing into moments of silence only punctuated by the intermittent noises of birds calling to each other.

My ringing cell phone interrupted one of those silences, and the sound echoed around us. Seeing that it was Mom's number on the screen, I sent it to voice mail. If she really needed me, she'd leave a message.

As the caller ID flashed off, I looked back down to see if it was lunchtime yet. Right on cue, my stomach growled. "Do you want to . . . go get a slice of pizza . . . or something?" I couldn't look Caspian directly in the eye. My shyness hadn't completely vanished.

He hesitated and stood up. "Abbey, I'm sorry, but I've got to go. I have some stuff to do this afternoon."

I'm cool, I'm calm. "Sure, no problem. Maybe next time. I should get going too, big science paper to finish and all that." I jumped up from my rock.

His smile was breathtaking, and heartbreaking, all at the same time. "Thanks, Abbey. I had a really good time with you today."

"Yeah, sure." We moved back toward the boulders. "When I wasn't launching into any speeches, maybe."

His eyes glowed with silent laughter, and a piece of stray black hair fell into one of them. He brushed it back haphazardly. "You didn't launch into any speeches," he reassured me. "Everything we talked about was cool. An exchange of wits."

We walked side by side on the path to the bridge.

He looked away for a moment, and then back at me again. "You have this way of viewing things, Abbey. . . . It turns my whole world upside down."

I didn't know what to say to that astonishing statement. *Should I say something complimentary back?* I didn't have to worry about it, though, because my phone rang again. Mom's name flashed across the screen for a second time.

"Sorry," I said to him. "I probably should get this. It's my mom. Again." He nodded, and I flipped open the phone. "Hey, Mom. . . . Yeah, your voice mail just popped up. I didn't get to listen to it yet. . . . Why? What's up? . . . Wait—what? You're breaking up. Hold on. . . . I said hold on."

We were almost to the bridge now, and I quickly walked underneath it to get to the other side. The reception was much better there.

"Okay, repeat that last part. You need what? Which file? . . . The one in the third cabinet. Okay, got it. Not the stack of green ones, though? . . . Wait a sec—hold on." I covered up the phone and turned back to Caspian. He had stopped to pick up his book. "I have to go. My mom needs some paperwork for a meeting she's in, and I have to get it for her. Thanks for . . . everything . . . Caspian. I had a nice time too."

I barely heard his whispered "Bye, Abbey" as I turned away from the bridge again.

"Yes, Mom, I'm still here. But why can't you get it? . . . Okay, fine. Give me about thirty minutes to get it to you, okay?" I peeked over my shoulder and mouthed another "Sorry" as I started climbing up the riverbank. Raising one hand in farewell, Caspian waved good-bye to me.

Shoving one hand into my pocket, I touched the crumpled-up violet that rested in there, and I couldn't stop smiling the whole way home.

Chapter Seven

HONORARY MEMBER

Such heaped-up platters of cakes of various and almost indescribable kinds, known only to experienced Dutch housewives!

—"The Legend of Sleepy Hollow"

To say I was distracted for the rest of the weekend would have been the understatement of the year. I had to keep pulling myself out of dreamland and back down to reality. And it was only because I really *did* have a science paper to finish that I didn't go back to the river on Sunday just in case he happened to be there.

After I handed in the completed assignment on Monday morning, I spent the rest of the class debating whether or not I should take the way home that passed by the river. *Will Caspian be there? What if he's waiting for me? Or what if he isn't there now but will come by later?*

There were so many variables to consider, I could go crazy trying to think of everything.

I forced myself to relax; I was putting way too much thought into this. He knew what school I went to. If he wanted to see me again, he could find me. Then panic hit. *Oh God, what if he shows up here, at school?*

I hoped Mr. Knickerbocker wasn't going over anything that would be needed for a test later, because I didn't hear a word he said during that whole science class. I was too busy trying to figure out what I should do.

Finally I came up with the tentative plan of hanging out by the outside steps after school for an extra fifteen minutes in case Caspian showed up, and then taking the way home by the river if he didn't. But by the end of the next period, I was completely convinced that I would look too desperate if I hung around school and stopped by the river again. I didn't want to look like I was chasing him around.

I went back and forth on it all day long, but ended up being slammed with so much homework that I was too busy to worry about whether or not Caspian would show up. I had a lot of books to shove into my tiny book bag, and it refused to cooperate. I forgot all about the whole idea to wait outside at the end of the day and quickly started home.

What I didn't forget, though, was my indecision on which way to actually take. I tried to convince myself that there were several valid reasons to go by the river.

I should stop there in case another piece of police tape had gotten stuck in a tree.

And I should probably make sure that no one stepped on that shiny thing I'd seen in the water.

Or what if someone *had* stepped on the shiny thing, which turned out to be glass, and there was no one around to help bandage their foot?

There were half a dozen excuses that I could have made, but I knew the real reason why I was going. I wanted to see Caspian again. That was the bottom line. No poorly disguised excuse needed. I held my breath in anticipation as I turned toward the river and tried to work out clever small talk in my head. *Hey, what are you doing here?*

Wow! What a surprise! I didn't expect to see you again so soon.

Come here often?

Good move, Abbey, I chastised myself. *Greet him with a pickup line used in bars.*

Yeah, I was *so* not good at this.

When I got to the riverbank and scanned the edge, no one was there. I looked several times under the bridge, but I didn't see him sitting there, either. Obviously I had a lot more free time on my hands than he did. And obviously I was the only one who was desperate for us to see each other again. Disappointment washed over me and I dragged my feet the rest of the way home.

I was *not* in a very good mood when I finally made it up to my room.

Homework sucked, and it took forever to do. If this was any indication of the upcoming school year, then it was *not* going to be an easy one. I didn't even want to think about the stack of glossy booklets and colorful brochures that Mom and Dad had started nudging my way. My brain couldn't handle any college drama right now.

It was after twelve thirty by the time I finished all my homework, but I was still too hung up on the disappointment at the bridge to sleep. So I started looking over my notes for Kristen's perfume, and sat down to tweak a few things. The next couple of hours flew by.

Because of that, I ended up with only three hours of sleep for school the next day, and that resulted in a disrupted nap during study hall and the shortest route home so I could finish that nap.

The rest of the week went by in much the same fashion, without me seeing Caspian even once at the cemetery, or the bridge, and I spent each night trying to distract myself with my perfume project.

But on Friday I was ambushed.

I had just slammed my locker door shut when I spotted one of the cheerleaders, Shana, trying to flag me down from one end of the hall. Hoping to avoid her, I did a quick half turn and started to walk in the opposite direction. Bad idea. Erika was coming that way, and she started waving at me too.

I froze, looking back and forth between the two, like a deer caught in the headlights. They must have sensed my urge to run, because they started waving frantically. They looked like two people stranded on a desert island, desperate to signal the only plane flying overhead. Their arms were jerking crazily over their heads.

Apparently I was the only one who noticed how crazy they looked, though, because no one else in the half-empty hallway paid them any attention.

Shana reached me first, and I knew I was doomed.

"There you are," she said, flashing a perfect, but very fake, smile. "We were trying to get your attention."

I just stared back at her. *Am I supposed to say something here?* I grasped at the first thing that came to mind. "Oh, yeah, I, uh, just remembered that I have to stop by English. I left one of my books there." I smiled weakly. Would it work? Would they leave me alone?

"Well, this will only take a minute. I'm sure you'll have plenty of time. You know Erika, right?"

"Hey," said Erika, who had taken much longer to make it over to my locker. Probably had something to do with the fact that she'd been stopped by no fewer than seven boys on her trip from one end of the hall to the other.

I gave her a forced smile. *If I don't talk much, will it encourage them to leave quicker?* I was clinging to the faint hope that it would.

"Anyway," continued Shana, with a bored look on her face. "What do you think about joining the prom committee this year? Of course, you'll only be an honorary member, but we'd like to give you the opportunity because of, you know."

I had no idea what she was talking about. "Sorry. I don't get it."

"Get it?" sneered Erika. "There's nothing to get. We're asking you a question. You say yes or no."

Yes, but why *are they asking me this question?*

Erika answered my unspoken thoughts. "Look, I don't give two shits about you, and I don't give two shits about whether or not you join the prom committee. Everyone knows you're milking the whole poor-me-my-friend-died thing, but for some reason all the teachers are buying it. And Principal Meeker most of all. He's forcing us to ask you as some messed-up way to pay respect to that Kristen girl's memory."

To give myself some credit, I actually did manage to hold in my snort of disbelief. *In what parallel universe does asking me to be an honorary prom committee member equal paying respect to Kristen's memory?* Before I could even attempt to follow that train of logic, Shana spoke again.

"Since the prom is in October, all the major planning was done last spring, of course. Now the *official* prom committee members just have to decide which color combinations to decorate with, what kind of favors to give out, whether or not there will be sherbet in the punch . . . stuff like that. As an honorary member, you'll get to, like, listen to us decide."

"Personally, I am voting for no sherbet this year," Erika butted in. "That stuff is disgusting. I don't care if it's not even as fattening as regular ice cream. It still goes straight to your hips."

"Don't worry, Erika, we are totally not having sherbet in the punch this year. I am putting my foot down on that one." Shana cast her vote on the sherbet issue.

I tried very hard not to think about all the pints of chocolate chip cookie dough ice cream that Kristen and I had polished off on multiple sleepovers. It had practically been a requirement for one. Nor did I think about the fact that I very much liked having sherbet in punch, and always made an extra effort to skim a piece of it when dishing up my beverage.

It didn't matter anyway, because there was no way in *hell* I was going to accept a position as "honorary" prom committee member. Or any other position, for that matter. *Prom planning is against my religion* would have to work. It was all I could think of.

"So." Shana was talking again. "Like Erika said, we don't care what you do. But Principal Meeker does, and he's promised us first dibs on the senior trip tickets if you join. So guess what? You're going to join. The first meeting will be tomorrow in the auditorium at nine a.m."

"Don't be late, loser," Erika said, with a vicious push to my left shoulder that sent me stumbling back into my locker door.

They both laughed and turned to leave as I rubbed my stinging arm with one hand.

My brain was still trying to form a coherent, sane sentence that involved me turning them down flat, yet all that came out was, "Ow." I looked down at my book bag, and then back in the general direction toward where they'd disappeared. "But—"

Only my locker door heard me, and it cared about as much as they did.

"Harsh," said a voice behind me, and I turned to see Ben coming my way.

I groaned inwardly. *Is this guy stalking me or something?* First he was at Kristen's funeral, then her house, and now here?

He stopped next to the locker beside mine. The empty one.

"Was this Kristen's locker?" he asked, staring at it like he could see through metal.

"Yeah," I said, momentarily distracted from my arm pain.

"It must be hard not seeing her here every day. I still haven't gotten used to it."

"Me either," I blurted out.

He just looked at me then. His big brown eyes were . . . sad. Like he really missed her.

The bell rang once, prompting us both into action. He took a step back and turned to move down the hall. "Don't let those bitches get to you, Abbey," he called out as he headed to his next class.

"O . . . kay?" I said awkwardly as I tightened my grip on my book bag. Then I shook my head. Was I wearing some kind of perfume that attracted weirdness? Today was turning out to be a very weird day.

I walked home as quickly as I could after school, all thoughts of the day's strangeness forgotten. Some new scent combinations had miraculously popped into my brain for Kristen's perfume, and I was eager to work on them.

Mom was using her laptop at the kitchen table when I got in. I grabbed an orange and headed up to my room to get busy. Two hours later, after several rounds of mixing, measuring, sniffing, and note taking, I had come up with a couple of new scents that I was pretty happy with. But I still needed a second opinion. Gathering up several tester vials, I headed back down to the kitchen.

"Mom!" I yelled, halfway down the stairs. "Are you in the kitchen?"

"Yes, I am," came her distracted reply.

I jumped down the last couple of steps and bounced into the room. "Will you smell a couple of these testers for me? I need a second nose."

"Yeah, sure." She pushed her laptop to the side. "I could use a break from all this Hollow Ball planning anyway."

"Sniff each one, and then tell me what you think," I instructed as I lined up the vials in front of her. "I've smelled them all so many times that the scents are running together on me."

She reached for the first one. "Okay. I'll give it my best shot. Has, um, anyone talked to you yet about the prom committee?"

I almost dropped the last vial I held. "How do you know about that?"

She didn't answer me but moved on to the next sample and sniffed. "Ooh, I like this one." She picked up the third vial while I stood there and stared at her like she'd just grown an extra arm.

"Mom!" I waited . . . then arched my eyebrow at her.

"What?" she tried to look surprised, but I didn't buy it.

"How do you know about that?" I demanded again.

"Principal Meeker called," she admitted. "He mentioned that the girls on the cheerleading squad were going to talk to you about it. So I guess they did."

I pushed the last sample over to her and pointed at it, indicating that I wanted her to sniff, not talk. "What do you think?" I asked. "Was there anything you liked, or didn't like, about them?" I waited for her reply.

"They all had a unique scent. Number two was my favorite, but I really didn't like number four."

"That's because sample number two had notes of vanilla in it," I informed her. "Which you definitely like, while sample number four had lavender in it, which you definitely do not like. Number two was my favorite too, so that's the one I'll go with. Thanks for helping me out." I started gathering up the vials to head back upstairs.

"You never answered my question, Abbey." Her tone stopped me dead in my tracks.

"Mom, I just . . ." I was exasperated. "The answer is no. No, I'm not going to join their stupid prom committee. End of story."

"But why, Abbey?" she pleaded with me. "What would it hurt? You and Kristen have been talking about your prom since you were little girls. Now you can actually help plan it. Kristen would *want* you to be on it. And besides, won't it be fun to talk to the other girls about their dresses? I know you didn't like that one I bought for you, but it's not too late to go get another one."

I didn't even go into the whole I-can't-believe-you-bought-me-a-prom-dress-I-didn't-pick-out argument again. That had been hashed out several times already.

"No, Mom. Kristen would *not* want me to be on some dumb committee run by some stupid, fake girls who haven't talked to either one of us since middle school. I think I know what my best friend would want me to do."

"If you don't want to do it for Kristen, then fine, do it for the school. Think about how this will look on your college applications. Besides, it would set a good example, Abbey. Your father and I have lived our lives always trying to be a good example for those around us. Maybe you need to accept the invitation simply because those girls took the time to think of you."

"They didn't think of me, Mom!" I exploded. "Do you even know how they asked me? *Do you?* They cornered me in the hallway and practically forced me to say yes. All because of Principal

Meeker. He wanted them to 'honor' Kristen's memory by asking me to be an *honorary* member. It's the stupidest thing I've ever heard of."

"Well, naturally you can't be a regular member of the committee; you have to be voted in. Being an honorary member is a special privilege. And I think it's an extremely nice way for them to honor Kristen. It was very thoughtful of them." Her voice had gotten louder.

"Very thoughtful?!" I was practically screaming. "They didn't do it because they were *thoughtful*. They did it so they could get themselves some stupid school-related privilege. And 'naturally' I can't be a regular member? Do you even hear yourself? I never asked to be on their freakin' committee in the first place. I don't care if it's an honorary position, a voted-in position, or president of the whole damn thing!"

"I just don't think its right for you to turn down an opportunity like this simply because you don't feel like it." Her voice took on a deadly quiet tone. "You can't stop living life, Abbey, just because Kristen had to. Over time it will get better."

"I am living life," I responded wearily. It felt like suddenly every muscle in my body had been stretched to the limit. "I'm still getting up and going to school, aren't I? I'm still doing my homework and eating my vegetables, aren't I? I'm still getting showered, getting dressed, putting on my shoes. . . . If I'm still doing all those things, then I'm still living life. But it will *never* get better. No matter how many prom committees I join, or college brochures I shuffle through, or . . ." I looked down at the vials in my hands. "Or how many new perfumes I make. This knot of coldness will always be inside of me. Always."

Mom's voice was quiet but firm. "I'm sorry, Abbey. I'm very sorry you feel that way, and if you need to talk to a professional about it, then we can arrange that for you. But you *will* accept their offer. No other arguments."

"Fine. Whatever, Mom." I jerked away. "But I don't need to talk to a *professional* about anything." One of the vials suddenly dropped from my hands and burst into tiny shards of glass on the ocher tile floor. The instant smell of lavender filled the air. *Sample number four.* I felt a perverse sense of satisfaction fill me, but I tried to squash it down.

"Just go," Mom said. "I'll clean this up. We'll continue this discussion later, Abigail."

Oh, goody, that's exactly what I wanted to hear: "We'll

continue this discussion later." What was there to continue? My mind had obviously been made up for me. I stomped up the stairs, wondering just how many bottles of lavender oil I could "accidentally" spill in my room.

I overslept on Saturday morning, and that was a great way to start off a crappy day that I was already not looking forward to. I didn't have time to eat breakfast, so I was in a royally foul mood with a growling stomach as I cut through the cemetery to get to school. *On a Saturday.*

"Hey, Abbey." His voice startled me.

I spun around. "Caspian, hi." My day instantly went from very bad to very good.

"How are you?" He was standing near the bridge.

"I'm good. How are you?" I gave him a shy half smile, not quite able to look him straight in the eye.

"I'm good. I'm really good. Are you doing anything today? Want to hang out for a while?" He gave me the cutest little smile.

Would it be bad if I called him adorable? Probably. Guys usually don't like those sort of girly terms associated with them.

"Yeah, I—" Then I remembered where I was supposed to be

heading. "I mean, I'd really like to stay, but I can't. I have this stupid school thing I have to go to."

"No big deal. Some other time, then."

Was it just my extremely hopeful imagination, or did he actually look disappointed? "What about next week? I can take you on that tour of Washington Irving's grave. We'll meet here, next Saturday around eleven thirty?" That should give me enough time to get back if I had another stupid prom meeting. The butterflies started swimming in my stomach. *Will he turn me down?*

"It's a date," he agreed. "Bye, Abbey. See you next week." He turned to walk away.

"Bye, Caspian!" I called out. He stopped, and threw me a big grin over his shoulder. I grinned back like the Cheshire cat. What was it about him that made me feel so ridiculously happy?

By the time I got to the school auditorium, I was in such a great mood, it was unbelievable. I wasn't even fazed by the death glares I received from Shana and Erika.

"I brought low-fat all-natural blueberry muffins and sparkling water for everyone," Shana begrudgingly told me, pointing to a nearby table. "Just try not to, like, eat everything, okay?" Erika laughed at what she said, but I just ignored them.

Personally, I would have chosen a dozen sugar doughnuts, but since I was starving, I couldn't afford to be picky.

I walked over to the table, grabbed a muffin, and slid an extra one into my pocket for later. Then I snagged a bottle of water. Finding a chair that was close to the others, but not within conversational range, I took a seat.

Scanning the room covertly, I counted a total of twelve, seriously twelve—was that necessary?—people there for the prom committee meeting. Over in another corner some tables and chessboards were set up. Two guys were bent over the boards, while a third stood off to the side, watching their every move. I noticed his brown curly hair about the same time he noticed me, and Ben glanced over, giving me a huge silly grin and waving like an idiot.

I tried to discreetly give him a brief wave back, and then turned my attention to the muffin in my hand. I should have guessed he would be here.

A minute and a half later I was *seriously* regretting that muffin.

"All-natural" must have meant "made with natural sawdust" or something, because that was what the thing tasted like. I tried to swallow it down with a huge gulp of water, but that only made the dry, crumbly mess in my mouth become a wet, soggy mess.

I fought back an automatic gag reflex and desperately wished I had picked up a napkin. At least then I could have spit out the shameful imitation muffin. Of course that was when Shana decided to announce my name as the special honorary member and everyone turned to stare at me. I prayed that no stray bits of muffin escaped my mouth as I gave a small closed-lip smile.

Most of them looked away when Erika started talking, and I frantically chewed what was left of the muffin mess. I gagged slightly as I swallowed, but I think only one guy heard me. He gave me a knowing look when he saw me set the muffin down on the ground next to me, still largely uneaten.

I looked closely at the other people in the room, wondering how many of them had also made the mistake of the muffin. No one else had any telltale crumbs or stray wrappers hanging around. Maybe they were all smarter than me.

Two agonizingly long hours dragged by *very slowly*, and I started contemplating whether or not I could choke myself to death on the muffin I had left in my pocket. The meeting, so far, had been one never ending conversation about what colors to decorate with and why.

When it seemed like they had made their final decision, I quickly scooped up the muffin remains and the empty bottle of water to throw away. I was *definitely* going to drop a bottle of lavender oil on the kitchen floor today. Mom should have to suffer as much as I had, since she was the reason I was here in the first place.

Passing the garbage can on my way out, I hoped to make my getaway without being stopped by anyone. Two more steps and I would be out the door. I was so close.

"Watch out for those muffins next time. They're killer."

I looked over my shoulder as I pushed through the door. Erika was the only one standing there. I felt my cheeks turn red, and she laughed out loud. But I didn't mind too much, because the last thing she saw was my middle finger aimed in her direction as I stepped outside.

On Monday, Shana informed me that the prom committee would no longer be needing my honorary services. I barely contained my joy.

But the rest of the school week felt like it would never end. It was like we were all stuck in some continuous *Twilight Zone* time loop, destined to repeat the same class over and over again.

Every second of the clock ticked by excruciatingly slowly, when all I wanted was for Saturday to hurry up and get here so I could finally see Caspian.

Finally, *finally*, Saturday morning arrived, and I was up and ready to go by nine thirty. Mom and I were still in the only-talking-to-you-when-it's-necessary stage, so I tiptoed around her as I made a cup of tea. A nice dose of warm vanilla chai was just what I needed. I was even happier when I found a package of unopened biscotti in the cupboard.

Then I spent the next hour baking cookies.

I had a strange urge to give Caspian something, and figured he'd probably rather have cookies than perfume. After the third batch had cooled, I slid a dozen of them into an empty fortune cookie box and grabbed one to nibble on as I turned to head out the door.

"Don't forget the Baxleys are coming over for dinner tonight, Abigail," Mom reminded me stiffly as I left. Since I would still have most of the day with Caspian, I just agreed and quietly shut the door behind me. It wasn't worth an argument.

I walked quickly to the river, and he was waiting for me under the bridge again. As I got closer, I shouted to him and waved the fortune cookie box. He smiled at me and the sun reflected off his hair.

My heart stuttered for a moment. I didn't know what stroke of good fortune had caused this, but I felt very, very lucky.

"Hi, beautiful," he said quietly.

I didn't answer him; I was too busy staring at his eyes. Was he wearing contact lenses to make them look even more vivid? If so, then contact lenses that color should be banned. They could make people think dangerous things. . . .

I realized he was waiting for me to say something.

"Here," I said, thrusting the cookie holder at him suddenly. "These are for you."

An amused look crossed his face. "You brought me fortune cookies? Do I need some luck?"

I laughed. "No, they aren't fortune cookies. It was the only small box I could find. Open it up. They're snickerdoodles. I baked them this morning."

His eyes lit up like a little boy with a new toy. "You made cookies for me?" He opened the box and sniffed inside. The look on his face was sheer bliss. "Ahh. How did you know they were my favorite? Thank you, Abbey. You don't know what this means to me."

I decided right then and there to make a snickerdoodle

perfume to wear, so that one day he would sniff me like that.

"You're welcome." I shrugged, trying to hide my extreme giddiness over the fact that the cookies had pleased him so much. "I'm just glad you like them. Ready to go?"

A very fine misting rain had started, and after assuring him that I didn't mind, if he didn't mind, we started on our tour. I took him to the Washington Irving plot first, and then showed him some of the other family plots that were favorites of mine. But I didn't take him to where Kristen was buried, or to the grave where the chair was. Today was about different memories.

We wandered slowly through the cemetery, talking some more about the history of the town, and the legend. When the conversation eventually turned to school, we laughed ourselves hoarse as I tried to imitate some of my teachers.

The last stop we made was to a double tombstone with the family name of Crane on it. It was a fairly recent grave, only a few years old, but the death dates listed for both John and Maria were the same.

"It's really sad that they died on the same day," I told him as we stood before it. "Must have been some type of accident or something; they weren't even sixty yet. But you know what I love?

Every year on the anniversary of their death someone leaves a single rose for them."

Caspian was silent, and I didn't know if I'd just killed the happier mood of the day. I turned away, scanning the hillside to my left to see if there was anything there I could talk about that would change the mood. I wasn't having very much luck, though. You don't exactly get "chipper" and "cheerful" vibes from a cemetery.

A figure on the far side of the hill caught my eye, and I just barely made out the gray hair. Nikolas! Putting one hand up to wave, I twisted my head back toward Caspian. "Look! Over there. It's—"

He interrupted me. "Let's keep walking, Abbey. I don't think we should . . . be out in this rain."

But he was looking at the figure on the hill as he said it.

O-kay. "We could go back down to the bridge," I suggested. He agreed, and we headed there, and spent another hour talking about movies, music, and more books.

At two thirty he said he had to go, and I was surprised at how fast time had flown by again. He walked me over to the underside of the bridge, and the rain gently kissed our faces.

"Thanks again for the cookies, Abbey. That was very sweet of you." He held the box in one hand and shoved his other hand into the front pocket of his jeans. "I wish I had something to give you in return, but all I have is my undying gratitude."

Oh. My. God. Was he getting his lines from the *How to Be a Perfect Gentleman* handbook or something? "You're very welcome for the cookies, and you don't have to give me anything in return," I said, silently telling myself not to swoon. "Try them with some tea; they make great dippers."

"I will," he promised. "Good-bye, Abbey." He stepped out into the rain and started in the opposite direction of where I was going.

I turned my back, and stepped out into the rain myself. Then I stopped suddenly. "Caspian!" I yelled. He was farther away than I thought he would be. I could hardly see his outline anymore. "I won't be able to meet you next weekend; we're going to our cabin upstate."

"Don't worry about it, Abbey," his voice floated back to me. "I'll see you again."

Chapter Eight

SHORT NOTICE

Something, however, I fear me, must have gone wrong....

—"The Legend of Sleepy Hollow"

Unfortunately, school did not start off well on Monday morning. I flunked a test *and* a pop quiz, and finally got yelled at for falling asleep in study hall.

I tried to stay on top of things—putting extra study time into my homework and really focusing on my project for Kristen, but the nightmares returned. There weren't any hallucinations this time, but I still wasn't getting very much sleep.

Then I started feeling guilty about Caspian.

I shouldn't be happy. Why did I deserve any happiness? My best friend was dead. And instead of telling him about *her*, all I could do was talk about *me*. Me, me, me, all the time.

I was an awful friend, and I felt terrible about it.

It was too much, and by Wednesday it all came crashing down on me. I wound up rocking myself back and forth on the floor again, just like before. I tried desperately to hold it back, but a cold feeling came flooding over me, freezing that black void inside and hardening it into a sharp ball of ice.

My heart was covered in tiny icicles that stabbed me with every breath I took. Ripping and shredding, until I was raw and bleeding inside. Nothing more than a quivering, aching pitiful excuse for a human being. That night was a very, very bad night.

I rigorously avoided the river and the cemetery the rest of the week. Taking the longest way home after school each day to avoid any accidental meetings, I tried very hard not to think about Caspian at all. This meant that *everything* I did seemed to trigger a memory of him.

First, one of my perfume creations smelled exactly like snickerdoodle cookies. I hastily shoved that sample into a drawer to be forgotten. Then there was the three-day repeat of the movie *Great Expectations* on TV. I didn't watch anything for those three days. *At all.*

I was starting to think that the universe was having a giant cosmic laugh at my expense.

Needless to say, I was extremely happy when school let out on Friday and Dad started loading our bags into the van. Away from all the distractions and reminders, I *might* actually be able to relax. I also had a good feeling about Kristen's perfume. Hopefully, it would all come together at the cabin.

I drummed my fingers impatiently on the armrest beside me, fidgeting in my seat and waiting for Dad to finish with the last of the bags. Once he was done, we both sat ready and restless, waiting on Mom, who was still inside the house. Three car honks and fifteen minutes later she came out the front door holding a briefcase with some papers spilling out the top. She started to lock up, and then suddenly disappeared inside again. When she stepped back out, she had the cordless phone.

"Abbey!" she yelled, motioning for me to go meet her. "There's a phone call for you."

I looked at Dad, but he just shrugged. "I'll try to keep it quick," I said, "and I'll send her out first so she doesn't find a million other things that have to be done before we leave."

He grinned at me. "Good plan. I'll distract her out here."

Jumping down from the van, I asked Mom who it was. She shook her head. "I don't know. Some boy."

My pulse raced and my heart soared as I grabbed the receiver. *Is it Caspian? How did he get my number? What should I say?* Mom stood guard over the sink, apparently finding some nonexistent stain that needed to be buffed or cleaned.

"Mom," I said sternly, holding my hand over the phone, "go to the van. Dad needs you out there. He said it was important."

I could see an argument forming on the tip of her tongue.

"Go!" I shooed, turning my back to her but waiting until I heard the front door open and close again before I spoke into the phone.

"Hello?" My tongue swelled, my throat closed up. I prayed that I would be able to form at least one semicoherent sentence.

"Is this Abbey?" The voice on the other end wasn't right. It wasn't him.

"Who is this?" I demanded, jerked out of my sudden euphoria.

"This is Justin Gaines. We go to school together? Uh, anyway, I know it's short notice and all, but I heard you don't have a date yet. So do you want to go to the prom with me?"

That was *so* totally not what I expected to hear. "Wait—what? What did you just say? Do I even know you?"

"Well, uh, we have math together. . . ."

"And?" I prompted.

"And . . . tha-that's it," he stuttered.

And yet my bafflement didn't cease. "So let me get this straight. We only have one class together, and you've never spoken to me before . . . correct?"

"Uh, yeah." His voice sounded slightly queasy.

"Okay, so one class, no actual conversation. . . . And what would be the basis for you to ask me to go to the prom with you?"

Something else he had said suddenly clicked into place. "And who *exactly* told you that I don't have a date?"

There was complete silence on the other end.

"Hello? Justin?" I had moved beyond confused and was now in the realm of pissed off.

"Shana Williams," was his quiet reply. "She told me that I should ask you, as a favor to her, since . . . you know."

"No, I do not *know*," I spat into the phone.

"Since, you know, Kristen Maxwell died. And since she was a friend of yours. The girls told me about the prom committee thing. Then Shana suggested that I ask you. Since no one else probably would."

Now the silence was on my end. *The cheerleaders are setting up pity dates for me?* It doesn't get any worse than that.

"A-Abbey? Are you still there?" It sounded like a full-blown vomit party was on the way.

"Justin," I said sweetly, "thanks ever so much for calling, but the next time you see Shana Williams, you can tell her to go to hell."

"Okay, so is that a no?"

"Yeah, that's a big fat no." I pushed the off button and stared at the phone in my hand. Clearly it would have to be burned. The weirdness had spread to it.

The shrill sound of it ringing again made me jump a mile. Did he not understand the word "no"? I pushed the TALK button. "Listen, I told you *no*."

"Uh, is this Abigail Browning?" another male voice asked. "It's Trevor McCreeless. I'm calling about the prom."

I rubbed my temples fiercely. I was getting a killer headache.

"Let me guess," I sighed. "One of the girls from the cheerleading squad suggested you call?"

"Well, yeah, Erika did. How did you—?"

"I'm psychic," I barked out, cutting him off. "The answer's no." I slammed the phone back onto the charger and turned the answering machine off. I *definitely* didn't need Mom to hear God knows how many more messages from strange boys asking me to the prom. She would *never* let me get out of that one.

Besides, there was only one prom date I would ever dream of saying yes to.

I grabbed the house key from my pocket and rushed to the door. The phone started ringing again; how many people did those girls know? But I ignored it and locked up. I only hoped that Mom and Dad couldn't hear it from the car.

"Who was it, honey?" Mom asked the instant I sat down and shut my door. Curiosity was written all over her face.

"Just someone from school. He needed to know something from the prom committee." It wasn't technically a lie, since Shana and Erika *were* on the prom committee, and they *had* suggested he ask me out.

"See?" She beamed at me. "Aren't you glad you made the right choice, Abbey? I told you it was a good idea to join the prom committee." She didn't wait for my answer but started talking to Dad about something spectacular she had done when she'd been on the prom committee in high school.

I just slid my headphones on and tuned out their conversation.

The soothing rhythm of a slow song relaxed me while I watched the trees pass by. I closed my eyes and concentrated on the music, feeling my body gradually drift toward sleep.

When we arrived at the cabin and I took my first step inside, memories from the last time we had been there overwhelmed me. The details of that terrible phone call came rushing back, and I needed a moment to steady myself. I struggled not to lose it right then and there. . . .

"I'll get it," Mom said, finishing off the last of her coffee. "Would you pour me another cup? And then tell me more about that dream you were talking about." She hurried into the living room to reach the phone in time.

"Never mind about the dream, Mom. It was nothing. Really, just forget about it." I raised my voice so that she would hear me as I got up to get the coffee refill.

I heard the muffled "Hello" and then a low murmur of conversation. I couldn't make out the words, and I wasn't really listening anyway as I went through the motions automatically to get the coffee ready.

I took a sip . . . Needed more milk.

My mind drifted back to that strange dream from the night before. Something about it really bothered me. Something in the back of my head that I just couldn't put my finger on.

A sudden rush of feeling washed over me. Pain came fast, clenching my insides. Sharp and stabbing. It was intense, and overwhelming. I was going to be sick.

I put down the coffee mug and headed back to the table to sit for a minute. Resting my forehead on the tabletop, I took several deep breaths, but the pain didn't go away.

"Mom," I croaked, then took another deep breath and tried again. "Mom! I think something's wrong." I turned my head and rested it on the side. The tabletop was cool against my cheek. Breathing slowly, I tried to concentrate. Another sharp pain came. This time it took my breath away, and I doubled over.

I was never going to drink coffee again.

As I sat there hunched over the table, the sharp pains eventually receded, but they left behind a terrible stomachache. All I wanted was some Pepto-Bismol and my bed, ASAP.

Opting for the bed first, Pepto second, I stood slowly, trying not to move too fast. The last thing I needed was to be throwing up all over *the kitchen. I hobbled over to the living room to let Mom know that I was going upstairs. Her back was turned to me, and she was still on the phone.*

Leaning against the door frame, I tried to get her attention. "Mom, I think I'm sick. I'm going to lie—"

"Yes. Okay. . . . I understand. I'll call the—Hold on, let me call you back."

That must have been when she heard me.

She hung up the phone and turned around. The first thing I noticed was that her makeup, usually so perfect, had started to smear a little. She was always very careful about things like that. "Abbey." She spoke calmly, in a low voice. "Abbey, I need you to listen to me. . . . It's Kristen. They don't know how it happened. . . . It's her mom. . . . I'm sorry, honey."

I didn't understand.

"What? What happened to her? Did something happen to Kristen's mom?"

She shook her head back and forth and grabbed a tissue from the box on the desk. "It's not Kristen's mom." She still spoke calmly but was now carefully dabbing under each eye to fix her makeup. "It's Kristen, Abbey. It's Kristen."

It's . . . Kristen . . . It's . . . Kristen . . .

I heard the words rhythmically, like the slow thud of a heart-beat.

It's . . . Kristen . . . It's . . . Kristen . . .

I forced back the memory and fought to regain my composure. Dad didn't even bother to unpack the bags from the car but suggested we go get some pizza instead. We drove around searching for anywhere that was still open, and found an old game arcade from the fifties that promised THE FUN IS FREE! When we got back to the cabin that night, I stumbled into my room and collapsed onto the bed, falling into a restless sleep.

The next morning Mom asked me if I wanted to make chocolate chip cookies. Even though all I really wanted to do was stay in my nice warm bed, I knew she was trying to help me replace the bad memories with good ones, so I agreed.

After dragging myself out of bed, I helped her get the kitchen ready, and dug through several cabinets to find a couple of mixing bowls. "Where are the measuring cups?" I asked, with one of my hands stuck in the junk drawer.

"I think we put them in the cabinet over the sink," she replied.

Then she pulled out some eggs and butter from the fridge. "Do you remember the last time we baked together here? I think you were, what, eight or nine?"

"Ugh, that's right." I grimaced. "You told me I'd actually *like* banana bread."

She laughed. "Well, you used to love bananas when you were a baby, so I thought you'd love banana bread."

"Liking mushy bananas when you are two years old and liking bananas and bread mixed together when you are eight years old are two entirely different things," I retorted, and then I shuddered. "I *still* can't eat regular bananas to this day because they make me think of banana bread. And I hate the color yellow because *it* reminds me of bananas!"

She looked shocked. "Really? I had no idea that's why you won't eat bananas."

"Yup, you scarred me that badly when I was a child. I'll never eat bananas again." Striking a dramatic pose, I put one hand to my forehead and tried to look neglected. But I couldn't keep a straight face.

Mom tossed a dish towel at my head, and I caught it one-handed. "Get to work, banana hater," she ordered with a teasing grin.

~ ~ ~

I spent the rest of the day working on Kristen's perfume, and wrote down the last couple of notes I would need for the project. It was a bittersweet moment, to finally finish it here at the cabin, but I was overwhelmingly relieved. I bid a silent farewell to the ghost of old memories as we drove away.

We were halfway home before I noticed the worried looks Mom and Dad kept passing each other. When I caught Dad looking anxiously at me for the fifty-third time in the rearview mirror, I knew that something was going on.

"Hey, guys?" I asked. "What's up with you two?" Neither of them would meet my eyes in the mirror.

"What do you mean, Abbey? Nothing's wrong between your father and me."

"Okay, then, what's wrong in general? You two keep looking all worried. The last time you looked like this you told me that someone had died. I think I'd rather hear you're getting a divorce than hear that again," I joked.

Dad looked over at Mom. "Tell her," he said quietly.

"Wait, it's *not* a divorce . . . *is it?*"

"Abbey," said Mom, "we have something extremely important

to tell you, but we're not sure how you're going to take the news."

"But it's not a divorce, right? Tell me it's not a divorce!" My head was spinning with the fact that I might have to deal with separate households and shared holidays. I had just a little too much going on in my own world right now to have to learn to deal with any of that on top of it.

"No, it's not a divorce." Dad spoke up, and nodded at Mom to continue.

Instant relief struck me like a wave of cold water and left me feeling almost giddy with joy. I wasn't getting hit with the D-bomb.

"Abbey . . . while we were at the cabin . . . Well . . ." Mom spoke hesitantly and very carefully. "We got a call from the police."

I felt my body go instantly still. "And?"

"They found her, Abbey. They found Kristen's body two and a half miles down the Crane River. She'd drifted, and had gotten stuck under a pile of branches. They're going to bury her tomorrow at nine a.m. We can write a note for school, if you want to go. . . . I'm so sorry."

Mom waited for my answer, but I shook my head and then

turned to face the window. "I'm never going back to that cabin again," I said softly.

Mom and Dad didn't talk any more after that.

I didn't go to the ceremony on Monday for burying Kristen's body. I couldn't do that all over again. And I didn't think about Caspian at all. He was the farthest thing from my mind.

Prom was coming up on Saturday night, and that was all anyone at school could talk about. But I couldn't wait until the prom was over. It took all of my concentration to stay focused on the mundane things in life.

Get up.

Get showered.

Get dressed.

Find socks that match.

Eat breakfast.

That seemed to be about all I could comprehend right now.

Most of all I was tired. I felt so tired all the time. I had to start setting two alarm clocks because one alone wouldn't wake me up. I took a nap after school each day, nodded my way through dinner, and then slept like the dead at night. I didn't have time to think about anything else; I was practically sleeping round the clock.

It didn't exactly help things when I started to look as exhausted as I felt. Deep purple circles formed under my eyes, and each eyelid felt like it would be stuck permanently half shut. My hair was dull and lifeless, and I didn't care what I wore anymore.

When I caught a glimpse of myself at school on Thursday, I was tempted to yank the mirror off my locker door. I looked awful. Then someone shouted my name, and I turned to see Ben waving at me. I groaned inwardly and briefly contemplated banging my head repeatedly on the locker door out of sheer frustration. It would add a nice purple bruise to match the circles under my eyes.

But I didn't have enough time to follow through on my plan; he had almost reached me.

The smile on his face turned to a look of concern when he finally got to my locker door. "Hey, Abbey. How are you? Are you feeling okay?"

I didn't smile back. "Perfect."

"You look like you have a cold or something," he suggested.

"Yeah, something like that," I said dryly.

"Okay." He shrugged. He had a funny look on his face, like he wasn't sure if he should continue or not.

"Look, Abbey," he said seriously. "I know it must suck for you right now, with prom coming up, and hearing the latest news about Kristen. I miss her too, but I know it must be a million times worse for you. And if you totally say no, I understand, but would you like to go to the prom with me? I know its short notice, and we don't have to go as a date. It can be just a friend thing. What do you think? In the midst of all this sucky-ness, want to try and have one night of fun? If you're feeling up to it, that is."

Ben looked so heartfelt and sincere that I didn't offer an automatic no. His big brown eyes watched me expectantly, like an adorable puppy waiting for his reward. It was really sweet that he was trying to cheer me up, but I had this nagging feeling . . .

"Did anyone ask you to do this?"

He looked uncomfortable. "Well, 'ask' isn't really the word. . . ." He saw my defenses going up and the shut-down that was coming his way. He tried to backpedal. "I mean . . . See, Shana said that some of the girls from the cheering squad were going to mention the fact that you needed a date to some of the guys they knew. But she didn't say it specifically to me. I swear. I only overheard the conversation. I was planning to ask you long before I ever heard them talking about it."

I felt my face grow hot. My utter mortification was now complete. Embarrassingly, my eyes started to burn with the sting of unshed tears.

"So why didn't you ask me before you heard them talking about it?" I asked him quietly, keeping my gaze averted to my locker door.

"I—I—," he stuttered.

"Sorry, Ben, but I just don't believe you. The answer is no."

"But, Abbey, I . . . lost my nerve," he said awkwardly.

I couldn't look him in the eye, so I shut my locker door and walked away. He called my name once, but I didn't turn around. I was trying to hold back the tears . . . at least until I made it to the safety and anonymity of the girls' bathroom.

Chapter Nine

PROM NIGHT

She wore the ornaments of pure yellow gold, which her great-great-grandmother had brought over from Saardam, the tempting stomacher of the olden time; and withal a provokingly short petticoat, to display the prettiest foot and ankle in the country round.

—"The Legend of Sleepy Hollow"

I avoided Ben for the rest of the week, and heard that one of the senior girls ended up asking him to the prom at the last minute. I really hoped that he would have a good time with her. Things would probably be awkward between us now, and I felt bad about that.

When Saturday morning, prom day, finally came, it was bright and sunny instead of cold and rainy like I thought it should be. I pulled the covers over my head and tried to stay in bed as long as I could, but eventually Mom dragged me out to help her get some costumes down from the attic.

Every year the town council held a Halloween party called the

Hollow Ball on the same night as the junior-senior prom. I always had a sneaking suspicion that the *real* reason behind this was for all the parents of juniors and seniors to distract themselves, so they didn't have to worry about what their kids were doing. Most of the time it seemed to work.

Mom and Dad always went to the party as Katrina Van Tassel and Ichabod Crane. They'd had authentic period clothing made, and the costumes were absolutely gorgeous. A bit cumbersome and heavy, but gorgeous. One year I had tried to convince Dad to mix things up and go as Mr. Irving instead since I felt that the storyteller deserved to have someone dressing up like him, but Mom didn't think it would be right for Katrina Van Tassel to show up with Washington Irving. *Whatever.*

We were in the middle of unpacking accessories when a large cloud of dust flew off the powdered wig I'd picked up, and I sneezed loudly.

"If this was supposed to be protected by storing it away properly, how did dust get on it?" I asked Mom.

She looked up from the jacket she was shaking out. "I don't know. It's probably leftover face powder from last year. But don't wipe it all off. It adds to the ambiance."

"If you want to have spiders in your hair, that's fine by me," I said, putting it to the side.

She laughed and threw a satin slipper at me. "Here, check that for spiders." Then she got serious. "Are you *sure* you don't want to come with us to the party tonight? Or you could go to the prom by yourself. I'm sure lots of your friends will be there. And you never know who you might meet. We could drop you off on the way."

I sighed. Had she always been this pushy? She seemed so pushy lately.

"I'm not going to the party tonight, Mom, and I am definitely not going to the prom. I know exactly who I'll meet there . . . someone who already has a date. Besides, I don't have any tickets for it, or even a dress that *I* chose, for that matter. And you know how much Kristen and I wanted to go together. I don't feel right going without her."

An excited look crossed her face. "What if we got a different dress? I didn't want to push you before, but this *is* your first prom. We're supposed to get all giddy and spend way too much money on the perfect dress." She cocked her head to the side. "I saw an adorable black satin gown in a bridal shop last weekend. I bet they still have it. I *know* you'll like that one."

It was like she didn't hear 90 percent of what I'd just said.

"No, Mom," I said forcefully. "Thanks anyway, but I'll be fine here. There will probably be some monster movies on, and I'll watch those. Plus, someone needs to be here for all the trick-or-treaters." I knew she wanted to argue, but thankfully she let it go.

After we finished unpacking the last of the costume pieces, Mom went to go try on her costume while I opened up candy bags. I had just finished arranging it all in bowls when she came back in.

"How do I look?" she asked.

"The same as last year," I replied. Then she pouted, and I threw a chocolate candy packet at her. "Oh, come on, Mom. You know you look great."

"I know." She ripped open the tiny package. "But you could have told me that first." Popping the candy into her mouth, she crunched loudly as she went to change out of the costume.

I wandered over to the couch and turned on the TV. Flipping blindly through the channels, I didn't really pay any attention to it. My eyes kept straying to the window. It would be getting dark soon. Almost all of the junior and senior girls were probably at a salon or makeup counter right now, getting ready for the prom. Kristen and I should be doing that too.

I tried not to think about white-blond hair on a green-eyed date … or beautiful black satin ball gowns … or sharing the excitement of prom with a best friend. . . . But I was failing miserably.

Kristen should be here, and we should both be going *there*. It wasn't supposed to be like this. I wasn't supposed to spend my junior prom alone, on a couch, without my best friend.

Depression settled on me like a heavy blanket. The channel turned to one that was playing a vampire movie, and I left it on. Stuffing a pillow behind my head, I put my feet up and closed my eyes.

"Abbey, I'm going to have to go get this hem fixed. It snagged on something when I was taking it off. Do we need any more candy? Soda? Anything?" Mom's voice interrupted the cheesy horror music from the television.

I didn't answer her but turned my face into the pillow. If I got lucky, she'd think I was sleeping. I heard her take a step closer to the couch, and then a moment later she walked away. I guess I got lucky.

There was a rustling noise, and I figured that she was putting her costume into a plastic garment bag, and then a minute later I heard the click of a locking door. I kept my eyes shut, still thinking about the prom, and it didn't take long for me to really fall asleep.

The prom dress was beautiful. An old-fashioned Victorian style. The fabric was blood red satin with a delicate black velvet embossed vine pattern that twisted and tangled its way across the bodice top before trailing down the sides. The lacings on the back were designed to mimic the strings of a corset, while a black netting underskirt peeked out from the bottom of the dress ever so slightly and completed the image.

It was something straight out of a Gothic fairy tale.

"Choose this one, Kristen. It's perfect for you." I grasped the hanger and turned to give it to her, but she wouldn't take it from me.

"I can't, Abbey. I already have a dress." She motioned to the dark gray tattered piece of fabric she had on. The jagged hem and ripped seams looked alarmingly like someone had tried to tear the outfit into two pieces. Horrified, I watched as the bottom of the dress began dripping water.

"No, no," I insisted. "Please, Kristen, put this one on. There's something wrong."

But she just shook her head and smiled sadly at me. "I can't, Abbey. I can't."

~ ~ ~

Mom was shaking my shoulder and calling my name when I finally woke up. My brain was still too foggy to process her costume, and I had no idea who the crazy person in front of me was. I just sat there, blinking, while her face gradually came into focus and Kristen's words faded from my mind.

"Are you awake now, Abbey?" she asked me. "We have to leave."

Mom was completely dressed in her costume, and Dad was polishing one of his shoes. I looked hazily around me. It was dark now, and the clock on the DVD player was blinking 5:30. I had been asleep for quite a while.

"Yeah, I'm awake, Mom. I'll see you guys later," I said.

She bent over to give me a hug, or the closest thing to it that her costume would allow, and I smiled sadly at her. "Go on," I whispered. "I'll be fine. Go have some fun."

"We need to get going sometime tonight," Dad called from the door.

Mom stood up. "I'm coming, I'm coming." Then she looked back at me. "Candy's on the table. We'll leave the porch light on. Be careful, and don't stay up too late." She patted her wig one last time and started toward Dad.

"Oh, and Abbey." She paused midstride. "Look behind your closet door." And with that they both gave me a final wave and stepped outside.

I wasn't really sure if I wanted to know what she had left me. Prom tickets taped to the mirror? A pumpkin costume for the Hollow Ball left by the door? I could only guess.

Unfortunately, for the next hour or so all I *could* do was guess. The doorbell kept ringing . . . and ringing . . . and ringing. It was a never ending flow of ghosts, goblins, witches, and one poor kid who'd gotten stuck trick-or-treating as a fire hydrant. I let him take two handfuls of candy.

When there was a lull in customers, I turned the porch light off so I could sneak upstairs to see what Mom had left. My jaw dropped when I opened the door and saw what was there.

Hanging on the back of the closet door was the most beautiful black ball gown I had ever seen.

I touched the skirt first. It had a fine layer of black tulle netting over ruched black taffeta that shimmered ever so slightly when the light hit it. The satin corset-style top felt cool and smooth under my fingertip as I traced a ribbon trailing down the front in an X pattern. She had even left a pair of black strappy heels that matched perfectly.

It was amazing.

I stared at the dress for a moment longer, then shook my head and closed the door very gently. She could be pushy, and aggravating to no end, but sometimes she was a very, very good mom.

As soon as I went back downstairs and flipped the porch light on again, the little monsters started lining up. They *really* wanted their candy. I started wondering if people were sending kids over from other towns, because the line kept getting longer and longer. The candy ended up running out before the trick-or-treaters did.

I tried turning out the porch light again, but that didn't work. They just rang the doorbell anyway. And after the eleventh sad little face turned away when I told the kid I was all out of candy, I just couldn't take it anymore.

Calling the closest drugstore, I found out that they were open till nine. And they had plenty of candy left. Since they were only five blocks away, it wouldn't take me long to get there either.

I thought about posting a GONE FOR MORE CANDY—BE BACK SOON sign on the door but decided against it. Might get the house egged by angry goblins who wanted their candy right then and there.

A nice cool breeze played along my face as I walked to the store, and a couple of wispy clouds filled the sky. I would have taken my time if I wasn't so worried about angry mobs of kids stampeding the house in search of candy. *That* terrifying thought made me walk just a little bit faster.

When I reached the drugstore, there was a black limo parked off to one side, and I couldn't figure out what it was doing there. Then I saw a window roll down and the brief flash of a tux inside. The prom, of course.

A group of guys had probably rented it and were on their way to pick up their dates. I tried not to give too much thought to the reason why they would stop at a drugstore on prom night. *Maybe they've run out of candy too?*

Grinning to myself as I opened the door, I walked down two aisles and then hit the jackpot. It was all 50 percent off too. Double jackpot.

I was trying to decide whether I should go with a variety or just one kind of candy, when a voice from the next aisle over caught my attention.

"... he asked that weird girl, Abbey, but she turned him down flat," a girl said.

"Yeah, and she was a real bitch about it too. I had to ask him, like, twice before he agreed to go with me."

"I thought you said you only asked him once and he—"

"Yeah, whatever. Look, let's just get the cameras and go. The boys are waiting."

I peeked around the corner of the aisle. There were two girls in prom dresses standing there, and obviously one of them was the senior who had asked Ben out.

They each grabbed a disposable camera and then went up to the registers. Three people were already in line ahead of them, and I could tell that the girls were *not* happy about it. I moved back to the candy section, grabbed ten random bags, and slowly walked to the front. Luckily someone else had gotten in line behind them, so I didn't have to worry about getting too close for comfort.

But I was still close enough to hear every word they said. And they had a lot to say.

"He'll have a much better time with you," the girl in the pink dress assured the girl in yellow. At least they were color coded, so I knew who was who.

"Of course he will," yellow dress said, with a toss of her head. As she did this, I noticed that the price tag for her dress was still attached, and sticking out of her side zipper for the entire world to see. I wondered if pink dress would tell her about it.

But yellow dress kept right on talking. "I mean, how rude is she? She should have been grateful that someone asked her to go to the prom at all."

"I heard that the entire cheerleading squad had to practically beg people to ask her to go, as a personal favor to them."

"How pathetic do you have to be to get other people to find dates for you, and still end up with no one?"

That one hurt. I felt the sting inside, and an instant rush of tears. *I'm not upset,* I told myself. *I'm pissed off.* But it didn't matter which one I really was; my vision still got blurry.

I stared down at the candy in my hands, not really seeing it. *Can't they get another cashier up there to help move the line along?* I tried to tune everything out and not listen to the conversation, but it was like a bad car wreck. I couldn't turn away.

They were next, but they still kept talking.

"Did you see her at school this week?" asked pink dress.

"Ugh, yes. She looked terrible. Someone really needs to

lay off the midnight margaritas on school nights."

"I know, right?"

"Someone should also tell her not to wear black all the time. It totally washes her out. What is she, a Goth girl? And it's called a haircut. Get one."

Pink dress laughed now. "Maybe she wears black because it's slimming. Could be hiding a few 'trouble spots.' You know, ever since her friend died, she has gotten weirder and weirder. She's *such* a loser. I wouldn't be surprised if she jumps off the bridge herself just to get some attention."

"She's totally trying to milk the pity," said yellow dress. "You know she is. First it gets her on the prom committee, and now I bet all the teachers are letting her turn in her homework late. She'll probably start skipping classes next so she can go sob on a counselor's shoulder about how much she misses her dead friend."

"Sometimes I think they planned this together or something, so that at least *one* of them would get some attention. It's not like the dead girl will be remembered for anything else. She was a bigger loser than Abbey."

My face went numb and my mind went blank. Nothing they said could hurt me. I was frozen inside. A wall of ice. I looked

178

blankly at the floor, until the cashier finally got my attention. They were gone, and I was next in line.

I spaced out again while he rang up my purchases, and it was like he was speaking a foreign language when he asked if I wanted everything to be double bagged. I shook my head no. And then nodded my head yes.

He double bagged the candy and handed it over to me like I was contagious. I stumbled out of the store and headed for home. I don't remember actually walking home, but the next thing I knew, I was standing in front of my door. I went inside, dumped the candy into several bowls, and placed them all on the front porch.

I just wanted to be alone now.

Turning out all the lights, I curled up on the couch. Another scary movie was about to start, and I turned it on. But it didn't hold my attention. Nothing did. I kept hearing their voices.

I thought about what they had said in the store. I thought about being alone and miserable on the couch. I thought about the prom I was missing. I thought about the fact that Kristen wasn't here for any of it, and never would be. I thought about how much I missed my best friend. I thought about how awful my life was.

And I think all those thoughts pushed me to an edge. Suddenly

I felt impulsive and full of wild energy, like I was teetering on the ledge of an impossible canyon and staring straight down. I jumped up from the couch and ran upstairs to my room. I knew what to do.

Opening the closet door, I grabbed the black gown off its hanger. Mom had taped a note behind it, and it momentarily stopped me. *Even if you don't get the prom, you still deserve the dress. Love, Mom.*

It only added fuel to the fire of my reckless abandon. I *did* deserve a dress. *And* a prom. A prom that I was going to give to myself. Changing into the ball gown, I passed over the strappy heels and put on my solid black boots. Then I took a moment to look at myself in the mirror. My eyes were stormy and bright, but my cheeks were deathly pale.

I quickly ran into the bathroom and teased my unruly curls, spraying them so that they really *were* wild and witchy. For a final accessory I tied a black ribbon around my throat. Now I was ready. I grabbed a vial of Kristen's perfume on my way out of the room and headed toward the door.

I was going to the cemetery.

~ ~ ~

The sky was filled with dark heavy clouds now, and it looked like rain. A slow rumble of thunder in the distance confirmed my suspicions. I didn't care.

Slipping into the cemetery, I wandered among the tombstones. My gown made a soft rustling noise with each step I took. Stopping in the middle of the pathway I was on, I spun around in a wide circle. Now the gown made a swishing sound. I liked that even better.

I spun around crazily until I was too dizzy to stand up straight, and staggered over to one side. I ended up in a sort of half curtsy directly in front of a tombstone. Looking at the name carved on it, I bowed even lower. "May I have this dance, Mr. Finklestein?"

For some reason, hearing those words out loud struck me as absurdly funny, and I found myself giggling uncontrollably. I couldn't stop. I didn't want to stop. So I waltzed my way down the hill holding my arms out in proper dancing fashion, all the while clutching my vial of perfume in one hand.

In between bouts of hysterical giggling, I hummed snatches of an old lullaby. Around and around I went, waltzing along several paths in order to get to my final destination. I was almost there.

Then my foot caught on the edge of a broken tombstone, and

it caused me to stumble. I tried to regain my balance, but I went down hard. Luckily, my outstretched arms took the brunt of the fall. Unluckily, that fall was against the edge of that tombstone. It scraped both of my hands raw.

I sat there on the cold, hard ground and stared down at my palms. The flesh had been torn away in jagged lines, and fresh blood was oozing to the surface. I didn't know what to do about it.

What I *did* know was that Kristen's perfume was missing. I searched the ground frantically for signs of broken glass, but there weren't any. I finally spotted the vial near a tree trunk and crawled over to it, just as the rain started.

The rain hit hard and fast, and my dress was quickly soaked. *Mom is going to be so pissed.*

I held my palms up to the rain, so at least they wouldn't be bloody anymore, and then picked up the vial. Somehow it had survived the fall.

When I spotted Kristen's tombstone, I gave up on any thoughts of saving the prom dress and plopped down beside it. It was the first time I'd seen the stone, and I reached out to touch it, half expecting to feel that same cold shock I'd felt when I'd touched her casket. But it just felt like stone.

I traced the deep outline of the smooth letters carved there. She was really here now.

Opening up the vial of perfume, I spilled a couple of drops onto the tombstone. It mixed with the rain and ran in tiny rivers down to the ground, soaking into the dirt below.

"Hey, Kris," I started softly. "I finally made you a perfume."

I grasped for the words. I was so numb inside that I didn't know what to say to her. "I hope you like it. I used grapefruit and ginger, with just a hint of vanilla. I think it suits you. It took me a long time to get it right, but I wanted it to be perfect." A huge fist of sorrow slammed into me, and my eyes started to swim. I felt it overwhelm me from the inside.

"It's prom night . . . tonight . . . Kristen," I tried to speak in between sobs. "We should be . . . together. But not this way. . . . It wasn't supposed to happen like this."

A gasping sob escaped, and I was lost for words again. I bowed my head, and my sorrow turned to rage, pure hate directed toward Kristen, the world, myself, anybody.

The thunder rolled again behind me, and I stood up, clenching my fists in anger. "Why aren't you here, Kristen? You're supposed to be here!" I screamed at the tombstone. "How could you just fall in? We never fell in the water!" The rain streamed down my face, and I ran.

I ran as fast and as hard and as long as I could down to the riverbank. I thought I saw a white shaped mist, and I ran after it until my legs ached and my lungs burned. *Is it her? Is she here?* I chased it until it disappeared, then I collapsed in a heap at the edge of the water.

My body struggled to fight for each breath, dragging in one short painful gasp of air after the other. I put an arm above my head, and poured the rest of the perfume into the dancing current, moving closer until I was right along the water's edge. Closing my eyes, I rested my head on the swirl of water beneath me. It whispered seductively, inviting me to lose my pain and sorrow, my rage and my fear, to feel still and calm.

To see Kristen again . . .

My hair floated around me, forming a dark halo. The water was freezing, and even though it should have made me cold, it didn't. Instead it felt like a soothing balm to my emotional wounds. I breathed deeply, imagining Kristen here, while the scent of grapefruit, ginger, and vanilla surrounded me.

But I was still numb inside. I lifted a hand and let it ride the current, watching as the empty perfume vial floated away. I kept breathing slowly, trying to still my mind. And then it started working. I was calming down.

The sound of someone shouting my name made me open my eyes.

Caspian was standing on the opposite side of the river. "Oh God, Abbey. I thought you were dead!" he yelled. He jumped out to a large flat rock in the middle of the water, and then another, to get closer.

I didn't move.

"Abbey," he said very calmly, "what are you doing? You need to get out of the water."

I laughed out loud. "I need to get out of the water? But Kristen didn't get out of the water, Caspian. How else am I supposed to reach her?"

"Come on, Abbey," he coaxed, crouching down closer to me, but still a couple of feet away. "I don't know what happened, but you need to sit up and get out of the water. Now." His voice turned hard.

I sat up abruptly, and water flew everywhere. The rain was still pounding down, and I saw he was soaked too. His hair was

185

plastered to his head, but that black streak stood out vividly against the rest of his pale hair.

"You don't *know* what happened?" I said hysterically. "What *happened* is my best friend died, Caspian. That's *what happened*. She drowned in this very river, remember? You were at her funeral. Only it wasn't really her funeral, because they didn't have a body to bury. But they do now. Or . . . they did. Her body was found last week, and she was buried. And that means it's all real. She's gone, and I wasn't there." The weight of those words hit me hard.

"I know, Abbey. I know the hurt you must be feeling. But why are you here now . . . and in a dress?" His beautiful green eyes pleaded with me to give him the answers he wanted.

I picked up a layer of the soggy, ruined gown. "This?" I held it out to him, and then let it drop. "This is my prom dress. Tonight's the prom. Because this stupid town can't do anything normal, our prom has to be on Halloween. Kristen and I were supposed to go together with our dates. But I guess she had a prior engagement." I laughed vehemently.

"Abbey, come on, please, get away from the water," he begged. "Come over here by me. You can talk to me about it."

"Talk to you about it? I can't *talk* to you about it. I shouldn't even *be* here with you, Caspian. I never should have met you here. This was *our* place. Mine and Kristen's. And what do I do? I forget all about her. I didn't tell you about what a good person she was, or how funny she was, and how much she loved her family. . . . She loved them so much, Caspian." I spoke furiously now.

"Kristen would have wanted you to be happy, Abbey. Even if that meant meeting me here and showing me around."

"You don't know what she would have wanted!" I screamed, standing up to face him. He stood up too. The wind whipped around us and took my words away, then threw them back into my face. My breathing was out of control, and I felt that pure rage pulsing through me again. "I knew what she wanted when no one else did. Not anyone at school, not anyone in this town, and not even you!"

My voice turned quiet now. The rage was still there, but it was focused—a quiet, raw rage. "Do you know that I dreamed about her, the night she died? That's how close we were. I knew when she was dying. I could feel it. I *felt* it, Caspian. *Everything.* But I wasn't here. I didn't stop it. I didn't even know what it meant the next morning. She needed my help, and I wasn't a good enough friend to help her. So I guess that means I wasn't really her best friend after all."

I turned away. My fury died down. I felt limp and ragged, cold again inside as my anger turned to grief.

"I didn't go to the prom tonight because she wasn't here to go with me," I said bitterly. "Oh yeah, and also because I'm such a loser, and so pathetic, that they have to set up dates for me. Do you know they begged people to ask me out? I'm washed out, and they said I need a haircut . . ." I trailed off.

"Abbey, I need you to slow down," he pleaded. "I don't understand you. Who asked people to ask you out? And who said you need a haircut?"

"The cheerleaders," I replied. "And some girls at the drugstore."

"It's okay that these things upset you, Abbey. Come over here and we can sit together. If you don't feel like talking, you don't have to." His voice was calm, but slightly unsteady.

I stared at him. He had a wild look in his eyes that matched mine, and I felt the desperate urge to make him understand me.

"Feel?" I scoffed. "That's where you're wrong, Caspian. I don't *feel* anything at all."

And then I saw something change in his eyes. A look of understanding that completely undid me. I took a step closer to him, and stumbled. "Oh God, Caspian," I said, horrified. "I don't feel anything."

That was when the wall broke. All that pain and numbness cracked, and shattered into a million tiny little pieces. Each one came tumbling down, revealing that huge hole left behind. A gaping black void surrounding my heart.

I started to cry. Uncontrollable tears consumed me from the inside out, and each one heaved, and rolled, and ached. Dropping to my knees, I cried, and cried, and cried.

I cried all the tears that I hadn't been able to shed at her funeral.

I cried all the tears that had been with me during those lonely nights.

I cried for the friend I had lost, and the memories we wouldn't get to share together.

And then I cried for me.

Hugging my knees to my chest, I sobbed all those tears that had been stuck inside. Every single heartache came pouring out in a twisted fury of anger and raw emotion, before slowly seeping away into the river until there was nothing left behind. As my tears stopped falling one by one, the weather took pity on me and offered its condolences. The wind died down, and the rain lessened.

Caspian waited silently. He just stood there patiently, until I was ready. When he finally spoke again, I looked up at him with wide eyes.

"The question to find the answer to is what Kristen was doing here the night that she died," he whispered. "So let's find out, Abbey. Let's find out."

Chapter Ten

CHOOSING SCENTS

It was the very witching time of night. . . .

—"The Legend of Sleepy Hollow"

Caspian walked me home from the river, placing himself as a silent barrier between me and the road. And even though we didn't pass any cars, the gesture left a sweet ache in the back of my throat.

I looked down at my wet, ruined dress as we walked. Mud smears and grass stains streaked down the front of it. Hopefully my face and hair didn't look as bad as the dress did. But then again, I was so tired I didn't really care what I looked like.

Well, maybe I cared a *little* bit.

The house was completely dark when we finally got there. I was so cold from being wet that I couldn't stop myself from shivering.

It was *freezing* out here. I grabbed the spare key from a brick next to the front door and quickly unlocked it, turning on several lights as I stepped in. Unlacing my muddy boots, I kicked them off and tried not to let the mud splatter everywhere.

Caspian hung back in the shadows of the house. I could barely see him. Even his light hair was hidden by the dark.

"You can come in if you want," I called out. "Just leave your shoes by the door." Glancing at the clock on the wall, I saw that it was almost eleven thirty. Mom and Dad wouldn't be home for at least another hour.

"Won't your, uh, parents mind?" he asked, echoing my thoughts.

"No, they're at the Hollow Ball. They always stay until the very end, like the good little council members that they are. And then they'll offer to be the designated drivers, or help clean up after the party . . . and so on. They'll probably be home around twelve thirty, or even one o'clock."

He stepped out from the darkness. "Would you like me to come in, Abbey?" His green eyes glowed, and he looked at me closely.

"Yes," I whispered. Then I cleared my throat and tried again. "Yes."

I looked down at my dress. "I need to change out of this and get into something dry. I'm turning into an icicle here. Why don't you follow me up to my room? I'm sure you're freezing too."

He took a step closer and was suddenly right beside me. "I'm not cold at all," he said. "It's warm right here." I stared at him for a moment before I realized that I *definitely* needed to distract myself with something.

Taking a step sideways, I reached around him and grabbed the now empty candy bowls from the front porch. Butterflies were swimming in my stomach, and I tried not to think about the fact that we would be alone together . . . in the house.

Chills went racing up and down my back. So much for not thinking about it.

"Just going to take care of these," I mumbled.

Caspian slipped off his shoes and then followed me into the kitchen, while I took longer than was necessary to wash each bowl. Once I had them dried and put away, there wasn't anything left to do. I cleared my throat nervously. "Well . . . my room's upstairs . . . so, I guess we can . . . go . . . there . . . now."

Argh. I was pathetic.

He didn't say anything but trailed behind as I walked to the staircase. The clock started chiming eleven thirty when we took our first step up, and Caspian paused, listening to its toll.

"Almost midnight," he whispered behind me.

The stairs creaked ominously as I made my next move. He was only a step below me, and I had to remind myself to watch where I was going. Tripping and falling down the stairs would *not* make a very good impression.

When we reached the top, and were only a few feet from my bedroom, I felt the oddest compulsion to stall. To prolong the moment before he entered my room and saw my personal space. *What if he doesn't like it? Should I have cleaned up my perfume samples? Does it smell too strongly of the oils I've been working with? What if he hates the red color I painted it?*

"Do you . . . Would you . . . like some dry clothes?" I burst out. "I mean, obviously not mine, but I could look through my dad's stuff. Maybe find an old pair of jeans for you?"

He looked at me with an amused smile on his face. "I'm good. Almost dry already." I glanced over at his clothes. They *did* look pretty dry. Silently I cursed my dress and the heavy layers of fabric. His tone turned teasing. "I promise not to sit down on your bed and get it all wet."

He meant the remark to be funny, but I didn't find anything funny about it. Thoughts of him ... on my bed ... turned dangerous, and instead of feeling cold now I felt hot.

Maybe this wasn't such a good idea after all.

My cheeks burned like they were on fire. His eyes weren't teasing anymore, and I couldn't tell if he was thinking the same thoughts about my bed that I was.

He stood to the side and motioned for me to lead the way. I rationalized to myself the whole time as I walked into my bedroom. It wasn't like we were dating. We hadn't even held hands yet. He'd never even accidentally brushed his skin against mine, for that matter. Nothing would happen.

I scanned the room quickly as I moved ahead of him, discreetly checking for dirty clothes and trying not to panic. Then I remembered that laundry day was yesterday. Not enough time for Mount St. Dirty Laundry to pile up again.

Casually making my way over to the bed, I tucked in the sheets and straightened the edge of the comforter. Then I grabbed a stray sock that was balled up next to my nightstand and swept a handful of stuffed animals from the window seat into the closet. I peeked behind me to see if Caspian had noticed.

He was busy looking around the room.

"I'm just going to get changed," I said, heading toward the bathroom. It felt a little weird to know that I would be literally undressing just a few feet away from him. The idea made me feel queasy and excited all at the same time.

Kristen had been the only other person to come into my room, besides my parents. Having Caspian here was like exposing an inner part of me. It was terrifying. I only hoped that he liked what he could see. The thought of him not liking my room, that extension of myself, made me squirm.

I stopped at my closet to grab some dry clothes but turned back to see him standing in front of the desk that held my perfume supplies. I started second-guessing whether or not I should have ever invited him in here, when his voice stopped me.

"Is this where you work, Abbey?" He sounded so intrigued that I forgot about panicking . . . and changing . . . and walked back over to him.

"Yeah, it is." I picked up the large briefcase that was sitting on the desk and popped it open. Several rows of glass tubes, jars, and vials were exposed. "Almost all of my supplies fit in here. Finished samples, test tubes, essential oils. . . . It even has a pocket for my notes."

He looked closely at the case. "So you use the oil from one tube and mix it with oil from another tube, and then you're done? The perfume is made?"

"It's a bit more complicated than that. See, when you make perfume, you need to have a top note, a middle note, and a bottom note. Then the three notes all blend together to create the scent. Once you've done that, you mix it with carrier oil, because essential oils can be dangerous if they're applied directly to the skin."

My hand wandered over several of the tiny clear glass tubes. "Most of the time I have pretty good luck with choosing scents that mix well. But every now and then I bomb. So I always take notes throughout the entire process."

"How many have you made so far?" he asked, gazing at all my sample vials.

"A lot." I laughed. "The possibilities are endless, really. It can boggle the brain to try to put a number on it."

"Boggle the brain, huh?" He laughed too. His smile was warm and inviting, and I didn't miss the opportunity to smile back.

"So what do you do when you create a scent you like?" He touched one of the tiny samples. "Do you just fill up a bunch of these small ones?"

Setting the briefcase down on my office chair, I opened a small drawer on the top of the desk. "That's where these come in handy." I picked up a larger cobalt blue bottle and held it out to him. The deep blue glass caught the light in the room, revealing its true gem tone. "They hold more than my sample vials, and I have a bunch of them stashed in my closet."

"Are they color coded?" He looked over at my sample case and then back at me. "I noticed that you have several different colored tubes."

"Very good." I was impressed. "Essential oils are kept in amber glass vials because it helps keep the light out. Sample scents that I'm working on are kept in the smaller clear glass vials. And finished scents are put into the cobalt bottles."

"Are these the perfumes you're going to sell in Abbey's Hollow?"

I nodded eagerly, and then I blushed. "Sorry if I rambled on too much. I didn't mean to give you a formal class on perfume making or anything."

He laughed again. "I'm sure that was the condensed version. It sounds like you put a lot of time and effort into your work, Abbey. You're obviously very dedicated. One of these days I'll have to be your first customer and ask you to come up with a scent for me. Do you think you can do it?"

I stared into his green, green eyes and immediately thought of snickerdoodle cookies and rainy nights in a graveyard.

"What are some of your favorite things?" I heard myself asking him. I wondered how difficult it would be to create a scent for him.

"Hmmm, let me think about that." He wandered away from me, stopping briefly at several different spots around my room. "Well, I love snickerdoodle cookies, but you already knew that. I also like pumpkin pie."

He wandered some more, and then came back to me. I held absolutely still.

"And vanilla, Abbey." His voice was low, barely above a whisper. "I like the smell of vanilla. You smell like vanilla . . . and ginger-bread cookies. And something else I can't quite figure out."

He was very, very close now. And so were his lips. His beauti-fully shaped lips. I watched them while he spoke, as he enunciated each word, and said my name.

"Grapefruit," I whispered, raising my gaze. I started at that stripe of black hair and followed it down to meet his eyes. They were changing . . . darkening. "It's Kristen's scent. I made it for her.

That's why I went to the cemetery tonight, to give it to her."

I could tell he *wanted* to touch me but something was holding him back. Maybe it was the same something that made me hesitate every time I thought about reaching out to touch him. Fear of rejection? Or fear that once our skin met it would fuse together and we wouldn't be able to pull it apart again?

He took an abrupt step back. The moment was interrupted, and I felt confused. I couldn't quite grasp what was going on here. He wandered away again, and stopped in front of the fireplace mantel, staring at something. I followed after him to see what he was looking at.

It was a picture of me and Kristen, taken that night we had put the red highlights in our hair. A slow smile crept across his face as he reached out to touch the picture frame. I watched him in utter fascination. There was something about him that captured my attention; I was like a moth drawn helplessly to a beautiful flame.

Caspian gently traced the swirl pattern decorating one of the frame's silver edges, and then he glanced over at the wall next to the fireplace. "So, I take it your favorite color is red?"

I grinned.

"What gave it away? The red highlights in the picture, the red stripes painted on the walls, or . . ." I glanced behind me. "The red comforter on the bed?"

"It was a completely random, totally wild guess on my part." He turned slightly and gave me a half smile. "I like your room, Abbey. It suits you. The colors in here are just . . . amazing. I've never seen anything like it."

He couldn't have said anything more perfect at that moment. My heart thumped erratically, and I prayed with everything inside of me that I wouldn't tear up at his words.

Then his expression changed. "You like astronomy?"

I was still enjoying the warm fuzzies his compliment had just given me, and was kind of lost on how we'd gone from red striped walls to astronomy. Taking a step closer, I saw my telescope propped up against the wall next to him.

"I haven't used it since I was younger," I admitted. "My dad bought it for me, and we used to look at the constellations together. That was how my parents met in high school, actually. Astronomy class. Dad loved it, and Mom took it for extra credit."

He bent down and looked through the eyepiece, fiddling with the knobs and running his hands over it like a little boy admiring a new toy. "And you don't use it anymore? Why not?" The look of pure astonishment on his face was adorable, and I tried very hard not to laugh.

"I just sort of forgot about it, really. Got busy, had other things to do. Plus, it kind of used to be a special thing for Dad and me. He would tell me all about the groups of stars and constellations, and every Saturday night we'd go to the top of the hill behind our house to look at the sky. Once he joined the town council, he never had any free time anymore. I guess that's when I stopped using it." Comprehension dawned, and I turned away, feeling that familiar sting. Great, now I was going to cry.

Caspian immediately caught on. He stood up and walked away from the telescope. "Meet me at the library tomorrow," he urged suddenly.

"What? Why?" I was still trying to blink away tears that I would not shed, and follow his train of thought at the same time.

"Do you know what the name Astrid means?" He switched gears again, and I was helpless to follow.

"No."

"It means 'star.' That's what I think of you as, Abbey. One day I looked up, and there you were. A fiery spot of light surrounded by darkness. You make me feel like anything is possible. And seeing that telescope over there only confirms it."

"That's beautiful, Caspian," I whispered. "But what does it have to do with the library?"

He gave a husky laugh, and the sound ricocheted through me. "I want you to meet me at the library tomorrow because I have to go now. But tomorrow I can . . . Just name a time and I'll find you."

Crap. I'd already promised Mom that I would help her reorganize the attic tomorrow morning. I *hadn't* promised her my afternoon, though.

"Tomorrow. At the library. Two thirty," I said in a whisper. I didn't want to speak too loudly. He nodded in agreement.

Something stretched and ebbed and flowed between us. In the back of my mind I wondered if it was electricity. If we kissed, would there be sparks?

Self-consciously I took a step closer. I wasn't sure what was about to happen, but I definitely wanted *something* to happen. There was this tug inside of me, and I was close. So close. Heart-breakingly, earth-shatteringly close.

I tried to control my breathing, but it came out faster and faster.

Downstairs the clock started to toll and I held my breath as it chimed once for every hour. Ten, eleven, twelve strokes. It was midnight.

His eyes started darkening, I could see the emotions in them. Reaching out one finger, he gently traced my cheek the same way he had traced that picture frame. Slowly, almost unsure of himself. And even though we were both fully dressed, with our shoes off, everything became more intimate. I felt small and dainty next to him.

"I really need to go, Abbey," he whispered to me. "Your parents will be home soon, and I . . ."

"Don't go. Stay." I sighed. I wanted to close my eyes and soak in the feeling of his touch. But I couldn't look away. Not even for a second.

My lips were suddenly very dry, and I licked them. He watched me. Intently.

Then he traced my lower lip . . . hesitantly again. My eyes lowered shut.

Now. It was going to happen now.

"I don't know if . . ." He groaned and suddenly pulled away. My eyes flew open, and I saw him running his hands through his hair almost desperately. That wild look was back in his eyes, coupled with something determined, and dangerous.

He paced around the room several times in an agitated manner. Then he seemed to make up his mind, and came back to me. Urgently grasping my face between his palms, he stared into my eyes. Searching for something in them.

"Caspian? What's wrong?" I opened my eyes wide, to show him whatever he wanted to see. Not even sure what that really was. He looked for a moment longer, and then spoke.

"Promise me you won't go to the river alone at night again. I don't want the same thing to happen to you, Abbey. Oh God, I thought you were dead in that water."

I knew what he was talking about. The desperateness in his voice spoke louder than any words ever could.

"There's so much I want, yet can't have. . . . The timing's not right." He closed his eyes and stroked my cheek once. "Just please, please meet me tomorrow, Abbey. Don't forget. Promise?"

"I won't forget," I promised. "And I won't fall in."

When he opened his eyes again, he looked relieved but still edgy. Casting a glance over at the clock on my nightstand, he said again, "I really do have to go."

I was lost. I didn't know what was happening now. I knew what had *almost* happened, and I was pretty sure I wanted to go back to that place.

"You don't have to go, Caspian. Not . . . yet." My gaze darted to the bed and then quickly back to him. I didn't know what part to play in any of this, what my role was.

"Yes, I do, Abbey," he sighed. "Believe me, it's not that I don't . . . I just need to go." He trailed a fingertip across my bottom lip for the shortest of moments. "What I meant about the star and the name Astrid . . . It's for you. You're my star," he said quietly. "Please don't forget about tomorrow." Then he cast a quick glance down. "And don't forget to take care of your hands. Sweet dreams, Astrid."

I heard him walk down the stairs, and then a door opened and closed, but I couldn't move. I was too stunned. My feet were rooted to the ground, while the words "my star" and "Astrid" played through my head. Then a huge smile spread across my face, and I laughed out loud as I tried to spin in a wobbly circle. My awkward movements reflected in the mirror hanging on my closet door, and I stopped short, and looked closer.

My eyes were shining and I had rosy cheeks, but the rest of me was wet and bedraggled. My hair lay in a limp, soggy mess around my shoulders, and my dress was stained by the mud and grass. I held my palms out in front of me. Each one bore several jagged scratches, and the edges were darkened with dried blood.

The implications of where I'd been, and what I'd done, suddenly sank into me.

I was insane; I had to be. I could have drowned in the river. Hit my head on that tombstone. Been attacked by someone hiding in the cemetery.

Astrid.

And then I realized who had been there with me, who had talked me off of that proverbial ledge and out of the water. Walked me home and made sure I was safe. Listened to me babble on like a crazy person. Waited by my side while I cried.

I needed to share this with someone, and I had the perfect person in mind.

Grabbing a notebook and pen off my desk, I curled up in the window seat. My prom dress had already started to dry, so it didn't bother me at all now, and I started writing a letter to Kristen. From the beginning, I told her everything.

I wrote about how hard it had been for me to go to her funeral, to believe that she was really gone. I explained how lost I'd felt during the last couple of months without her. The feeling I'd gotten when I touched her casket. I described the sensation of that crinkly yellow police tape in my hand. Then I told her about the cheerleaders, and what they had done. About prom night, and the girls in the pink and yellow dresses. How I'd danced wildly through the cemetery, and made her a perfume.

But what I wrote about the most was someone with vivid green eyes, and white-blond hair with a streak of black. I explained how we met, and how he'd kept me company at her house. The tour I'd given him of the graveyard, and our talks about classic literature. I told her that he'd been there for me tonight, when I finally hit the bottom, and how he made the lost feelings disappear.

The only thing I left out was the special name he had given me. I needed that to be my own private memory for now, and it was the first time I had ever consciously kept something from Kristen.

By the time I finished writing, I had filled up an entire notebook and my pen was running out of ink. Mom and Dad still weren't home yet, and the clock told me that it was one a.m.

I got up from the window seat and grabbed the blue glass bottle with Kristen's name on it from my desk. Then I sprinkled a couple of drops over the notebook pages. My lower desk drawer yielded me a half-used book of matches and a new red candle, so I grabbed those, too.

After lighting the candle, I carried it back over to the window seat. I set it down carefully on the ledge and pried open the old window. The night air was clear and cool. I took a deep breath and felt calm. Very, very calm.

I slowly tore out the pages from the notebook, and held the candle out the window as I fed it scraps of paper, one by one. I watched each wisp of smoke spiral up into the sky, and the ashes scatter to the wind. The scent of the perfume mingled with the smell of the candle and created a hazy veil around me.

I thought about a specific memory with Kristen as I burned each page, and hesitated when I finally reached the last one. "I won't say good-bye, because I hope some part of you will always be with me. So I'll say . . . to a new beginning. It's an end to our old way of making memories, but I'll find a way to make new ones, I promise. I'll never forget you, Kristen. Never," I vowed as the last notebook page disappeared into ash in front of me.

Blowing out the candle, I sat it on the floor and got up to turn off the lights. I was feeling sleepy, but I didn't want to go to bed just yet. So I stepped out of the messy prom dress and left it in a heap on the floor. Then I threw on some shorts and an old T-shirt and returned to my window. I decided to leave the dress where it was until morning and then stash it in the closet before Mom had a chance to see it.

It was going to cost a fortune to get it dry-cleaned and repaired.

The next thing I knew, my alarm was chirping that it was eight a.m., and my face was wearing the imprint of the window sill. Cracking one eyelid open, I saw that my window was now closed and the dress that had been on the floor was gone.

Chapter Eleven

THE LIBRARY

From the moment Ichabod laid his eyes upon these regions of delight, the peace of his mind was at an end. . . .

—"The Legend of Sleepy Hollow"

My head started pounding the minute I stood up, and I had a terrible cramp in my neck. Sleeping on the windowsill had *probably* not been the brightest idea I'd ever had. Moving very slowly, I double-checked the floor again, and then my closet, to make sure I hadn't dropped the dress in there.

No luck. The dress was definitely gone.

I was having a hard time caring about that, though. Breakfast and some headache medicine were first on my list . . . and then I would worry about the dress.

Creeping downstairs took all of my effort, and I had to

concentrate very hard to not miss any of the steps on the way down. Mom was making coffee when I reached the kitchen, and she turned when I stumbled in.

"Morning, honey. Want some coffee?" She held up an empty mug.

"Egghhh," I grunted, hoping she would take that as a no. I pulled out a cereal bowl and then cringed as the cabinet door slammed shut and the sound echoed through my head.

"Headache," I grunted again while I moved at a snail's pace to pour the cereal and some milk.

Barely making it to the table, I sat the bowl down and rested my head in my hands. Then I groaned loudly.

"Rough night?" asked Mom, coming to sit beside me.

"Don't ask," was my muffled reply.

She didn't get the chance to, because just then an even louder groan came from the living room. She patted my back and rubbed the top of my head. "Poor baby. Your father is feeling your pain. Apparently he can't handle mixed drinks like he used to. I ended up being the designated driver last night."

A horrible, pitiful on-the-edge-of-death's-door moan erupted from the living room again.

"I better go check on him," she said, putting her coffee mug down and getting up from the table. "I don't want him to ruin the couch."

She hesitated for a moment, and I almost heard the gears start clicking in her head. She was a loud thinker. "You don't . . . have a headache for the same reason your father does . . . do you, Abbey?"

"No, Mom." I lifted my head a fraction of an inch. "It's called falling asleep in a window seat with my neck propped up at a weird angle. *That's* why I have a headache."

I swear she actually sighed with relief.

"That's good. Let me go check on your father and then I'll bring you back some aspirin, okay?"

She really was a good mom.

I tried to say thank you, but it came out as another groan. I debated whether or not I could just stay where I was for the rest of the day, but I knew I needed to eat my cereal. It wouldn't take long for it to get all soggy.

Reaching for my spoon, I lifted my head up and saw the angry red scratches on my hand. They were still bloody. I never cleaned them last night. Focusing on the tabletop beside the bowl, I shoveled cereal into my mouth as fast as I could. I *definitely* wanted to skip the round of ten questions that I knew would come from Mom if she saw the scratches.

Gulping down the last of the cereal, I got up to drop the bowl into the sink. Then I ran some cool water over my palms and wiped them gently with a washcloth. Once the dried blood was washed away, they didn't look so bad.

My head started pounding out a symphony again, and I staggered back from the sink. I held one hand to my throbbing temple and waited for the pain to ease up. I must have really been distracted by my hands if I'd forgotten about my headache.

I managed to walk back to the table and resume my head-in-hands position. It wasn't long before I heard Mom come in again.

"So what were you doing sleeping by your window last night? It was wide open. I had to shut it so you didn't fall out."

I cracked open an eyelid and glared at her. "Headache," I pleaded pathetically. "Medicine?"

She threw her hands up into the air. "I get it, I get it. You don't want to talk about it. But if you tell me why, I'll get you a nice big cup of orange juice to go with your aspirin."

I cracked open my other eye. She had her eyebrow raised.

"Mothers are not supposed to bribe their sick children," I

mumbled. "But if you must know, I fell asleep by the window because I was enjoying the night air. There was a nice breeze. That's it. Are you happy now?" I put one hand up to my temple and groaned.

Yeah, I might have been faking it a bit, but I really did have a killer headache. I closed my eyes again, and a minute later I heard two pills and a glass being plunked down onto the table. Keeping my eyes tightly closed, I groped for the pills and washed them both down with the juice.

"Thanks, Mom." I took a break from the juice and opened my eyes again. "I'm feeling pretty awful here. Is it okay if I go take a nap before we start on the attic?"

She must have felt bad about the bribery thing, because she let me off the hook for the attic reorganizing and didn't even bring the dress up at all. I dragged myself back up the stairs, set my alarm for twelve thirty, and collapsed in a heap on the bed.

I was asleep before I even hit the pillows.

"Come on, Kristen." I kicked my foot up from the water and playfully splashed her. "Take off your shoes and come on in."

She was sitting at the edge of the riverbank, reading a book. "Not right now, Abbey. I'm busy."

I splashed her for a second time. "What are you reading? What can be more important than your best friend?"

She smiled and laughed but didn't say anything.

Wading closer to the edge, I tried to see the title of the book. But Kristen used her hand to cover one of the pages. "You'll get water on it," she said.

"No, I won't," I protested. "Look, I'm not even close." I tried again to persuade her to come into the river. "Put the book down, Kristen. You'll have plenty of time to read it later."

"I can't. I have to read it now."

I let out a frustrated sigh. "What is it? I swear I won't get it wet."

Kristen smiled again and held the book up for me to see. The pages were soaked. All the ink was running together, and water ran from the spine. "You already did."

Even after my strange dream about Kristen, when the alarm went off, I woke up ready to go. Whether my good mood was due to the nap, my headache being gone, or the excitement of who I was going to see, was debatable. But I was excited . . . and happy. Somehow I knew that from now on I was going to be having a lot of good days.

I spent a couple of hours making quite a mess in the bathroom trying to revive my faded red highlights, and narrowly avoided a whole tub of bleach going down the drain. The highlights had been gone for a very long time, and I pretty much had to start from scratch. None of that mattered, though, when I saw the final result. It was perfect.

When I was ready to get dressed, what was *supposed* to be a quick trip to my closet turned into an agonizing thirty-minute debate over what I should wear. I heavily debated forsaking the color black for something different, but eventually settled with jeans, a long black T-shirt, and a black cropped jacket.

I checked my palms and was relieved to see that the scratches almost blended in. I dabbed a tiny bit of ointment on each one, to make sure they stayed that way, and blew on them to dry. I still had about fifteen minutes before I had to leave, so I went back down to the kitchen and heated up some leftover Chinese noodles. I got so caught up in a magazine Mom had left on the table that before I knew it, the noodles were gone, and so was my time.

Dashing back upstairs, I grabbed my cell phone, shoved a twenty into my back pocket, and wondered what else I was forgetting. When my eyes landed on the desk, I knew.

I hurried over and dug through a pile of tiny sample vials all crammed into the desk drawer, cursing myself the whole time for not labeling them better. But finally I found it.

Liberally dousing myself behind each ear and on my throat, I breathed in the fragrance of snickerdoodle cookies. After one last look in the mirror, I was on my way.

I made amazing time actually getting to the library, and was surprised to see that I was ten minutes early. The comforting smell of books surrounded me as I stepped through the massive wooden entrance door and walked into the familiar space. Caspian had said he would find me, but I didn't know where I should wait.

The basement archive room beckoned to me, and as I descended, I wondered how Caspian would ever find me if I didn't stay in one place.

Flickering lightbulbs sputtered overhead, and the room had a stale smell to it. I walked among towering shelves, endless and mazelike, literally stuffed with old books. Every now and then a bare spot would be revealed, like the gap of a missing tooth. I moved quietly, almost reverently, through this room that held so much history.

I don't know what made me look over when I did, but Caspian was standing there in a corner. He was dressed in jeans and a dark green shirt. He must have heard my footsteps, because he turned toward me at that exact moment, and a huge smile broke out on his face. It was full of happiness.

"Astrid." It was a whisper. I shouldn't have been able to hear it, but I did.

At that moment—in that small, concise, perfectly clear moment of time—I knew. It was *that* moment I fell in love with him. It actually caused me to stop, and time froze for just a second. But the feeling was so right, and so strong, that I knew I wasn't wrong.

Then everything went back to normal. I walked toward him, and he kept smiling at me. A million thoughts were racing through my head as I kept walking.

Can he tell? Is it showing on my face? Am I giving it away somehow? When should I tell him? How should I tell him? What if he doesn't feel the same? What if he does?

I tried to be cool and keep my smile steady, but I couldn't stop the extra spring in my step. "Hi," I said shyly as I got closer. *How do you say hello to someone when you've just found out that you love*

219

him? I smiled again and tried to put some of my newly discovered feelings behind that smile.

"I'm glad you could make it." He was still smiling too. "And really glad you didn't forget. Today is . . . a good day."

It was strange how relieved he sounded, and it threw me slightly off balance.

"How could I forget after everything you did for me last night?" I must have looked as confused as I felt, because he turned slightly pink and ducked his head. Reaching for one of my hands, he turned it palm-side up and slowly traced one of the scratches.

I had to hold back a gasp as his fingers gently grazed the delicate skin. He hesitated a little, like he was still afraid to touch me. My whole arm tingled in pleasure. Was this even legal in public?

A shiver ran through me, and tiny goose bumps stood up on my arms as his fingers released my hand. I laughed lightly and tried not to beg him to touch me again.

"I only wanted to protect you, Abbey. To make sure you were okay, and that you got home safely," he said. "I don't want anything to happen to you." The look he gave me went straight to my heart.

He started stroking my palm again. His fingers were long and lean, and so very, very warm. I tried to think of a way to steer the conversation to something else, but it was useless. My brain was quickly turning to mush.

Good Lord. All he was doing was touching my hand, and I was ready to tell him my heart was all his. And I was pretty sure that I was getting to the point where I didn't even care if he would ever love me back, as long as he promised to never stop touching me.

I don't know if my face showed what I was thinking, or if he somehow read my mind, but he let go of my hand and gave me a crooked smile.

"I want to talk about Kristen today. Is there anywhere we can go where we won't be disturbed? That has chairs? I don't really know my way around here."

My brain was still slightly foggy from the sensory overload of just moments before, but it cleared up quickly. "There's a room upstairs for private tutoring, but no one uses it. I can go talk to a librarian that I know about it, if you want."

He nodded his agreement. "I'll wait for you there. Which way upstairs?"

I walked him over to the wooden staircase leading out of the archive room. "Follow these all the way up to the fifth floor. It's at the end of the hall, to your left. You can't miss it. I'll be right up."

He nodded again and started up the stairs.

I went to go find my favorite librarian, Mrs. Walker. She didn't have any problem letting me use the room, so I headed up to meet Caspian. The banister definitely got cobwebbier the farther up I went, and it seemed like every other step groaned with old age. There was hardly anyone in the library, and I didn't pass a single soul on my long journey.

When I finally reached the room, Caspian was fidgeting in his chair. His fingers were drumming softly on the table in front of him, and his eyes moved constantly, never settling on one thing for too long. Even from the doorway, I could tell that he was filled with a restless energy.

He seemed to calm down the instant he saw me, though, and pulled out a chair right next to him. I had been planning to sit across from him, but I wasn't going to argue about that seating change.

"So I guess we won't be able to get away with anything in here," he said seriously, pointing to the KEEP THIS DOOR OPEN AT ALL TIMES sign posted above the light switch.

I eased the door shut so that it was cracked open only a little bit before I made my way over to the chair. "Well, they never said anything about keeping it *wide* open," I offered back, just as serious. We both grinned at the same time.

"Now tell me about this dream you had," Caspian said. "About that night at the river."

I took a deep breath and looked down at the table, focusing my mind back.

"We had gone to the cabin for the weekend," I began. "We got there Friday evening and didn't really do anything out of the ordinary. Unpacked our stuff, got a couple of things out of storage, had dinner, and then went to bed. I looked over some notes right before I fell asleep, for a new perfume I was trying to make at home. Rose, lavender, and cloves."

I looked up at him, and he was paying close attention, completely centered on everything I said. His eyes were focused and intense. I forced myself back to the matter at hand.

"I remember waking up a lot that night. I was having nightmares. But they weren't different nightmares; it was always the same one. Every time I fell back to sleep, I would just fall back into that same nightmare." A warning bell started ringing in the back of my brain.

"Do you remember anything specific about the dream?" he prodded gently.

The bell got louder, and I knew the answer to that question was yes.

I closed my eyes and immediately slid back into the memory. Vivid pictures sprang to my mind in a wild cascade of imagery, and I had to fight my way through to tell which way was up.

They didn't make sense, almost as if I was viewing them out of order. Slowing each image down, I dug deeper and tried to remember the beginning of the dream.

"I can't do it. It's all messed up in my head." I let out a frustrated sigh and opened my eyes again. My head was starting to ache from all that damn ringing. "I'm having a hard time piecing it all together now, but that morning, I remembered every detail. Like I had actually *been* in the dream." I looked over at him.

"Try again, Abbey. Look at what's around you in the dream, and then think about what you are physically feeling." His voice was soft, and it calmed the warning bell that was clanging so loudly in my head. That bell told me I knew what had happened in the dream, even if I didn't want to remember it.

I closed my eyes and concentrated hard. Suddenly I was there. Back in the dream again . . . the night she died.

The library room fell away, and I was in a new place. The

emotions I felt were large and heavy, pressing down on me. This must have been what it had felt like to be Kristen.

"Panic. Terror," I blurted out. "It's cold and I have to fight it." Something exploded in the back of my skull, erupting into a terrible pain that danced along my brain.

I peered dimly at my surroundings in the dream, through that pain-filled memory. "There are shadows all around me. But I can't see anything else. It's too dark. Everything is dark." I felt another surge of feeling, one last desperate attempt to fight. "I'm trying to fight it, but it hurts," I said. "It won't let me go." The pain in my head was joined by an ache in my chest. I couldn't breathe. I was going under.

His hand gripped mine, and I held on to it like he was my lifeline. I wanted to stop. I didn't want to do this anymore. There was another rush of pain, and fear . . . and then nothing. She was gone. Just like that.

I slowly opened my eyes and saw Caspian staring at me. His eyes were filled with compassion.

"I'm sorry, Abbey. I'm so, so sorry. I didn't know it would be like that for you. Are you okay?"

I blinked away hot tears and gave him a shaky laugh. "Wow.

That was a head trip I hope I don't have to repeat again anytime soon."

He squeezed my hand, and we sat there in silence. I was glad for the quiet time to collect my thoughts. He waited, casting anxious glances at me every couple of seconds.

"I'm okay, Caspian," I finally said, holding his hand tighter and looking him in the eye. "Really, I'm okay."

"Should we stop talking about this?" Worry filled his eyes. "I don't want to cause you any more pain, Astrid."

That name banished any second thoughts I was having, and I squared my shoulders. "It's not you, Caspian. It's never you. If any of this gets too hard for me, just give me a moment to work through it, and I'll deal. Kristen deserves this. She deserves some sort of sense made out of her death. I know that we'll get through this . . . together."

It was the boldest thing I had said to him yet, referencing us together. I held my breath and prayed that he wouldn't crush my heart with his response.

"It's a deal," he replied, gifting me with his beautiful smile. His thumb stroked the back of my thumb, and my heart swelled. He looked thoughtful for a moment, and then asked, "What about before the dream? Did Kristen act strange, or did anything unusual happen?"

I replayed those weeks before her death in my mind, but came up with a blank. "I don't remember anything unusual happening. Nothing that sticks out to me, anyway. We were supposed to go shopping for school clothes when I got back from the cabin, but that's pretty much it."

"It's so strange," Caspian mused, absentmindedly running his fingers through his hair. "What was she doing at the river? Did she decide to go for a walk? Did she slip and fall in? I wish I could have been there."

"We made a pact when we were little to never go to the river alone at night, in case something happened," I said softly. "I don't know what would have made her break it." I stared off into space, trying to figure out the answers. "I guess we'll never know."

I gulped away a sudden lump in my throat and took his hand again. He seemed surprised by the contact, and looked directly at me. His eyes were very wide and clear.

"Thank you," I said. "And thank you for finding me last night." It was heartfelt and sincere, and he bowed his head in response.

"Now," I teased, giving his hand a short squeeze. "Enough of all this sad talk. When are you going to tell me how much you like my hair?" I shook my head and sucked in my cheeks, doing my worst fashion model pose.

He laughed and tugged on one of the red tinted curls. "I like your hair, Abbey. But the real question is: Do you like mine?" He finger-combed his shaggy blond hair forward until it completely covered his face, and then he peeked out at me with one barely visible green eye.

I returned the favor by tugging gently on the black stripe. "I especially like the black."

"It's been there since third grade. I went to a swimming party for this kid's birthday and almost drowned. After that it just sort of grew in." He shrugged nonchalantly and looked away, but there was some sadness behind the gesture.

He shook his hair, and I briefly wondered what hair god had decided to give guys the ability to shake their heads and have their hair fall perfectly into place, while girls have to work so much harder at it.

"It's very rock star," I teased. "All the third-grade girls must have loved it."

"Not very many people liked it back then," he said. "It didn't take me long to learn that I should start dyeing it. Over the years, well . . . I guess the dye just stopped working."

I pictured him in third grade, being picked on by the other kids for something he had no control over, and my heart broke a little for him.

Then he smiled again and gave my hair another tug. The sadness disappeared. "All that matters now is the fact that you like it, Abbey."

My heart somersaulted. *He is the most perfect man on earth.*

I didn't know what to say, so I quickly launched into the tale of my narrowly avoided mishap this morning involving the bleach and the bathtub. He started laughing really hard. And then I found myself regaling him with other hair misadventures from my youth. I think he liked the let's-cut-our-own-bangs-Kristen story the best.

We spent the rest of the afternoon talking and holding hands, taking turns to see who could make who laugh the loudest. This involved many wild hand gestures and snorts. I especially liked the fact that as soon as he realized he was no longer holding my hand, he would grab on to it, almost desperately. I had totally been missing out the other times we'd met.

It wasn't until I was actually wiping away tears of laughter—one-handed, of course—that I realized I had no idea what time it was. I took my cell phone out of my pocket and checked the clock. The library would be closing in less than an hour.

"Wow," I could hear the surprise in my voice. "It's five thirty already."

Caspian stopped laughing. A look I was starting to recognize crossed his face. "I hate to say it, Abbey, but I need to go."

"I know. I figured." I hadn't meant for my answer to come out sounding so depressed, but it sort of did.

"I'll tell you what. I have to meet my dad at eight tonight, but what if we meet afterward? I promise I'll have you home by midnight."

"I can't," I groaned. "My parents are still living in the dark ages. Not only do I have to ask them, like, three weeks in advance to go on a date, but my 'official' curfew is nine o'clock."

"No big deal, Abbey. I'll see you again soon," he promised, getting up from his chair.

"Yeah, sure. I'll see you again by the river sometime." I stood too, not really sure if I should try to hug him or wait for him to hug me.

"That will be *at* the river, not *in* the river, right?" He looked deadly serious.

"Right," I agreed, and then I winked at him.

He grinned, and we stood there for an awkward moment. I started to take a step toward him but then kind of just jerked and froze.

"Well . . . bye, Abbey. I'll see you later." He didn't seem to notice my strange movements, and left the room.

I stood by my chair, feeling like an idiot. Maybe I should have asked for his phone number or something.

Then he called my name.

I ran out of the room, but forced myself to slow down before I came to the banister. He was waiting on the steps below.

He put one finger through the stair railing and beckoned me down to his level. Ignoring the cobwebs, I knelt between the badly painted wooden spindles and gripped them tightly. I was only inches away from his face.

He motioned for me to come closer, and I moved a fraction of an inch. His eyes held that desperate look again, and I searched them, not sure what was going on. We were so close, and I wanted that moment we had almost shared, back again. My eyelids slowly drifted shut, and I waited, holding every part of my body absolutely still.

His lips barely touched mine. It seemed like everything he did around me was hesitant, as if he was afraid I would break . . . or tell him no.

Like *that* would ever happen.

That explosion in my skull happened again, only this time it wasn't pain; it was pleasure. My heart stopped beating. My toes curled. And I held on for the ride.

He kissed me like I was delicate and fragile, an easily breakable thing.

I heard a soft moan, and my eyes flew wide open. I was mortified that I had made such a sound. His eyes opened too, and he stared at me, his mouth still pressed to mine. Then his eyes darkened and he whispered my name against my lips as he ran a finger down my cheek.

I closed my eyes again, and sank everything I had into that kiss. His hand moved from my face to the back of my hair, and he was holding my head, almost cradling it.

The kiss suddenly turned harder, and more desperate. I tasted the urgency in it and thought that I would die from the pleasure. Would they lock up the library for the night and find us dead in each other's arms? Perished from pleasure? That thought sent delicious goose bumps traveling over my entire body.

This is a million times better than holding his hand. I never wanted it to end.

As soon as I thought that, he tore away from me, and I felt the separation all the way through to my soul. He really was some sort of mind reader.

I looked into his eyes, panting slightly, and tried to catch my breath. I fervently hoped that I wasn't a disappointment to him.

He was staring back at me, hair slightly disheveled, and he brushed the hair out of his eyes. "Abbey, I lo—" His voice was a hoarse whisper. He broke eye contact with me and looked briefly down the stairwell. Then he looked at me again. "I really do love your hair, Astrid."

And with one final tug of a red-tinted curl, he vanished down the steps.

Chapter Twelve

SECRETS

He was always ready for either a fight or a frolic. . . .

—"The Legend of Sleepy Hollow"

When I woke up Monday morning from dreams of long white dresses and houses with white picket fences, I realized that my subconscious was really rushing things. But that didn't stop me from daydreaming during school that day.

Sure, I *might* have relived that kiss a thousand times. Or *maybe* thought about what we would name our first dog. And *possibly* even scribbled our names together surrounded by hearts.

I seriously needed to get a grip.

Caspian had never said he loved me. I didn't even know if he really *liked* me. We hadn't gone on any official dates yet, and it wasn't exactly like I'd told him how I felt. Yet I still doodled, and daydreamed, and smiled happily at everyone around me. Not even the ten million hours of extra homework that every teacher so eagerly assigned could ruin my good mood. All was right in my little corner of the world.

On Tuesday I passed a history test that I had totally forgotten to study for. On Wednesday the soda machine in the cafeteria wouldn't take my quarters but after a quick shake spit out a soda anyway. Although grape soda wasn't *exactly* what I wanted, it was free, so I wasn't complaining.

Even lunch seemed to have gotten marginally better. I moved to a table where small talk was mutually hated by several other people. We spent the whole time working on homework, reading a book, or, in the case of one, playing with our food. And I was *not* the one playing with my food. It wasn't the most exciting time in my life, but it was better than it had been.

On Thursday afternoon I found a note from Ben in my locker asking me to meet him in the gym after school. It really surprised me; I thought we were avoiding each other.

When the last bell rang at the end of the day, I wasn't entirely sure if I should go see Ben or not. I kind of felt guilty about it. What would Caspian think? Would he mind that I was meeting another guy? I mean, it wasn't like I was going to hook up with Ben or anything, but still . . .

My overflowing book bag felt like a fifty-pound weight on my back, wearing me down with each step I took as I paced back and forth in front of my locker trying to make a decision. If I went to go see Ben now and only stayed for a couple of minutes, then I could apologize about the whole prom thing ending badly and stop by the river on my way home to see if Caspian was there. It was a win all the way around.

That idea seemed to lighten my load, and my spirits, and I headed toward the gymnasium to look for Ben. As soon as I stepped into the room, I saw a couple of track runners warming up in one corner and felt an immediate sense of relief that we wouldn't be alone. Then I scolded myself for thinking that, and repeated the phrase "I will not feel guilty" out loud. I was young, and carefree. Or at least I was supposed to be.

Right.

I took my young and carefree self off toward the other end of the gym, still searching for Ben. Was he not here yet? I rounded the bleachers, and that was when I saw him, leaning against the wall watching the runners. As I got closer, I could see that he had a perfect view of the door I'd come in. Great. *Did he see me talking to myself?*

A strange feeling of nervousness washed over me as I approached him. Was he mad at me for what I had said to him about the prom? What if he'd had a terrible time with his date and wanted to blame me for it?

He saw me, and smiled. "Abbey, I'm glad you got my note."

The nervousness melted away. My answering smile was wide, and I felt a slight blush rise to my cheeks as he gave me a quick once-over.

"Hey, Ben," I said, walking over to him and dropping my heavy book bag against the cinderblock wall. "I swear that thing wants to kill me."

He laughed. "Yeah, all the teachers are really piling it on this week. I hope we don't get any homework for Thanksgiving break."

"Only in a perfect world," I sighed.

"True." He smiled at me again. "Hey, you changed your hair. I like it."

I blushed furiously and reached up to touch my curls. "Thanks. I was feeling . . . festive."

"It looks good," he said.

I glanced down at the wooden floor, still feeling the heat in my cheeks. We stood there silently, and I wondered what he really wanted to say. *Maybe I should go first*, I thought.

"Look, Ben." I tried to look anywhere but into his eyes. "I'm sorry for what I said to you about the prom. You were trying to do a nice thing, and I shouldn't have acted like I did."

He shook his head. "It was stupid. I'm sorry. That's why I sent you the note to meet me here. I should have asked you back when I first wanted to. You had every right to turn me down." He gave me a hopeful look. "Will you give me a second chance if I ask you out again?"

Hmm. How best to skirt *that* issue?

"You don't have to pull the puppy dog look on me, Ben." I tried to laugh it off. "Apology accepted." I turned to pick up my book bag, but his voice stopped me.

"How about a hug, then?"

I peeked over at him, sternly telling myself not to make a bigger deal out of this than it really was. People hugged all the time. It didn't mean anything. "Sure." I stepped closer, and he folded his arms around me. I briefly raised mine to hug him back, and had started to pull away when he leaned down close to my ear.

I could feel his warm breath, and I froze.

"I really like your hair, Abbey," he whispered, gently touching a curl that was near my cheek. I turned my head and came face-to-face with him. His big brown eyes were only inches away from mine. But in my head a different voice was saying those words to me, and for a moment the eyes were green.

A split second later, I realized what type of position I had placed myself in. If I didn't move *very* soon, he was going to get the wrong idea. "I'm sorry, Ben," I said, pulling myself back from him. "I have a . . . boyfriend." The term tripped on my tongue, but I felt a warm sensation inside as I said it. I rolled the word around silently, liking the way it sounded.

"Oh, but I th-thought . . . ," he stammered. "I mean, you do?" He pulled back too. "I haven't seen you with anyone. Does he go here?"

"He graduated two years ago," I said proudly.

"Oh. Well, I . . . I didn't mean anything by it. I didn't know. I just thought that you and I . . . since Kristen."

I felt terrible. "No, it's okay. No one really knows about it. It's kind of a new thing." Had I known this was going to happen? Was that why I felt so guilty about meeting him? I tried to make it better. After all, he didn't *really* want me. It was obvious

 239

that Kristen had been the one he'd had the crush on.

"If I didn't have a boyfriend, things might be different. I'm actually really flattered that you thought we would be—well . . . I hope this doesn't ruin our friendship, Ben."

"Oh, Abbey, you're killing me," he groaned. "First the I-would-have-picked-you-if-I-hadn't-already-picked-someone-else line, and then the friendship zone? That's like the kiss of death."

I was stricken, but I didn't know what else to do.

Ben gave a heartfelt sigh, and then he laughed. "It's okay. I'm just teasing you. If you're happy, then I'm happy. I'm still glad to be your friend."

I turned away from him and bent to pick up my book bag. When I turned around to face him again, he had a smile on his face. But his eyes looked sad.

"I'm sorry," I whispered, reaching out to give his hand a quick squeeze. He nodded, and I started to walk away. So much for my good mood. It was now completely gone as I thought about the person I was leaving behind.

I decided to tell Caspian how I felt when I finally made it to the river. I had to know whether or not he felt the same way about me.

Hopefully, my confession wouldn't be in vain, or else I'd be joining the recently rejected club.

My determination fell away, though, as I passed by the river, and then the bridge. He wasn't here.

I wandered through the cemetery, looking everywhere in case I saw him. But once I realized I had no hope of finding him somewhere he obviously wasn't, I stopped looking. Dejected, I kept my gaze to the ground and followed the familiar pathway home.

It was when I looked up to step around a deep rut in the road that I spotted him.

"Caspian, what are you doing here?" Happiness crept into my question, and I couldn't stop myself from blushing.

He was sitting next to a large monument in a family plot, drawing on a piece of paper. He had black smudges on his hands, and he looked just as surprised to see me as I was to see him. "Hi, Abbey." A strange look passed over his face, and he shoved the paper behind him. "I'm just . . . sitting."

"Wow." I laughed. "You must like it here even more than I do." I shifted my book bag awkwardly. "I know we just saw each other a couple of days ago and all, but . . ." I blushed again at the memory of our last meeting and then stopped abruptly when I realized I was rambling.

He didn't say anything. Silence rose between us, and I started to get concerned.

"Have you . . . been waiting here . . . for me?" I was hoping for a no to that question, but I could see the answer in his eyes.

"Yeah. I stopped by the cemetery and river each day. But I didn't wait long. Other stuff to do, you know." He blew it off.

I got a sick feeling in the pit of my stomach. "I'm really sorry I didn't stop by, Caspian. I . . . I didn't know." I found myself repeating Ben's words.

"It's not a big deal. We'll catch up another time, okay?" He picked up his drawing and stood up.

"Caspian, wait," I said. He had started to turn away already. "When . . . Where do you want to meet next?"

"I'm busy this weekend, but I guess meet me here next Saturday at noon," he replied over his shoulder. "Bye, Abbey."

I watched him walk away, and was confused by his dismissive tone. Okay, so he was mad that I hadn't stopped by, but it wasn't like we had set a date and time. And if I actually had his phone number or something, then I could have called him about it. I made a mental note to ask him for that next Saturday.

Upset, and not even really knowing why, I went to Washington Irving's grave. As usual, there wasn't anyone there and I let myself in through the gate. I stalked around the length of the fenced-in area, too disturbed to sit still on the ground.

"How was I supposed to know he'd be waiting here?" I muttered, half to myself, half to the empty graveyard. "Did I ever claim to be a mind reader? No, I did not. So how can I be expected to read his mind?" Angrily, I kicked at a stray leaf on the ground. "It's called a phone number. Get one."

As I heard those words come out of my mouth, echoing those hateful words once said by someone else in a prom dress, I immediately stopped pacing. Hanging my head, I went to sit down next to the carved initials tree. I buried my head in my arms and tucked my legs up underneath me. *Why did he act that way today?* It was all so confusing.

Soft footsteps disturbed the grass around me, and I looked up to see the old caretaker coming toward the tree. He was wearing the same patched blue overalls, but he had a brown shirt on. I forced a smile to my face and got to my feet. "Hello, Nikolas."

His whole face lit up, and the smile he gave me almost made

me cry. He looked so happy to see me. "Abbey, how wonderful to meet you here again! How have you been?"

I shrugged my shoulders and stuffed my hands into my jeans pockets. "I guess I'm fine. It's been kind of a rough day."

"Is there anything I can help you with?"

"I don't know. It's just . . ." I hesitated. "It's not like there's anything specifically wrong, you know? I just don't get how someone can act a certain way that's really positive, and then all of a sudden be different."

"Like changing your mind about something?" he asked.

"No," I said, at a loss as to how to describe my dilemma. "Never mind. It's just . . . boys. They're aggravating. That's all."

He got that mischievous look in his eye again, and said very solemnly, "Well, speaking as someone who was once technically a boy . . ." I blushed, completely embarrassed now. "I don't want to make any excuses for whoever this is you are speaking of," he continued on, "but . . . he is obviously crazy."

My eyes grew wide, and he chuckled. "I am just teasing with you. I hope you don't mind."

I couldn't hide my grin, and I shook my head at him. "You're just as bad as the boys," I teased back.

He smiled. "I only wanted to see you smile. I hope you don't mind indulging an old man. Truthfully, though, give your young man some time. I am sure he's confused, or unsure of himself. A man's pride is a very powerful thing."

"That's definitely true," I agreed. "So do you think that maybe it wasn't me, but him? Maybe he's just dealing with something on his end?"

Nikolas leaned closer and said quietly, "I can tell that you have a very wise and kind soul, Abbey. And I am an excellent judge of character. I don't think it was anything you could have done. Besides, if he can't get over whatever is bothering him, send him to me and I will set him straight."

To my total embarrassment, I burst into tears. Then I leaned over to hug him. "Thanks, Nikolas," I whispered. "That means a lot to me."

He let out a soft breath, almost like I'd surprised him, and hesitated before awkwardly trying to hug me back. He seemed a bit rusty at it. I hastily dashed away my tears, scrubbing both hands across my face.

"You know," he said, "sometimes we put on a facade because we are afraid of how those close to us will react if they see our true selves. Just because someone does this, doesn't mean he wants to put you off in any way, or he doesn't like you. I don't see how anyone could *not* like you, Abbey."

Taking a minute to compose myself, I leaned down and acted like my shoe was untied. After fidgeting with it for a while, and hoping that my eyes weren't all red and splotchy, I stood back up to face Nikolas. "I . . . um . . . should go. Mom's probably waiting, and I have a lot of homework to do. So . . . thanks. I really appreciate it."

He patted my arm gently and beamed at me. "You are most welcome, Abbey. I hope I'll see you again soon."

I nodded, trying not to be too embarrassed that I had just cried in front of a total stranger, and headed to the gate. After briefly stopping to wave to Nikolas, I stepped down the stairs and started home. This had been one hell of a day.

On Saturday morning I asked Mom if she wanted to go with me to the Maxwells' house. It had been a while since I'd seen Mrs. M., and I wanted to check on her. I was shocked when Mom told me she didn't have any plans and actually agreed to go. I think the last time she had a free weekend was, like, a decade ago.

We debated on whether or not we should call ahead of

time, before agreeing on the just-drop-by approach. Luckily the Maxwells were home when we arrived. It was nice to see them again and be in that familiar environment, but it was also awkward. We tried not to talk about Kristen very much.

When Mom got up to pour herself a cup of coffee, I took that as an invitation to talk to Mrs. Maxwell alone.

"How are you *really* doing, Mrs. M.?" I asked her quietly.

She took my hand and held it. I could tell that she was putting on a brave face. "I'm okay, Abbey. It's hard, obviously. And God knows that I haven't even thought about doing anything with her room yet. But we're taking it one day at a time."

An idea popped into my head. "Would you mind if I went up there?"

"You don't have to ask me to go to her room, Abbey. You know that. You practically lived here when—" She broke off and looked away.

Standing up, I gave her a brief hug. "Thanks, Mrs. M. I won't be long." I turned to leave the room, and she called out to me. "If there's anything in Kristen's room that you want, Abbey, go ahead and take it."

I smiled and nodded, then headed for the stairs.

It felt like a long trip up, and I took a deep breath to steel myself before I finally reached for her door. In my own room I may have been able to deal with my thoughts and emotions regarding her death, but actually going into *her* room was a whole different story.

I slowly pushed the door open, and the familiar sight of petal pink wallpaper—that Kristen had hated with a passion ever since she'd turned eleven—greeted me as I entered the room. It hadn't changed very much since the last time I'd been in here. The only major difference was that the floor and bed, usually covered in dirty laundry, were now both completely clear.

But her small computer desk was still cluttered. And the old white dresser still held her stereo with its tower of empty CD cases next to it. Her favorite red shirt was hanging on the closet doorknob too. Almost like she'd be back for it at any minute.

Sadness sank into me as I realized that she would never *be* back . . . but I pushed it away. We had spent a lot of time up here, and it wasn't hard to associate practically everything in the room with some sort of happy memory. I clung to that thought as I moved around the room.

Was there anything in here that would tell me why she had been at the river that night?

I glanced in her closet first, but nothing looked out of place in there. I skimmed over her desk next, and that revealed the same result. Her cell phone was propped up beside the charger next to a lamp. I turned away from it and kept looking.

The only thing the dresser held was clothes, and I moved through them as quickly as I could. They still smelled like her favorite shampoo, and that almost brought me to my knees. I sat down hard on the edge of her bed, trying to concentrate on the good memories.

The bedside table beside me had a small drawer, and I opened it. A diary was inside. Picking it up, I skimmed through the pages. I felt kind of bad about peeking through Kristen's private thoughts, but desperate times call for desperate measures.

Nothing caught my eye, though. It didn't look like she had written down anything about the river.

Then I noticed one of the corners of the bedspread was hanging against the edge of the bed frame at an odd angle. I leaned down to straighten it out. My fingers brushed against something hard, tucked in between the mattress and the box spring, and I scooted closer to see what it was.

Stuck under the corner of the bed was a little book about the size of a . . . diary. I had to shift the edge of the mattress and wedge my hand next to the frame, but I was able to reach it.

When I pulled it out, it was a carbon copy of the book I held in my other hand. Only its cover was red, while the cover of the first diary was black. *Now* I was intrigued. Had I found several of Kristen's diaries? I opened the first page of the black book and scanned it for a date. The first entry read April 19. Then I opened the first page of the red book to check for its date.

April 19 . . . of the same year. *Why would she have had two diaries for the same year?*

Sitting back on my heels, I flipped the red one open, intent on finding some answers. I felt that twinge of guilt again, but my curiosity was too strong.

I tried to soothe my conscience by making a deal with myself. If I read through the diaries only once, then put them back, I wouldn't really be doing anything wrong. And Kristen's mom *had* said that I could take anything I wanted. Of course, she probably meant more along the lines of clothes, or CDs, but that was beside the point.

Before I had the chance to start reading, Mom called my name from below. I jumped at the sudden interruption and scrambled to my feet, quickly glancing around the room. I needed something.

The red shirt on the knob of the closet door. Perfect.

I grabbed it and carefully wrapped the diaries up inside. As I passed Kristen's desk on my way to the door, a piece of crumpled-up notebook paper caught my attention. A tube of lipstick was resting next to it. I scooped the lipstick up and removed the cap, revealing a dark red shade.

Wanting to leave my mark, my final good-bye in some way, I carefully smoothed out the paper and scrawled "Memories Last Forever" on it. Then I signed my name in a big, bold script and re-capped the lipstick before tucking it with the note into the top drawer.

Shutting the bedroom door carefully behind me, I walked down the stairs to where Mom was waiting. Memories *definitely* lasted forever.

Once we got home, I went straight to my room, and locked the door behind me for privacy. Then, thinking twice about it, I went inside my closet and locked *that* door. I settled down on a huge pile of stuffed animals and got comfortable. I wouldn't be interrupted here.

I carefully laid both diaries side by side and then started with the black one. The first page was innocent enough.

April 19th—Friday morning

This weekend Abbey and I are going shopping for some essential oils and bottles that she needs. There's a new store that opened up right next to the mall, and she can't wait to go. I agreed on the condition that we stop at the mall for some new shoes, and possibly a cinnamon pretzel.

She acted like she wanted to give me a hard time about it, but she couldn't keep a straight enough face. She's so funny. After we get back, I have to start on my end-of-the-year science paper. I can't afford to get anything lower than an A-, so I need to get a jump on it.

I wish school was easier. Sometimes I think that one day my brain will explode from all the algebra, biology, and history I'm being forced to cram in there.

Oh well, another day.

Kristen

P.S. Just got back from the mall, and I am now

the proud owner of the *cutest* brown sandals. Hurry up, warm weather, so I can show off my gorgeous new shoes!

I smiled as I read what was written in her small, neat handwriting. It was so typically Kristen. I turned to the red diary.

April 19th—Friday evening

I have decided to start this alternate diary to talk about D. in. I'm afraid that if I commit any of this to my real diary, it will be taken away from me, like a dream.

D. called me tonight. We talked for over an hour, and he wants to meet tomorrow. I'm so nervous. I can't believe that he's actually interested in me. Am I dreaming? Will I wake up and find this was all a lie? God, I hope not. I don't think I could handle the heartbreak.

It's so hard to keep this from Abbey. I want so badly to share all of this with my best friend. But I know I can't. And that's the hardest thing of all.

K.

I sat in stunned silence. My best friend had been keeping secrets from me? A swift and piercing hurt filled me, and I shoved the diaries away, burying my head in my hands. How could this be true? I'd never kept any secrets from her.

My mind tried to grapple with the impossibility of the situation. April 19. She had been keeping secrets from me since April 19.

Who is D.? Why didn't Kristen tell me about him?

Tears welled up, and I allowed them to fall. I didn't know how to deal with this. What was I supposed to do now? Part of me wanted to read further, to see if she revealed her secrets. But another part of me was too hurt and furious, and wanted to rip out all the pages and tear them into tiny shreds. She had betrayed me.

I didn't know what I should do.

When Mom called me down for dinner that evening, I went somberly and didn't say very much. I had come to terms with the fact that it didn't matter how or what I felt. I had to keep reading the diaries. They might explain why Kristen had been down at the river.

And secrets or not, I owed it to her.

Chapter Thirteen

A GOOD REASON

...and a book of dreams and fortune-telling; in which last was a sheet of foolscap much scribbled and blotted in several fruitless attempts to make a copy of verses in honor of the heiress of Van Tassel.

—"The Legend of Sleepy Hollow"

I had a hard time going back and forth between the two diaries, so I stopped reading the black one and put it away. In some ways it was harder to read that one. In the black diary she acted so normal. Like the Kristen I thought I knew. It was an abrupt shift switching over to the red diary. The whole tone was different. Even her writing style had changed.

From what I could piece together so far, Kristen had met this guy who insisted they keep their relationship a secret, and had spent hours talking to him on the phone. They'd even gotten together a couple of times.

She never said how she first met him, or when and where they had been meeting, but I couldn't stop myself from wondering where *I* had been all of those times. It felt like such a personal betrayal. She had obviously gone through a lot of extra effort to make sure I didn't find out about him. I couldn't understand why she would do that, if he'd made her so happy.

So I kept reading to find a clue ... Any clue ...

April 23rd—Tuesday afternoon
I think I'm in love! D. is so romantic. He pretended to tuck a piece of hair behind my ear and gently touched my cheek. And then it happened . . . our first kiss.

Not being with him is torture—every hour we're apart I die a slow death of agonizing loneliness. I can't stand this feeling. I wish we could spend every day together. I wish we were free to tell the world. I wish he would agree to let me tell Abbey.

I hope he calls me again tonight. Please call me, my love. Put me out of this misery.
K.

May 17th — Friday evening

Today D. told me I'm beautiful. I'll never forget that moment. As I looked into his eyes, I could almost believe him. Then he made me cry when he gave me a flower he found. But I had to leave it behind. I didn't want anyone to see it. So he promised me dozens of roses instead.

  Maybe one day . . .

  K

June 2nd — Sunday morning

It's been exactly one month since D. and I made it official. I love him so much! Sometimes I can't believe that he picked me. I don't know why he did, but I <u>do</u> know that we'll be together forever.

  I know what he wants, but I'm scared. The thought of that is . . . terrifying . . . and exciting . . . and exhilarating . . . but mostly terrifying.

  What scares me the most about all of this, though, is the fact that I can never go back. I wish I could talk to Abbey about it. How do you not tell your best friend something like this? I don't know if I can keep that kind of secret.

    K.

I thought back to our last couple of months at school, trying to analyze all the time I had spent with Kristen. Why hadn't I paid closer attention?

And then my thoughts turned to other things. Like, how many times had she wanted me to go away so she could meet this guy? Or, did she tell him any of *my* secrets?

This diary cast shadows of doubt onto every word she had ever said to me, and my mind started picking apart all the things we had done together. I couldn't help but wonder: *If I had asked her about any of this, would she have lied to me?* Unfortunately, the answer appeared to be yes. And that hurt.

I wished I had never found this side of her. I just wanted things to go back to the way they were. Before I found out that my best friend was keeping secrets from me and lying every day. Before I had to question every motive behind her actions. Before I had to ask whether or not she really *had* been my best friend after all.

July 26th — Friday evening

How can I make up my mind about a decision like this? If I say no, what will he do? I can't say no. I try to convince myself that it's not a big deal. Everyone goes through this at some point in time. I can do this. I can do this.

    K.

August 13th — Tuesday morning

We talked about what we're going to do, and agreed on it. I want to ask him for more time to think about it, but he's given me almost three months already. I'm afraid that I'm going to lose him. It's all I can think about lately. I find myself obsessing over it.

    I wonder if Abbey knows what I have planned. She has to have guessed. How can I keep a secret like this from a best friend that can practically read my mind? I hope D. doesn't figure out that Abbey might know something. I don't want him to . . . I don't want to lose him.

    Oh God, please don't let me lose him.

    K.

August 16th — Friday afternoon

Tonight's the night. We're meeting at the park, like usual. I have to get ready soon. I'm so nervous. I hope I can make him happy.

K.

August 18th — Sunday evening

Just had another fight with D. I don't understand why this keeps happening. Sometimes I wish Abbey would just come out and tell me if she knows what's going on. She might not forgive me for keeping all of this from her, but I have to talk to someone.

K.

August 18th — Sunday evening II

Every time I think it's over, that we're just too different, he says something that changes my mind. I'm starting to wonder if I'm with him because _I_ actually want to be or because _he_ wants me to be.

K.

August 19th — Monday morning

I can't do this anymore. The secrets . . . the lies . . .
I told D. that I wanted to tell Abbey about us, and we
had a huge fight. I had to beg him to give me another
chance. He agreed, as long as we stop meeting at the
park. I don't know where else we can go. Sometimes I
wish we had never . . .

I don't know what to do. I can't live without him.

K.

That was it. The last entry.

I threw the diary down onto the bed and angrily shook my head, rejecting this new information. There was no way she would have kept any of these things from me. We were too close for that. But proof in the form of a red diary told me I was wrong.

Kristen *had* kept secrets from me . . . several of them.

I woke up unusually early on Saturday morning. The week had flown by, but I couldn't stop thinking about the diary. It was like trying to solve a puzzle when I didn't know what the picture looked like.

 261

Forcing myself out of bed, I went down to the kitchen to make some more cookies for Caspian. After our last conversation, I was hoping they'd suffice as a peace offering. I followed the recipe in the cookbook automatically, not really paying any attention to what I was doing.

It wasn't until the second batch was being taken out of the oven that my distraction caught up with me, and I ended up reaching for the hot cookie sheet with my bare hand instead of with an oven mitt. The searing metal registered immediately, and I dropped the tray back onto the oven rack. Luckily, I'd only managed to lift it up an inch or two, so it didn't have very far to fall. I cursed my way over to the kitchen sink, and then cursed some more when the phone started ringing.

Deciding that my burned appendage needed more attention than the phone right now, I blasted the cold water and felt immediate, blessed relief. Ten seconds later my hand was barely throbbing, but the phone was still ringing.

I grabbed a washcloth and ran it under the water before applying it to the blister that had already started to form. Turning to reach the phone behind me, I juggled the washcloth into a better position. "Hello?"

"Hi, honey," came a cheerful voice on the other end. "It's Mrs. Maxwell. I thought I'd get the machine."

"Oh, hi, Mrs. M." I snapped to my senses immediately. *Is this a sign? Should I tell her about the diary?*

"I was just calling to tell your mom not to worry about the reservations tomorrow night. I've already taken care of them."

"Okay," I replied. "I'll tell her. Are you guys doing anything special?"

"We have a meeting with the head of the historical society. Should be fun. The last one was a blast."

The heavy sarcasm in her voice made me laugh. "I'm sure it will be excitement all around."

"At least the food will be good," she sighed. "We're meeting at Callenini's. They have the *best* chicken Alfredo linguini there."

"Ooooh, yeah," I agreed. "Tell Mom to bring me home some of their garlic knots. I love those things."

"Will do."

We talked about the restaurant a bit more, and then Mrs. M. said she had to go. I didn't bring up the diary. I couldn't do it.

But as I hung up the phone, all those feelings of hurt and betrayal resurfaced and I felt a tear run slowly down my cheek.

Another tear followed, and I hung my head, wallowing in a moment of self-pity.

Suddenly the timer on the oven beeped loudly, and startled me. I had set it to go off every fifteen minutes for a new batch of cookies. Rubbing my hands across my face, I quickly dried my eyes. I didn't have time for a pity party. I still had a whole bowl of cookie dough left, and a couple dozen more cookies to make.

So I turned on the angriest music I could find, cranked it up until it echoed through the house, and sang along at the top of my lungs as I got back to work.

Four sheets of cookies and thirteen kick-ass songs later, it was time for me to get ready to go see Caspian. Exactly one hour after that, I was dressed in jeans and a red sweater, and back downstairs putting some of the cookies into a paper bag.

Since neither of the parental units had yelled at me to turn down the music earlier, I figured they were both probably out of the house already and at one of their endless meetings. I left a few cookies on a plate next to the coffeepot for them to find. That should earn me a couple of "good daughter" bonus points. Then I double-checked the oven to make sure I had turned it off, grabbed the bag for Caspian, and shut the door behind me on my way out.

I didn't feel the cold at first as I briskly stepped into the wind. But it didn't take long before I started wishing that I had grabbed a heavier coat and some gloves to go with it. The wind blew hard, and I felt its cold breath whipping against me. I shuddered and bent my head slightly, trying to ignore it as I walked to the cemetery.

Making my way through the gates and toward the path that lead to the river, I found Caspian at the Irving family plot. His back was turned, and he was dressed all in black, but I would have recognized that hair anywhere. I slowed down, moving carefully and silently until I was directly behind him.

"Caspian," I whispered. If he heard me, he didn't let on. He held perfectly still. I took another step, and was now right next to him. He was staring at Washington Irving's grave. I reached out to touch his arm.

"Coins. Why do you think they leave coins?" His quiet voice sent a chill through me, and for some reason I pulled my hand back. He turned his head to look at me, and his eyes were slightly unfocused. "Do you think it means anything? To him, I mean?" He looked genuinely perplexed at the question.

I wasn't sure if I should answer or not.

Then he blinked and his expression changed. A smile lit up his face. "Astrid. I'm glad you came."

My head spun. Did he know how much his smile made my heart melt? Or the way his voice sent tingles up and down my arms, and butterflies fluttering wildly inside my stomach? *Someday I'll be able to tell him how he makes me feel. But not today.*

I smiled back. "Hi, Caspian."

Did my smile make him melt? Did my voice make him feel funny, or send chills racing through his body? I vowed to ask him those things someday. But not today.

"I hope you're not still mad at me." I peeked shyly at him.

"Mad at you?" he asked. "Why would I be mad at you?"

"Because I didn't meet you here last week. I thought you were pissed about that."

He shook his head. "I wasn't mad at you. How were you supposed to know that I'd be here?"

"I don't know. I guess I just thought . . ." I shrugged. "I don't know."

"I wasn't mad, Abbey," he reassured me. "Believe me?" He had that serious little-boy look on his face again.

Yeah, like I could resist that.

"Okay," I sighed dramatically. "I believe you." I grinned to let him know I was teasing and was rewarded with a smile in return. Remembering the cookies, I held the bag out and gestured to them. "I made you some cookies so you wouldn't be mad at me. But since you weren't ever mad, I guess I'll just have to keep them."

He tugged the bag playfully out of my hand. "On second thought, if they're snickerdoodle cookies, then I think I *do* need them to help me get over my anger." He gave me a mock scowl.

I laughed at his act. "Of course they're snickerdoodle. I wouldn't make you any other kind. Do you want to go sit under the bridge to eat them? It should be warmer there." I shivered and rubbed my hands together. It was really cold out here.

He immediately looked contrite. "You're cold? Why didn't you wear a heavier jacket?"

"Like you're one to talk? You don't even have one on."

He looked down and seemed surprised. Then he laughed. "I never wear one. I guess I'm warm-blooded. But you're right about the bridge; we'll go there."

We turned away from the gravestone and started to walk down the hill. We didn't talk, but it wasn't an awkward silence. It was comfortable. Tiny pebbles crunched under our feet as we followed the path to the riverbank. It was colder by the water, until we stepped underneath the cover of the bridge. I felt warmer already just being with him.

Another moment of silence passed by. I stared at a jagged crack in the concrete wall that made up part of the support pillar for the bridge.

"So I went to see Kristen's mom last week, and I found something hidden under Kristen's bed. She was keeping two diaries." Focusing on that crack, I tried to give my mind something else to dwell on. "One was written like the Kristen I knew, but the other one . . . It was filled with some stuff I wasn't expecting to find."

I could hear the quiet rush of the river next to me, and I looked over at the water. "Did you ever think you knew someone, and then find out it was all bullshit?" The words exploded out of my mouth. The thoughts were tumbling out of me, and I was helpless to stop any of it. The dam had been breached. I shoved my hands into my pockets out of sheer frustration. "I thought I knew Kristen. She was supposed to be my best friend, and I told her everything. *Everything!*

"She was lying to me the whole time, and I never even knew it.

I'm such an idiot! I mean, how can you do that to someone? How can you pretend to be someone else, and hide who you really are? How can anyone do that?" I scuffed my shoe in the dirt.

"Maybe she didn't have a choice," Caspian said softly. "Some people don't have choices about the secrets they keep."

I dismissed his logic. "Kristen had a choice. No one *forced* her to keep a secret boyfriend from me. She could have told me about him anytime. Besides, it's practically one of the requirements of being a best friend. You *don't* keep secrets from people you care about, and you *definitely don't* keep secrets like that." My voice shook, and I felt dangerously close to that tear threshold. I blinked quickly and took a deep breath. I was *not* going to embarrass myself by blubbering like a baby.

"So Kristen had a secret boyfriend, then, I take it?" Caspian asked. "Do you think she was meeting him here that night?"

"I don't know. But I think they were . . . really involved."

Caspian glanced over at me, but I couldn't look him in the eye. Ahh, embarrassment. Always a friend of mine.

"Did she mention a name anywhere?"

I shook my head. "Only the initial *D*. There was definitely something up, though. Her whole writing style changed, like she

269

was getting depressed. I never noticed it in person," I said sadly. "I don't know how she managed to keep it from me. It must have been a difficult thing to do."

"I'm sure she had her reasons," Caspian said. "She must have. I don't think she would have kept something like that from you without having a very good reason. Trust her, Abbey."

"Trust her? After she lied to me for months?"

He didn't reply. But it didn't bother me. I just needed someone to vent to, someone to listen to my frustrations. I obviously didn't have a best friend to fill that role anymore. We were both quiet for a long time, so I leaned against the wall and slid to the ground.

Okay, so maybe I *was* looking for someone to talk back, to tell me that I wasn't crazy and had every right to feel the way I did.

But we didn't talk about anything else, and a moment later he slid down beside me. We were both caught up in our own little worlds.

My world was interrupted when my cell phone buzzed. Voice mail message. I flipped it open and saw that I was in an area that didn't have any reception. I checked my missed calls folder, and Mom's number was listed there.

"So are you going to eat any of your cookies, or wait until

you get home again?" I asked Caspian, trying to lighten the mood before our day ended badly.

He looked over at me like he had been startled from a deep thought. "What?" Then he looked at the bag between us. "Oh, yeah." He laughed. "Are you kidding? I can't wait to dig in." He carefully opened the bag and took out a cookie that was broken in half. As he took a bite, I glanced at my phone again.

"I'm going to go check my voice mail. I'll be right back."

He nodded, and continued chewing. I stood up and walked out from under the bridge to an area farther away where I would get better reception. Mom's voice came in loud and clear through the voice mail. I sighed heavily, not even bothering to listen to what she had to say, and quickly punched the save button as I walked back toward the bridge.

"You know," I said, closing my phone once I got closer to Caspian, "if you gave me a cell number, it would make finding you a whole lot easier."

There was a sheepish look on his face as he stood up. "I know this is going to sound very twentieth century, but . . . I don't have one."

My jaw dropped.

"You don't have a cell phone?"

"Nope."

I couldn't believe what he was saying.

"Okay, then what about your home phone number?"

He shook his head again. "That one's not really any good either. My dad keeps it off the hook. He sleeps strange hours."

"Screen name, e-mail address . . . So I can text you?" I could see the answer coming before he even got it out. I was in a state of shock.

"Look, Abbey," he said. "I'm not trying to be weird here or anything. It's just that I don't spend very much time at home. And I don't hang around the computer when I *am* there. Don't worry so much about it. We'll find each other."

Caspian held the rest of his cookie half out to me. "Cookie? They're some of the best I've ever tasted."

I took the peace offering and smiled. Putting it into my mouth, I felt a secret thrill that his lips had just touched this cookie. So that almost translated into him kissing me again. I munched away happily, being careful to swallow very thoroughly, and then ran my tongue over my teeth to get rid of any stray crumbs.

"I'm going to be kind of busy over the next couple of weeks," he said, "but we'll work something out."

I opened my mouth to protest, but he cut me off.

"I already told you not to worry so much, Abbey. Relax." He was smiling at me, and I couldn't help but smile back. I think he was starting to figure out that I would agree to pretty much anything for that smile.

"Okay, okay," I replied. "Enjoy the rest of your cookies, and I'll see you around."

"See?" he said with a wide grin. "That's not so hard, is it, Astrid? No worries." He bowed his head slightly. "Thank you very much for the cookies. I'm pretty sure they'll be gone before I get home. Now before you leave, close your eyes and hold out your hand."

I stared at him.

He waited.

I sighed dramatically and stuck out my hand while I closed my eyes. Nothing happened.

"Are you sure you have your eyes closed?" he asked.

"Very sure."

"Do you promise to open this at home?"

That was a tough promise to make. *He has something to give me?* It was a very, very long walk home.

"Abigail Astrid?" he prompted.

I laughed. "Yes, yes, I promise. Even though I will be dying of curiosity, I promise not to open whatever you give me until I get home."

Something small and soft dropped into my open hand. It felt like a piece of cloth, and before I opened my eyes, I put it right into my pocket. The temptation might be too great if I saw it.

"Bye, Abbey," I heard Caspian call out. "Remember your promise."

My eyes flew open, but he was already walking away from me in the opposite direction. I smiled when I felt the small thing in my pocket. *Maybe I should try running home,* I thought.

"Bye, Caspian," I called out, turning to go the other way. But my mind went back to the cell phone conversation, and something he had said bugged me. "Wait, Caspian!" I spun back around.

He was far away, but he heard me and turned back. "You know, I don't even know your last name!" I shouted. Even from a distance I could see the gleam in his eye.

"Crane!" he shouted back. "It's Caspian Crane."

Chapter Fourteen

NEW FRIENDS

❦

Several of the Sleepy Hollow people were present at Van Tassel's, and, as usual, were doling out their wild and wonderful legends.

—"The Legend of Sleepy Hollow"

I barely made it home. The suspense was absolutely *killing* me. I alternated between a half run and a half walk that quickly left me gasping for air. I was *so* not in shape for this. Several times I was tempted to look at what was in my pocket, but then I would hear Caspian's words, and my promise to him, and the guilt stopped me.

When the front door finally came into view, I was extremely relieved. I ran up the steps to the porch, panting heavily, and anxiously searched my pants for the key. After fishing it out of my back pocket, I stuck it into the keyhole. Then the knob turned on its own and the door opened. Startled, I looked up into Mom's face.

"Oh good, you're ho— What's wrong with you?" she asked. "Were you running?"

My eyes immediately dropped to the ground. I couldn't exactly tell her I was meeting a boy in a graveyard. I took several gulps of air, trying to calm my breathing back down, but it wasn't helping.

"What happened?" Mom's voice was rising, and I put up a hand to try to stop her worry.

"Nothing's wrong," I gasped. "I just walked home . . . a little too quickly. I remembered . . . some homework . . . I have to finish."

"But it's Saturday."

My breathing started slowing to a somewhat normal level. "Mom . . . nobody wants to do homework on Sunday." I headed to the kitchen and grabbed a bottle of water before I flopped down onto a bar stool next to the table. I chugged the water as fast as I could.

"Careful," she warned. "You'll get sick if you drink that too fast."

I sat the now empty bottle down on the table and smiled wryly at her. She was *soooo* helpful. Feeling around in my pocket for the millionth time, I wondered again what the surprise could be as I ran my fingers over the soft edges. I glanced at the clock on the wall, and judged how quickly I could make an escape to my room.

The curiosity really was going to kill me any second now.

"I'm glad you got my message about tonight, Abbey." Mom's voice interrupted my plans.

Message? *Right.* Mom had left me a voice mail message at the bridge. I squirmed in my chair. I hadn't exactly listened to what she'd said.

I bluffed. "Yeah, I got your voice mail, but I had terrible reception at the bridge." I left it at that, hoping she would assume I hadn't heard the entire message because of the bad reception.

"You've been spending a lot of time at the bridge by yourself." She frowned. "I know it was your favorite spot to go with Kristen, but it's not healthy for you to be alone there all the time. Maybe you should see if any of your friends from school want to get together. We could plan something fun, like a girls' night out type of thing."

If only she knew how not *alone I am when I'm at the bridge . . .* But that wasn't something I was going to share with my mother. I deferred. "Yeah, maybe I'll ask them."

Maybe in another lifetime.

But it put a happy look on Mom's face, and she started chattering away again. "Okay, so for dinner tonight with Aunt

277

Marjorie, I was thinking about roast beef, but then I realized I don't even know if she likes beef. What if she prefers chicken, or lamb?"

I tuned out the rest of the conversation. Dinner . . . Tonight . . . Aunt Marjorie . . . I smiled weakly and tried to nod at all the appropriate moments as Mom babbled on, while I also fidgeted in my chair, anxious to get to the privacy of my own room.

Mom beamed. "It's really nice that you're looking forward to this, honey. Aunt Marjorie will like that."

I could be opening Caspian's gift right now . . . At this very second, holding it in my greedy little hands . . . My leg started twitching on its own, ready to race upstairs at a moment's notice.

"You're awfully restless." Mom scowled. "Why don't you go take a nice hot bath to calm your nerves? I know we haven't seen Aunt Marjorie for several years, but there's no reason to be anxious about it."

I hopped up from the stool, glad to have an excuse. "Sounds like a good idea, Mom. I'm all sweaty and gross from running too." I don't know if she heard me or not. She was already moving on to something else, probably checking the fridge for ingredients for dinner, or whatever. "What time are we eating?" I asked as I tossed the empty water bottle into the recycling bin.

"Six o'clock," was her distracted reply. "And try to wear something nice for Aunt Marjorie."

I made a face at her as I walked out of the kitchen. "Wear something nice." *What am I, ten?* I let that thought go, though, as soon as I realized where I was going and what that meant.

Present. From Caspian. Opened soon.

Sprinting up the stairs, I told myself the whole way that I was almost there. It was almost time to find out what his surprise for me was. My heart skipped a beat when I finally made it to my room, and I locked the door behind me. Carefully taking the small item out of my pocket, I laid it reverently on the bed. It was wrapped in a piece of red fabric.

I kicked off my shoes and sat down cross-legged, readjusting myself until I was in a comfortable position. Then I picked the piece of cloth up. A sudden knock on the door interrupted me, and I almost jumped off the bed. "What?" I called out, shoving the present under my pillow.

Mom's muffled voice came echoing through the door. "Abbey, I need your opinion on something. I just called the store to order the roast beef, and they're all out. Do you think I should get chicken, or lamb? Or what about fish? Do you think Aunt Marjorie would like a nice baked—"

"Mom!" I exploded, cutting her off midsentence. "I don't care! Get whatever you want. I'm pretty sure Aunt Marjorie will eat anything you put in front of her. Or, why don't you make like . . . meat loaf . . . or something."

"That's a good idea," she said. "Do you think she'll like that?"

"Yes, Mother, I do. Now go start making it. I'm getting in the bathtub, remember?"

"Okay." She laughed. "Thanks, Abbey. Enjoy your bath."

I held my breath until I heard her footsteps fade away. Reaching for my pillow, I pulled out the present and cradled it in my lap, exhaling deeply. I stared at the door for a couple of minutes, waiting to see if there were going to be any more interruptions, but it looked like everything was clear.

I think I forgot to breathe while I slowly unwound several layers of red cloth. It kept getting smaller and smaller, until the last fold revealed the treasure inside.

It was a necklace. He had given me a necklace.

Very gently I picked it up. It appeared to be made out of tiny square glass plates, and the edges were soldered together all the way around. A small ring had been attached to the top, and a black satin ribbon was threaded through it. But the best part was what was underneath the glass's surface.

On the front, with a background of midnight blue, was the name *Astrid* etched in deep red flowing cursive letters. I traced the graceful lines with my fingertip, and carefully turned it over, eager to see the other side.

The back had the same brilliant blue background, but it was dotted with tiny white stars, and each one hung like a perfect diamond, dazzling against the nighttime canvas. It was absolutely exquisite. The most beautiful thing I had ever seen.

Tying the ribbon around my neck, I jumped up from the bed and ran over to the mirror. The pendant lay in the hollow of my throat, and the black ribbon hugged my neck in a graceful V.

I couldn't stop staring at it. This *had* to mean he felt something for me. There was no way you would give something so personal to someone you were "just friends" with.

That thought filled me with a strange joy, and I gleefully danced around the room, only stopping when I came perilously close to knocking over my nightstand. I went to go look in the mirror one more time, and suddenly remembered the bath I was supposed to be taking.

I made my way over to the bathroom, pulled the plug on the tub, and turned on the water, wiggling the knob until it reached the temperature I liked. Then I added a heaping scoopful of bath salts and shut the door behind me as I left the room to take the necklace off.

I slowly untied the ribbon and held the small pendant in my hand. The metal edges were rough and bumpy, a stark contrast to the smooth plated glass. I was amazed at the perfect detailing. Where had he gotten it from? It was truly a masterpiece. A tiny work of art certainly worth more to me than any piece by Monet or van Gogh could ever be.

The sound of running water reminded me of my forgotten bath again, and I put the necklace down on the bed and raced into the bathroom. I was about an inch away from having an overflowing tub, but I made it in time.

I turned the faucet off and stripped out of my clothes before dipping a bare toe in. I shivered at the contact. It was so hot, it actually gave me chills. Giving myself time to adjust to the temperature, I sank in bit by bit and exhaled a happy sigh when I was fully immersed. *This* was heaven in a tub.

Reaching for the orange burlap bag that held my bath salts, I added another spoonful to the bathwater. A yummy pumpkin pie scent immediately filled the bathroom, and I leaned my head back and closed my eyes. The rough edges of the salts brushed against my skin while they sank to the bottom, and I swirled my hands gently around me, creating tiny waves to help them dissolve faster. The water was warm and soothing, and I felt my body slowly start to relax.

My mind drifted, and I found myself thinking about the last couple of months. So much had happened—good and bad. While I had come to terms with Kristen's death, in some sort of way, I was still troubled by everything I had learned from the diaries. And what about the plans for my shop? Would Kristen really want me to go through with them?

Then I thought about Caspian, which immediately brought a smile to my face. I hadn't completely worked out when, or how, I was going to tell him what I felt, but I still had plenty of time to figure it out. The right moment would come. Eventually.

I stayed in the tub until my fingers were pruney and I had relived that library kiss over and over again. Begrudgingly I climbed out and dried off, then marched over to survey my closet for something

283

nice to wear. I ended up choosing a pink shirtdress that mom had bought for me last year for school. I would wear the dress for her, and my black combat boots for me. That was a good compromise.

After I got dressed, I put the necklace from Caspian back on and tied a black scarf around my neck to cover it up. I really wasn't in the mood to explain to Mom and Dad where it had come from, but I certainly wasn't going to *not* wear it.

Dragging my feet, I headed downstairs, looking forward to what was surely going to be the most boring night of my life.

Mom had gone with my suggestion of meat loaf, and I gave Aunt Marjorie a polite smile when she arrived. Dinner was fairly normal, while Mom and Dad did most of the talking. Aunt Marjorie completely shocked me, though, as she was holding the peas, when she announced that she used to wear black combat boots too, and she really liked mine.

The look of surprise on Mom's face was priceless, and I decided right then and there that Aunt Marjorie was officially my new favorite great-aunt.

She spent the rest of the evening telling me stories about her rebellious younger years, and how she used to be a pilot. She still had her own plane and everything. I kept urging her to tell me story after story, until dinner had ended and several hours had passed without either of us realizing it. When she gathered up her coat, I was genuinely sorry to see her go, but I promised to visit soon. And she promised to take me up in her plane and teach me a thing or two about flying.

Then she was officially my new favorite relative of *all time*.

I'd had no idea someone that cool was related to me.

I couldn't wait to go visit her.

It felt like I had only shut my eyes for a couple of seconds when nine o'clock came the next morning. It certainly did *not* feel like I had just spent the last seven and a half hours in a comfortable bed, surrounded by soft pillows.

But once I got in the shower, the hot water did wonders. I had a feeling that Caspian might be at the cemetery today, and I wanted to thank him for the beautiful necklace.

I peeked out the window to gauge the weather, and saw the wind whipping through the trees, stirring up brightly colored maple leaves on the ground and making each one dance. I grabbed a red belted trench coat on my way out the door. I wasn't going to get caught in the cold this time.

The air outside was crisp and clean, and I breathed deeply. Everything looked so shiny and new. It was like a whole different world out here. I felt light, and pretty, and completely happy. Nothing could ruin my good mood . . .

. . . except wandering through a cemetery all morning, searching for someone who wasn't there.

To make matters worse, I'd skipped breakfast again, so that meant I was beyond hungry. "Hungry" had been an hour and a half ago. Now it felt like I could eat breakfast, lunch, and dinner all piled on top of each other.

I trudged along the cemetery path one last time, toward the river, with my hands tightly fisted in my pockets. *One more sweep.* I would make just one more sweep down by the bridge, and then I was totally out of here. Several hot fresh pizza slices were calling my name from the pizzeria downtown, and I didn't want to deny them.

Disappointment weighed heavily on my mind as I scanned under the bridge, desperate for a glimpse of Caspian. *He isn't here.* I slowly made my way back up to the main cemetery path, but took a right when I normally would have taken a left. The path split, and I started walking toward the other half of the cemetery, telling myself that there was no *particular* reason why I was going this way. This path would lead me out of the cemetery and to the pizza . . . eventually. It wasn't like I was going to see if Caspian was over on this side. That was something I was definitely *not* doing.

I almost had myself convinced, when I spotted someone. My heart sped up until I saw that it was Nikolas. Disappointment set back in. I opened my mouth to say something, but realized awkwardly that I didn't know what to say.

I don't know if I made some type of weird noise with my mouth hanging open like that, or if he just sensed I was there somehow, but suddenly he turned and looked my way. A wide grin split his face and he put up one hand in a wave. I smiled back and quickened my pace.

"Hello, Nikolas," I said once I got closer.

His hair was even more windblown than it had been before, but his eyes were still warm and friendly. He nodded his head in greeting. "Katy, look, we have a visitor. The young lady I told you about," Nikolas called out.

I turned in the general direction where he seemed to be speaking. Farther down another path an older woman was placing a single flower along each gravestone. She looked our way, and I could see her wrinkled face light up with a smile. Her long strawberry-golden hair was tied back in gentle waves, and she was wearing an old-fashioned skirt that should have looked completely out of place, yet suited her perfectly. She bent to pick up her basket from the ground, and then lifted it high and started toward us.

Nikolas reached out his hand to help her when she reached us. She gave it a quick squeeze, and Nikolas made the introductions. "This is Abigail—er, Abbey, sweet." He turned to me. "And this is my wife, Katy."

"It's very nice to meet you," I said. Her eyes were just like his—friendly, and crinkly in the corners—but they were clear blue. Even brighter than my own blue eyes.

"How lovely to meet you, Abbey," she replied. "Nikolas told me that you helped him tend to Mr. Irving. They so enjoyed the company. Would you care to join us for some tea this afternoon?" She looked at me hopefully.

"Do you have any peppermint tea?" I asked, grinning at Nikolas. They both chuckled.

"Ahh, yes, of course. It's our favorite kind," said Katy.

"Then I would love to," I agreed.

Katy passed the basket she held over to Nikolas. "If you will carry that for me, love, we'll lead the way." Then she gave him a questioning look, and he nodded once.

Grabbing my hand, Katy tucked it into the crook of her elbow. I didn't know where we were headed—there weren't any houses close to this side of the cemetery—but she just started walking, and I tried to keep up. She was surprisingly fast for someone who was probably sixty years older than me.

We walked for a while along that path. Every now and then it would wind sharply to one side or the other. The farther we walked, the more frequent the twists and turns became. The foliage also started to get denser. Trees seemed to stand closer together, with their branches interwoven tightly among each other, filtering the daylight so that it broke through only in small patches.

The ground was overflowing with springy moss and sparse flowers. Wild ferns pushed their way onto the pathway, invading our space. They seemed to be reaching out to grasp the edges of our clothing as we passed by. I suppose the changes in the scenery should have made me a little apprehensive, but being with Nikolas and Katy put my mind at ease.

I could hear the shrill chirping of birds, singing along to a scattered melody that only they knew. A sharp *tap, tap, tap* indicated a woodpecker was nearby, and as we passed a giant tree trunk, I caught sight of it. His head was fiery red, and he took a moment from his pecking to look back at me, as if astonished to see someone so near his claimed space.

It was all so . . . amazing. I had spent plenty of time outside, and had certainly seen trees and plants and birds before, but this . . . this was completely different. Out here was wild and untouched. Nature as it was meant to be.

What surprised me the most, though, was that I had never noticed this place. I thought Kristen and I had explored every inch of the cemetery grounds.

All of a sudden Katy slowed, and indicated that we were going to cross a small wooden bridge that was just ahead. The rickety old slats of the bridge jumped and rattled beneath our feet as we crossed, causing a *clip, clop* sound to echo around us. It created an eerie ambiance, and I glanced behind me more than once to make sure I wasn't being followed by an actual horse. And perhaps a headless rider . . . ?

I looked down at the shallow stream below me and felt silly. The Horseman couldn't cross water. What was I thinking? Forcing a laugh as we stepped off the bridge, I breathed a not-so-silent sigh of relief. Nikolas was a step behind us, but he caught up quickly.

My jaw dropped when I looked up and saw what was waiting in front of me. It was the most perfect straight-from-the-pages-of-a-storybook cottage I had ever seen.

The walls were built with large, uneven rounded stones, while the roof looked like it had been laid with thatched shingles. Various plants grew abundantly underneath each leaded glass arched window. A trailing vine of purple flowers was creeping up the massive stone chimney on the left of the wooden front door.

"Wisteria," I said softly to myself. I recognized it from the Irving estate. "Your home is absolutely beautiful!" I breathed in with awe. "I didn't know that anyone lived back here."

Katy nodded. "Thank you for your compliment. I know my home appreciates it." There was a twinkle in her eye.

"I'm glad your home enjoys compliments," I said with a smile. I took another moment to gaze at my beautiful surroundings, and Nikolas stepped around us to place the basket he had been carrying next to the front door. Then he gently pushed the door open, and held out his hand, waiting for Katy, who had stooped down to snap off a dead leaf from one of the wisteria vines. She placed her hand in his, and they crossed the threshold together, sharing a look that made me fiercely miss my own long-dead grandparents. "Please make yourself at home, Abbey," Katy called from inside the house.

I took a deep breath and walked in, unsure of what I'd see. But it didn't disappoint. It was just as beautiful on the inside as it was on the outside.

There were flowers absolutely *everywhere*. The house looked like it could have been a flower shop. Bunches of dried flowers hung from the exposed rafter beams and from the walls, while fresh flowers filled ancient glass bottles that covered every spare surface.

The counters were neat and clean, uncluttered by snacks or junk food like the ones at my house. Not even so much as a loaf of bread was sitting out. An old spinning wheel hung on one of the white walls, but the obvious gathering place was a massive slate table, worn with age, set up in front of the brick fireplace.

I stood there awkwardly, not really sure what to do now that I was actually inside the house, but Katy told me to have a seat and gestured toward the table. Pulling out an ornately carved wooden chair, I did as I was told.

Nikolas puttered over to a metal teakettle hanging next to the fireplace, took it to the sink, and spoke quietly to Katy while he filled it with water. She took some leaves out of a bowl on the countertop and brought them over to him. Smoothing down his wild hair with one wrinkled hand, she gave him a look that made me feel like I was intruding on a very personal moment. I looked away and let my mind wander.

I could totally see myself here. Surrounded by my bottles, and oils, and glass jars. Making my own peppermint tea, with someone who had white-blond hair and green eyes, and a smile that made me melt. We would set up a little work space underneath the window by the sink, and I would create my perfumes all day long with a perfect view of the garden outside. A fat lazy cat would lie in front of the fireplace, and in the afternoon Caspian and I would take our tea together. He would help me label scents, and fill bottles, and lift all the things that were too heavy for me, and we would talk about anything and everything while we worked side by side.

The sudden metal clang of the teapot hitting the hook it would hang from in the fireplace interrupted my daydreams, and I mentally reigned myself in. Was I really rearranging someone else's house to fit my needs and planning out Caspian's future for him? What was wrong with me? What if he didn't want to live in a cozy cottage and fill bottles, or lift heavy things, or take afternoon tea breaks? What if he wanted to do something entirely different with his life?

What if he didn't want . . . me?

I was seriously freaking out, and getting way too ahead of myself, so I took a deep breath and tried to calm back down. I looked around and saw that Nikolas was making his way over to a rocking chair in the corner with a small knife and a piece of wood in his hand, while Katy wiped off the counter in front of her.

Seeing them both here, in a place obviously well loved and suited to them, brought a dull ache to the middle of my stomach. They really did remind me of my grandparents.

Since my grandparents had died within days of each other when I was six, I had only a handful of memories of them. But the overall feelings of love and tenderness had always been there. I could vaguely recall how much they'd seemed to truly enjoy each other's company. It was a far cry from the grandparents on my dad's side. *They* had been divorced longer than they'd been married, and didn't even like to hear each other's name mentioned.

I fervently hoped that would never happen to me. I wanted a happy ending and a stone cottage in my future. I never wanted to end up hating the one person I had sworn to love until death parted us. I would rather not love anyone at all than have that happen to me.

Thoughts of divorce and unhappily-ever-afters were certainly not adding to the cheerfulness of the afternoon, so I decided to try my hand at small talk. After all, it couldn't get any worse than sitting in a chair depressing myself with my own thoughts. I said the first thing that came to mind. "So, do you guys like the legend?"

Katy and Nikolas both stared at me like I was speaking a foreign language.

"The legend?" they asked innocently.

"You know," I elaborated, "'The Legend of Sleepy Hollow'? Since you guys live here . . . I just wondered if you liked the legend."

"Yes, we do enjoy the legend." Nikolas spoke before I had a chance to hang my head and apologize for how socially inadequate I obviously was at small talk. I glanced over at him, and he was concentrating on whittling away tiny slivers of wood.

"Because we have lived here all of our lives, it *is* a story that is near and dear to us," agreed Katy, pulling out the chair next to me. She held a tangled pile of multicolored yarn, and I could see two shiny silver knitting needles poking out of the side. "What about you, dear?" she asked. "What do you think of it? You seem to have a strong connection to the Hollow."

"Oh, it's one of my favorites," I said quickly. "I've lived here all my life too, and I think it's great that the town embraces history like it does. My parents are both on the town council, so I go to a lot of the meetings with them, and I get to see firsthand all of the work that goes into preserving Sleepy Hollow."

Katy nodded as she started sorting her yarn piles. "Awareness for the town has certainly grown over the years, but there's always been something special about this place. I don't think anyone could spend time living here and not feel its magic . . . the pull of living history all around us. We feel a special bond with the cemetery ourselves."

A clicking noise echoed through the room as she picked up her needles and began to knit. I folded my hands in front of me and watched her fingers fly through the motions, looping and pulling, over and over again.

"Have you been to the Sleepy Hollow Museum lately?" I asked, leaning forward slightly, still unsure of what to do with my hands. "The genealogy exhibit has a lot of new stuff in it that's really interesting. I like the—" The teakettle whistled sharply, interrupting my sentence, and I jumped at the unexpected noise. Nikolas got up to grab a dish towel for the hot kettle handle.

"Just a minute, dear." Katy patted my hand before she reached for three identical teacups. "Let me fix the tea, and then you can continue."

Nikolas brought the teakettle over for her, carefully poured the steaming liquid, and then returned the kettle to its iron hook.

Two matching smaller silver serving pots were resting in the middle of the table, and I moved them closer to us. Katy brought a third matching silver pot out from the refrigerator and sat it down next to the other two.

"Milk is in this one, and those two are sugar and honey," she explained, picking up her teacup.

I watched as she poured a small amount of milk and a couple drops of honey into her tea, and then thanked Nikolas when he placed three spoons on the table. Nikolas made his tea the same way, except he used a bit more honey. Katy smiled in mock disapproval at him, and he grinned like a little boy who was grabbing a second piece of chocolate cake.

My cup was next. Usually I made my tea like I used to make my coffee. Three milks and two sugars. But today I tried the honey. I added a couple of extra drops, like Nikolas, figuring the sweeter, the better. While I was briskly stirring my spoon in my cup, Katy settled back into her seat and Nikolas returned to his rocking chair.

I took a cautious sip.

It was surprisingly good. The mint taste was clear and strong, much better than a generic peppermint tea bag, and the honey added just the right amount of flavor, giving it an edge. I took another sip. Larger this time. I could really grow to like this stuff.

We sat there in silence, and it almost felt as if I'd known Katy and Nikolas my whole life and had spent every day having tea with them. But then I started to feel like I had to make up for lost time, and that scared me a little. *These are not your grandparents,* I sternly reminded myself. Although they seemed like they were very nice people, they probably had their own grandchildren who really did come to visit them for tea. I was only a stranger passing through.

"Go ahead and finish what you were saying, dear," urged Katy with a warm smile, and I forced myself to shake off the melancholy.

"I was just going to tell you that I really like the exhibit they made based on Washington Irving's life. That's all." I wrapped my fingers around the warm teacup in front of me.

"You must be a fan of his," said Katy. "Not many people your age would help an old man take care of a grave."

"Oh, I'd do it anytime," I blurted out. "I mean, for any grave, but particularly for his grave. My best friend and I used to spend a lot of time there. Talking to him and stuff." I looked down at my drink, realizing how crazy that made me sound. "I mean," I said hastily, "not like crazy or anything. Just like . . . pretend." I heard my words and cringed inside. Yeah, like *that* was going to make them think I'm *not* crazy.

Katy smiled at me over her clicking needles. "We know what you mean, Abbey. I think it's wonderful. He was very important to us, too. His works are a piece of American history, and I think you do his memory a great service to remember him like that."

"That's exactly how I think of him too! 'The Legend of Sleepy Hollow' is one of America's only ghost stories, and I get to live right here, in the middle of it all. It's amazing. We are literally living in history, and that just leaves me in awe."

Nikolas chuckled at my obvious enthusiasm, and I blushed. "Sorry," I said. "Sometimes I can get a little carried away."

Katy disagreed. "Nonsense. There is nothing wrong with loving history. I bet your friend feels the same way, doesn't she?"

"Well, she did. She . . . died." I stared down into what was left of my tea.

"There are those sad memories again," Nikolas said from the corner.

I gave him a brave smile and shook my head. "Not today. I won't let the sad ones in today."

"You said before that you've lived here all your life. Where is your house located?" asked Katy.

I was glad she changed the subject, and I willingly accepted something else to talk about. "I live across the street from the other side of the cemetery, by the main gates. It's the big white Victorian with green gables. Can't miss it."

They both asked lots of questions, and seemed genuinely interested in what I had to say, so I spent the rest of the afternoon telling them about school, and Kristen, and even my plans for the shop downtown. I hesitated several times, unsure of how much to tell them, or how long I should keep talking about myself, but they urged me on every time I came close to stopping.

The sunlight in the room had shifted positions several times before I realized that I was probably wearing out my welcome. So I quickly said my good-byes and left their house with a promise to stop by for tea again.

It was surprisingly easy to find my way back to the main cemetery path. As I crossed through the entrance gates and headed home, I couldn't help but think about how weird it was that they had lived back there all this time and I'd never met them before.

Strange.

Chapter Fifteen

THE JOB OFFER

His notable little wife, too, had enough to do to attend to her housekeeping and manage her poultry; for, as she sagely observed, ducks and geese are foolish things, and must be looked after, but girls can take care of themselves.

—"The Legend of Sleepy Hollow"

I stopped by the river almost every day over the next week, but Caspian wasn't there. I knew he'd said he would be busy, but why couldn't he squeeze a five-minute break into his schedule? I visited Katy and Nikolas again, but only ended up staying for a couple of minutes. I wasn't very good company.

One afternoon I even found myself heading to Kristen's grave. I hadn't been there since prom night, and I really *wasn't* in the best of moods, but I felt the urge to go. It had been too long since I'd seen her.

As her stone came into view, my breath caught. I could feel

the ache go straight to my heart. Would it ever get easier? Would I ever be able to get used to the fact that my best friend lived *here* now?

I knelt down and touched the top of her tombstone. "Hey, Kris." Tracing the rough edges of her carved name, I sat in silence. It was nice to connect with her in this quiet way.

After sitting for a while, I started talking about the letter I had written to her on prom night. Then I brought up Caspian and how I'd spent the last couple of days looking for him. I didn't mention the diaries I had found, or the secrets she'd been keeping from me. I wasn't ready to talk about that yet. Maybe I never would be.

It started getting dark and I knew it was time for me to get home, so I rose stiffly from my position on the ground. One of my legs had fallen asleep, and I hobbled my way out of the cemetery, leaving Kristen with a quick good-bye and a promise to visit again soon.

While I walked home, I made excuses to myself for Caspian. He must have gone away for the holidays. He had gotten sick. His family decided to spontaneously move to Africa . . . But I knew none of them were true, and depression sank in. I had a hard time concentrating. I didn't sleep very well. And even my appetite was gone.

When school finally let out on Monday afternoon for Thanksgiving break, I was overwhelmingly grateful. My daily trip to the cemetery didn't yield anything new, and I ended up lying in bed that night wide awake. After an hour spent looking up at my ceiling, I knew I had to find something to do before I went insane. Flipping on the lamp, I gazed around the room. A half-filled suitcase propped up next to the door caught my eye.

Since we were going to be bouncing around from relative to relative for most of the Thanksgiving vacation, I needed to make sure I had enough stuff to keep me busy so that I could spend as little time as possible actually *with* the extended family.

I spent the next two hours going through my perfuming supplies and sorting through different notes from old projects that I hadn't finished yet. I packed plenty of tester vials, an extra half dozen cobalt blue tubes, and almost all of my essential oils. Then I packed another bagful of books, CDs, movies, and a couple of magazines.

Once everything was ready to go, I looked it all over again, satisfied with what I'd chosen. Feeling a sudden ache in my back and heaviness in my eyelids, I piled my now full suitcase and two bags into the corner, and then staggered to bed. Hopefully I'd be able to fall asleep soon; I had an early wake-up call coming my way.

Considering that I got only four hours of sleep that night, I felt surprisingly good the next morning. Jumping out of bed, I hurried to claim my seat in the van. If I didn't get there before Dad finished loading it up, I'd be forced to endure an uncomfortable ride crammed between stacks of suitcases.

Luckily, success was mine, and I made sure that everything I'd need for the seven-hour trip to Ohio was close at hand. Dad must have been rushing Mom, too, because a scant thirty minutes later they were both buckled up and we were on our way.

I pulled a pair of headphones out of my bag, settled them over my ears, and set my music volume to low. The melody was slow and mournful, but soothing. I leaned my head back and stared out the window as we left the house behind; I was content to just let my mind wander. The trees passed by in a blur, one after the other, and it became hypnotic. My eyes jumped from limb to limb while my brain tripped from thought to thought.

Why did *I* have to be the one to find out Kristen's secrets? Why did *I* have to be the one to have a best friend betray me? Why did

I have to be the one dragged from home and carted halfway across the country to see relatives I only saw once a year? Why couldn't my parents tell everyone that turkey would taste *just* as good at our house as it would at theirs? And *why* couldn't Caspian have a damn cell phone number so I could reach him?

Clearly the entire world was plotting against me.

Unfortunately, my mood wasn't given any chance to improve once we reached the relatives' house. I got stuck sleeping on a lumpy couch, was pestered to no end by meddling fifth cousins, once removed, and was reminded again and again by several aunts why I needed to concentrate harder on my schoolwork "because college is no picnic to get in to." I was now depressed, angry, *and* insane from being cooped up with all that family.

Mercifully it came to an end, and we were soon moving on to the relatives in New Jersey. They, at least, had a spare bedroom and an extra DVD player. The time passed all too quickly there.

The final stop on our Thanksgiving journey was back to New York to see Uncle Bob. He lived only about an hour away from us and owned an ice cream shop that was less than twenty minutes from our house. Once I found out we were going to see him at the shop,

I eagerly looked forward to that. Uncle Bob + an ice cream shop = all the free samples I could eat.

Oh yeah, I couldn't *wait* for that visit.

The drive didn't take very long, but I was pretty tired from the past week of relative-hopping, and I crashed on an old leather couch in Uncle Bob's office as soon as we got there. When I woke up, I could hear Mom and Dad talking to Uncle Bob out in the actual shop part of the ice cream shop, so I quietly made my way back to the supply room to help myself to some of those free samples. I knew Uncle Bob would let me have all the ice cream I wanted, but Mom, on the other hand, was a different story.

The supply room was dark and cold, but the freezers were surprisingly shiny and new. They were probably the *only* new thing around here. Uncle Bob had attempted to decorate most of the shop in a vintage 1950s decor, but it had ended up more old and drab than old and vintage.

Eleven samples later I couldn't eat any more ice cream, so I wandered back into Uncle Bob's office. A bunch of old pictures decorated the walls, and most of them had been signed by people who had stopped in at one time or another. I recognized a couple of celebrities, and two singers, but the rest I couldn't place. The picture frames were chipped and dusty, and looked like they should have been replaced several years ago.

I shook my head at the further signs of neglect as I continued my tour of the office, and I swore to myself that my shop would never look like his.

Once I reached the desk, I saw more evidence that upkeep was obviously not very high on Uncle Bob's "to do" list. Boxes were *everywhere.*

Each one was stuffed haphazardly with papers, receipts, and unopened envelopes. Wedged underneath the desk next to a chair was a huge file box marked DUE in black letters. It was overflowing too. A filing cabinet against the wall had one drawer halfway open, and upon further inspection, I found that it contained nothing but empty folders.

As I looked around the room, I realized that someone should really straighten up a little. An office couldn't stay this messy and still be functional. And if Uncle Bob wasn't functional, he could lose the shop. I didn't want that to happen. Plus, it was something to keep me occupied while Mom and Dad told him every single detail of every single thing that had happened since the last time we saw him. *That* was bound to take a while.

So I tossed my almost empty sample cup into the nearest trash can, vowed never again to try peanut butter pineapple ice cream, and got to work.

The first thing I did was get started on the desk, which was completely covered with a stack of mail about a foot high. Pretty much anywhere mail could be laid, or stacked, it was laid and stacked. And then laid and stacked some more. It was one giant mess. I got so involved with my project that I lost track of time and didn't stop again until I heard voices getting louder. When I realized they were calling for me, I raced out of the room to meet them.

Mom gave me a strange look as she asked if I was too busy to go get some lunch. I glanced down at my jeans, completely lost on what she meant, but then I saw a streak of dust running up one leg. I hurriedly brushed it off, trying to think of an explanation. "I was just . . . dusting some . . . pictures on the walls," I said weakly.

She must have bought the lame excuse, though, because she let it drop. Dad and Uncle Bob brought up the rear of our party, and we all headed out for some pizza.

The pizzeria we went to was practically empty, and the owner personally made and delivered the pies to our table. Uncle Bob was in the middle of telling us a story about the turkey he set on fire last Thanksgiving, when the little bell over the door jingled and in walked Ben.

I guess I should have been surprised to see him, but I wasn't. I tried not to make direct eye contact, and slouched down in my chair, but he saw me anyway. A second later the bell jingled again and in walked a familiar-looking girl. I figured that I probably went to school with her.

"Do *not* look over there," I whispered to everyone at the table. On cue, their heads all turned to the door. "I *said* don't look," I groaned. "There are some kids I go to school with over there, and I don't want them to see me."

But it was too late.

"Hey, Abbey," yelled Ben. "Can we come sit with you guys?"

The girl he was with did *not* look very happy about his request, and I wasn't too happy with it either.

"Sure, honey," said Mom before I had a chance to say no. "We've already ordered some pizzas, so why don't you two kids come right over?"

Ben grinned and grabbed the girl's hand, hauling her to our

table. I forced a smile and scooted my chair all the way over to the opposite end. They might be sharing our food, but that didn't mean I had to sit next to them.

Proclaiming the girl he was with to be Ginger, Ben sat down, and I begrudgingly made the round of introductions, starting with Dad. He and Mom seemed happy to have more company, and Uncle Bob was thrilled to have a bigger audience as he launched right back into his turkey story.

Consoling myself with a slice of cheese pizza, I tried to hide my humiliation while Ginger stared at me with daggers in her eyes, and I pondered exactly how long this meal of shame would last.

As soon as we got back to Uncle Bob's place, Mom and Dad resumed their conversation and I hurried back to my project. I hoped it would be enough to wipe the terrible memory of that pizza place from my brain.

I changed over all the calendars to the current month and straightened up a pile of magazines strewn across the coffee table next to the couch. The last thing I did was heave a giant stack of unopened mail onto the worn leather recliner that served as a desk chair.

By the time I was done, I was covered in more dirt and my back was killing me, but the office was starting to look great. Plopping down on the couch, I took my shoes off and leaned my head against the cushion. Professional cleaners would have charged an arm and a leg for what I had accomplished. It was a good thing I liked ice cream so much. Uncle Bob could just pay me in scoops.

I felt for the necklace I wore under my shirt, touched it for a moment, and thought about Caspian. *What is he doing right now? Is he thinking of me?* I closed my eyes and tried to rest, but thoughts of double mint chocolate chip and rainbow sherbet kept dancing through my head. Forget resting. It was time to go get my pay.

Slipping my shoes back on, I brushed my arms and legs to get all the dust off. Then I briskly clapped my palms together. Once all traces of dirt were removed, Mom shouldn't be giving me any more strange looks.

I headed back to the supply room and started loading up two scoops of double mint chocolate chip ice cream and rainbow sherbet in the same bowl, remembering the last time I'd eaten rainbow sherbet. It had been with Kristen last summer. We always had a race to see who could eat the most ice cream without getting a brain freeze. She usually won.

A sudden knock came from the outside door next to the freezers and interrupted my thoughts. Holding the scooper in one hand and my bowl in the other, I nudged the door open with my foot.

"It's not like it's cold out here or anything," a snotty voice said. An arm wearing a silver Rolex shot out to grab the door.

I almost dropped my bowl.

A guy stepped through the door and immediately crowded into my space. His blond hair had that carefully highlighted and styled look to make it appear like it was just naturally perfect, and his leather jacket looked brand-new. I felt my eyes widen.

"My dad asked me to drop these papers off. He needs them signed and returned by Monday." He glanced over and suddenly seemed to see me for the first time. "Who are you?"

"I'm . . . uh . . . his niece. Bob's niece." I put the bowl and the ice cream scooper down onto the freezer lid.

"Yeah, whatever. Can you just make sure he gets these papers? They are ve-ry im-por-tant." He said the last two words slowly, like he was spelling it out for a child.

Jerk.

"I sure can," I said cheerfully. I forced a bright and shiny fake smile to my face. *And you can kiss my . . .*

"Great." He slid the papers onto the freezer and turned for the door. "Thanks *so* much," he said sarcastically as he made his way out. The door slammed shut behind him, and I stuck out my tongue. The nerve of some people.

After scooping out the rest of my ice cream, I closed the freezer door and headed to Uncle Bob's office. I laid the papers on his clean desk and then went to join the rest of the family in the main room. We stayed for another hour, and Uncle Bob walked us out to the van when we were ready to leave.

The ride home was quiet, and it passed quickly. I couldn't wait to climb those stairs to my room and finally get to sleep in my own bed for more than one night. All I wanted was to be home and stay there forever.

I didn't even complain about having to carry my own bags up when we finally got there. I happily banged my way up those stairs and threw off my shoes almost as quickly as I dumped open my suitcase. I think I actually felt myself falling to sleep as soon as my head hit the pillow and my body snuggled under the sheets.

God, it was good to be home.

313

~ ~ ~

On Sunday morning I woke up early and couldn't figure out why I had slept so well, until my sleep-induced stupor cleared and I saw that I was in my own bed. I'd never known how much I really loved my bedroom until I had been forced to leave it. I swore it would never happen again. At least, not until next Thanksgiving anyway.

As I stumbled out of bed to get dressed, I waded through the mound of dirty clothing that had exploded from my suitcase, and quickly realized that laundry would have to be number one on my priority list for the day. I sure hoped Mom was up to the task.

Gathering as much as I could carry, I hauled the dirty laundry downstairs, staggering under its weight. I figured that the least I could do was carry it down for her, since she was going to take care of it all. I dropped it off by the washer door and then went to raid the kitchen for some breakfast. Hauling laundry really works up an appetite.

After I inhaled two bowls of cereal, I went back upstairs and slouched over my work desk. I was a little tired, but I didn't feel like going back to bed. I didn't really know what to do.

Shuffling past a few stray papers, I grabbed an old perfume

notebook and idly flipped through it. A tiny thought started wiggling at the back of my brain and I kept flipping, not really seeing the pages in front of me anymore but thinking about this new, shiny idea forming inside my head.

I got up to grab my perfume case from my overnight bag but stopped short. *Maybe I should go to the cemetery instead. Caspian might be waiting for me there,* I thought. And I still hadn't thanked him for the gift.

Pride sparred with common sense, and I debated over just how good the odds were that *this* time I would actually find him. Common sense told me those odds weren't very good. Pride told me that *he* should come find *me*.

So I sat back down at the worktable with my perfume case in hand. School started again on Monday, and I could cut through the cemetery on my way home. I would look for him then. All I had to do was make it through today.

I forced myself to focus on one of my unfinished perfume projects, and it was a growling stomach that finally broke through my concentration. I pushed my notes and bottles away as I stood up to stretch my legs. Wandering downstairs for a snack, I was just crossing into the kitchen when Mom called my name.

Yelling back that I was busy, I searched the fridge for something edible. All I came across were leftovers and lunch meat. Why couldn't I find anything to eat? We *never* had any food in the house. I was standing in front of the pantry when she called my name again, this time more insistently. Grabbing a bag of chips with one hand and a bag of pretzels with the other, I stomped my way into the living room.

"Busy, Mom, on my way upstairs. No time to talk."

She was sitting on the couch with her laptop propped up beside her, but she paused for a moment and looked up. "You have a phone call, Abbey."

"Who is it?" I asked, dropping my snacks onto the nearest chair and running over to pick up the phone.

"It's Uncle Bob."

My finger paused on the TALK button. "Uncle Bob?" I croaked. "Did he, uh, say, at all, why he wanted to talk to me?"

She shrugged, paying more attention to her screen than me. "Don't know. He just asked if you were available."

I swallowed down my fear, counted to ten, and pushed the button. "Hello? Uncle Bob?"

His booming voice echoed loudly through the receiver, and

I held it about an inch away from my ear. "Hi, Abbey. How's it going for you?"

"Fine, Uncle Bob. It's going fine for me. How's it going for you?"

"Good, good," he boomed. "Listen, Abbey, I was calling to ask you something. I hope you won't mind. Well, I guess you won't mind, maybe, if I thought right."

Sometimes following Uncle Bob's train of thought was easier said than done. It was a trait that everyone around me seemed to pick up sooner or later.

I furrowed my brow. "What is it, Uncle Bob? What did you want to ask me?"

"Well, see, it was about my office. I couldn't help but notice what you did in there—"

My heart sank to my feet. *Oh, no. Here it comes.* He was probably calling because I'd moved something important and now he couldn't find it.

"Look, Uncle Bob," I interrupted. "I'm really sorry about that. I just thought you would like it. I can come by and . . . I don't know . . . try to put it back somehow?" Yeah right, like I could put back dust and grime. *Way to go, Abbey. Good move.*

"Are you kidding?" Uncle Bob spoke again, loud and clear. "I love it! You did such a great job that I was hoping maybe you would come do it again. Only sort through all the papers and stuff. Maybe even file a little? I would pay you, of course. Like an after-school job. What do you say?"

What did I say? I was speechless. I thought he was calling to yell at me, and he was offering me a job instead? How cool was that?

My speechlessness didn't go unnoticed.

"Abbey? Are you still there? If you're worried about money, I can pay you ten dollars an hour. How's that?"

I was still completely stunned, but I found my voice. "Um, yeah, sure, Uncle Bob. That all sounds good to me. When do you want me to start?"

I *think* he asked me if I wanted to start next week. I just kind of made agreeing noises every now and then. I couldn't believe this call was actually happening.

After I hung up the phone, Mom must have noticed the dazed look in my eyes when I grabbed my snacks. "What was *that* all about? Is everything okay with Uncle Bob?" she asked me.

I laughed loudly. "Yeah, it is. Everything's okay. I think . . . I think he just offered me a job."

 318

Chapter Sixteen

A VISIT

❧❧❧

... a kind of buzzing stillness reigned throughout the school-room.

—"The Legend of Sleepy Hollow"

On Monday morning I woke up to snow. As I lay in bed watching the sparkling flakes float down slowly to earth, I snuggled deeper into my warm nest of covers. I really did *not* want to get out of bed. Maybe I could talk Mom into bringing me some hot chocolate.

I started to doze off again, but Mom's voice jerked me out of my drowsy slumber. I sat straight up, losing the covers briefly, and regretted it instantly, as a shock of icy cold air blasted over me. Shivering, I snatched up the covers again and burrowed back down, ignoring Mom when she called a second time.

It was the banging on the stairs ten minutes later that was

too hard to ignore. I rolled out of bed, threw on two sweatshirts and an extra pair of sweatpants over my pajamas, and jammed my feet into a thick pair of socks. I was not happy at the thought of having to leave my warm bed. I ran to the top of the stairs, but Mom was already halfway up them. She didn't look very happy either. "I was just about to come yank you out of bed myself, Abigail."

Oh crap, the full name.

"You only have forty-five minutes to get ready for school, and then I'm leaving."

"Sorry, Mom," I yawned. "I'm up now. Going to get dressed. Could you make me some hot chocolate for breakfast?" I threw a hopeful look over my shoulder, but she was shaking her head and muttering to herself as she started walking back down the stairs. "Okay, scratch that whole hot chocolate idea," I mumbled.

I flew to my bathroom and took a speed shower. I didn't want to leave the cascading spray of hot water, but I knew that I was running short on time. Grumbling about hot showers and cold mornings, I dried off briskly and ran to my closet. Once there, I grabbed a long black sweater and a pair of red boots that I'd never worn before.

When I made it downstairs, I looked forlornly at the kitchen table, where a mug was sitting, stuffed with an instant hot chocolate packet. Not quite what I'd had in mind, but I guess it's the thought that counts, right? I glanced over at the clock on the oven. Two minutes to go. I didn't have time for hot chocolate of *any* kind. Reaching into one of the cabinets, I grabbed a granola bar and stuffed it in my bag, then snagged an apple from the fridge. I guess it would be breakfast on the run today.

A car horn honked impatiently from the driveway. With breakfast firmly in hand, I juggled my key and quickly locked the front door on my way out.

Ahhh, Mondays. Have to love them.

The snow was beautiful as I stepped outside, and it made a soft crunching noise. I hurried to the car, grateful for its heat, and bit into my apple as we pulled away. The crisp zing inside was tart and delicious, but I mourned the fact that it wasn't warm and soothing . . . like hot chocolate.

"Do you want me to pick you up after school today? The weather's getting colder." Mom said.

"No, thanks," I replied instantly. I had plans that involved a cemetery and, hopefully, a visit with Caspian. "It's not too cold. Besides, I like walking in the snow."

"Okay. See you when you get home, then."

The car came to a stop and I pushed the door open. Taking one last bite of my apple, I climbed out and waved. "Bye, Mom!"

She smiled as the door slammed shut behind me, and then she sped off. I looked up at the imposing gray structure looming in front of me, hoisted my book bag higher, and reluctantly started trudging toward it.

Where's a blizzard when you need one?

As I made my way into the school hallway, everyone else around me looked like they'd enjoyed climbing out of a nice cozy bed this morning and braving a cold world about as much as I had. Red noses and teary eyes shuffled in, one after the other. Streaks of muddy slush covered the wooden floors, and more than one glove had been abandoned, lost out of a jacket pocket, never to see its mate again.

Considering that this was the last place on earth I wanted to be right now, I felt oddly cheerful in this sea of misery.

The rest of the school day passed like many other school days had passed before it. Midterms were coming up in January right after

Christmas break, so all the teachers spent their time explaining what we would review over the next couple of weeks.

When the last bell rang for the day, the snow had already stopped. Most of what had been on the ground was gone, with the exception of a few tiny patches that still glistened, tucked away in the shade. Shouts of joy filled the parking lot as the collective school body was finally released from its prison for another day. I slipped away from all the noise and headed toward the cemetery, fervently hoping that Caspian would be there.

Passing by the riverbank, I saw brown flowers at several grave sites while I followed the cemetery pathway. I couldn't tell if the flowers were dead because they had been here too long or if they were dead because of the recent cold snap. Either way, it was sad.

I almost stopped once or twice to get rid of them, but then thought better of it. The families might want to do that themselves. It was a funny thing. Some people wouldn't mind if a complete stranger got rid of the dead flowers on their loved one's grave, while others would be deeply offended.

I chose the least offensive path and moved on, uttering a small "Sorry" to each grave with brown flowers that I left behind.

A familiar hill came into view, and then the small iron fence that marked the Irving family plot. Watching for icy patches, I climbed up the stone steps and pushed my way through the gate. The stacks of coins were still near Washington Irving's grave, but now a brown glass bottle crudely marked ABSINTHE was lying on its side at the foot of the stone. Someone had also placed a bright red poinsettia on top of his marker that was dangerously close to tipping over. I stepped around the brown bottle and fixed the plant, brushing away stray pieces of dirt.

Crouching down next to the headstone, I traced the worn lettering as I had done so many times before. "Good day to you, Mr. Irving. Nice to see you again." A cold wind blew around me, and I stuck my hands in my pockets, sincerely regretting the fact that I had left my gloves at home. "I hope you had a nice Thanksgiving." I rocked back slightly on my heels. "We spent our entire holiday visiting the relatives. It was terrible."

I looked up at the sky. Grayish clouds were rolling in. Not the kind that meant a thunderstorm was on its way but the kind that meant more snow was on its way. Hopefully many, many feet of snow.

Silence enveloped me, and I shivered again in the cold. I knew I really should get going. It was all too obvious I wasn't going to find Caspian. Maybe I wouldn't ever see him again.

That thought filled me with a piercing ache, and I fought back tears. It had only been two weeks; it was way too soon to give up all hope. I was just being silly and overly dramatic. I bowed my head and waited for the catch in my throat to disappear before I spoke again. "We, um . . . got some snow today. First snow of the season. It looked beautiful glistening on the ground everywhere. And someone left a poinsettia for you. Everything else is neat and tidy around here. Nikolas does a good job."

The grating noise of the gate being pushed open surprised me. I twisted around to see what had happened, and slipped. Catching myself before I hit the ground, I looked up.

It was Caspian.

I leapt to my feet, a little too excitedly, and almost ran to him. My *God*, he was gorgeous. Forcing myself to slow down, I silently repeated over and over again that I would *not* jump into his arms. I *would not*.

His hair was windblown and messy, like he had just run his fingers through it. And those eyes . . . To hell with not jumping into his arms. With the look he was giving me right now, his arms were the only place I wanted to be.

I lost my nerve about six inches away from him.

"Hi," I said softly.

"Hi, Astrid." He had his hands in his pockets, and I wanted to reach over and put them in mine.

"I tried to find you but I cou—," I started.

"I really missed you," he said at the same time.

I could feel my cheeks turning red, and I shuffled my feet, digging my toe into an imaginary hole in the ground.

"You go first." He laughed.

I laughed too, but I was replaying his words in my head. *Me? I said something?* I thought back to three seconds ago. *Right, okay.* "I tried to find you, to thank you for the beautiful gift, but I couldn't. And then my parents dragged me around to go see the relatives for Thanksgiving, so I was gone for a while. You weren't, uh, waiting here for me . . . were you?"

A mischievous gleam came into his eyes before he shook his head. "I should totally say yes, but no, I wasn't. I was busy too. Thanksgiving with the family and all that."

An instant wave of relief and giddiness washed over me, and I briefly looked him over. It was so good to see him here, in the flesh. My imagination hadn't done him nearly enough justice. Hmmm . . . imagining him . . . in the flesh . . .

I was afraid my face would stay red forever. Hastily I turned my attention elsewhere. He raised one mocking eyebrow at me and chuckled wickedly, and I swear he knew what I was thinking.

Guiltily looking around me, I willed my cheeks back to their normal color. "Anyway." I cleared my throat loudly. "Thank you, again, for the beautiful necklace. It's perfect, and I love it. Where did you find it? I've never seen anything like it before."

It was his turn to look embarrassed, and he ducked his head. "That's because I made it." He peeked up at me, and my heart melted. *Am I dreaming? This has to be a dream.*

"You *made* it?" Something wet hit my cheek and I brushed it away, impatiently waiting for his answer.

"Yeah," he said shyly. "I did."

Another wet spot hit my nose, and I shook my head in disgust. Really, couldn't the rain hold off for just a bit longer? Then something white and fluffy got trapped in my eyelash. I looked up at the sky. Millions of tiny wet flakes suddenly started hurtling down, evaporating on the grass as soon as they hit. "Snow!" I exclaimed. "It's snowing again!"

Caspian looked up too, and I laughed at him as he stuck out his tongue. The snow changed from tiny wet sprinkles to big, fat fluffy flakes that landed on our hair and clothes. I put out my hands and spun around delightedly before coming to a graceful halt.

My heart started racing when his gaze drifted down to my lips. *Yes, do it!* my mind screamed. *There would be nothing more romantic in the world right now than a kiss in the snow!*

He just stared at me, his green gaze burning a hole in my heart. I pleaded with my eyes for him to kiss me. That was *exactly* what I wanted right now. He took a sudden step back and looked around us. I took a sudden step forward.

Obviously this was one of those stupid guy moments and he didn't understand what I wanted. I was going to explain it to him very, very soon.

But he took another step back, and I stopped, suddenly confused. Were we not on the same page here again?

"You need to get home, Abbey. I don't want you to get caught in this storm," he said urgently.

I reached out a hand; I couldn't seem to stop myself. "Okay," I said boldly. "Why don't you walk me there?"

A pained expression filled his eyes. He reached out a hand too, but let it drop. "Abbey, I . . . I can't," he said, sounding genuinely sorry. "I have to go the other way, and I'm going to be late."

His eyes looked so sad, it broke my heart. "It's okay, Caspian. Forget about it. I never mentioned it." I lowered my hand. "I'll see you around."

He took a step toward me, but then stopped. "Are you sure?" His face was concerned, and my heart flooded with warmth.

"Yeah," I replied. Then I decided to test the waters. "But you know, if you just so happen to be free tomorrow night, my parents will be gone. They have a town council meeting that they're going to. You could come over . . . if you wanted . . ." I blushed again.

He didn't answer me at first, and I tried not to hyperventilate. He was *so* going to reject me. What had I been thinking?

"Okay," he said fiercely. His eyes looked determined. "What time do you want me?"

Oh, the multitude of meaning behind those words. "Seven fifteen?" I said softly. *Am I doing this? Am I really doing this?* "The meeting starts at seven and my parents leave about ten minutes early to get there. How does that sound?"

"Sounds like a date," he said, just as softly. "See you then, Abbey."

He put up a hand in farewell as he passed me by, and I did the same. For an instant our hands almost touched. We were two frozen statues with so little, and yet so much, dividing us. But then the moment broke and he was moving on.

And I was walking home alone. Thrilled to the tips of my shiny red boots.

Chapter Seventeen

MIXED SIGNALS

❧

. . . and though his amorous toyings were something like the gentle caresses and endearments of a bear, yet it was whispered that she did not altogether discourage his hopes.

—"The Legend of Sleepy Hollow"

I walked back and forth between the front door and the stairs, fixated on the large grandfather clock nearby as time slowly ticked away second by second.

Tuesday evening had finally arrived, and I was a bundle of nerves. Mom and Dad had just left for their meeting, and I felt like I was in overdrive mode. Checking over the whole house, I managed to eliminate anything that might be embarrassing, paying special attention to any stray laundry piles.

7:01 rolled around. Then 7:02. By 7:03 I was ready to scream. 7:15 would never get here. My eyes scanned the living room one more time, and then I looked down at my clothes. *Was this outfit really the right choice? Should I go change it again? Maybe I should put on a dress. . . .*

The ringing of doorbell chimes echoed through the house and made me jump out of my skin. He was here. My heart began to beat wildly, and I tried to control my breathing. *Oh. My. God.* He was really here. At my house.

The doorbell chimed again, and I hurried to answer it. This was no big deal. He had been here before—in my room, no less. Not a big deal at all.

As I moved quickly, I wished I had grabbed a couple of breath mints. I tried the hand-to-mouth test, but that didn't really work too well, and the doorbell rang again. If I didn't answer it soon, he was going to think I'd stood him up.

Crossing my fingers, I opened the door.

The hinges creaked eerily as the door swung outward, but Caspian was standing there with a smile on his face. It was snowing, and a few glistening flakes rested on the shoulders of his black coat.

"Hi, Caspian. Come on in," I said nervously. I would *not* think about Mom and Dad right now, and how they would probably kill me if they knew about this.

He stepped inside and ran his fingers through his hair, dispersing the flakes of snow. "Nice to see you again, Abbey."

I led the way into the living room, unsure of whether or not I should take his coat or leave it up to him. "You too," I said, tucking a stray piece of hair behind one ear. "Do you want to sit down or . . . ?"

"Yeah, sure." After shrugging off his jacket, he folded it up and draped it over the back of the couch before taking a seat. "Is this okay here?" he asked.

"It's fine." Waving my hand in what I hoped was a show of casual disregard, I took a seat on the opposite end of the couch. "I'm just surprised you're actually wearing one." Tugging self-consciously at my own gray and black striped sweater, I noticed he was wearing a heavy gray rolled-edge sweater and blue jeans.

Silence loomed between us and I tucked my feet up under me, glad that I hadn't put any shoes on. Settling more comfortably onto the couch, I looked around. The atmosphere was warm, and cozy, and romantic . . . but I couldn't think of a thing to say.

Caspian was steadfastly studying the room, looking everywhere but at me.

I sighed inwardly. This was not going as planned. Of course, I hadn't exactly *made* any plans, but I certainly didn't invite him over here to stare at my living room walls. I needed something to talk about *now*. "So how was your Thanksgiving?" I ventured. "You said you spent it with your relatives, right?"

He turned to look at me.

"In a manner of speaking," he said slowly. "I went to go see some family that I hadn't visited in a while. It was nice to see them again. I guess you never really know how much time you have left, so it's good to catch up every now and then."

Well, that was just a little bit morbid. "Um, yeah, I guess you don't. So, did you do turkey at the relative's house, or yours? I mean, if you guys even make a turkey. I don't know, maybe your family likes ham for Thanksgiving. Or tofu burgers, if you're a vegetarian. Are you a vegetarian?"

He grinned and shook his head. "No, I'm not a vegetarian. We usually do turkey at anyone's house but our own. Dad's not the greatest cook in the world. He does okay with cooking out and ordering in, but turkey is a bit of a stretch."

"Is it just you and your dad, then?" I asked hesitantly. "You haven't mentioned your mom."

He toyed with the fringed edges of a blanket resting next to him on the arm of the couch. "Yup. Just me and Dad. My mom took off when I was a baby, and I haven't seen her since. Dad never talks about her. I don't have any idea where she is."

I looked down at my jeans and pulled off a nonexistent piece of fuzz. My parents weren't really home all that often, but I always knew they'd be there for me. I couldn't imagine what it would feel like to have one parent taking off like that. Caspian had probably grown up wondering if it was somehow his fault that she'd left.

"I'm sure she thought she had a good reason." I didn't look up from my imaginary fuzz. "There was nothing you could have done to stop her. And nothing you did made her choose to leave." I glanced at him then, and he was staring off into the distance with a strange look in his eyes.

"I know," he said softly. "But still, sometimes I wonder if . . ." He didn't finish, and it was almost like he wasn't talking to me. It sent a shiver down my spine, and I wanted to bring him back to the here and now, with me.

"Didn't you say before that your dad is a mechanic? And he was getting his own shop?" That brought him out of his daze, and he looked over at me again.

"Yeah, Dad will take over the shop as soon as the owner retires.

I drew up some of the floor plans for him so he could have a visual."

"What's the name of his place?" I asked. "Is it around here?" Then a word he had said stuck out to me. "Wait, what? You *drew* the floor plans for him?"

He nodded, looking pleased with himself. "Yeah, I drew the floor plans for him. Mike, the owner, does auto repair right now, but Dad plans to change it to more of an auto body store, and stock it with stuff to customize cars. He has some really great ideas."

"Ohhhh." I was getting lost in all of the car talk. They really weren't my thing. "So you're kind of a car person, then?"

A look of surprise crossed his face. "Me? No. No way. My dad is the one into cars. Although I *do* like using a blow torch every now and then, I'm more into my art. Much to his everlasting dismay," he added ruefully.

I perked up. "Do you have an artwork portfolio or anything?"

"I have my collection from when I worked in a tattoo shop. Before we moved here, I designed some stuff for them." He looked happy now; his eyes were blazing with pride.

That piece of news was *very* interesting.

"A tattoo shop?" I stretched my legs out from under me and moved closer to him on the couch. "Wow. You've had quite the exciting life." I tried to give him my best you're-so-sexy-and-I'm-impressed look, but I don't think it worked.

He just laughed and ran his fingers through his hair again. "I don't know if I'd call my life exciting, but it was cool."

"Were you drawing in the cemetery that one day? Your hands were all black."

He looked away for a minute, and I thought I saw a slight blush rise to his cheeks. But it could have been the room. It *was* getting pretty warm in here.

"You must have seen the charcoal," he said. "When I draw, I use charcoal. I picked up the habit making sketches for the tattoos, and then I just stuck with it. I like the texture it gives me. The only drawback is that I forget to wash my hands afterward a lot."

So that was what the blush was for? Because he was admitting he didn't wash his hands? I thought it was like some guy requirement to be dirty most of the time. But I didn't want him to feel bad, so I admitted, "I get pretty caught up with my perfumes, too. When I'm not careful, I can spill my oils, and no amount of washing will get that smell out."

He gave me a half smile, and the room felt like it shot up to 112 degrees. *Good Lord, it's warm in here.* Desperate for a cool breeze, I thought about cracking open the door but decided against it. I went to look out the window instead, using the pretense of watching the still falling snow so that I could feel the coolness of the window pane.

"Does getting a tattoo hurt?" I asked, turning back to him after a minute of faux snow gazing. "Do you have any?"

He stretched out his legs underneath the coffee table in front of him and shifted slightly to face me. "I can't speak for anyone else, but mine didn't hurt. I felt a slight pressure, and then a dull sting, but it didn't really hurt. It all depends on where you get them placed, who's doing it, and what your pain threshold is."

I put my hand against the window pane and felt the coolness seep into my skin. "Where do you . . . have yours?" I asked the window in front of me, too shy to face him.

"Two of them are on my back, and another one is on my left arm."

My window trick suddenly stopped working, and I decided to be bold. I walked back over to the couch. "Can I see them?"

Caspian looked startled. I waited, considering whether or not

I should just laugh it off as a joke or tell him to forget about it. But I didn't want to forget about it. There was a lot that I . . . wanted. It was time to see if he wanted any of those things too.

He didn't answer me, but held my gaze intently as he stood up and slowly started to reach for the bottom of his sweater. He turned around and lifted it up over his shoulders, and I forgot how to breathe. The sweater slid off of him in one long smooth motion and messed up his hair, leaving it tousled and sexy-looking.

An interlocking chain of small black circles and triangles was etched onto each shoulder blade, ending halfway down his back. It was a beautiful design that looked both enticing and exotic, and I ached to put one hand out and trace it. He turned back around to face me, and his green eyes stared right through me.

I broke his gaze and looked down, gulping hard. His chest was muscular, but not bulky, and his hips were lean. A fine trail of pale blond hair ran down from his belly button and disappeared underneath the waistband of his jeans. I gulped again and tried *very* hard not to drool.

He lifted up his arm to show me the black interlocking circles tattooed there. "I've always been fascinated with patterns," he said while staring down at it. "With circles, there's no beginning and no end. It just goes on forever. I like that."

I heard my heartbeat echo loudly around us as I dragged in each suddenly painful breath.

"Do you have any tattoos, Abbey?" he whispered.

"Not yet," I said. "Where do you think I should get one?"

Without any effort, we seemed to have gotten closer to each other. The room grew hotter again. My eyes dropped involuntarily to his bare chest and I pictured myself running a finger over that tattooed design. Then I looked at him again and put everything I felt, and everything I wanted to do, behind that look.

He shuddered and closed his eyes. The moment was powerful, and so overwhelming that I closed my eyes too. He *had* to know. He *had* to have seen how I felt about him. I couldn't give off any clearer of a signal. I wanted him to kiss me *now*.

I felt a sudden breeze wash over me, and I shivered in the cold draft. My eyes flew open, and I watched as he pulled his sweater back on. I could sense reluctance about him now. "Why?" I cried out. "Why do you do this? Is it me? Is there something about me? I thought you, that we felt . . ." I sighed out of sheer frustration and stood there waiting for his answer.

He didn't say anything.

"Do you not like me? Because I thought after that kiss in the library, and the necklace, and all the times we've met . . . and prom night! You were in my room on prom night! I thought maybe you lov—" I broke off and looked down at the floor. I was babbling. Again.

"Abbey, I'm sorry. That's all I can say." Looking at me with sorrow in his eyes, he tried to explain. "I don't mean to be this way. I just don't know how to . . . Forgive me, Astrid."

An apology *and* my special name? It was hard to stay mad at that. "Forgive you for what, Caspian? For acting like you like me when you really don't? I just don't get you sometimes. You take two steps forward and then five back. You act like you want me to get home safely, but won't walk me there. We never meet anywhere normal, like a restaurant, or a mall, and you always have to be 'somewhere else.' What's going on? Do you want to be with me or not?"

Hot tears filled my eyes, but I refused to look away. I wanted him to see all the hurt and confusion I was feeling. Then maybe I'd get a straight answer.

He turned away and started pacing between the couch and an armchair. Back and forth he went. "Please don't cry, Astrid," he begged. "I'm not worth that. I'm sorry. Really, I am. Things are just complicated right now. It's not that I don't . . . I *do* want to be with you. I didn't mean to give you mixed signals. I just need you to work with me somehow. Give me some time to figure it all out. Let's take it slow."

Take it slow. The kiss of death. I suddenly remembered Ben's words from another time and place, and understood exactly what he meant. This felt suspiciously like a dumping that wasn't really, but really was.

But my heart wanted Caspian, and was willing to do whatever he asked.

"Okay." I nodded, blinking away the tears. "Okay, we can take it slow." I laughed shakily and tried not to think about what page we were on now. That path was way too confusing. "Do you want anything to eat? Or drink? I'm going to the kitchen. I'm starving." I waited for his reply, but he shook his head.

Walking into the kitchen took a lot of effort, and I breathed deeply, trying to compose myself. This was just one teeny, tiny hurdle to get over. No big deal. I grabbed a can of soda out of the fridge and put it on the counter before crossing over to the cupboards. I ended up passing on everything inside. My appetite was suddenly gone. I wasn't even all that thirsty, but I needed some sort of an excuse to go calm myself down.

On my way back to retrieve the soda, I came to a halt when I saw my reflection in the microwave door. My eyes were wide and my cheeks were pale. I patted my face, and then pinched both cheeks to bring some color into them. Running a hand through my wild curls, I fluffed and rearranged them. It wasn't a miracle, but it helped a little.

Squaring my shoulders, I stood up straight and marched into the living room, drink in hand. Caspian was by the window looking out at the snow, and I sat down on the couch while simultaneously popping the top of my can. "Did I tell you that my uncle wants me to work in his ice cream shop?" Changing the subject was the only thing I could think of.

I took a large, but still ladylike, sip from the soda can and continued on. "I'm going to be keeping his office for him. Or something like that. We haven't quite worked out all the details yet, but I'm supposed to start this weekend."

Caspian turned away from the window and came to sit back down on the couch, keeping a large distance between us. I tried not to let that sting.

"That's great, Abbey," he said. "I know you'll do a good job."

I sat up and placed the now forgotten soda can on the coffee table. "Do you think so? I mean, I'm really worried. What if I screw something up? This is an actual business here, not just one I've thought about in my head. What if I can't do it?" I hadn't really given much voice to my fears, but they were right there, bubbling under the surface.

"You'll be able to handle it," he assured me. "I have faith in you, Abbey. You won't screw it up, and it'll give you practice for when you're ready to open Abbey's Hollow."

I leaned back against the couch, wondering if I would ever see that day. It seemed so far off. And how did he have a way of making me feel so comfortable again?

"You know, I've been working on this idea for a new line of perfumes." Excitement filled my voice. "It's based on 'The Legend of Sleepy Hollow,' and each character has a unique scent. But not only do the characters get scents, so do the feelings, emotions, and settings. I had planned to—" The sound of a key at the front door stopped me cold.

We both froze. I could hear muffled voices outside.

"Parents!" I squeaked. "Quick, go out the back door. They won't see you that way."

Caspian stood up and grabbed his coat while I rushed him along. Any second now they would be opening that door, and I would be *so* grounded.

He opened the door quietly and I hurried behind him, hastily shoving my feet into an old pair of boots left outside. "Bye, Caspian," I said in hushed tones. "Thanks for coming over. Now go!"

He waved a silent farewell and stepped off into the night. I did a quick shuffle through the snow as I watched him leave, but I was having a hard time getting rid of all the tracks. The snow wasn't falling fast enough to cover them up completely.

That was when inspiration hit.

I lay down on the ground and waved my arms and legs frantically, creating an impromptu snow angel. Then I chose another spot and did it again. A third one did the trick, and all the "evidence" was cleared. I tried not to worry about the fact that his tracks led away from the house in the direction he had gone. I just hoped Mom and Dad would stay inside for the night.

It was absolutely freezing outside now, and my heart was

racing ninety miles a minute as I barreled through the back door to confront bewildered-looking parents.

"We were just looking for you," Mom said. "We thought you'd fallen asleep."

"Nope. I was outside in the snow. Just noticed it and I couldn't wait to go make a snow angel." Would they actually buy that? I wasn't seven anymore.

"Without your coat?" asked Dad, with a puzzled look on his face.

"I, uh, just thought I'd be a minute . . . so I didn't grab my jacket. I'm pretty beat, though. Time for bed. See you guys in the morning." They both watched me as I grabbed my soda can and headed up the stairs. I cast a discreet glance over my shoulder to make sure there were no visible signs that I had had a guest over.

I was good to go.

"Night. See you in the morning," I called again as I ran upstairs to my bedroom. I would be awake all night.

Chapter Eighteen

UNWANTED CONVERSATION

Our man of letters, therefore, was peculiarly happy in the smiles of all the country damsels.

—"The Legend of Sleepy Hollow"

Imade it through most of the week, and *thought* that I'd pulled it off. Mom and Dad would never find out that Caspian had come over when they weren't home. But it was not a good sign when I went downstairs for breakfast on Friday morning and saw Dad sitting in a chair reading the paper.

Dad *never* stayed home this late. He should have left for work almost an hour ago.

Stumbling into the kitchen, I pretended to be half asleep. "Hey, Dad, what are you doing here? Aren't you going to be late for work?" *Say you're going to work. . . . Please say you are going to work.* I rubbed my eyes sleepily and looked at him.

He folded the paper in half and tucked it under his elbow. "Why don't you stay home from school today, Abbey? I think we should have a little chat. I'll write a note for you."

I almost missed the chair I was aiming for. This was it. I was in deep trouble.

"Stay—" My voice cracked. "Stay home? From school? Can't we just talk right now? You know, over breakfast. I've got midterms coming up, and I really shouldn't miss any of the stuff we're reviewing in class." *Think, Abbey. Think very fast. Come up with a really good reason for why Caspian was here. With you. Alone.*

My brain started spazzing.

New student in town?

Study buddy?

Mandatory student exchange program participant?

My brain kept spazzing.

"I don't know, Abbey," he said hesitantly. "Your mother and I have gone over a couple of things that we feel need to be discussed with you."

Oh. My. God. Legs. Turning. To. Water. Brain. Spazzing. Again. Can't. Think. Complete. Sentences. "Gee, Dad," I finally spit out, after a

 348

full minute of brain malfunction. "I really don't want to miss out on anything for the exams. Can't we just talk tonight, after school?"

After I have had the time to think up many, many excuses, to enlist the aid of many, many people at school, and/or possibly run away. Of course there was the very small problem that I didn't know many, many people at school. But that was a bridge, and it could be crossed.

I bit my thumbnail. How many weeks would I be grounded if I made up some excuse having to do with school? Probably the least amount. It was the only way to go.

"I know!" Dad said suddenly, practically giving me a heart attack. "If you stay home today, I'll make you pancakes and we'll go bowling. Besides, I'm sure your teachers won't cover very much material that you'll miss. It's a Friday. They never do much on Fridays."

Well, he was right about that. Plus, with pancakes and bowling, I couldn't be in all that much trouble. At least I hoped not. Dad beamed and patted my hand happily as he waited for my answer. Interesting . . . *Very* interesting.

I felt my hopes start to rise. Surely Dad would have on his stern disciplinarian face if I was about to be grounded for the rest of my natural life. And maybe during the pancake eating I could use the time to think up a killer school excuse if I really *was* in it deep. *I might actually be able to make this thing work,* I thought.

"Oh, all right, Dad. You can write me a note for school today. But don't forget, extra, extra chocolate chips in my pancakes."

"You got it," he said. "I'll take care of the note now so you have it for Monday. Then I'll start on the pancakes. You go get dressed. They'll be ready in about fifteen minutes."

I flashed him my bravest smile as I stood up. Bowling and long chats with Dad.

Yeah, this day was sooo going to suck.

As I stood in front of my closet trying to pick the best outfit that would say *No, really, I didn't have that boy over because I wanted to. I had to do it for a school project,* I tried to think of what it was they could take away in punishment.

I didn't have a car or my license yet, so that was out. And they couldn't exactly ground me from seeing Kristen either, so that was out too. I guess they could take away the job from Uncle Bob, and all the cash that would bring. But seeing as how I hadn't even started that job yet, there wasn't any cash to miss.

The only other alternative was being stuck in my room. And while that definitely presented a certain sucky-ness regarding not seeing Caspian, if it wasn't for very long, then I could work on my newest perfume project. Yup. *Definitely* use a school excuse.

I gave up on finding an outfit that would lessen my grounding time and settled for a dark blue sweater and a pair of jeans. After throwing on my boots, I clomped slowly back downstairs. My fifteen minutes was up and my trial awaited me. *Maybe I should compliment Dad's bowling skills . . .*

"Something sure smells good, Dad!" I said brightly, with a fake smile pasted onto my face as I entered through the kitchen door. "I hope you made a lot of pancakes, because I'm starving." I headed back to the chair I'd been sitting in earlier, making a quick pit stop along the way for the orange juice container. *So far, so good.*

Dad brought over a heaping stack of pancakes piled at least ten high on a bright yellow plate. "Here you go, Abbey. Save me a couple if you can. I'll put a second batch on."

I gulped as I stared at the huge pile making its way toward me. Maybe I had overplayed the whole I'm-so-hungry bit just a tad. "That's enough, Dad. Why don't you come help me eat these while they're still hot, and then you can make us some more?"

He seemed to like that idea and grabbed a fork for himself.

"Don't forget the cups," I reminded him. "I've got the O.J."

Dad made his way through his first and second pancake before I was even halfway done with my first. "Come on, Abbey," he teased me. "I thought you were hungry."

I smiled back and forced down the rest of my first pancake, already dreading the second. It wasn't until he was finishing the last bite of his entire stack before he spoke again. "Are you going to make it through the rest of those? If you're still hungry, I can make more."

I shook my head and paused with my fork in the air. "That's okay, Dad. Guess I must have still been full from dinner last night. You can have these if you want, instead of making another batch." He willingly took the rest of my pancakes, and I gladly handed them over. I wasn't going to make it through a third one of those.

Slumping against the chair, I let my leg swing back and forth, taking small sips of orange juice to keep myself occupied. I wondered how long it would take for the talking to begin. My heart sped up and I forced myself to keep taking small sips. Who was I kidding? I was totally screwed.

I didn't have long to wait, because Dad polished off the rest of my pancakes faster than he'd polished off his, and pushed the plate away. "Abbey," he said, in between mouthfuls of orange juice. *Oh God, here it comes.* My heart hammered out a tap dance, but he launched right into it.

"Your mother and I have been talking about this a lot lately, and we wanted to get your thoughts on it." Pushing the juice aside, he folded his hands and settled into his chair. "How have you been . . . coping . . . lately? How have things been going for you since the accident? I mean, now that Kristen's gone?"

It was a good thing I was sitting down, or I would have missed that chair again. *This* was what he wanted to talk about? *Kristen?* Totally didn't see that one coming.

I thought hard, and chose my words carefully. I couldn't tell him about prom night. That would just bring up too many questions. And lectures. There would definitely be lectures. "I've dealt with it in my own way. It was a lot harder when they found . . . her. But I've managed to wrap my head around it. I've made my peace."

He was paying very close attention.

"How have things been at school? I know it can't be easy to go through your entire junior year with your best friend suddenly gone. And your mother told me about the prom committee. Have those girls settled down a little?"

I was completely shocked at the questions he was asking. They were actually intuitive and insightful. "School pretty much sucks," I admitted, "but that's any school. Everyone leaves me alone for the most part. Once the prom was over, those girls didn't have two words to say to me. I'd expected it, though. They were just doing it for the attention."

I played distractedly with the handle on my cup. I had been so wrapped up with Caspian lately, and obsessing over what Kristen had been hiding from me, that I hadn't given much thought to school. Each day really *was* lonely. Funny how I'd never noticed that.

Dad cleared his throat, and I looked up at him. His hands were still folded together and he looked somewhat embarrassed. "Abbey, arrangements can be made," he said, leaning forward to pat my hand awkwardly. "If you need to change schools, we can do that. I know your mother won't like it very much, but I want you to be comfortable. And if you ever need to speak to anyone, a psychologist, or a counselor, we can arrange that, too. It's nothing to be ashamed of."

Did I have some sort of invisible sign around my neck that said WARNING: TWO STEPS AWAY FROM CRAZY or something? Everyone always assumed I needed professional help.

I patted his hand back just as awkwardly. "No, Dad, I'm okay. Really. Thanks for the offer on the school, but I'm good there, too." He gave me a questioning look, but I shook my head. "I really am fine, Dad. If I ever need . . . anything . . . then you'll be the first to know. Deal?"

He nodded and I removed my hand, glad that this conversation was not what I thought it would be.

"So, since everything is okay at school for you, then, have you given any thought to what comes next?" he asked.

I groaned inwardly. The "future" talk. I should have known this was coming. I geared up my defenses and tried to think of the best way to talk around the situation.

"Well . . . ," I started slowly, trying to think fast. "You know that I had talked about wanting to run my own business. I've been giving that a lot of thought lately. Researching different aspects and laying the groundwork, that type of thing."

He didn't look impressed. "I meant specifics. What type of field are you looking at entering? What type of major are you going to choose? Any specific colleges you want to apply for?"

His questions caught me off guard. Truthfully, I hadn't given any thought to *those* specifics. "I still have plenty of time yet, Dad.

There are a lot of options out there, and I want to make sure I choose the right one. You know?"

Now he was looking unhappy.

"You don't have that much time, young lady. If you're going to get accepted to a good school, then you need to start thinking about applications, and essays, and tuition fees. There's a lot of work involved in getting into college, and it's not easy."

A frown line was starting to work its way across his forehead, and I knew my ship was sinking quickly. I thought about my perfumes, and what it was *I* wanted to do with my life, and then Caspian's words crystallized in my head. *If you tell your mom and dad what your ideas are now, then maybe they won't waste their time planning a different future for you.*

"Look, Dad," I said, "I know you and Mom only have my best interests at heart—I really do know that—but what I do with my life is my decision. *I'm* going to be the one stuck with the consequences of the choices I make. I *could* go to a college you choose, or pick a major that you like, and maybe even get a job somewhere that you approve of, but I won't be happy about it."

He started to say something, but I held up a hand. "Please just let me finish here and then you can rebut everything I say, okay?"

He nodded, and I continued. "Of course I want a great job and a secure future, but I want to do it *my* way. I don't want to become a doctor, or a lawyer, or a PR person, or a publicist. Those things might lead me to the most money, or they might make *you* happy, but they won't make *me* happy. Don't you want me to be happy, Dad, above all else?" I gave him my most sincere look, and he nodded slowly.

"I just want to be happy with my choices in life. And like I said, I *have* given a lot of thought to my future—a lot more than most of the other kids my age. I want to have my own shop downtown. I've even picked out the place and everything. I know how much rent will be, what types of overhead costs I'll have . . . Plus I have a list started for inventory, and how much of it to keep in stock. Everything I have so far is written down in a business plan. I know it still needs a lot of work, and I know it will be tough at first, but I'm bound and determined to see it through. *My* way."

I was hoping that I'd covered all my bases, when something else popped into my head. "Oh, and I *do* plan on taking some courses on business, maybe even get a degree in that, but it will probably take a while and will be at a local college. I want to work as an apprentice to someone who already has a store in a similar field while I take my classes, and use that as a hands-on approach to my education. That's one of the reasons why I'm so excited about working at Uncle Bob's, too. It will give me some practical experience."

Sitting back, I took a deep breath. It was all out now. He would either love it or hate it. Any second, the screaming could begin.

He had a thoughtful look on his face, and I couldn't tell if he was actually thinking about what I'd said, or thinking of ways to rebut it. But he didn't say anything and I started to get nervous. This could end up being very, very bad.

"I think it's a great idea, Abbey."

"You do?"

"Yes, I do," he said. "You laid out your plans in a very clear, concise manner. You've obviously taken the time to give it a lot of thought. And if you really have accomplished everything that you just told me, then you're already ahead of the game. I'm very proud of you."

Wow. Today was turning out to be the most fantastic day *ever.*

"Thanks, Dad," I gushed. "You have no idea what that means to me. I thought you and Mom would totally flip out when I told you. Thanks for being so cool about it."

He looked slightly uncomfortable, but he patted my hand

again. "Well, I don't know how your mother will react, but I'll break the news to her gently. After all, you are right about it being your decision, and we both want you to be happy. And if this means you'll be staying closer to home, then I'm sure she won't mind that."

I beamed at him. This talk was going *very* well.

"I'll tell you what else I'll do," he said abruptly. "If you finish your business plan, say by the end of the school year, then I'll give you three thousand dollars as seed money to help you get started. Deal?"

He stuck out his hand, and I quickly shook it. "Deal."

Like I even had to think about that one. Three grand just to finish my business plan? I was so there.

Dad looked pretty pleased with himself, and I was feeling pretty happy too. I smiled at him and jumped up to give him a spontaneous half hug. He was surprised, but returned the sentiment, and I grinned like a fool, feeling absurdly happy for the moment. Then he cleared his throat gruffly and set me to the side.

"You know, you've seemed happier lately. Even with Kristen's death. Is there anything you want to tell me?"

Let's see . . .

I was in love for the first time. I hadn't gotten in trouble for having a boy over to the house when I was there alone. Tomorrow I was going to start a sweet job that paid really well. And I'd just gotten offered a bunch of money to write a business document.

Is there anything I want to tell him?

"Nope," I said with a grin.

"Are you sure?" he asked me, with a wickedly teasing glint in his eyes. "There's no one special in the picture? A boy you haven't told us about?"

I tried very, very hard not to blush, but I felt my cheeks go red. "Aw, Dad," I played it off. "You know us girls. We always have a crush on some boy or another. It's just a silly thing."

He chuckled and pushed his chair back from the table. "I know, I know. But be sure to introduce us to anyone special. Your mother and I will want to meet that young man."

"Okay, Dad." *Yeah, right.*

He started gathering up the dishes, and I moved fast to help him. "Why don't we go bowling now?" I asked, trying to change the subject. "Then we can stop for Chinese food on the way back."

Still chuckling, he gave me a quick wink. "Okay. We'll leave the dishes here, and I'll take care of them when we get back. Race you out to the car."

I piled up the dishes and headed to the sink, letting him have a head start, while telling myself that this was all for a good cause. Anything I had to do to stay on his good side was completely worth it. Even if it was bowling . . . with Dad . . . in public.

Bowling went surprisingly well. There was only one other person in the far left lane, so we pretty much had the run of the place. We ended up playing three games, and Dad happily gloated about how he'd won two out of the three games, but graciously offered me a rematch.

Much Chinese food was had, and enjoyed by both of us after that, and we decided to go back for a couple more rounds. It was almost six o'clock by the time we got home. I was pleasantly surprised at how cool Dad ended up being. It was actually a fun day. Not that I'd ever admit that to anyone, though.

Mom was home, and had dinner waiting for us as we stepped in. I hungrily slurped down several bowls of steaming clam chowder and ate half a loaf of French bread along with it. I fell into bed a little later that night exhausted, but warm and full. It was a great feeling.

~ ~ ~

The next morning, however, did not feel as great, since it was still freezing out, and I had to force myself out of a cozy bed once again. It was Saturday, and I had a job to do.

I yawned and rubbed my bleary eyes while Mom kept saying how she had things to do on the weekends too and they didn't involve being my personal taxicab, as she drove me to Uncle Bob's shop. But she changed her tune when I gladly reminded her that I could go get my license at anytime and drive myself around. Then she quickly agreed to drive me each weekend.

I knew the license thing would work.

Mom pulled up to Uncle Bob's with an abrupt stop and told me she'd be back to pick me up at five. I was dumped rather unceremoniously at the front door, and she drove off. I could have sworn I heard her tires squeal.

Turning to face the shop, I pushed my way through the glass doors. Bells jingled softly overhead as I called out for Uncle Bob.

"Back here," was his booming response, somewhere from the general vicinity of the office area. "I'm glad you came. Are you sure this is going to work for you? I know how you young kids want to spend time with your boyfriends and girlfriends on the weekends.

I mean, that is, if you have a boyfriend. Do you . . . do you have one of . . . those?"

I rolled my eyes as I walked back to meet him. I was almost afraid to answer. God only knew where *that* would lead me. How could I explain my on-again, off-again relationship with Caspian? "No, Uncle Bob," I called back. "I don't have one of those."

On Wednesday afternoon I found myself sitting cross-legged under the bridge, staring aimlessly into the water. Christmas was only two weeks away, and I didn't know what to get for Caspian.

The crunch of gravel caught my attention, but I didn't have to look up. I knew who it was. A second later Caspian came over and sat down next to me, nodding his head in silent greeting. I nodded back. He didn't say anything, and I turned back to the water and my thoughts.

He had a sketchpad in one hand and something skinny and black in the other, and I watched out of the corner of my eye as he started drawing on one of the pages.

Frowning, he stopped drawing, shook his head, and rubbed a finger repeatedly over the page, causing a dark smear to bloom. He looked at it for a moment longer, then flipped to a new, fresh page and set his charcoal to work again.

I abandoned all previous thinking and angled my body to watch him more closely, now completely caught up in what he was doing. It didn't take long for a tree, then a riverbank, and finally the water itself to start taking form on the paper.

His lean fingers flew across the page, and I watched in amazement as short, bold strokes took up residence next to long, smooth ones. Creating a scene that ebbed and flowed together, mirroring its true-life counterparts. It was beautiful to watch.

"How did your first weekend at your new job go?" he asked me softly, never looking up from the paper. I couldn't stop staring at his hands. They were moving so fast, yet he never faltered. I wondered if the next time he touched me, would it be with confidence, or hesitance?

"It went great," I said, trying to force my thoughts elsewhere. "All I did so far was open and sort all of my uncle's mail, but he had a ton of it. This weekend I'm going to set up a new filing system for him and show him how to use it." His hands kept moving. Shading now. Blending the edges of one harsh line into another.

"Then the weekend after that I'll start compiling all his

364

invoices and vendor information and make a database for them. He told me that eventually he wants me to completely take over the office end of his business. I sort of can't believe it."

"I told you that you'd be great at it," he replied. "So, will your uncle be paying you with ice cream? Because I'm totally available if he wants to hire a second employee."

I snorted. "No, he won't be paying me in ice cream, but I do get all the free samples I want. One of the perks of working there."

I turned a delighted grin toward him, catching his eye for a brief second when he looked up. "And you know what else is cool? I spent Friday with my dad, talking some things over. Like school and stuff, and I told him about my plans for the shop. Get this: He actually took it well, and thought it was a great idea. He even offered to give me some start-up money if I finish my business plan!"

He smiled. "See? I was completely right."

"Yeah," I laughed. "Yeah, you were."

Caspian resumed his sketching, and I turned back to the water. "You know," I said quietly, "it's actually kind of nice to be working at Uncle Bob's. Kristen and I had planned to get after-school jobs together this year, and I think she'd like the fact that I'm working there." Out of the corner of my eye I could see him nod his head.

Then he asked, "Have you learned anything new about Kristen's secret boyfriend?"

I picked up a small handful of pebbles, slowly shifting them from side to side in my palms. The unexpected thought of Kristen's diaries made me twitchy, and angry, and I needed something to distract myself with. "No, I haven't." I readjusted my legs and then tossed the pebbles into the water.

"Tell me what I should do, Caspian," I said suddenly, desperately. Surprising even myself. "I don't know what to do. There's no one to ask, no way to get any answers. I don't know who this guy was, or how involved he might have been with what happened. What if he was there with her at the river that night? What if he could have saved her? What if he stood her up and she did something stupid and desperate? I'm not even sure that I *want* to know what happened anymore."

I put my hands to the ground and pushed myself up to my feet. "But I *need* to know, Caspian. I need to know the answers to these questions."

He just sat there. Working on his page.

"Caspian?" Still no answer.

I snapped my fingers as I called his name again. "Caspian! Tell me what I should do . . . please."

He finally looked up. "I don't think you want me to tell you that," he said slowly.

I waited impatiently, eyebrows raised, for him to continue. "Why not?" I prompted.

"Because," he said, in that same slow tone, "you won't like it."

"Please, tell me," I begged. "If I didn't want your advice, then I wouldn't have asked for it."

His fingers stilled, and he looked at me. I could see a storm gathering in his eyes. "Do we have to do this, Abbey?" he asked fiercely. "Do you really want to go there? Why don't you just let it drop, and we'll pretend this never happened. Just go back to the way things were, before we talked about any of this. I never should have brought it up." He trailed off, and it sounded like he was getting angry.

Where the hell did that come from? I didn't think. The words just started flying out of my mouth. "Oh, no," I said very calmly, stewing in my anger. "Let's go there. Let's *definitely* go there. I'm a big girl. I can handle it. So tell me what it is you think I should do. Go on, tell me," I goaded.

With a shake of his head he put the pad and piece of charcoal on the ground. "I don't want to do this, Abbey. I don't want to fight with you. Tell me what to say to make it all go away, and I will. Tell me what to do to make it better."

I started pacing; I thought I'd wear a hole in the ground. I didn't want to do this either, but something was wrong with me. Some perverse part of my mind delighted in torturing myself. There was no turning back now. "Just tell me what you were going to say. Simple as that and this will all be over."

He shook his head again and heaved a large sigh. His eyes found mine and locked into place as he stood up too. We faced each other, drawn to the heat of the moment. Our anger was large and deadly. Something that should not have been between us.

"Okay, you win," he said simply. "You'll always win, Abbey. I didn't want to tell you what to do because I think that you should just let it go. Allow Kristen to keep her secrets. Everyone has secrets, Abbey, even you, and some need to be protected more than others. Maybe this is one of those. Maybe your questions will never *be* answered, but I think you should let it stay that way. Are you happy now?" His shoulders sagged and he turned from me to face the river.

I felt like I'd just been punched in the chest.

"Let it go? You think I should just let it go? I can't do that, Caspian. She was my best friend, and I have a right to know. What if this secret boyfriend was involved? I can't just let that go, and you have no right to ask me to."

I was breathing fast now, rage building up inside of me. And yet even as I said those bitter angry words, I wanted to take them back. To say "I'm sorry" and beg his forgiveness. To make him understand that it was Kristen, and myself, I was really mad at. Not him.

But I didn't say those things, and the ugly words hung between us. I never was any good at small talk, or apologies.

"I'm sorry, Abbey, but that's not your choice to make," he said. "You don't know if this guy is responsible for any of those things, and Kristen isn't here to tell you any differently. They were her secrets to tell . . . or keep. And she made her choice."

My hands were shaking and I fought off the urge to cry. They weren't tears of sadness but tears of anger, and frustration. I hated the fact that if I gave in, it would make me look like a blubbering baby. "So first you want me to find out why Kristen went to the river, but then when I do, you tell me to let it go? I *thought* that you would support me in this, not go all . . ." Words failed me, and I didn't know what to say. "Well, like how you went. All non-supportive."

I hated to finish that weakly, but I was too blindsided, too overwhelmed, to finish eloquently. I held up my hands to stop him from answering. "You know what?" I said tiredly. "Just don't. Don't answer that. Don't give me your opinion. Don't 'go there.' I can't deal with any more of this right now. I have to go. I'll—I'll see you later."

I didn't give him a chance to speak, but I saw the sad look in his eyes. Turning away, I jammed my hands deep into my pockets. A small rock must have been left behind from when I'd picked them up, because as I shoved my fists into my jeans, I felt the sudden slice of a pebble's rough edge against my palm. Oddly, I didn't mind the dull ache. It was a welcome distraction from what I was leaving behind.

And besides, it was nothing compared to the pain in my heart when I heard him whisper "I'm sorry, Astrid" as I walked away.

Chapter Nineteen

THE PERFECT PRESENT

Another of his sources of fearful pleasure was, to pass long winter evenings with the old Dutch wives . . . with a row of apples roasting and spluttering along the hearth, and listen to their marvellous tales of ghosts and goblins. . . .

—"The Legend of Sleepy Hollow"

I cried myself to sleep over the next couple of days, and avoided the cemetery and river at all costs. I felt depressed, and awful, and sick at heart. Between this most recent fight and the earlier conversation on "taking it slow," things were not going very well for Caspian and me. The fact that it was almost Christmas made it ten times worse.

Uncle Bob must have picked up on my mood, because he kept asking me if I was feeling okay while I set up the filing system for him. I told him that everything was fine, and I felt great, but I don't think he believed me. Not like I really blamed him, though. I was withdrawn and silent, with permanent purple bags under my eyes. Not exactly the picture of glowing health.

I finally gave in to his persistent badgering and left early on Sunday afternoon. He insisted on paying me for a full day's work, and even threw in a Christmas bonus. I just tried not to cry, and gave him a big hug before meeting Mom outside. The crying thing was getting annoying, but it was happening a lot these days. Luckily, I managed to keep the blubbering to a minimum.

Mom surprised me by stopping at the mall on the way home, saying that I was in dire need of some spontaneous seasonal shopping therapy. I strongly disagreed with her. The *last* place I wanted to be right now was in a crowded shopping center watching all the happy couples strolling by hand in hand sharing Christmas cheer with each other.

Yeah, I definitely wasn't in the mood for *that*.

But Mom has always been a brilliant tactician, and she wore me down with promises of free food and new shoes. As we pushed our way through the revolving doors, she made a beeline for the food court, and snagged us some fresh cinnamon rolls and steaming hot chocolate.

As I willingly munched away, I couldn't help but think that

Mom should have been a war general or something. She had totally missed her calling. Leaving no room for doubt, she herded me to the shoe store, and, unwittingly, I found myself the new owner of the cutest pair of brown boots.

Damn it, she was good.

We walked past bell ringers, present wrappers, and Christmas carolers dressed in old-fashioned costumes. From time to time we'd stop in and check out a store, but mostly I was just browsing. We even saw Santa and one very tall, very bored-looking elf, but we thought better of stopping. After we came to the pet store window display and spent a sufficient amount of time ogling the baby kittens, Mom and I decided to split up for a while, and we each went our separate ways.

It didn't take me long to find a new laptop carrying case for her Christmas present, and an electronic baseball trivia thingamajig for Dad. I didn't really have any idea what to get for the Maxwells, and nothing jumped out at me as I continued to look around, so I decided to wait and give their gift some more thought.

As far as Caspian went . . . I still didn't know what to do there.

On the one hand, I didn't even know if we were still talking, let alone whatever we were boyfriend-girlfriend-wise. But on the other hand, it just didn't feel right to not get him anything for Christmas. I had to be able to find *some* small gift to give him.

I trekked across the mall and ended up in a sports store, an electronics store, and even a men's clothing store along the way, but still didn't find anything. When I started to seriously eye up tube socks while wondering if I could get them gift wrapped, I knew it was time to stop.

Lugging my bags back to the food court, I stopped to get another hot chocolate before finding a bench. For a while I just sat there at the edge of the crowd and watched the throng of people go by while I blew gently on my drink.

Just as I was taking a tester sip and checking my cell phone to see how much time I had left before I had to meet Mom, someone plopped down next to me. I jerked in surprise, and tried to hold on to the Styrofoam cup. My bags jostled against my legs and I turned, ready to give whoever had sat down an earful.

Mrs. Maxwell sat there, frowning slightly. "I'm sorry, dear; I thought you saw me coming. I never would have snuck up on you if I knew that hot drink was in your hand."

"Not a problem." I tried to casually wave it off, but the drink was still in my grasp. So I took a sip. "How have you guys been? I haven't seen you in a while. Did you get some Christmas shopping done?" I noticed her lack of bags and mentally kicked myself. She had one less person to buy for this year, and I had probably just reminded her of that.

"Mostly window-shopping today," she replied. "I haven't bought anything yet since, well, you know. Things will be different this year."

I busied myself with my drink again, and we fell into an awkward silence.

"So . . . can you believe we got snow already? I hope it's a white Christmas this year." It was lame to talk about the weather, but unfortunately, it was all I had.

"I know," she said. "The snow is so beautiful. I hope it's a white Christmas too. But just snow, not ice. I hate ice."

Sipping slowly, I looked around me, nodding in agreement. *Will it always be this awkward between us?* Kristen's mom had been like a second mother to me, but now it was like we were only the barest of acquaintances. A death could change so many things for so many people. It was heartbreaking.

"Are you going to the New Year's party at the museum?" I asked, hoping that was safer territory.

She shook her head. "I don't think so. We'll probably just stay home this year and keep things quiet. It's for the best."

A sad look crossed her face, and I could tell she was fighting not to cry. I placed my almost empty cup on the ground next to me and reached for her hand. "I know this Christmas will be difficult for you. Losing Kristen was like losing a limb, and I can *especially* feel your pain. It's going to be hard on all of us." I took a deep breath, and vowed then and there never to tell Kristen's mom about the diaries. She didn't need that hanging over her head.

"I'll see you guys at our house for Christmas dinner, though, right? You can't skip that. And you know *someone* has to help me eat all those dozens of cookies Mom will inevitably make in a fit of madness. You don't want to leave me alone in that, do you? I'll end up gaining, like, fifty pounds, and then I'll definitely be mad at you guys when I'm forced to buy all new clothes."

She laughed and squeezed my hand. "Your mother does whip herself up into quite a cookie frenzy every year. I guess it wouldn't be fair to leave you alone in that misery."

I heaved a large sigh. "You *do* understand. Thank you for taking pity on me and my poor waistline."

She laughed again, and my spirit soared. *Maybe I can get rid of that awkwardness after all.* A smile on her face was a definite improvement over tears.

"Same time, same place, then?" I asked in invitation.

She nodded, and the smile stayed on her face. It was so good to see her happy. I wanted to make her stay that way forever. "You know," I said softly, "if you ever need to adopt a daughter, even for, like, a couple of hours, I'm all yours. You've always felt like a second mother to me, and I would be honored to repay the favor."

Her eyes misted over at that, and she mouthed "Thank you" before giving me a shaky hug. "I need to get going, honey. I told Harold that I'd meet him in ten minutes. If I don't find him in time, we'll be stuck here for hours looking at the electronics store. You know how men are."

I nodded, and she looked at me for a minute longer, then turned and walked away, quickly becoming a melted shadow lost among all the other shoppers. Since I had a couple more minutes to kill, I decided to go check out the perfume store.

Mom found me ten minutes later, happily sniffing away at

several samples. "How did I know I would find you here?"

I didn't even turn around. "Hey, Mom. Are you all done with your shopping?"

"Yes, yes," she said hurriedly. "But we need to leave now. I forgot that I have fifty-four red bows to make for all the shops participating in Christmas in the Hollow. I have to get back home and start those."

"I'm ready to go whenever you are. Do you think my perfumes smell better than these?" I held out the tester tube. "Mine have a stronger scent to them, and not so much of an alcohol after-smell."

She leaned in for a quick whiff and made a face. "Yep, yours smell better. Now get your bags and let's go."

I capped the sample and picked up my bags before turning to leave. Mom was babbling on and on about how glad she was that only the shops on Main Street were participating and that it wasn't every street, because then she would have five hundred bows to make . . . blah, blah, blah.

I wasn't paying much attention to her rambling. I was too busy thinking about my Sleepy Hollow perfume project and how I could tie in a holiday theme with it.

 378

We were five feet away from the exit doors when a tiny hole-in-the-wall shop caught my eye. It was a bookstore called Hallowed Words, and the sign on the door stated that they specialized in vintage books. I skidded to a stop, bags flying wildly around me. Mom didn't notice at first, but then she turned back when she hit the outside doors alone.

"I need to make a stop in here," I said quickly. "I'll only be five minutes, I swear."

Her look was disbelieving. "You had all the time in the world earlier, Abbey. Why didn't you go then? I told you I have a lot of work to do tonight."

"Please, Mom? Only five minutes. You can warm up the car and bring it around. I *promise* it will only be five minutes."

She glared. "You better be at the door when I get there. *Five minutes.*"

"Okay," I called over my shoulder, already walking toward the store. I didn't know if I would find anything in there, let alone find it in five minutes, but I had a good feeling.

Stepping through the glass doors was like stepping back in time. The store had a papery old-book smell, and it was nice. I breathed deeply, briefly wondering if I could make a perfume that smelled like old books, but then I was quickly moving on. My five minutes were ticking away, and I realized there was no *way* five minutes would be enough time to spend in here.

Books were literally *everywhere*. Floor to ceiling, row after row. Bookcases were lined up one behind the other, and each one was practically groaning under its full load.

I was doomed. I'd never make it out in time.

Wandering down the first aisle, I kept telling myself that I should leave. It was a waste of time. But I kept walking, and the first aisle led me to the second aisle, and that led me to a third, and then I made a right turn. I was just trying to turn around and give up, when I came to a corner display.

There, on two small brass shelves, were several old books, and the prize was in the center. An antique telescope. As I got closer, I could see that it was a display based on astronomy. My head got a weird buzzing sensation, and I felt a tiny shock run up my spine as I gazed in mute adoration and awe.

This is it. I had found the perfect gift for Caspian.

The telescope was in amazingly pristine condition. Made of antiqued glass and old metal beauty, it looked like something to be found in a mad scientist's laboratory. It was perfect.

I held my breath as I picked it up, feeling its heavy, solid surface under my fingertips, and I prayed that it was a price I could afford. Visions of price tags marked two hundred, three hundred, and even five hundred dollars kept running through my head, and I desperately hoped that I was wrong.

When the tag revealed the price of fifty dollars slashed in half, and twenty-five dollars marked next to it, I practically broke out into a song and dance. Oh yeah, it was totally mine.

Carefully tucking my treasure under one arm, I turned to the books and picked up one that was beautifully illustrated with drawings of the stars. It was from the early 1900s, and I couldn't believe my good luck. The price tag on that little beauty showed a mere eight dollars, and I quickly added it to my loot.

Knowing that my time had probably come and gone, I tried to find the front of the store, and anxiously waited for the salesperson to come ring up my purchases.

"Did you find what you were looking for?" she asked as she slowly rang things up for me.

"Yes," I replied with a large grin. "I found *exactly* what I was looking for."

Chapter Twenty

'TIS THE SEASON

Books were flung aside without being put away on the shelves, inkstands were over-
turned, benches thrown down, and the whole school was turned loose an hour before the
usual time, bursting forth like a legion of young imps. . . .

—"The Legend of Sleepy Hollow"

The last couple of days before Christmas vacation were brutal,
and I wasn't the only one tired of studying for midterms. Once
class started, attention would quickly turn from what was being
written on the board to who was wearing what for the upcoming
Christmas dance.

It was bad enough to see the colorful posters leering down at
me everywhere with their obnoxious cheerfulness, but that was
nothing compared to the stab of loneliness I felt whenever a snippet
of conversation would reach my ear.

"Oh my God, I have the most perfect dress! It's red and white ..."

Did *I* care that the theme of the dance would be winter wonderland romance?

No.

"I heard they're going to make it snow ..."

Did *I* care that there would be delicate glass icicles and mounds of fluffy fake snow covering everything?

No.

"Can you believe there's going to be sleigh rides ..."

Did *I* care that a horse-drawn buggy would be available so you could take a romantic ride outside with your date?

No.

Did *I* want to go to the stupid dance?

Yes. *Desperately.*

It really wasn't fair. I had a boyfriend now. Sure, we weren't exactly seeing eye-to-eye at the moment, but *I* was supposed to be one of those girls deciding what dress I would wear to the dance. Not standing on the outside looking in.

A pang of guilt hit me when I realized that only two months ago I hadn't gone to a dance because Kristen would never have the chance to go. Feeling like a terrible best friend, I promptly banished all thoughts of the dance to the back of my mind, and swore not to think about it again.

The final bell buzzed loudly overhead, and jerked me out of my thoughts. Doors suddenly burst open up and down the long hallway, while voices filled the air. Most of the students didn't even stop at their lockers. They had two weeks of freedom ahead of them, and they wanted out.

I couldn't blame them.

Alone now in the empty corridor, I threw my book bag to the floor and left the zipper wide open. My locker door slammed into the door next to it, but I didn't care. I picked up my English Lit book and tossed it in.

Stupid Christmas dance.

My algebra book was next.

Stupid icicles and fake snow.

Then science.

And the horse will probably poop everywhere.

The dull thuds were strangely satisfying, and I threw in the last couple of books with vehemence. I was completely out of ammo now, and my locker looked hollow and forlorn. Then I looked down and saw dozens of gum wrappers, balled-up pieces of notebook paper, and chewed pencils scattered along the bottom.

Time for a quick clean-out.

Taking advantage of the clear hallway, I dragged over the nearest garbage can. It was made of very old, very loud monstrous metal and it made an ungodly screeching noise. I fought and pulled and generally pleaded with the thing to please cooperate with me, even if only a little. Fortunately, it chose to cooperate, and half the battle was over once I parked it next to my locker.

I started hurling in gum wrappers, forgotten class notes from last semester, an old science test that I had looked everywhere for, a handful of ratty pencils, a picture of Kristen and me—

The picture went sailing by before I even had a chance to recognize it, and then it was too late. As I stared down into that deep pile of nasty garbage, I knew I couldn't leave it there. The picture had been taken last year on a school field trip, and it was the only copy I had.

At first I tried to just reach my arm in, staying carefully away from the goopy sides. But I came up short. About six inches too short. I wished for someone tall to still be hanging around who could suddenly appear and get it for me, but a quick glance down the hall told me there was zero chance of that happening. I was alone and it was up to me.

So I went in . . .

Holding my breath, and placing a piece of scrap paper as a barrier between my shirt and the can, I bent over and lunged for all I was worth. There wasn't much light once I was inside, so I was reaching blindly until I felt the photo. I also managed to somehow grab a half-eaten candy bar while I was at it, but I quickly let that drop and hauled ass out of there.

I lifted myself up and out of the trash can, trying to swing my hair out of the way. Then I backed up a step, picture firmly in hand, and promptly ran into someone. Dread instantly bloomed in the pit of my stomach as I realized that whoever was behind me had just witnessed my Dumpster dive.

Not exactly one of my finest moments.

I turned around slowly. Ben's laughing brown eyes began to come into focus, and he had a strange look on his face, like he was holding in a snort and a laugh at the same time. I hung my head as my cheeks went red. "It's not what you think. I dropped something accidentally in there and had to get it out. That was the only way."

He shook his head and still had that strange look on his face.

Only at my insistent "Go ahead" did he double over and burst into gales of laughter. But at least it didn't last long.

"I'm sorry, Abbey," he said, wiping away tears. "Really, I didn't mean to laugh *at* you. It was just a funny picture. I thought maybe you were going after a sandwich in there or something." He gave me a silly grin, and I grinned back. It was infectious.

I leaned against my locker and wedged my hip against it for support, abandoning all attempts to look cool. What possibly could have made Ben choose *this* moment to find me?

He gave me a serious smile and glanced over at my locker door nervously. "So, how are things going for you, Abbey?"

For a moment, déjà vu hit. Hadn't I already been asked this before? "Things are good," I answered, after the feeling passed. "What about you?"

"Good . . . They've been good for me, too," he said. "I started dating Amanda Reynolds. We've been going out for the last month or so."

Amanda Reynolds. The name tickled the back of my brain, but I couldn't place it. "Sorry. I don't think I know her."

He looked back at the locker and then down at the garbage can. "We, uh, went to prom together."

My lips made the sound before I even thought it. "Oooooooh."
Yellow dress. From prom night. The one who'd said I was a bitch.

"It's not like it's serious or anything." He shrugged. "But who
wants to be alone at Christmas?"

I nodded my head slowly. *Yeah, who wants to be alone at
Christmas?*

He looked me in the eye for a second and hesitated, almost
like he was waiting for me to say something. I stayed silent, and
he continued on. "So anyway, how are things with you and what's
his name?"

"Caspian," I supplied. "His name is Caspian. And things are good,
I guess. We're trying to figure some stuff out. But it's all good."

He nodded, and we both stood there in an awkward silence.
Ben was the one to break the stalemate. "Here." He pulled
something out of his back pocket. "This is for you." He held out a
red envelope, and I looked at it in surprise.

"It's just a Christmas card," he said, answering my silent question.
"Not a big deal. Just, you know, cuz 'tis the season and all."

I looked down at the card again, dumbfounded. He had gotten
a Christmas card for me? I hadn't gotten one from anyone else. It
was a high school tradition that you exchange Christmas cards with

all of your friends each year, but since Kristen and I had only been friends with each other, that had left our card list fairly short.

"I don't know what to say." It was true, I really didn't. I hadn't even taken the card yet.

"Don't say anything. Just take the card." He held it out closer to me, and I took it, pathetically grateful.

"Thank you, Ben. This means a lot to me."

Seeing that the picture I'd worked so hard to rescue from the garbage can was still in my hand, I thrust it at him. "I want you to have this."

He tried to protest at first, but I wouldn't budge. Finally he accepted it. I didn't miss the fact that he touched Kristen's smiling face before he tucked it into his pocket. Ducking his head, he turned shy on me. "I have to go. You take care, Abbey, and Merry Christmas."

"Yeah, you too," I called out to him as he turned and started to walk away. "Happy Holidays."

I waited and didn't open the envelope from Ben until I started walking home. There was just a generic Happy Holidays card inside, signed with his name, but it really *did* mean a lot to me. I felt terrible that I didn't have one for him, but it was too late now.

If I gave him one when we got back to school, I'd look like someone who was obviously just returning the favor.

Oh, well. At least there was next year.

When I finally got home, I heaved a sigh of relief as I shrugged the book bag off of my aching shoulders and let it drop to the floor in a graceless heap. I didn't even care that Mom would probably yell at me later for leaving it in the middle of the hallway. It just didn't matter.

I walked toward the kitchen and went through the motions of grabbing a snack before heading up to my room. After turning on the computer, I rested my head in my hands as I waited for it to boot up. I was so tired. Exhaustion was a constant companion of mine.

The computer clicked and beeped and whirred, and when all the noises stopped, I knew it was good to go. I signed on to the Internet and took my time checking my e-mail. Then I browsed through a couple of familiar shopping websites. Most of them were offering FREE! EXPEDITED SHIPPING! for the holidays, and once again my mind turned to presents. I mentally checked off the list in my head of who was already bought for, and that left me with only Mr. and Mrs. Maxwell.

Still unsure of what to get them, I typed "unique gifts" into a search engine box and hit enter. Within seconds dozens of listings popped up on my screen. I was unhappy with all of them until I finally came upon a site advertising to name a star after someone.

Ten minutes later I was sold. Naming a star for Kristen would be the *perfect* gift. The Maxwells would *love* it. I quickly clicked my way to the checkout, wincing at the fact that FREE! EXPEDITED SHIPPING! was not offered on *this* website, and in order to get my certificate of notice in time for Christmas, it would cost me an extra thirty-two dollars.

But I chose it anyway, since it was Christmas after all, and Uncle Bob *had* given me a bonus. As I entered Mom's credit card number from memory, I sternly reminded myself to give her the money for it later.

Thoughts of Uncle Bob brought to mind the fact that I had totally forgotten about getting a gift for him, so I started clicking my way through more websites. It was even harder finding something for him, and a couple moments later I turned the computer off, frustrated to no end. When had shopping become so difficult?

I shoved my chair back and stood up, pacing over to the window seat. Outside, a light snow was falling, and the frosty scene was beautiful and calm. Inside, though, I felt nothing but worry and anxiousness. I desperately wanted to go to the cemetery and find Caspian.

Deciding that a distraction was in order, I grabbed my coat and headed downstairs. To keep my mind off of things, this time I would go in the *opposite* direction of the cemetery. Main Street. And maybe I would even find something for Uncle Bob while I was at it.

I remembered my gloves this time, and quickly pulled them on as I walked. Within minutes the first shop came into view. It was absolutely beautiful, and I stopped to gaze at the decorations. Tiny red bows and green garland accentuated by silver glass balls hung from the outside of the store, while strings of popcorn and twinkling white lights covered the inside.

Looking around me, I noticed that this wasn't the only decorated storefront. The neighbors had really gone all out. I strolled slowly, observing the big red bow on each shop's front door. That was surely Mom's handiwork. She had created the perfect bow of course, and it definitely added the right touch.

Even the street corners had been decorated, and a large old-fashioned gas lamp sat on each corner. The dancing flames flickering behind the covered glass shade starkly illuminated the still-falling flakes of snow. It was a sight to see, and I briefly felt like I had been transported back in time.

The next window I passed was bare and empty, but I stopped. It was my shop. Or my future shop, anyway. I reached out one hand and lovingly ran my finger over the dirty glass. The painted wooden frame was chipped and peeling, but I didn't care. It was waiting for me. This would be my baby one day. I daydreamed about how I would set it up.

Maybe I would use an old claw-foot bathtub and mismatched armoires to display my wares. I could have a reading section, with a library of old books, featuring all of Washington Irving's works. Or perhaps there would be antique tables, and apothecary bottles. An old-fashioned beauty store of sorts. The possibilities were endless.

My thoughts ran wild, but I reluctantly pulled myself away from the window. I didn't have very much time left before all of the shops would start to close, and I'd be seeing Uncle Bob tomorrow. I needed to find him a present, and I needed to find it fast.

A tiny florist shop yielded me the perfect gift for Uncle Bob, and he was thrilled with the WORLD'S BEST BOSS mug that I presented to him at work on Saturday. He made sure to bring it in each time he came to check on me, holding it up so I could see he was using it. I barely got any work done at all.

On Sunday he seemed content to let the mug sit on his desk, and I finally got to start a new project. When it was time for Mom to come pick me up that evening, I reminded Uncle Bob that I would see him in two weeks, and told him yet again that he was very welcome for the mug. I hurried out of there before he got the chance to go pick it up again.

I was finally free for the holidays and ready for the relaxation to begin.

Over the next three days I slept in till noon, made dozens and dozens of cookies with Mom, and drank hot chocolate by the gallon. It was completely blissful.

Christmas Eve came before I knew it, and I spent most of the morning helping Mom box up cookies for all of our extended family members. Which probably explained why Mom always went a little cookie crazy every year. We had a *lot* of relatives.

After we finished packaging the last of them up, I went to my room to wrap some presents of my own. The name-a-star certificate had arrived just in time, and I was thrilled to see that it came in a beautiful black frame. I added a little bit of gift wrap and a red bow and had it finished in no time. Next up were Mom's and Dad's gifts, and they didn't take very long to wrap either.

I dug deep into my creative side to find a unique way to wrap Caspian's gifts. After finding some dark blue wrapping paper, and adding some strategically placed tiny silver star stickers, I drew on a couple of swirling designs with a gray marker. The result was perfect.

Trying to find a red pen to write his name with, I dug around in my perfume supply box. I stopped for a minute when my eyes landed on the sample I'd made for Kristen. Uncapping the blue glass bottle, I poured a tiny amount into a tester vial and added it to the present pile.

I couldn't forget my best friend.

Once that task was complete, and I had found the red pen, my thoughts wandered back to the cemetery. I struggled with the decision of whether or not to go there, while I absentmindedly wrote names on each present. It *was* Christmas, after all. And it didn't really matter who said what, as long as everything was okay between us.

Indecision had me chewing my lip with worry, so I decided

to distract myself with more cookies. Cookies had always worked before, and hopefully, they wouldn't let me down now.

I went downstairs to the kitchen and threw myself into the process of making another batch, but soon realized that being arm-deep in cookie dough left my mind plenty of time to wander and worry. Utterly disgusted with myself, and feeling extremely dejected, I gave up on the cookies, put the dough in the refrigerator, and trudged back up to my room to think about what I should do.

Then the perfect excuse hit me. Presents for Nikolas and Katy.

I knew instinctively what Katy would love, and I dug through my perfumes, impatiently looking for a scent that I hadn't used before. I came to an older mix, and after a quick check on the description label, I unscrewed the lid and took a deep whiff.

The scent, with hints of violet and honeysuckle, had been sitting for over a year and had aged very well. It was almost old-fashioned-smelling, and I knew right away that it was the perfect one to give to her. Then I sat back and pondered what to do for Nikolas.

I wasn't entirely sure that he would enjoy getting perfume as a Christmas gift. Plus, I didn't want him to get the wrong idea and think that I was giving him the hint that he needed a new scent. The smell of fresh cookies still lingered on the air, and it distracted me as I inhaled appreciatively.

Inspiration hit again, and I headed back downstairs. Just as I knew that Katy would love the perfume, I knew that Nikolas would love some freshly baked cookies. Choosing from the selection of gingerbread, snickerdoodle, and Russian thumbprint cookies Mom and I had made earlier, I put them all into a brightly colored round tin. When it was stuffed full, I snapped the lid shut and added a bow.

It was time to play Santa.

I navigated the streets outside carefully, trying to avoid any patches of hidden ice. The snow was still falling, and a fine film stuck wetly to the ground. I slipped and slid every now and then, but I successfully managed not to drop my bag of loot along the way. It didn't take me long to get across town, and the Maxwells' house soon came into sight.

I stepped cautiously up the narrow stairs and stomped my feet once I'd reached the landing. There had always been a slight gap in the sheer white curtains that covered the front window overlooking the porch, and I peeked through it as I sat my bag down on a dry spot.

Both of the Maxwells were sitting on a small couch, and they appeared to be in deep conversation. I watched as Mr. M. gestured wildly with his hands while Mrs. M. shook her head. When I peered closer, I could see that her eyes were red, and she had a bunched-up tissue in her hand. Obviously this was not the best time to interrupt.

Quietly I dug into my present bag and withdrew their gift. Fluffing out the edges of the slightly crushed bow, I looked around for the safest spot to put it. The door frame caught my eye. It was large, deep, and dry.

I wedged the present in so that it sat propped at an angle, and readjusted it once or twice before knocking softly on the door. Even if they didn't answer right away, I knew they would find it sooner or later. Picking up my bag and giving a final glance over my shoulder, I crept off the porch and headed toward the cemetery. On to my next destination.

I pulled my coat tighter around me as I walked, feeling the sting of the biting snow. I didn't realize how much of a difference it had made standing under a covered porch for those couple of minutes. It was *freezing* out here.

Instead of turning back, though, I trudged on, gripping my bag tightly. When I came to the large cemetery gates, I picked up my pace. I still had quite a walk in front of me, and the weather was getting worse. Taking the main path, I made my way past the Irving grave site and went farther on to the other side of the cemetery. The route was still fresh in my mind, and I followed the winding road, making several turns when I needed to.

With the cold breath of winter in the air, the forest around me was gray and ominous. There weren't any birds out this time, and most of the plants had withered away. It all looked so barren and empty; it was a vast difference from the last time I'd been here.

I turned my eyes ahead, continuing down the path in front of me. I couldn't afford to stop now. Stuck in a snowstorm was *not* somewhere I wanted to be.

Spotting the large stone chimney, I ran the rest of the way and knocked loudly when I reached the front door. It swung open immediately, and Nikolas stood there looking concerned, with Katy by his side.

Their eyes lit up when they saw it was me, and they tried to wave me in, but I put up a hand. "I can't stay long. I just wanted to wish you guys a Merry Christmas and give you these." I pulled their gifts from my bag and thrust them into their hands.

A huge grin broke out on Nikolas's face as he passed the perfume back to Katy. She held the bottle up to the faint light behind her and examined it eagerly.

"It's perfume," I explained. "Remember I told you that I make perfume? This scent is for you, Katy. You just unscrew the top and hold your finger over it while tilting it upside down. That's how you get some out."

She unscrewed the lid and did as I'd instructed, then held her finger up to her nose to smell. "It's wonderful!" she exclaimed, a look of pure delight on her face. "I smell honeysuckle vines and wild violets. Two of my favorite things. You have quite a talent, Abbey. Thank you very much for my beautiful gift."

I nodded, impressed with her ability to pick out the individual scents.

Nikolas quickly turned the attention to his gift, by loudly popping off the tin top. Katy and I laughed at the expression of glee on his face when he saw what was inside. "Cookies! Did you, by chance, happen to make any of these, Abbey?"

I nodded again, in response to his question. "Yeah, I helped make them."

 400

"They look delicious. Thank you, Abbey. It means even more to me knowing that you have put your time and attention into them."

I blushed, overcome by their words of praise. "It was nothing. Really. You've both been so nice to me that I just wanted to give you a small token of my thanks."

"Why don't you come in and warm up for a while?" suggested Katy. "I'll make us some tea."

I shook my head regretfully. "I'd love to, but I can't. I have one more stop to make, and then I have to get home for dinner. In fact, I'd better be on my way."

Katy leaned forward to give me a quick hug. "All right, dear. But come see us again for a visit after Christmas, okay? We have much to talk about."

"Okay." Nikolas stepped forward to give me a side hug, and I got lost for a moment in a memory of my grandfather and his bear hugs. I squeezed Nikolas tight, wishing even as I let him go that he was my grandpa. That would be a nice Christmas gift.

Katy disappeared for a minute and then returned. She had a small bundle in her hands. "I almost forgot. This is for you, dear. We weren't sure when we would see you again, so we've been holding on to it. Merry Christmas."

I accepted the bundle she held out to me and tucked it safely into my bag. "Thank you. Thank you both. And Merry Christmas to you, too. I'll definitely be back to see you after Christmas. Save some peppermint tea for me."

They laughed and waved as I started down the path that led away from their house. I threw one last grin over my shoulder and called out "Merry Christmas to all, and to all a good night!" but the wind tore my words away and scattered them to the trees around me. Looking up at the ever darkening sky, I hunkered into my coat, and set off to find my way back to the cemetery.

I was almost out of time.

When I finally made it back to the trail, I followed it until it brought me to a familiar tombstone, and I stopped short, struck again by the vivid reminder that my best friend was dead.

I grabbed Kristen's perfume vial, and then dropped my bag to the ground. Uncorking the vial, I held it carefully, trying not to spill any. Then I carried it over and knelt directly in front of the tombstone. I brushed away some snow caught in the etched lettering carved onto its surface before I spoke. "Hey, Kris, Merry Christmas Eve. I brought you a present." Dumping the perfume onto the frozen ground, I watched it slowly eat through a thin layer of snow and ice.

402

The sweet scent of grapefruit, ginger, and vanilla rose up around me. "I have to go now," I said, "but I wanted to let you know that your mom and dad won't be alone on Christmas. They've agreed to come over for dinner. Oh, and I gave them their gift already. I had a star named for you."

I tucked the now empty vial near some fake flowers at the foot of her tombstone then stood up. "Bye, Kristen. See you tomorrow. I won't forget our tradition."

The wind roared again, and I turned away, stooping to pick up my bag as I went. The fastest way out of the cemetery was to pass the Irving family plot, so I chose that way, sneaking a quick peek as I walked by.

I noticed immediately that the metal gate was open, and wedged with a large rock to keep it in place. I climbed up the stairs, intrigued as to who would have left the gate that way. A quick scan of the enclosed area revealed that it hadn't been done by anyone intent on vandalizing the graves. Nothing was disturbed.

Instead, it appeared to have been done for *me*....

A long, flat box was propped up next to Washington Irving's grave, and my name was boldly scrawled on it. Or rather, as I could tell when I got closer, my nickname was scrawled on it.

A bittersweet pang struck my heart while I gazed around me. The package had definitely not been here when I'd passed by earlier. It must have been dropped off while I was at the cottage. Apparently the giver had decided not to stick around, though, because he was nowhere in sight.

Scooping it up, I shook off some snow and held it reverently. The words DO NOT OPEN TILL CHRISTMAS were written in big block letters under the name *Astrid*, with several stern exclamation points. I smiled and looked around me again before withdrawing Caspian's gifts from my bag.

Unwinding the long black scarf from my neck, I used that as an extra layer of protection for Caspian's small pile. I had no idea how long it would be before he found them, but I hoped they wouldn't get too wet. Placing them in exactly the same spot as he'd placed mine, I kissed one fingertip and touched it to the pile. If I didn't get to see him at all for Christmas, then this would have to be my silent message to him.

The cold snow started settling rapidly on my bare neck and quickly reminded me of where I was, so I tucked the gift from him into my bag and stepped away from the grave. "Merry Christmas, Caspian," I whispered to the wind. "I love you."

Chapter Twenty-one

A TRADITION

If ever I should wish for a retreat, whither I might steal from the world and its distractions . . . I know of none more promising than this little valley.

—"The Legend of Sleepy Hollow"

The snow made a cold companion while I hurried home. Dinner was beef stew with freshly baked bread, and it smelled heavenly. Mom and Dad seemed to be just as distracted as I was, and we all shuffled along one by one into the kitchen, where we filled up a soup mug and then wandered off to our own little corners. It was obviously a buffet night.

I carried my dinner and my bounty up to my room, eager to look at my gifts. The stew was still way too hot, so I set it down on the desk and put the bag of presents on my bed. I shrugged out of the wet jacket I still had on, hung it up on the back of my door, and kicked my soggy shoes off. After finding a warm pair of sweatpants and a long sleeve T-shirt, I was dry once again and quickly settled in.

Picking up Caspian's gift, and then the one from Nikolas and Katy, I laid them side by side and sank down onto the bed to look them over. Caspian's was hard to inspect because all I could see from the outside was just a plain brown box. The warning to wait until Christmas ate at my conscience, and I glanced at the clock. Four and a half more hours to go until midnight. . . .

Technically, if I waited till then, it would be Christmas morning and I could open it without violating the rules. It was a minor technicality, but it worked for me. I pushed Caspian's gift off to the side and distracted myself with Nikolas and Katy's bundle. At least I could open one gift early.

The bundle turned out to actually be some type of long red quilted material, and once I started unwinding it, the package inside got smaller and smaller. A beautiful china teacup was revealed when I pulled away the last of the fabric. It was small and dainty, with a fluted edge and handle, both rimmed in gold leafing. Tiny pink roses were scattered over the surface, and it looked like each one had been painted on by hand.

I picked it up and admired it from every angle. There appeared to be something stuffed inside the cup, so I tipped it over onto the bed. A smaller bunch of red material, a piece of wood, and a sheet of paper all came fluttering out. I examined the paper first, grinning excitedly when I saw a recipe for peppermint tea was handwritten on it. It touched my heart that they had put so much evident thought into this gift. They couldn't have picked anything more perfect to give me.

The small bundle of cloth was next, and I held it up and stretched it out a bit. I could tell immediately that it was a pair of knitted red gloves, and I turned back to the longer piece of cloth, belatedly realizing that it was a matching scarf. They were lovely, *and* had been made in my favorite color. Katy was a good guesser.

I donned the gloves and scarf and reached for the piece of wood. It fit into the palm of my hand and was an exact replica of the sign on the iron gates that read SLEEPY HOLLOW CEMETERY.

The details were *amazing*. Obviously hand carved, each letter was bold, and stood out with a shadowed background. The word "Caretakers" had been etched onto the back. I could tell that Nikolas had spent many hours laboring over it. Touched again by their kindness and generosity, I reminded myself to stop over to see them as soon as I could. Maybe I'd even bring some more cookies with me.

Getting up from the bed, I placed the teacup and wooden carving on my desk, and then reached for the stew. It was a bit awkward with the gloves on, but at that point I didn't really care. Exhaustion was setting in, and I just wanted to eat my dinner as quickly as I could.

After finishing the last couple of bites, I set the empty mug on the desk again and went to lie down next to Caspian's presents. My stomach was pleasantly full, and I felt drowsiness hit me like a jackhammer. It would be okay if I took a *little* nap. After all, I had almost four hours to kill. . . .

When I woke up, the clock was blinking 12:48 and I was danger-ously close to rolling over onto the box that Caspian had left me. I sat up groggily and pulled an extra blanket around my shoulders before peeling off the gloves I still wore. Glancing over at the clock again, I picked the cardboard box up. The time had finally come.

A nervous feeling hit my stomach, but I forced it back and ripped one end of the box open.

A thin spiral bound notebook and a tiny package wrapped in

red paper were inside, and I slid out the tiny package first. It was similar in shape and size to the red fabric that my necklace had been wrapped in before, and I decided to open that one first. As I tore the paper off in one long strip, another necklace was revealed.

I gazed at it in awe and held it up to the light.

Made in the same fashion as the first one, this pendant had a drawing of the Headless Horseman on one side and a fat orange pumpkin on the other. The Horseman was a bold, black charcoal outline, beautiful and dramatic, while the pumpkin was fully colored and shaded in. It looked like it had been plucked from the nearest pumpkin patch.

Both drawings were flawless, and completely lifelike. To say that I was merely happy with it would have been a huge disservice. It was a perfect representation of the legend that I loved. I couldn't *believe* that he'd made me another necklace.

Jumping off the bed, I ran to put the necklace on. I turned from side to side to look at it in the mirror, marveling at its beauty. Then I remembered the notebook.

I ran back to the bed to return my attention to it, and tilted the box over. The notebook slid out, making a dull thumping noise as it hit the covers. A drawing of a pencil was on the cover, but the back was made out of cardboard. I opened it up, and the first page was titled simply "The Sketchbook."

I was stunned when I flipped over to the next page.

Caspian had drawn a gorgeous picture of the cemetery with sharp jagged lines of tombstones accented against the softer curves of grass and trees. He had captured every minute detail, down to the inscriptions on the tombstones and the curled edges of stray leaves that had drifted down from the trees.

The paper crinkled slightly when I touched it, and I sat back in silence. Maybe I should have made him something too. This gift was so personal, so . . . *amazing*. What if he didn't like the telescope and book I'd gotten him? How could anything store-bought compare to the obvious time and effort he had spent creating this?

Worry and doubt set in, and I started flipping through the pages to distract myself. It looked like the whole notebook was filled with drawings. There was one of the bridge, and one of the river. Another one was of Washington Irving's grave, and the one after that was a picture of the tall iron gates guarding the cemetery entrance. They were all done in charcoal, ranging from simple black outlines to scenes with countless amounts of light and dark gray shadows.

I was startled when one of the last pages revealed a drawing of me, and I looked at it closer. Caspian had drawn me sitting next to Kristen's grave, looking out into the distance. A couple strands of hair blew slightly in a nonexistent breeze, and the sadness was clearly evident in my eyes. He had titled it "Abbey & Kristen."

I slowly flipped over to the next page, unsure of what I would find.

There was another drawing of me there, this time at the river on prom night. Caspian had captured the rushing water perfectly, and me in my black dress, lying in the middle of it with my hair floating all around me. He had even drawn the black choker necklace I'd worn that night, and my eyes were blazing. This portrait was titled "Abbey's Pain."

The second-to-last page showed a picture of a storefront, downtown on Main Street. I hadn't given him very many details, but it was drawn exactly like the shop I'd picked out for my own. He'd also added a sign on top of the store that said ABBEY'S HOLLOW. This portrait was named "Abbey's Future."

A tear suddenly rolled down my cheek, and I wiped it away, trying very hard not to let it smear any of the lines on the page. Hesitation made me stop before I flipped to the last page, but I knew I couldn't *not* look at it. So I counted to three and held my breath as I turned to the drawing.

It was just me, my hands at my hips and my hair pushed off to one side, in jeans and a tank top. He had written "Abbey the Brave" at the bottom of the page, and I couldn't figure out why. Then I saw a slight gap between the waistband of my jeans and the bottom of my shirt. At first I thought I was imagining it.

But I wasn't.

Right where my left hip bone would be, Caspian had drawn a tattoo. The design looked like some type of triangle and circle pattern, a replica of his. I smiled and shook my head, feeling a warm glow settle over me. How was I going to tell him "Thank you" for *this*?

As I carefully closed the notebook, a letter fell out from the pages, and I picked it up, wondering how I'd missed it. Paying close attention to every word, I eagerly started reading.

Dear Abbey,

I hope you like the Christmas presents. I wanted to get you something that reminded you of me. I don't know where to go from here. I don't think this is working. What I want and what I can have are two very different things. I'm sorry. It just has to be this way.

Merry Christmas (I hope).

Love, Caspian

My heart stopped beating and sunk like a rock at those words. The warm glow faded, and I felt chilled to the very depths of my being. Was he breaking up with me? Did we even have something *to* break up? I lowered my head to my hands and thought about it calmly for a minute before the tears came. But then they really came.

Pushing the pictures over the edge of the bed, I removed the necklace and shoved it under my pillow. I buried myself under a mountain of covers and used my pillow to muffle my sobs as I cried myself to sleep.

It would definitely be a blue Christmas for me.

My eyes felt crusty and swollen when I woke up the next morning, and a glance in the mirror confirmed that they looked as bad as they felt. My nose was stuffed up too, so I crawled back into bed to lie under the covers for a couple more hours.

Mom was the first one to try to get me up, asking over and over again why I wasn't downstairs opening any presents yet. When the thought of free things didn't even faze me, I knew I had it bad.

Eventually I crawled out of bed and stumbled downstairs like a zombie. Mom's and Dad's faces were all happy and excited, and I went through the motions of unwrapping gifts, but I didn't really care what they'd gotten me.

As the pile of clothes, books, shoes, CDs, and perfume supplies grew, I felt worse and worse. I tried to put on a happy face when I gave them their gifts, and they both seemed genuinely excited to get them, especially Dad. But even that didn't last long, and I think Mom was starting to see it was all an act.

"Are you feeling sick, Abbey?" she asked me, taking her time to sort, fold, and arrange each piece of torn wrapping paper that she came across.

I nodded my head, too miserable to say anything else. With my red eyes and stuffy nose, I *looked* sick. And inside, I definitely *felt* sick. I made my way over to the window, leaned against the glass, and stared outside. It was a white Christmas after all. Mom continued to work around me, stopping once to feel my forehead with the back of her hand and mutter something about temperatures.

414

Dad had started cooking breakfast, and it didn't take long for a plate of extra, extra chocolate chip pancakes with a side of bacon and eggs to appear in front of me. I didn't feel hungry, or full, or anything else. I just felt blank and empty inside.

I picked at the pancakes so Dad's feelings wouldn't be hurt, but ignored everything else. After a couple minutes, though, I handed the plate off to Mom, told them both thanks for the gifts, and headed back upstairs. Today just felt like a stay-in-bed kind of day, and I wasn't going to fight it.

When I made it up to my room, I just lay there for a while. I couldn't get to sleep, and my thoughts seemed to roam from one topic to the next. It was like I couldn't shut my brain off. Finally I pulled the sheets all the way over my head and tried to make a cocoon of sorts, to curl up and die in. My hand hit something cold and hard when I moved the pillow, and I grabbed at it, feeling a pit of dread fill up my stomach as I pulled whatever it was free.

As soon as my eyes recognized it, the floodgates opened again. Instantly more tears came, and I cried softly to myself as I sat there stroking the smooth glass. I turned it over and over again compulsively. And while I don't think it's actually possible to cry *while* you're asleep, I couldn't tell the difference. My tears felt like they would never end.

 415

Hours later I felt a slow pull, that lazy urge that tells you it's time to get up because you've been sleeping for far too long. But I wanted to fight it. I wanted to stay where I was forever, and never move another muscle again. *Ever.*

However, the pull was strong and I became more and more awake, even as I lay there with my eyes tightly closed. I could tell that it was later in the day because the light had shifted. Shadows played behind my eyes, and I opened them to a darkened room with a blinking alarm clock that let me know exactly how late it really was.

Sitting up slowly, I took in my surroundings. Everything looked different half cloaked in the dark, and I tried to shake off my grogginess. Something nagged at the back of my mind until I remembered what day it was. I didn't have very much time left.

I climbed wearily out of bed and pulled on a pair of jeans and a sweater as quickly as I could. But I had to stop several times to give myself a break. Every muscle in my body ached. *Who knew crying could take so much out of you?* I grabbed my gloves and scarf and slid them on while I took the stairs two at a time. I was really going to have to hurry to get back in time for dinner with the Maxwells.

I hit the kitchen, and headed for the cabinet that held the old Tupperware and extra lunch boxes, and nearly tripped over a chair. I dug through all the containers near the back of the cabinet and pulled out a small insulated traveling thermos. Just what I was looking for. Then I made my way over to the fridge and pulled out several juice containers.

Mom came in when my back was turned, but there was a tone of disapproval in her voice. "What are you doing, Abbey?"

I tried to act like I didn't hear her, while I looked for my prize. Time was ticking away, and I had to do this before Christmas night was over.

"And why do you have gloves and a scarf on? Are you that cold? Let me feel your forehead again."

I was searching desperately now, moving egg cartons and bowls of cookie dough out of the way. "I'm not cold, Mom. I'm just looking for the eggnog. Did you buy any this year? You always buy some." I risked a quick glance in her direction. "And why do we have three cartons of milk? Who drinks that much milk?"

She stepped closer, trying to reach out and feel my forehead.

"It's on the left, two tubs of butter and one bag of celery over," she sighed. "But maybe you should have some hot tea instead. I don't know if eggnog would be good for you right now."

I held up the thermos while I moved the butter tubs and grabbed the nog. "It's not for me, Mom. It's our tradition, remember?"

A stern look crossed her face and she was already shaking her head before I'd even finished talking. "Not this year, it's not. You're not going outside in this weather. The Maxwells will be here any minute."

I looked pointedly at the clock on the wall behind me before unscrewing the thermos lid and pouring in the eggnog. "They won't be here for another twenty-three minutes, at least. And I won't be gone long. You know I have to do this, Mom. I can't let Kristen down. I already told her that I'd be doing it for both of us this year."

The thermos lid slid back on and it screwed on tight before clicking into place with a loud *pop*. I put the eggnog and the juice and milk containers back into the fridge, then slammed the door.

"You told *who* already? What do you mean by that?" Mom looked befuddled.

"I told Kristen. You know . . . at her grave. I told her that I would be doing it for both of us today. Look, I'm all bundled up, and I'll even button my coat all the way to the top. But I have to

418

go. It'll be quick, and I'll be back in time for dinner, but in order to do that, I have to leave now."

I kissed her on the cheek and scooped up the thermos. Then I headed over to the closet for my jacket. She was standing there with her mouth wide open. She spluttered for a minute and held up a finger to me. "Fine, Abbey. But if you get pneumonia, don't say I didn't warn you. And if you are late for dinner, we're *not* waiting."

"Okay, Mom," I called back from the doorway as I buttoned my coat one-handed. "See you soon. Love you, too."

Her final words came drifting out to me, half mumbled as I closed the front door. "Don't think I'm going to spend all day making chicken soup when you *do* get sick!"

I smiled to myself. Who did she think she was kidding? There would probably be hot chocolate waiting for me when I got home tonight.

Holding my thermos in one hand and my coat with the other, I kept my head down and walked quickly. The snow was still falling, swirling all around me and crunching loudly beneath my feet. If it kept up at this rate, we'd have a blizzard in the morning.

As I trudged onward, I thought about the first time I'd done this. . . .

~ ~ ~

"Hurry up, Kristen. The sun will be going down soon. I wanted to do this in the daylight."

"Why don't we just do it at night, Abbey? It'll be spookier that way. And are you sure the low-fat sugar free eggnog will be okay?" she called out to me. "That's all my mom bought this year."

I laughed at her question. "Of course the sugar free kind is okay. It's not like he's actually going to drink any of it. It's just symbolic. And it's not supposed *to be spooky. Leaving letters on his grave on Halloween night was spooky. But Christmas? Not for the spooky."*

"Yeah?" Kristen giggled. "Well, tell that to Tim Burton. He thinks Christmas is all about the spooky."

We both laughed as we walked uphill and pushed through the cemetery gates. As we came closer to his grave, Kristen leaned in and whispered, "I think we should make this a yearly tradition."

"Agreed," I whispered back.

I smiled at the memory. We'd had so much fun together. It was hard to believe it wouldn't happen again. The thought sobered me, and when I reached the main gates, my fingers slipped on the cold, wet iron. Frustration welled up inside me and I slammed my thermos against the gate in a sudden burst of anger. "Damn it!"

It did nothing, of course, except send a clanging pain through my arm and my shoulder blade, and I lowered my head for a minute before trying again.

This time, as I concentrated, the gate moved forward just enough for me to slip in, and I was grateful for small favors. I rushed down to Kristen's grave first, skidding to a halt in front of it. "I'm here, Kristen. I brought the eggnog." I held up the thermos. "I'll let him know that it's from both of us. Merry Christmas."

I felt a strange feeling of release as I stared down at her stone. Maybe it really *was* okay that I didn't know all of her secrets and would never find out who D. was. Maybe the important thing was the fact that she had *wanted* to tell me, but for whatever reasons just couldn't. Maybe that had to be enough.

Lifting a hand, I waved before I turned and headed in the direction of Washington Irving's grave. The snow was getting harder and harder to see through, so I hurried to get over there as fast as I could.

Once I made it up the stairs and through the gate without slipping, I swept a glance over the family plot. I was glad to see that Caspian's gifts were gone, but sad to see that he was nowhere in sight. My tattered and bruised heart gave a little shudder, but I brushed the feeling aside and bent to the task at hand.

Next to the gravestone I hurriedly unscrewed the lid to the thermos. It was not an easy task to do with my gloves on, but it was way too cold to take them off, even for a couple of seconds. A minute later I had success, and I poured a small amount into the lid before holding it up to the grave. "Happy Christmas to you, Mr. Irving. It will have to be quick, but this one's from me and Kristen. May all your yules be merry."

I tapped the stone gently with my mug, and then swigged my eggnog before dumping the contents of the thermos into the frozen dirt before me. I waited a brief second in silence, and nodded my head once. "See you in the new year."

Getting to my feet, I re-capped the thermos as I navigated my way out of the family plot. The daylight was almost gone, and I took small steps, mindful of the possibility of dangerous hidden ice. When I was finally clear of the cemetery, I picked up my pace, so the walk home didn't take very long. I arrived at the front door at the same time the Maxwells were stepping into the hallway to clean off their snow covered boots and coats.

I gave them both quick hugs and welcomed them before Mr.

Maxwell went in. Kristen's mom had a quizzical look on her face when she saw the thick layer of snow I had on my coat. I held up the thermos as my answer to her unspoken question. "Just had to go drop by an old friend's place. It's a tradition."

She smiled a little as she nodded her head. I could tell by the look in her eye that she knew exactly what I was talking about. She reached out for another hug and held me tight for a moment, then loosened her grip. "I wanted to say thank you for the beautiful gift, Abbey. It really meant a lot to us."

"You're welcome," I replied.

She linked her arm through mine, and we walked to our seats. Mom had really outdone herself, and the table, covered by various plates, platters, dishes, and bowls, was literally groaning from the weight of the food.

I sat down to the left of Mrs. M. and picked up my glass of water when everyone else held up their champagne flutes for a toast. "To happy holidays, healthy new years, and good memories of the ones we love," bellowed Dad.

"To the ones we love," echoed the rest of the table.

Looking out the window at the snow, I made my own silent toast. "To the ones we love . . ."

Chapter Twenty-two

A NEW PARTNER

He who wins a thousand common hearts is therefore entitled to some renown; but he who keeps undisputed sway over the heart of a coquette, is indeed a hero.

—"The Legend of Sleepy Hollow"

January came in with a bang. Or at least it did for everyone else. Mine was more of a dull thud. I spent New Year's Eve alone, too depressed to even wait for the ball to drop. Mom and Dad went out to celebrate with some friends, so I went to bed early. It wasn't like I had anything to be happy about.

My boyfriend didn't want to be my boyfriend. My best friend was still dead. And midterms were about to start as soon as I went back to school.

Definitely nothing to be happy about.

In my last few fleeting days of freedom, I worked nonstop on my Sleepy Hollow perfume project. I'd decided to make one scent for each of the main characters, but first I wanted to create scents that evoked the settings and emotions of the legend. I had the perfect combination in mind for one I wanted to call the Midnight Hour, and I spent long hours trying to perfect it.

I thought about working on my business plan, but the temptation to play with perfumes was too strong, and the distraction from my thoughts was therapeutic. Overall, it was a somber and quiet yet productive holiday.

When school started up again, we had two final days of prep before midterms began. I was actually glad for the extra schoolwork, and I buried myself in books the entire time. It seemed like I had forgotten almost everything that we'd reviewed before the holidays. My brain felt hollow and stuffy. Uncle Bob probably would have joked about my head rattling.

In the end I surprised even myself by managing to pass all my tests. I barely squeaked by in math, pulling in a low C, but I got a B in history, and everything else was in the A range. Mom and Dad gave me a well-rehearsed you've-got-to-apply-yourself-more speech, of course, but I let it go in one ear and out the other. They probably would have given me that same speech if I'd brought home all A minuses.

We didn't get much of a break at school once our midterm week was over. The next bombshell was dropped on us the following Monday morning in science class. Mr. Knickerbocker waited patiently until everyone was seated and had their textbooks out before he made the big announcement.

I was fidgeting with my pencil, rolling it back and forth on the desktop, when I heard him clear his throat. "Ladies and Gents, if I can please have your attention."

The quiet chatter came to a stop and the room grew still.

"I know you're all very sad that midterms are finished." We groaned on cue, and he gave a wide fake smile. "But I have some good news for you."

His stiff brown tie bobbed slightly and he started pacing in front of the chalkboard, hands clasped behind his back. There was no way this was good news. Science did *not* equal good news.

He came to a halt and held one finger up. "It's science time, people." Another groan filled the air, but he kept right on talking, like he didn't hear us. "To be precise, it's science fair time. That wonderful time of year when you get to rack your tiny little brains and then dazzle me with your brilliance."

I rolled my eyes. This was *definitely* not good news. Mr. Knickerbocker had a reputation for not letting people pick their own partners for science fair, and with my luck I'd get stuck with one of the girls from the cheerleading squad.

"This year, instead of devising an alternate way of picking partners, I'm just going to do it alphabetically starting from Z. As soon as you and your partner are paired up, I'll expect you to change seats. You'll be sitting next to your partner for the rest of the school year."

Now I *really* held my breath, and even said a silent prayer. Mentally working my way through the alphabet, I breathed a sigh of relief when I realized that none of the cheerleaders' last names started with an *A*, *B*, or *C*.

Mr. Knickerbocker continued on. "You'll have three months to work on your project. Entries are due during the second week of April. At that time we'll be holding the science fair and you'll be responsible for giving a presentation on your project. This will make up twenty-five percent of your grade, people, so think long and hard. Any questions, please see me after class."

I tuned out when he started assigning partner names, and the room quickly filled with the sounds of scraping chairs and squeaking desks. It took him a surprisingly long time to get to my name, and I pasted a bored expression onto my face, hoping that whomever I got stuck with would get the hint that I did *not* want to make any new friends.

Chairs were still scraping loudly, and students were settling in, when he finally called my name, so I missed who was supposed to be my partner. I sat frozen in my seat, hoping that the person who would be sitting beside me for the next couple of months was making their move. Because I sure wasn't.

Glancing discreetly over my shoulder, I saw a girl sitting behind me with an identical look of boredom on her face, and an empty chair next to her. I turned back around to move my books and go sit by her, when all of a sudden Ben plopped down next to me.

"What are you doing?" I asked him. *I'm confused* was probably written all over my face.

He just raised his eyebrows and grinned at me. "I'm Bennett. You're Browning, right?"

Comprehension still hadn't dawned. "Yeah, so?"

"I'm your partner," he laughed.

My cheeks turned red. "Oh," I said lamely. "I must not have been paying attention."

He shook his head and piled his books neatly over to one

side. "So, any ideas for what we can do? Or were you not paying attention to anything Mr. Knickerbocker said?"

I kicked his foot under the desk, and felt a gleam of satisfaction when he doubled over. He was still laughing, but I could tell he wasn't being mean about it.

"No, Mr. Hotshot Listener, I don't have any ideas. What about you?"

He rattled off an idea involving math, DNA, and some type of space travel, but I was already shaking my head. "Come on. Get real, science nerd. It's a science project, not science fiction. If you want to be responsible for the entire project, then by all means be my guest and go for that one. But if you actually want *me* to do any work, then we have to pick something a little less *Star Trek* and a little more . . . normal."

Crossing his arms in front of his chest, he leaned back on two legs of the chair. "Well, if you don't have any ideas, then how can you contribute?"

I shrugged. "I don't know. I'll go to the library and look in a book or something. There's got to be a ton of ideas in there."

Now he shrugged. "Whatever. But I don't want you to skip over any cool ideas, so I'll come too."

"Do you have a free study hall last period?" I asked.

He nodded.

"Okay. We'll go then."

He leaned his chair back down onto the ground and winked at me. "Great! It's a date."

I just buried my face in my hands and shook my head. It was going to be a really *long* three months.

I had agreed to meet Ben by the main school doors at the end of our last class, and I tugged impatiently on the strap of my book bag while I waited for him. The bell had rung ten minutes ago, and I was ready to get out of here before anyone questioned what I was doing just hanging around.

He showed up five minutes later, grinning shamefully and spouting off some sorry excuse, but I was already sailing through the double doors, content to leave him behind. He caught up with me a minute later, and tugged on my book bag when I started to turn left, in the direction of the library. "Where are you going?" he asked. "Parking lot's in the other direction."

I came to a stop. "It's not that far to the library. I just figured we'd walk."

Ben shook his head. "I'm not leaving my car here, and it's freezing. Come on."

I exhaled loudly as I followed him to the student parking lot, navigating the maze of cars as we went.

"What am I looking for?" I called, scanning in several directions.

"It's right over here."

I couldn't see him anymore, so I followed the sound of his voice and stopped when I came to a battered green Jeep Cherokee. He was sitting inside, revving the engine.

"Your chariot waits," he said over the loud noise. "Come on, get in." I tried not to laugh when a puff of black smoke shot out the exhaust.

Chucking my bag into the backseat, I shook my head as I climbed in on the passenger side. "You know, you're really pushy."

He slowly pulled out of the parking space, and I struggled with the seat belt at my shoulder. "Here," he said, reaching over and giving it a sharp tug, "you have to find its sweet spot."

I burst out laughing. "Your car has a sweet spot? You're kidding, right? Next you'll tell me that you've named it too."

He kept his eyes on the road, but nodded. "Of course. All good cars have names. This here is Candy Christine."

I couldn't help it. I exploded with more laughter. "Candy Christine? Did you come up with that name when you were twelve?"

His cheeks turned a bright red and he took his time checking all of his mirrors before answering me. "How'd you guess? I got the car when I was twelve, helped my dad piece it back together, and when it came time for a name, I . . . uh . . . just put my two favorite things at the time together. I was going through a real Stephen King phase."

I kept laughing. The image was just too much. Twelve-year-old Ben naming his future car Candy Christine was absurdly funny to me.

"I'm sorry," I gasped in between bouts of laughter. "I guess we can be glad that you didn't wait until you were older to name her. Candy probably isn't number one on your list of favorite things anymore."

He shrugged. "You're right. If I would have waited to name her until I got my license, then she would have been a different kind of Candy." Grinning wickedly, he laughed when I turned red as I realized what he meant.

Yeah, I probably should have kept my mouth shut on the whole naming-of-the-car thing. But he took mercy on me and stopped teasing. "So what are you driving?"

"I'm not." I sighed ruefully. "My parents are making me wait to get my license until I'm seventeen."

"Man, that sucks. No wheels equals no freedom. I can't imagine what I'd do if I didn't have Candy Christine. She's like family."

"It's not too bad," I said. "My parents are pretty loose with the rules, so I go wherever I want. And since I grew up walking everywhere, I kind of just got used to not having a car of my own. My mom drops me off at my job on the weekends."

We had reached the library, and he guided the car along until we found the first open parking spot. "You have a job? That's cool. Where at?"

I explained as we got out of the car and walked up the library steps. He listened to what I said, and held the door for me while we stepped inside. I didn't get the chance to ask him whether or not he had a job, because we were immediately greeted by a stony-faced librarian who gave us a very stern look.

Stopping midsentence, I lowered my voice. "What section do you think we should start looking in first?"

"Let's see if they have a section for students," he suggested. "We might find something there."

I agreed, and we quickly set out looking for that section. We didn't find anything on the first floor, and the second floor turned out to be a bust too. But the third floor gave us exactly what we were looking for. "Over here." Ben gestured as we rounded the banister and took the last step up. "I can see a student section." I followed him in through an archway, and we split up, each taking an end.

"It looks like there's a whole section on science project ideas," I called out from my half of the shelf.

"I found some different books specifically on math and science," echoed back to me.

I spent a couple more minutes browsing. I must have been concentrating really hard, because I jumped a mile when Ben came around the corner and surprised me. His arms were loaded down with books. "Here. I'm going to go see how many we're allowed to check out."

After dumping the books in a pile at my feet, he jogged off, and I turned my attention back to the shelf. By the time he returned, I'd added several books of my own to his sizeable pile.

"The librarian said we can only check out eight books at a time," he said, eyeing the stack in front of me. "And even if we *both* check out eight, we have a *lot* more than that here."

I looked at the pile and quickly counted. We had thirty-two books between us.

"The librarian also mentioned some type of study room a couple of floors up, and she said we could reserve it for two hours," he continued on. "So I just told her we'd use that for now. Feel up to carrying some books with me?"

My stomach dropped. And not because I was frightened of carrying books. No, it had a little something to do with the fact that I knew exactly what study room he was talking about. I faltered for a moment, but then shook it off. "Sure," I said nonchalantly. "Let's go."

We each gathered up an armful of books, and Ben made sure to pick up twice as many as I did. I gave him a scornful look, but he just turned away and started walking toward the door. "It's the manly thing to do," he called over his shoulder. "I have to carry more books than you."

I readjusted the stack in my arms and followed him, trying to keep my thoughts to myself. *This won't be too hard. It's just a room. I can totally do this. I will not think about Caspian at all, and instead I will focus solely on what type of project Ben and I should do for the science fair.*

When we finally came to the room, I heaved my books down onto the table. Momentarily distracted by the sharp ache in my arms, I swore to myself that I would start working out one of these days. A couple more trips like that would kill me.

Ben set his books down too, and gave the room a brief once-over. "I guess this is it for the next two hours." He glanced up at the peeling paint on the ceiling, and the faded pictures on the walls. "Looks like they blew their decorating budget on all the *other* rooms in the library."

I gave him a wry smile as I spread my books out in front of me and sat down. Then I carefully gave his books a gentle nudge over to the opposite side of the table. He was still prowling around the room, and I tried to ignore him, picking up a particularly heavy-looking book before opening it up to the table of contents.

"They obviously don't want anyone getting away with anything in here," he said, pointing to the KEEP THIS DOOR OPEN AT ALL TIMES sign.

I froze.

Caspian's words came back to me, and in my head I heard my response. *Well, they never said anything about keeping it* wide *open.* Ruthlessly banishing the memory, I forced my attention back to the book and stared down at the page in front of me.

But I wasn't seeing words. I was seeing a memory of white

blond hair and deep green eyes that sparkled above a wide smile. That vivid black streak stood out, and for a second I swore that I could almost touch it.

Ben's hand waving in front of my face broke the moment, and my thought was shattered. I looked over at him and raised an eyebrow. "Yes?"

He was sitting down now, over where I had pushed his books, and he looked aggravated. "I was calling your name, but you didn't answer me. Are you okay?"

No, I'm not okay! my brain screamed, but I just gave him an annoyed look. "Sorry. I was concentrating. We *do* have to get some work done here, you know."

He leaned back in his chair and flipped open a book. "Fine. Let me know when you find something."

I shrugged and turned back to the page in front of me, half-heartedly flipping through a couple of different sections. I knew I should be paying attention to what was in front of me, but it was really hard to make my brain cooperate.

Reminding myself once again of the no-thinking-about-Caspian rule, I started reading about a project that used different scents and a blindfold to test the five senses. I quickly got caught up in that section. It sounded like an interesting idea.

Ben interrupted my train of thought. "Do you think we could get our hands on petroleum, alcohol, and ethanol? It would all be used strictly in the name of science, of course. I think that we could make our own gasoline."

Placing my finger on the spot where I'd been reading, I looked over at him. "And the point of that would be . . . ?"

"To not have to pay for gas for my car anymore," he said. "Do you have any idea how much a gallon of unleaded is going for right now?"

I rolled my eyes. "We are *not* going to figure out how to make gas for your car as a science project. Now keep reading."

Returning to my spot, I tried to finish reading, but I ended up casting glances over at Ben. I knew exactly when he'd find another idea that he liked, because his eyes lit up and he wiggled in his chair like a monkey.

Sighing, I put my book down again and looked straight at him. "What is it this time?"

He looked up at me, practically bouncing in his seat, and said, "How do you feel about the space-time continuum? If we were able to take some mirrors, and refract the light, I think we could calculate a quantum physics theory, and then we could . . ." He trailed off when he noticed my expression. "Does that fit into the not-normal category?"

I nodded.

"What about time travel?" he countered.

I shook my head. "Leave that to NASA, or wherever it is they figure that stuff out. Here. I think I found one." As I read to him from the book I held about a project based on nose sensitivity and the power of compensating for lost senses, he stared at me blankly.

"Did you listen to any of that?" I asked when I'd finished. "I think it would be a really neat project to do. I've always wondered how strong the sense of smell is. When I'm making my perfumes, at times I swear I—"

He cut me off. "You make perfume? I didn't know that."

I ignored him and kept talking about the project. "Can you just focus here, Ben? Please? I think this is the one for us. It won't be boring. And you'll get to make people smell gross things. How much more fun can you get?"

He looked intrigued by the idea, and I took the opportunity to read some more to him from the book, but he interrupted me again. "Are you going to put those red streaks back in your hair, Abbey? I really liked them."

The breath sucked right out of me, and I felt like a fish, gasping for air. It was a blow aimed straight at my heart, and it bruised all the way down to my soul. He didn't have any way of knowing. No way to tell that his question could hurt me so.

"What do you think of mine?" Ben asked. "Should I put some red streaks in it? They could match yours."

He gave me a smile, but I just sat there in frozen shock. To my immense horror, a tear spilled down my cheek, and I immediately brushed it away, ducking my head in shame. I felt the table shift beneath me, and then there was an awkward touch on my arm.

"Hey," Ben said softly. "We can do the smelly stuff project. It's cool. I was just teasing you about the other ones. I didn't really mean it."

I laughed shakily, and wiped another tear away before lifting my head. "It's not that, Ben, but thanks." I looked around the room and gestured hopelessly. "This room . . . It has some memories for me . . . and when you said that about the red streaks, well . . ."

He dropped his hand and took a step back. "It reminded you of him, right? Is that a good thing? Or a bad thing?"

I shook my head and pushed a hand through my hair, tucking a stray curl behind one ear. "Honestly? I don't really know." My nose was feeling runny, and I tried to sniff it as discreetly as possible. "Things have been kind of messed up, and I don't know what to do. It's just that being in this room again . . . The memories were a lot happier back then, and I thought I'd be okay. . . . But I'm not."

He stepped around the table and put his hand on my arm again. "Abbey, it's all good. You should have mentioned it to me. We don't have to stay here."

I stood up and started pacing back and forth. "Would it be okay if we left? We can go back to my house or something. Maybe order a pizza?"

He nodded and started to gather up the books. "I'll go return these to the librarian. You take whatever time you need and meet me downstairs when you're ready, okay?"

"Thanks, Ben." I pushed the book I'd been reading over to him. "Check this one out for me, and we'll take it with us."

He picked up all the books from the table, including the ones that I'd been carrying, turned to the door, and then turned back to me. "Are you going to be all right now? No more tears? I don't know how to handle crying girls. Every time my five-year-old sister turns on the waterworks, I end up buying her a Barbie. You don't need a new Barbie, do you?"

I shook my head. "Shut up, Benjamin Bennett. Don't forget, I know the car naming story. You wouldn't want it to get told to the entire school, now, would you?"

He vanished out the door, and his laughter echoed up to me from the stairwell. After taking a few deep breaths, I forced my chin up and squared my shoulders back. So the no-thinking-about-Caspian rule hadn't gone very well. At least it couldn't get much worse than breaking down and crying in front of a classmate.

No, I told myself as I flicked the light off and left the room behind me, *it definitely can't get worse than that.*

I took my time walking down the five flights of stairs, and ran my finger over the dusty banister as I went. It was while I was stepping down to the first floor that something familiar caught my eye. My eyes registered it before my brain did, but as soon as I realized what it was, I took off in the same direction. I followed it down to a lower floor, and found myself in the poorly lit archives room.

The air was still stuffy, and towers of books loomed out at me from every turn. I walked down each long aisle, glancing wildly in all directions. I'd seen a flash of white blond, and there was only one person I knew who had that particular shade of hair.

Caspian was here.

I searched all over, firmly convinced that I'd seen him. There were only so many places down here for someone to hide. I rounded the last corner before the stairs for a second time, and that was when I saw him sitting at a small table with a book in front of him. He didn't hear me coming, and I was almost right beside him before he looked up.

"Hi," I said softly. I looked down at what he was reading, and saw illustrations of stars. It was the book I'd gotten him for Christmas.

"Hi," he said back. "I got your gifts." He pointed to the book, and I nodded. "They're great. Thank you, Abbey."

My poor bruised ego soared at the way he said my name. "I got yours, too, Caspian. The drawings are . . . amazing. And the necklace, it's beautiful."

Of course I hadn't worn it yet, because just seeing it drove me to tears every time. So it had found a new home under the pillow, hiding away from view but close to my dreams.

He looked back down at the book, and awkwardness filled the space between us. I racked my brain for something to say, but only succeeded in remembering that Ben was waiting for me and that I should probably be on my way to meet him.

"I've got to go. Someone's waiting for me," I blurted out. He glanced up from the book again, meeting my gaze, and I went weak in the knees. I knew that at that precise moment I would have given *anything* to go back in time and be up in that study room with him again.

"Okay," he said, flipping a page and breaking eye contact. "See you around sometime."

"Y-yeah, see you around," I stuttered. He was back to reading his page again before I even finished my sentence. I hardened my resolve and turned away. If this was how he wanted to act, then two could play that game.

Climbing up the stairs, I peeked over my shoulder one last time before he was completely out of sight. I almost stumbled on the step when I saw that he was staring back at me. My eyes locked with his before I tore my gaze away and continued up the stairs.

It didn't mean anything. I couldn't let myself think that it meant anything.

Ben was waiting for me at the checkout desk, and he looked confused when he saw me on the stairs leading up from the archive room. He did an exaggerated double take. "I thought you were upstairs."

"I was," I replied. "But I saw someone I knew and stopped for a minute to go say hi." I led the way out the front door and into the cold sunshine. Ben followed me down the steps.

"Was it Caspian? Is he cool with me going over to your house? I don't want to step on any toes."

I looked both ways before crossing into the parking lot and heading for his car. "You're not stepping on any toes. *Trust me.*"

Ben didn't say anything as we climbed in, and he started Candy Christine up. I gave him directions to my house and we rode in silence. When we got there, I made hasty introductions to Mom and Dad, who *happened* to be home at the same time, and then called in to order the pizza.

Ben and I got right to work, outlining what we'd need for the project, and we spent the next hour going over everything. Mom and Dad stayed pretty much to themselves, and I was completely amazed at their restraint.

Even when Dad started winking at me whenever he could catch my eye, and I had to give him the stern I'm-going-to-kill-you-if-you-don't-knock-it-off look, they managed to keep their cool. I was shocked.

When Ben told me that he had to go, I grabbed my coat and

offered to walk him out to his car. I gave Dad the look as I went, but he didn't wink at all. The brisk winter air felt cool on my face as I stepped outside, and I pulled my coat closer and buttoned it up. Ben opened the door and sat down, sliding his book bag along to the passenger seat next to him.

I stood by the driver side window. "So how do you want to do this? I have to work weekends at my uncle's, but I'm free after school."

Ben revved the engine, and the exhaust made a puff of white smoke in the frigid air.

"Do you want to meet Wednesday and Friday afternoons?" he asked. "Amanda has cheerleading practice those days, and I don't start work until seven each night."

I looked down at the gravel driveway beneath my feet. *Nice to know we're planning our science project around his girlfriend.*

My thoughts must have shown on my face, because he spoke up a little defensively. "Or we can do something else. Whatever works for you."

I picked at a stray piece of string on my jacket before looking at him again. "That's okay. It works for me. We'll just meet during that last study hall of the day."

He nodded.

"Okay," I said. "I'll see you tomorrow at school. And thanks for being so nice about everything today, Ben. I really appreciate it."

I caught his eye so he could tell that I meant what I said. But he just looked embarrassed, and shrugged it off like it was no big deal.

"So where do you work?" I asked with a teasing grin. I wanted to turn the topic of conversation as far away from me as possible before he left. "Maybe I'll come torment you sometime."

He laughed and put the car into drive, keeping his foot on the brake. "I'm a waiter at the Horseman's Haunt restaurant. Well, a glorified busboy is more like it. If you stop in, I'll make sure you get a free glass of water. On the house."

I grinned. "That's too good an offer to pass up."

He smiled and waved as he slowly pulled the car forward. "Bye, Abbey. See you around."

"Bye, Ben," I called back. "Take care of Candy Christine."

I heard his whoop of laughter as I walked back into the house. Dad was standing there near the door, winking one eye at me, and I sighed while I hung up my jacket. I was obviously going to have to give him a lecture.

Chapter Twenty-three

CONFUSION

He appeared to be a horseman of large dimensions, and mounted on a black horse of powerful frame.

—"The Legend of Sleepy Hollow"

January flew by and rapidly turned into February. On Wednesdays and Fridays, I met with Ben for an hour or two at school, and on the weekends I worked for Uncle Bob. I steadfastly ignored the cemetery, and every free moment I had I spent on my business plan. If I ever wanted to get that money from Dad, it was time to get serious about it. I had only a couple months left until the end of the school year.

It was during a short break from working on it one Thursday evening that I found myself in the mood for some peppermint tea. Grabbing my new, and still unused, teacup off my desk, I realized that I hadn't gotten the chance to thank Nikolas and Katy for their Christmas gifts yet. I'd been so wrapped up in the science fair project, and my perfumes, and my heartbreak that I hadn't stopped by for that visit.

I felt bad about that. They had both been so nice to me, and had seemed extremely eager for my visit. It was terrible that I hadn't stopped by yet. As my water came to a boil and I plunked a peppermint-flavored tea bag into the cup, I promised myself that if I finished my work early today, I would go see them.

With my plans firmly made, I went back upstairs and sat down at my desk, continuing my calculations of estimated gross profits for three years. When my screaming neck muscles and aching eyes finally reminded me that I'd been working for far too long, I looked at the clock on the wall with dread. It was almost midnight.

Way too late for a visit, and with school the next day, it was time for me to climb into bed. I wearily pushed my papers to the side of the desk and left my empty teacup there. It could wait until tomorrow to get washed. Fighting back several large yawns, I changed into a pair of warm fuzzy pajamas and snuggled under the covers. *Tomorrow,* I assured myself.

I'll go see them tomorrow.

~ ~ ~

But when Friday afternoon rolled around, I found myself working on the project with Ben at school, and my plans changed again. If I could get him to give me a ride to the cemetery and drop me off at Nikolas and Katy's house, then I'd tell them a quick thank you and make plans for a longer visit another time. It sounded like a solid idea to me, and I quickly got caught up again working with Ben.

We were making our list of all the different things we'd need for people to smell, and he was doing a thoroughly disgusting job of grossing me out. Readjusting my seat at the empty table we were using, I looked over our list of categories again. They were divided up into yes, no, and maybe.

"I think we should add a new category on here, Ben," I said. "The 'hell no' category. That's where the rotten eggs should be."

His shoulders shook with laughter, and the grin on his face was contagious. I started laughing too.

"I'm serious, Ben," I said in between giggles. "There is *no way* we can make people smell rotten eggs. Do you want them to throw up all over the project?"

His eyes lit up, and I threw my hands into the air, knowing

immediately that I'd just given him another idea. "No. No. Definitely not."

He put on his saddest expression. "Come on, Abbey, you're not making this any fun. I thought you said I could make people smell really gross things. Weren't those your exact words?"

I sighed in defeat. He was right.

"Okay, okay." I gave in. "You can have the rotten eggs, but no vomit. And if people start puking from the smell, I'm going to make *you* clean it up. Okay?"

His wide grin was the only answer I got, as I shook my head and wrote "rotten eggs" under the yes category. Once I was done writing, he leaned over and scrawled "B.B." next to it. I stared down at the paper, trying to make sense of why he'd just done that. I looked over and raised an eyebrow at him.

"I give up. What does that mean?"

He pointed to the B.B. "Ben Bennett. My initials. I didn't want you to forget whose awesome idea that was."

I stared at him like he'd just turned green in front of my very eyes.

"Awesome? Oh, yeah. I'll be sure to remind you of that when you're knee-deep in puke piles."

The look he gave me was so comical that I doubled over laughing again, and a couple of seconds later he joined me. "Your laughter is catchy, Abbey," he told me after I'd gotten control of myself.

I nudged him on the arm. "It's all your fault, you know. You make me forget everything and laugh way too much. We'll never get this project done if we don't put some serious work into it."

He took the pen from my hand and started scribbling on the paper. "It's better to laugh than cry, though, isn't it?"

The seriousness of his question hit me, and I sobered, nodding my head slowly. He continued to look down at what he was doing, and kept scribbling. Tension settled around my shoulders, and I thought back to the scene in the library, regretting that moment yet again.

Ben kept silent, until he looked at his watch and then jumped up suddenly. "Oh, man, I'm late. I have to go. I'm supposed to pick up Amanda at five tonight. We have a date."

I pulled my cell phone out of my pocket and saw that it was 4:53 already. "Go ahead. I'll see you on Monday."

He picked up his book bag while I put the list we had made away, and he turned to face me before heading toward the door. "See ya, Abbey. It's been fun. You're the best science fair partner I've ever had."

I laughed. "I'm the *only* science fair partner you've had. Up until now, we haven't even had to participate in the science fair."

Grinning, he lifted one shoulder in casual concession. "Same difference."

"Go," I said. "Get out of here." He waved before he went, and I finished zipping up my bag, making sure that everything was sealed tight.

Ben could be a handful, but at least for the most part he kept my mind occupied.

Hoisting my bag onto my shoulders, I walked over to the door and stopped when I realized that I'd forgotten to ask him for a ride to the cemetery. I hesitated, unsure if I should stick to my plans and just walk to Nikolas and Katy's house or if I should call Mom for a ride home.

Peeking out the nearest window, I tried to gauge the weather. It was getting dark outside, but it looked clear. I pulled out my phone again and dialed Mom's number, waiting for her to pick up. Her tone of voice sounded distracted, and when she told me that dinner would be late due to some last-minute paperwork, the decision was made for me.

I told her not to worry about it. I would walk home and get something to eat on the way. After checking to make sure I had enough money, she breathed an audible sigh of relief and quickly hung up the phone.

With that settled, I put my phone back in my pocket and walked out of the classroom. It was a bit strange to still be in school this late, and I hurried through the hallways and toward the main doors. The distant buzz of a floor buffer hummed in the background, and a couple of teachers looked up from grading their papers when I passed the rooms they were in. I gave them a fake smile and kept moving, anxious to be on my way.

Once I was outside, an immediate sense of freedom enveloped me. Rearranging my bag, I shoved my gloveless fingers into my pockets and turned to the cemetery. I had a stop to make.

I chose the direction that would take me directly to the cemetery by crossing the river. It was a dangerous choice, and it was the first time I'd ever broken the pact with Kristen, but it was the quickest route. I walked quickly, and soon came to the rocky banks that marked my destination ahead.

Watching the swirling angry water for a minute, I sent out a brief prayer that I'd make it to the other side without falling in. All I had to do was watch my step on the rocks, and I'd be across it in no time. Anchoring my book bag more firmly across my back, and holding out my arms to steady myself, I took a small test step onto the nearest rock to check for slipperiness. It seemed like most of the snow had melted, but in the freezing weather, ice was my biggest concern.

I placed a second foot on the rock and stood still for a minute. So far, so good. I had to step on only four or five more rocks to make it to the other side. The rushing water moved fast, and I tried not to look down directly at it. Keeping my eyes on the other side of the riverbank, I hopped to the next rock.

Choosing only the largest and flattest rocks was a bit tricky, but I stepped out onto the next one and found myself in the middle of the river. I looked around me, seeing the shore I had just come from, so far behind, and the shore I was trying to reach, so far away.

The next rock jutted out in a sharp, angular manner, and I knew that it would probably be hard to get to safely. I made my move, but my foot slipped off the rock and almost landed in the water. I jerked myself upright and back, trying to keep my balance. Trying again, my foot slipped for the second time, and I almost lost my book bag.

That shook me up, and I had to force myself not to panic. I

didn't know if I should keep going or just turn around. The water was making a loud rushing noise all around me, and I felt surrounded. It was almost like my dream that night Kristen had died.

I stared down at the clear river. I knew it would be cold. Mindnumbing, breath-taking, and icy cold. And fast. The current would swell around me and carry me off if I should happen to fall in.

A thought struck me, and I looked at the rock I was perched on. *Is this the one she hit her head on?* Did Kristen's blood still stain this water somewhere?

The sound of someone yelling something pulled me out of my contemplation, and I glanced over at the opposite bank. A dark figure stood there, waving at me, and I could just barely make out the outline of overalls. Cupping my hands around my mouth, I called out, "Nikolas, is that you?"

"Yes, Abbey, it's me," echoed back.

"Hold on!" I yelled. "I'm almost across!"

Eyeing the rock in front of me, I slowly slid one foot out, trying for a different angle this time. It worked, and I was able to plant my foot more firmly. I straddled both rocks, held on to my book bag, and then swung myself over.

I didn't stay still for very long but tried to keep moving. The next rock was the largest of them all, and I quickly crossed it. When I stepped out to the last rock that stood between myself and dry land, I could see Nikolas standing right next to the water's edge. A frail hand was extended in my direction, and I latched on to it as soon as I hit the riverbank, grateful for the lifeline.

After casting one long last glance behind me, I turned to him and let all the gratefulness I was feeling show in my eyes. "Thank you, Nikolas. You're the second man to come to my rescue at this river. A girl could get used to this sort of thing."

He shuffled his feet, and made disapproving noises, but I think he was pleased by my words. When I finally let go of his hand, he pulled his worn flannel jacket a little closer around his shoulders and gave me an anxious glance. "You shouldn't be crossing that river, Abbey. If you had slipped, or fallen in, I don't know what I would have done. It's not your time yet." His lined face looked worried, and I was overwhelmingly sorry for causing him any concern.

I patted his hand soothingly and put one arm around his shoulders. "I promise I won't cross the river again anytime soon, Nikolas. Once they finish the construction work on the Washington Irving Bridge, I'll be able to take that each time. Okay?"

457

He nodded and looked relieved.

"Besides," I said, "what are *you* doing out in this weather? Katy's not out here too, is she?" I cast a glance around me, but I didn't see anything.

He looked affronted at the possibility that Katy would be roaming around out here in the cold darkness. "My lady love is safe and warm at home, tucked in front of a roaring fire. She wasn't feeling much like herself, so I volunteered to come out and gather some firewood, and along the way I took a small walk."

I grew concerned at the thought of Katy being ill. I couldn't bear the thought of something happening to her, and I gripped both of his hands urgently. "Is she okay? Do you need me to do anything?"

Nikolas shook his head. "She's fine. Just a slight winter chill." Tucking one of my hands under his elbow, he turned to the gently sloping bank. "Nothing more, nothing less. I will tell her about your concern for her, though. I'm sure she will appreciate it." With only a slight hesitancy we climbed the bank together and stood near the top, close to the path that led over to his house.

"If there's anything I can do, please let me know," I replied. "Can you also tell her thank you for me? The gloves and scarf are absolutely beautiful. And the teacup is exquisite." He waited patiently while I babbled on. "Oh, and thank you for the carving! I love it! The detailing is amazing. And how did Katy know red is my favorite color? She must be psychic or something."

Nikolas beamed at me and squeezed my arm. "I will certainly pass along the kind words to her. She had a hunch that you would like the red. I will be glad to tell her she was right."

I smiled and gave him a spontaneous hug. "I hope you two had a very Merry Christmas," I said into his ear. He hugged me, and then stepped back, looking a bit embarrassed.

"Now, then," he said, straightening his jacket, "I must get back to my lady. Tell me, when can you come for a visit?"

I cocked my head to the side and gave him a serious look. "Well, since you don't want me to cross the river at night . . ." He held up a finger and shook his head. "And you want me to give Katy enough time to rest . . ." I acted like I was pondering the question for a minute. "How about this coming Thursday, after school? I don't have any plans that day. Does that sound okay to you?"

Nikolas agreed, and I carefully removed my hand from his arm. "Okay. Then I'll see you on Thursday. Put some peppermint tea on to boil that day."

A happy look filled his eyes, and I expected him to leave, but he didn't. So I waited, wondering if he'd forgotten something. He turned to glance back at the water. "You're not going to cross that river again to get home, are you?" I thought I heard him mutter something about "falling in again," but I wasn't sure.

"No," I said, shaking my head. "I'm going to follow the other path up to the main gate an—" A noise from behind me interrupted us, and I turned to see what it was. It sounded like something had been thrown.

Caspian stepped out from the shadows of a mausoleum to the left of me, and my jaw dropped in surprise. I wasn't expecting to see *him* there.

"Walk away, Abbey. Walk away from him now." His tone shocked me, and his green eyes were cold. Everything grew crystal clear when I saw a rock in his hand, and I felt all my senses shift. A tiny ribbon of fear ran down my back, and I snapped my spine straighter. This was very real now, and I had to deal with it.

Turning my back to Nikolas, I moved to stand in front of him and held out a hand to Caspian, taking a cautious step forward. "What are you doing here, Caspian? What's wrong?"

His grip visibly tightened on the rock, but what confused me were his eyes. They were fixed hard on Nikolas, but when they shifted to me, they softened, almost pleadingly. I stopped and stared. *What is going on here?*

He held out a hand, the one not holding the rock, and beckoned me to his side. His voice was very, very soft. "Just come over here by me, Abbey."

I took an automatic step toward him, but then stopped again. The rock frightened me, and I couldn't make sense of anything. My head was spinning, and I put my hands out to try to get some control of the situation.

"Why do you have a rock, Caspian? I don't know if you think I'm in some type of danger here, but I'm not. This is Nikolas, and he's—" The next interruption came in a form that I was not expecting.

A hand grabbed my wrist from the side—gently, but the grip was solid and strong. I looked behind me in surprise.

It was Nikolas.

There was something different about him, an undercurrent of power and authority, and for the tiniest second I wasn't sure who to be more afraid of. I shook that feeling off, and glanced down at my arm. Caspian shouted something, but I couldn't hear him. Nikolas was speaking now, and it was for my ears only.

"Don't be afraid of him, or me," he said quietly. "The young man thinks he is protecting you. He feels very strongly about you. I know you don't understand all that is going on here, Abigail, but you will. The time has come."

He released my arm and took a stand by my side. "Don't worry," he called out to Caspian. "She isn't in any danger. I promise."

Caspian tossed the rock from hand to hand and took a step closer. "Back off, old man. If she's not in any danger, then why don't you let her come to me?"

Nikolas turned and gave me a gentle push forward. "Go on," he whispered. "Show the young fool that I am not a liar."

I stepped closer to Caspian and stood less than a foot away from him. His eyes were anguished, and I searched them, looking for answers.

"Astrid, please. Please come over here. I'll protect you. I promise," he pleaded with me.

For a moment I wavered. I pictured him scooping me up in his strong arms and carrying me safely home. We'd get to the front door, and he would gently lower me to the ground as we—

Suddenly I whacked myself on the forehead. *Focus, girl. Focus.* I didn't need rescuing. I was with *Nikolas*. The man I thought of as a grandfather. Something was very, very wrong here, and I needed to fix it. *Immediately.*

After making a time-out gesture with my hands, I put both fists on my hips and turned to Caspian. "First of all, you need to put down that stupid rock. *Now.*"

I crossed my arms and waited for him to listen to me. When he hesitated, I tapped my foot against the ground until he complied with my orders. "Thank you," I said sweetly. Then I got down to business. "Now, I don't know how things are between *us* right now, Caspian, but you sure as hell are *not* going to come here and frighten me half to death, and then threaten a friend of mine."

Nikolas took a step forward, and I whirled on him. "In a minute, Nikolas. I'll get to you next." He shuffled back to his spot with a chastised look on his face.

I turned back to Caspian. "I didn't get to make the proper introductions before, but this is Nikolas. He and his wife Katy live near here. They used to be caretakers, and they have both become good friends of mine. And Nikolas, this is Caspian. He's my, well he used to be . . . He's just a friend. Now, why were you holding a rock in your hand like that, Caspian?"

He looked agitated, and ran both of his hands through his hair before speaking. "They're not what they seem, Abbey. There's more to whatever bogus story he told you. He's dangerous."

I snorted in disbelief and turned to face Nikolas. "Are you dangerous, Nikolas?"

He bowed his head, looking for all the world like a frail old man, and then he looked up at me. "Have I ever hurt you, Abbey?"

"Point taken," I replied. "Now, will you please explain to Caspian here, who has taken some kind of crazy pill today, that you are just a caretaker who lives in the woods."

Nikolas inclined his head again and spoke to Caspian. "No matter who, or what, we may have been in another lifetime, everything we have told her about us is true."

"That's a lie," Caspian spat. "I know the truth. I've seen the horse. And I've seen you talking to *them*."

My mind was positively spinning now, and I was starting to feel the bite of the cold night air. I had no idea what Caspian's words meant.

"I am nothing more than a man," countered Nikolas, "and right now I am a man who needs to get home to see his beloved."

I shook my head and gave each of them a disgusted look. "Wait.

Just wait a minute. I don't know what's going on here between the two of you, but when you feel like you're ready to stop talking in a secret code, then you'll know where to find me."

Caspian spoke before I could stomp away in a dignified manner. "I'm sorry, Abbey. I didn't want you to get caught in the middle of this."

"*This?* What is *this*, Caspian?" I asked angrily. "I never know what I'm doing with you. You're never where I can find you; you're keeping things from me all the time. . . . I just can't wrap my head around any of this. I can't keep it all straight. And now you're *here*, with a *rock?* What were you going to do? Throw the rock at a horse, at Nikolas . . . or at me?"

He looked sad, like his feelings had been hurt, and that just made me mad. *I* was the one with the hurt feelings here.

Caspian shook his head. "I would never hurt you, Abbey. You know that." I felt a pang of guilt, because somewhere deep down I *did* know that. "I threw that rock to get your attention. To get you away from *him*. I aimed for the bushes over there." He pointed to a clump of shrubs that were at least twenty feet away from where Nikolas and I had been standing.

"Still," I said, "you really frightened me, Caspian. I can't deal with that on top of everything else weird going on here. I have to . . . I just have to go."

"Let me walk you." He started forward.

I put out a hand to stop him. "I think you should leave me alone for right now. Let me be alone."

I looked back over my shoulder as I strode away from all the confusion, and I couldn't see Caspian at all. Even his bright hair had melted into the darkness.

But Nikolas was there, and I swear I saw the dark outline of a horse nuzzle up from behind him, while he patted its head. And that made the scariest thing of all happen. I started to question myself, and just how sane *I* really was.

Chapter Twenty-four

THE LEGEND

Ichabod was horror-struck, on perceiving that he was headless!—but his horror was still more increased, on observing that the head, which should have rested on his shoulders, was carried before him on the pommel of the saddle. . . .

—"The Legend of Sleepy Hollow"

My concentration was blown for the weekend and the following week. But I guess a nighttime stroll through a graveyard with the crazy people showdown would do that to anyone.

Ben really stepped up to the plate and helped hold down my end of the science project, though. He even refrained from asking me any questions, and I was grateful for small favors. Especially since I didn't have any answers to the questions I was already asking myself.

When Thursday afternoon finally came around, I bolstered up my courage to stop by his locker for some advice. He was chatting with a couple of friends, but they quickly dispersed when they saw me approaching. Ben slammed his locker door shut and waited for me.

I didn't know where to begin. "Ben, I wanted to tell you that . . ." I hesitated. *Do I tell him everything? Or nothing at all?* "Look, I know I've been a big flake this week, and I'm sorry about that. Next week will be better. I promise. I'm going to take care of something today that I think will help."

He didn't seem to know how to respond, but just fiddled with the bottom of his dark brown shirt. "Don't worry about it, Abbey," he said after a moment. "It's cool. You deal with it and make sure everything's good on your end. I'll cover for you."

I looked down at my boots, embarrassed that it had come to this.

"Some partner I've been, huh?"

He shook his head. "I'm not playing the Blame Abbey game. Just deal with it, move on, and come be my partner again, okay?"

"Agreed," I replied. "And, hey, I'm sorry about shooting down your ideas before about the space and time travel thing."

Someone called his name from the opposite end of the hallway, and he yelled out a greeting. "Not a problem," he said to me. "I've already forgotten about it."

"Can I just ask you one more thing?" I said suddenly.

"Shoot."

"Do you and Amanda trust each other? I mean, if you found out she was keeping secrets from you, would you ask her about it?"

He looked puzzled by my questions, but answered anyway. "Amanda and I trust each other, I guess, to an extent. Our relationship isn't, like, all deep and meaningful, but I trust that she's not going to cheat on me. As far as whether or not I would ask her about something I thought she might be hiding . . . yeah, I would." He shrugged. "Without trust, what kind of relationship can you hope to have with anyone?"

I nodded. His words were exactly what I needed to hear, and they echoed my own thoughts on the matter. "Thanks, Ben. I'll see you later. I know your friends are waiting for you."

I turned away, but he caught my hand and looked me directly in the eye.

"Don't let that boyfriend of yours give you any shit, Abbey. There are a lot of other guys out there. You don't need a loser."

I sighed, and pulled my hand from his as I started to take slow steps away from his locker. "That's the problem. He's not a loser . . . and he's the only one I want." Ben gave me a sad smile. "I know what you mean," he said softly.

Shrugging hopelessly, I waved good-bye as I headed to the opposite end of the hall. It was time to go see Nikolas and Katy, and get some answers to these questions once and for all.

I rehearsed what I was going to say the entire walk over to their house. As I wandered along the pathway, I told myself to relax and play it cool. Stepping up to the front door, I nervously gave it a knock. Katy came to answer, and greeted me with a warm smile as she opened the door to let me in. Nikolas was seated in his rocking chair in the corner, and I gave a little wave to him before taking off my red scarf and gloves and setting them down on the table.

The teapot was already bubbling over the fire, and three place settings had been arranged at the table. I seated myself at the spot I'd sat in last time, and glanced around the cottage. Nothing had changed; it still felt warm and cozy inside.

"We're glad you came," Katy said, sitting down at the table, with her knitting needles in hand.

I gestured to the pile of yarn in front of her. "I'm glad to see you're feeling better. Did Nikolas pass along my well wishes and words of thanks to you?"

She beamed. "He did, and I'm so happy that you liked the gifts. Something just told me red was your color."

I smiled at her. I didn't know when, or how, to start asking my questions, so I turned to face Nikolas in the corner and plunged in. "I'm really sorry about what happened the other night. I don't know why Caspian was acting that way. Did you get a chance to tell Katy about it yet?"

He nodded once as he spoke. "I've told her everything. I'm sure you must have some questions for us."

I nodded in return. "Yeah, I do."

"Before you begin, though," he said, "I want to let you know that Katy and I have come to admire you a great deal in this short amount of time, and we think of you as we would our own granddaughter."

I couldn't contain my megawatt grin. "Really? I'm honored. I think of you the same way. It feels like we've known each other for much longer than we actually have."

"That may be because in some ways we share a very special bond."

I stared at him, wondering what that might be exactly.

"You see, Abbey, there is something . . . unique about you, and your young man sees it too."

"His name is Caspian, and I certainly hope he sees something special in me." I grinned at Katy, but she didn't smile back. It was then that I got the faintest twinge of uneasiness in my stomach.

"Go on," I urged Nikolas. "I didn't mean to interrupt."

He turned to watch the fire as he continued speaking. "The other night, when your—when Caspian was trying to defend you, he only thought he was doing what was right. Like I said, there are strong feelings there, and I think that might be the reason behind his actions."

I was getting frustrated now and wanted him to get to the point, instead of telling me things I already knew. I barely managed to keep my mouth closed and my thoughts to myself.

He picked up again. "When I first met you at Washington Irving's grave, I was surprised when you talked to me. Other people . . . don't. Do you understand at all where I'm going with this?"

Impatience reared its ugly head, and I sighed. "I really want to, but I don't. What do you mean?" ·

"Your ability to see me and talk to me, when no one else can. It's because we're all a part of this place. . . . We have a connection to Washington Irving and 'The Legend of Sleepy Hollow.'"

I began panicking, but stubbornly clung to the small hope that he was joking for some strange reason. "I don't get what you mean, Nikolas. You're talking gibberish here." I looked to Katy for some sort of confirmation, but she was looking back at me without an ounce of expression on her face.

"Don't you see, dear?" she said. "Caspian was afraid of Nikolas because he still doesn't fully understand us."

I felt my heart start to beat harder, and my breath came quicker. Was I hyperventilating? Was this what a heart attack felt like? I tried to keep calm, but the crazy talk in the room was starting to go to my head.

"What's there to understand?" I asked Katy. "He's just a harmless old man, and you're harmless too, right?" I immediately thought back to the peppermint tea I had consumed here. *Good God, do these people put crazy leaves in their tea?*

I stood up and paced around the room. Nikolas and Katy seemed to be waiting for me to calm down. They were watching me with guarded expressions, and I heard Caspian's words in the back of my head. *They're not what they seem, Abbey. There's more to whatever bogus story he told you.*

I stopped pacing midthought and turned back to them with

a big smile on my face. "I get it. You two are like some of those people who pretend they're part of living history or something, right? You get dressed up and go to battlefields and stuff like that. Only, since we live in Sleepy Hollow, you pretend you're a part of that. I get it." Relief flowed through me when I'd figured it out. They just took their acting a bit too far.

Katy shook her head at me. "We don't pretend we're from the legend. We *are* the legend."

Rolling my eyes, I looked over at Nikolas. "Seriously. Come on, guys. I need you to be straight with me."

Nikolas rose from his chair and stepped closer to me. I felt that change happening again, and power filled the air.

"I know its hard, Abbey, but you must believe us," he said gently. "Katy's full name is Katrina Van Tassel. We have proof. A birth record, pictures, and more . . ."

I scoffed at him. This was going too far. "And who are you supposed to be? Ichabod Crane? Or Brom Bones? The legend says that she married Brom, but I always had my suspicions that Ichabod came back into the story."

"Neither. I'm the Headless Horseman."

My jaw dropped to the ground. I actually looked down to see if

I needed to pick it back up. "The Headless Horseman?" I repeated with a gulp. "But you . . . you . . . have . . . well, a *head*."

I mentally chastised myself as I came up with that lame logic, but apparently I was in the land of crazies now, so hopefully it was anything goes.

"Appearances aren't always what they seem, Abbey," Nikolas said softly.

At this point I started eyeing the door and calculating how far it was to the only exit. If I started moving closer, I could make a run for it.

"Okay," I admitted, humoring them while I started my slow advances. "So if you're the Headless Horseman, the *real* one, from the legend, how did you end up here?"

"Well, the legend is true," said Nikolas. "Up to the point that I *was* a soldier, and *did* die in battle. But then I fell in love with Katrina. She could see me when no one else could."

I nodded like I was following along, and turned to Katy. "So the Headless Horseman was a ghost who fell in love with you. But what about Brom Bones? The end of the legend says . . ." I was moving closer and closer to the door, and I nodded at her to finish.

She got an excited expression on her face, and I felt a tiny sliver of guilt for making them think I believed their craziness. "Washington Irving wrote the legend that way to protect us. He changed the ending."

Reaching behind me, I felt for the doorknob and twisted it slowly.

"So you really ended up with him—the Headless Horseman— instead, and you both decided to stay in Sleepy Hollow together forever?"

Katy smiled. "Yes, dear, we've been caretakers for the cemetery ever since. I'm so glad you believe us."

Pushing the door open, I stood framed in the afternoon sunlight slanting in on us. "Actually," I said, "I think you're a nice old couple who have deluded yourselves into thinking these things because you don't want to face reality. I'm sorry if things got too strange and too busy for you, out there in the real world, but that's where I live, and that's where I'm going back to."

I turned and sprinted down the path for all I was worth. Leaving my gloves and scarf behind. Leaving behind the warmth and friendship I'd thought I had. And leaving a piece of my broken heart behind for those poor lonely people.

Chapter Twenty-five

THE TRUTH

❧❀❧

The old country wives, however, who are the best judges of these matters, maintain to this day that Ichabod was spirited away. . . .

—"The Legend of Sleepy Hollow"

I threw myself into the project with Ben to keep me busy. It kept my mind occupied, and I tried to make up for the time I had spent before not holding up my end of the work. I didn't allow myself to think about cemeteries, or old people who were crazy, or peppermint tea, or boys with green eyes, or dead best friends.

Every time my thoughts started to wander, I immediately pulled out a notebook and started writing down ideas for new scents for the science project. Sure, we already had our main list completed, and it was a pain in the ass to scramble for a notebook in the dark at night in bed . . . but it was the only thing that worked.

When Valentine's Day was less than a week away, I begged off working at Uncle Bob's for the weekend. I was not in the mood to see happy couples gazing into each other's eyes while sharing sundaes together. I planned to stay home and continue my process of not thinking about anything at all.

By Saturday afternoon I was moping around the house. The weather was cold and nasty outside, and there had been thunderstorms off and on all morning. Not very conducive to a bright and shiny happy day. I really should have just climbed back into bed with some hot cocoa and a good book, but I was restless.

After wandering aimlessly from window to window in the living room, I dragged myself over to the couch. Mom was reading a book there, so I flopped down next to her. I picked up the remote and started to channel surf, but it seemed to take her forever to recognize my boredom.

I kept sighing dramatically after every commercial, until she finally shut her book forcefully and glared at me. "Okay. I get it. You're bored, or upset, or something. Want to talk about it?"

I shook my head stubbornly and kept flipping.

"Why don't you go up to your room, then? Some of us were enjoying the peace and quiet around here."

I shut the TV off and crossed my arms in front of me. Mom picked up her book again and went back to her reading. Tilting my head back to gaze at the ceiling, I tried to follow a tiny crack from one end of the room to the other. It was a painfully boring exercise, but I didn't have anything else to do.

I sighed again.

That must have been too much for Mom, because she slammed her book shut and got to her feet. "Silence just isn't silence with you, is it? Get your coat. Let's go see a movie or something."

I jumped up off the couch to get my jacket. "Can we see something that has bombs or explosions in it? I am *so* not in the mood for a romantic comedy."

"We'll see what's there." She joined me at the door and slipped on her jacket before scooping up her keys from the small hallway table.

We stepped outside, and I ran to the van. The rain had stopped for a moment, but the air was still chilly. As soon as I heard those doors unlock, I scrambled up into the front seat and waited impatiently while Mom started it up. My teeth were chattering, and I quickly turned the heater up to as high as it would go.

Once the interior had warmed up slightly, and my nose no longer felt like it was caught in the freezer, Mom put both hands on the wheel and shifted to drive. Then she turned to face me and put it back into park. "Why don't you drive today?"

"Me? D-drive?" I sputtered. "But I don't even have my permit yet, and you only took me out to practice in that empty parking lot, like, twice."

She shrugged. "So? Your seventeenth birthday is coming up in a couple of months, and you'll have your permit then. Besides, it's only fifteen minutes to the theater, and there aren't that many people out today. The practice will be good for you."

"Okay." I jumped at the chance and threw the passenger side door open. Mom switched seats with me and I carefully adjusted my mirrors then put on my seat belt.

"Nice job," Mom told me. "Now just pull out slowly, and take it easy. You know the way."

Looking both ways as I pulled out of the driveway, I put my blinker on, signaling a left turn. *This is a piece of cake.* I took my time on the side roads but really poured on the gas when we hit highway nine. The sign posted said fifty-five, and I intended to make sure I hit every bit of that speed.

I cruised along, hitting my speed, and my stride, and glanced over at Mom. She was actually grinning and nodded at me. "You're doing great, Abbey. Nice driving." I smiled back. I only took my eyes off the road for a second, but that was why I didn't see it until it was too late.

Straight ahead, lying in the road mere inches away, was a two-by-four with several rusty nails sticking out of it.

I hit the brakes hard and swerved to the left. There was an angled curb there, and for a couple of seconds we were airborne before touching down again. I held on tight to the steering wheel, even as I heard the dull thuds, and I braked again until we came to a stop in a gravel parking lot.

"What the *hell* was that doing in the road?" I exploded.

Mom didn't say anything, but she had a sickly expression on her face.

"Sorry, Mom," I said quickly, "I didn't mean to—"

She cut me off. "Don't worry about it, Abbey. Are you all right?" At my brief nod, she glanced into the side mirror. "You did what was necessary. Once you saw that braking wasn't going to work in time, you got out of the way. It was the smartest thing to do." She sighed heavily. "Let's go look everything over and see what the damage is."

I turned the engine off and slid out of my seat. Mom was already walking around to her side of the car and looking it over from top to bottom. "Everything looks fine here," she called out.

I looked at my side and immediately saw it. "It's over here, on my side. Both tires blew out." A sick feeling flooded my stomach. This could be really, really bad news for me and my future license.

Mom came around to inspect the damage. She crouched down and looked at each tire before instructing me to pop the trunk. I did as she asked, and she went to go peer inside.

"Damn it," I heard a minute later. There was a loud clunking sound, and I walked back to see what she was doing.

"Well, we have a jack but no spare," she informed me. "Not like one spare would have done us any good, anyway, but that's beside the point. I *told* your father that we needed to replace the one we *did* have, and did he listen to me? No, he did not."

She kept ranting, even as she pulled out her cell phone and dialed information to get the nearest tow truck's number. Then she called the insurance company to give them some information, and I heard her ranting to them, too. I went to go move the board out of the road so no one else would hit it. Giving it a ferocious kick with my foot, I muttered several angry words before heading back to the car.

Mom had finished making all of her phone calls, and she told me that we might as well wait inside the car since it could be a while. I heeded her advice and climbed into the passenger side, a safe distance away from the steering wheel.

The rain started up again, and we sat there, huddled in miserable silence. Two hours passed, and several more phone calls were made, before the tow truck finally showed up. We stood out in the rain with him while he loaded the van up.

"Guess we won't be seeing that movie after all," I said to Mom. She just rolled her eyes and told me to go get inside the tow truck. I squeezed my way around crumpled-up fast-food bags and a gazillion empty soda cans before Mom and the tow truck man climbed in.

"So is the repair shop close to here?" Mom asked the guy as she elbowed me over to make a little more room.

He ran a greasy hand through his straggly hair before answering. "Yup. About five miles up the road here is Mike's Auto Repair."

Mom breathed an audible sigh of relief. "If you could just take us over there, we'd really appreciate it." He nodded and then shifted gears as we lurched bumpily down the road.

It didn't take me long to discover that five miles spent squeezed next to a gear shift was entirely too long for my comfort, and I happily disentangled myself when we arrived at the auto shop.

 483

Mom paid the tow truck driver, and we both hurried into a small gray rectangular building. While she went over to the parts counter, I wandered down a back hall, looking for a waiting area. I found it easily enough but sighed in despair as I noted that all it had to offer was an old TV, a gross-looking coffee machine, and a couple of car mags.

Not exactly how I'd pictured spending my afternoon.

But I took a seat and stretched my legs out over the empty orange plastic chairs next to me. I tried to ignore the scent of stale grease that permeated the air, and reached for the television remote. The television had a grand total of seven channels, and three of them were fuzzy. "Of course, of course," I said to the empty room.

Closing my eyes, I leaned my head back against the wall behind me, pretending I was at home on our couch. *Maybe this will all be over when I open my eyes again.*

Someone entered the room, and I opened my eyes to see that it was Mom.

"Well," she said. "The good news is that they have our tires in stock, and it should only take about an hour and a half to get to it."

I groaned. "How long will it take them to put the tires on, once they get to it?"

"Oh, it won't take that long. But that's not the best part. The best part is that with parts and labor, it will end up costing me a hundred and fifty bucks."

I groaned again, louder this time. I could envision myself doing infinite amounts of laundry and handing over portions of my paychecks from Uncle Bob for the next five years. "I'm really sorry, Mom. I'll pay for it. I didn't mean to do it. It was a complete accident."

"Don't worry about it," she said. "I know I'll probably regret this later, but accidents happen to everyone."

I almost hopped up and hugged her right then and there, my relief was so overwhelming. "Thanks, Mom. Really, thanks. But I *was* driving pretty well before that, right?"

She glared at me. "Don't push it. I could still have you doing a lot more dishes from now on," she warned.

I shut my mouth and closed my eyes again. Whatever she wanted, just as long as I didn't have to pay for those tires.

"What do we have to entertain ourselves with in here?" she asked.

Lifting a hand, I pointed in the general direction of the TV, or at least where I thought the TV was, since my eyes were closed.

"A TV that gets four channels, some old coffee, and a couple of magazines."

Her voice perked up. "Magazines?"

I opened my eyes briefly, and then shut them again. "You won't want them. Not unless you secretly read *Car and Driver* or *Auto Enthusiast*.

Her voice fell. "Oh."

I readjusted my feet, and she grew silent. I kept my eyes closed, oblivious to whatever she was doing, and tried to will myself into sleep.

The next thing I knew, I was jerking awake, and catching myself before I slumped off the chair. I gazed sleepily around the room. I must have drifted off after all. Mom was furiously typing away on her PDA, and I yawned loudly before getting to my feet. "I'm going to take a quick walk around to stretch my legs a bit, maybe see how far along they are on the car."

"Okay," she murmured.

I left the waiting room and found my way back to the main part of the shop. Our car was still waiting to be put up on the lift, so it was bound to be a while. Exhaling loudly, I turned the corner and walked to the end of the hall, where another room appeared to be. I didn't mean to snoop or pry, but I was bored out of my mind. That had to count as extenuating circumstances or something.

I poked my head into the room and saw a dark-haired man sitting behind a large desk. He was wearing mechanics overalls, but I couldn't read the name badge sewn onto them. I knocked twice on the wood frame outside the door and waited.

He looked up with a blank expression on his face, and I spoke hesitantly. "I'm sorry to bother you, sir, but my mom and I are waiting for our van to be fixed, and I was wondering if you had anything else to read around here. *Not* car related?"

The man stared at me, then pointed to the corner. "There's a box of old magazines. They were donated, so I don't know what's in there. I think we might have thrown in a book or two from the last time we cleaned out the shop. But you're welcome to look through it."

I smiled at him and went to grab the box. "Thanks. I'm sure this will help pass the time."

"You're very welcome," he said. "Glad to be of service."

The box was kind of heavy, but I managed to carry it out of the office. I only made it three whole steps toward the waiting room before I dropped it, though. Since there was no one else nearby, I sank to my knees to see what was inside.

Digging through all kinds of magazines, including some that dated back to the eighties, I quickly realized there was a *lot* of crap in that box. A thick, stout book was buried near the bottom, and I picked it up, only to read *Chilton's Car Guide: Toyota 1984* on the side before dropping it back in.

I kept on digging.

Moments later my fingers struck something else smooth and hard, and I lifted out a dusty yearbook. It was facedown, but when I turned it over, I was surprised to see that it was from White Plains High. And it was only two and a half years old.

Jackpot.

I drew my legs up underneath me and sat cross-legged with my back to the wall. All of my yearbooks at home had several signatures scrawled throughout, each one wishing me various ways to "Have a Good Summer," but I noticed that this book's pages remained signature free.

Interesting.

Flipping through slowly, I wasn't surprised to see that most of the pictures were dominated by the pretty people. I thumbed past them until I saw individual photos. One of the teachers, in a rumpled suit and on obvious hairpiece, caught my eye, and I remembered a game Kristen and I had played in history class last year.

"It's time for another round of Guess When Mr. Ives's Toupee Will Fall Off," I murmured to myself. "You were really good at that game, Kristen."

Poor Mr. Ives had been the brunt of a lot of jokes that year. Every time he'd cross the room too fast, his poorly attached hairpiece would go flopping off his head. Now he'd moved on from bad toupees to even worse hair plugs. The man obviously had no idea how cruel high schoolers could be.

I shook my head, smiling at the flying toupee memory. God, that had been a fun year.

I kept flipping, and finally came to the last couple of pages. Sitting up straighter, I squinted my eyes as I stared at the group of seniors that heralded the end of their school years. It was a grainy black-and-white shot of the gymnasium right before graduation, and the faces were hard to make out, but I scanned over them, looking for Caspian. He should have been there. This was his graduating class.

I searched the lines of names to the far left of the picture, cursing the tiny size-four font that they had chosen, and looked for the *C*s. He'd be listed there.

But in between Carlotta and Cruz, there was no Crane.

I looked through all the *C* names again, thinking that I must have missed it, or it might have been mis-alphabetized, but I couldn't find it anywhere. Then I went line by line, skimming until I came across Caspian's name listed with the *V*s. They had his name down as Caspian Vander.

The mistake puzzled me. Sure, he had been a new student and all, but hadn't anyone checked the school records to make sure they didn't mess up last names before they labeled the pictures? I checked the yearbook again more carefully, but I didn't see any other pictures that he was in.

Then I flipped over to the senior portraits section, figuring that at least *they* had to be labeled correctly. But the *C* names listed there yielded the same results as before. They had a listing under the *V*s once again, for a Caspian Vander, but in the little box where there should have been a picture were the words "Sorry, no picture available." I had no way of knowing if it was really him or not.

Gently closing the yearbook, I set it on my knee and rested my chin in my hand. This was weird. I didn't seriously think that there were two guys named Caspian, who just *happened* to go to the same high school. It was a fairly uncommon name. Yet I distinctly recalled the Caspian that *I* had met telling me he'd gone to White Plains High, and his last name was Crane.

There was no Caspian Crane in this yearbook.

Footsteps echoing loudly in the hallway interrupted my thoughts, and I looked over to see the man that I'd talked to earlier. He had obviously just come from his office and was walking my way. I said "Hi" automatically as he passed, but my thoughts weren't on him at all. My brain was too busy trying to sort out the pieces of this puzzle I'd stumbled upon.

He gave me some type of return greeting that didn't even register with me, and took two more steps before stopping to turn around. I looked up at him in a daze, with the yearbook still resting on my knee.

"Was that yearbook in the box?" He looked confused. "I didn't mean for it to get put in there."

I looked down at the yearbook, and then back at him before even realizing he was talking to me. My brain was acting fuzzy. "Oh, yeah," I blurted out, looking over at the box. "It was." Ahhh, my brain was back. "Do you know whose it is?"

A small, sad smile played across his face. "Yes, I do. It was *my* son's."

For the third time in my life time froze. I could see his name tag clearly now, and it said Bill Vander. When my words came out, they slow and distorted, like I was speaking underwater. It sounded funny even to my own ears.

"Your ... son's ... ?"

He nodded, and suddenly things sped up again. Time whooshed around me, and I knew it was moving too fast. I had to slow this down ... to stop it from coming ... but I couldn't.

"He used to go to White Plains High School," the man said. "He graduated almost three years ago."

Don't ask him, Abbey. Just don't ask him.

"What was his name?" I asked him.

"Caspian Vander. Why? Did you know him? Did you go there too?"

I couldn't stop myself.

"No. But I think I saw him around once or twice. Blondish hair, with a black streak in it ... and green eyes?"

The man laughed, but it was a sad laugh. "Yep, that's him all right." He shook his head and spoke softly, almost to himself, "That damn black streak . . ."

Don't do it, Abbey. Just don't do it.

My brain was absolutely freaking out now, spazzing with little tiny aftershocks of thought. I didn't want to do it, but I had to know.

I stuck out my hand, or rather stuck my hand up, since I was still sitting on the floor. "I'm Abigail Browning—Abbey."

He grasped my hand and shook it. "Bill."

"So, did Caspian leave this behind when he went off to college or something?"

"No."

Don't say it. Please don't say it.

"He died a little more than two years ago in a car accident. Right after Halloween."

Something exploded in the back of my head, and my ears actually rang from the force of it. I dropped the yearbook. "I have to g-go now," I stuttered, stumbling to my feet. "I'm sorry for your— My mom . . . I have to go." Blindly, I turned and felt my way back to the waiting room, holding on to the wall for support.

493

"Are you okay?" he called out after me. But I ignored him. The edges of my vision were blurry, and tiny white spots danced behind my eyelids when I closed them, but I held on to the wall and desperately tried not to cry.

Mom was standing over by the coffeemaker, doing something with the lid when I entered. "Oh good, you're back," she said. "They just let me know that it will only be another twenty minutes or so."

I sat down numbly on the plastic chairs and pulled my knees up to my chest. I didn't say anything out loud . . . but my mind was screaming.

When they finally came to get Mom twenty-five minutes later, and she had paid the bill, I settled into the passenger seat of the car and stared out the window. Mom started it up and turned the radio on low before heading in the direction of home.

"Let's not say anything about this to your father just yet. Okay, Abbey? I want to tell him about it myself, when he's in a good mood."

I shrugged, still facing the window, and kept silent. That was fine by me. Dad and the new tires were the farthest things from my mind right now, considering the mechanic just told me that my boyfriend was dead.

The rain started pounding again right as we pulled into the driveway, and Mom made a mad dash for the front door. I stayed where I was. The rain was falling hard and fast, and I watched the big drops splatter and then roll across the windshield.

I tried to collect my thoughts, but failed. It felt like all the wires in my head had been fried, like a fuse had gone haywire. But I knew there was one thing I could do that would make it all better. Climbing from the car, I walked slowly to the house, heedless of the rain. I didn't step inside, but only opened the door far enough to catch Mom's attention. She was pulling something out of the freezer that looked like a bag of frozen meatballs.

"I have to go do something, Mom," I said. My tone of voice was normal, which kind of surprised me. "I don't know how long it's going to take, but it's important."

She looked up from the bag in her hand. Something in my tone, or face, must have let her know how serious it was, because she didn't say anything. She just looked outside at the falling rain. "You'll get sick if you stay outside too long. Try to hurry."

I nodded and turned away, but she called my name. I glanced

back. "I hope one day you can tell me what's going on, Abbey. I'm worried, *really* worried for you."

Tears filled my eyes and I looked at her, trying to show her what I couldn't say at the moment. She took a step toward me, her eyes wide, but I turned away and let the door slam shut behind me. Mom couldn't help me right now. Only one person could.

The rain pounded down, and I lifted my head to let it wash over me. I didn't care if I was soaking wet. My jacket would cover my body, but as far as my face and hair ... I just didn't care.

I kept my pace slow and steady, with my chosen destination in mind. I tried to work everything out in my head, but I still couldn't think clearly. It was like trying to read a book written with numbers instead of letters. I couldn't make sense out of anything.

In time I came to that large iron fence marking the entryway, and I took the familiar path, running now as I went farther and farther along. Every pounding footstep echoed the sound of my heart against my chest, a pattern that went round and round inside my head. *Please be here, please be here,* it chanted.

I didn't stop running when Irving's plot came into view, but kept right on going toward the river. My feet slid on the wet muddy trail, but I kept pushing forward. I *had* to find him. I had to know *now.*

Before I even realized it, my mouth started sounding out the words echoing inside my brain. "Please be here. Please be here," I panted, trying to pace myself. Rounding the downward slope that led to the Old Dutch Church and Crane River, I stayed my course.

The river came into sight. I slowed to a walk when I finally reached its rocky bank. Skidding my way down it, I looked the entire area over. But he wasn't there. I threw my head back and howled out my frustration to the wind. *Where am I going to find him?*

Something quiet inside caught hold and told me to shut up and pay attention. I pushed heavy hunks of wet hair away from my eyes and immediately calmed my breathing. Then I stood very still. After exhaling once, I breathed in deeply and turned to look toward the bridge again.

A dark figure was leaning up against the concrete pillar, almost blending in completely. I knew without a doubt that my search was over. I took off running, and came to a halt under the safety of the bridge. Only a foot away from him. He looked surprised to see me.

"Abbey, what—"

"Why haven't you kissed me again?" I interrupted. "Since that day in the library? It was real, right? I didn't make it up, did I?"

He didn't say anything, and I took a step closer. Now I was only six inches away from him. "Is it because you don't want to?" Silence again. "Or because you *can't*?"

He took a step away, and I matched it, suddenly wanting the confrontation. "I talked to Nikolas and Katy. They had some interesting things to say. Like how they think they're really characters from 'The Legend of Sleepy Hollow.'" I gave an exaggerated laugh at the absurdity. "Nikolas thinks he's supposed to be the Headless Horseman, who fell in love with Katy—which is short for Katrina, as in Van Tassel—while he was a ghost. Pretty crazy stuff. How much did you know about it?"

I stared him down, waiting for a reaction.

"That would explain a couple of things about them," he said quietly. Then louder, "I didn't know any more than you. I swear, Abbey."

"What about you, then, Caspian?" I asked. "What's your last name? Your *real* last name?"

He looked at me, but didn't answer. I felt like stepping up to him and poking him while I enunciated every single word.

"My mom and I stopped at an auto body shop today," I began. "Met a man who's name was Bill. I also found a White Plains yearbook there from two and a half years ago. Funny thing, though, there's no one named Caspian *Crane* in there. Only a Caspian *Vander*."

His look told me everything, and I stumbled back, almost falling.

"It's true, then?" I whispered. "But how—why . . . ?"

He ran his hands through his hair. A gesture that I'd once found endearing was now heartbreaking. "I don't know why, Abbey. I don't even really know how. All I know is that I'm here, and you're here, and somehow . . ." He didn't finish.

"But your dad. He said you were . . . in a car crash—" I put one hand up to my mouth to stifle a sob, but it was a pointless act. No use trying to hold back a tidal wave with a single bag of sand.

He nodded, and pain filled his eyes.

"I don't believe you," I said fiercely. "Everyone in this whole entire town has gone crazy, and I'm the only sane person left. I don't know why that man said that today, but I don't believe him. And I don't believe *you!*" I pointed an accusing finger at him.

He held out one hand. "Abbey, I'm sorry. I didn't want you to find out this way. I had hoped that we could find a way to . . . I don't know. And then I thought it might be better if I tried to make you stay away from me, but that just . . ."

I tried not to look into his eyes. That was too overwhelming right now. "Is your last name Vander?" I asked him.

He nodded once.

"Then why did you tell me it was Crane?"

He looked out over the water next to us, rolling and swirling under the relentless onslaught of rain. "For some reason I was drawn to this river. One day, early last year, I saw you and Kristen here at the cemetery, and ever since then . . . It's become kind of my refuge, has brought me some sense of peace. So when you asked me my name, it just sort of came out that way."

I couldn't look at him. "And the rest? If that was your father . . . was that all true?" I addressed my questions to the river; I didn't want to see his face.

"I don't know," he whispered. "I've seen the newspaper articles, but I can't remember anything. It's all black. All I know is that I'm drawn to this place, and to you. You're so beautiful . . . Everywhere you go, I see these colors. You're the only one . . ."

I turned to face him now. "Maybe it's not really true, then," I said eagerly. "I mean, maybe you just had a concussion or something, and that's why you have the no memory part. Or maybe they got the ID wrong."

He shook his head. "Abbey, no."

"But you don't know!" I screamed at him. "You just don't know!"

He stepped closer, until he was right next to me. "Take my hand," he commanded softly.

I looked at him incredulously. "What?"

"Take my hand," he said again.

I sighed and reached out to touch him. But my fingers slipped right through. I backed up, out into the rain, horrified.

"What did you do?" I screeched, dancing perilously close to the edge of hysterics. "Why did you do that?"

"That's how it is, Abbey," he said. "That's just how it is."

Now I was shaking my head frantically, back and forth. It felt like I was on the verge of a nervous breakdown. Something was broken in my head; some sort of wire was messed up.

"What about that night in my room?" I demanded, trying to cling to some small thread of sanity. "You touched my face. And at the library I held your hand. And *kissed* you. And you kissed me back, damn it. So do whatever you did then now." I was sailing beyond hysterical breakdown, clear on through to pissed off and angry.

He walked closer to me, until he was just under the edge of the bridge. "I can't do it again, Abbey. That's why I've stayed away from you. It was only for a day. That day specifically."

I stepped back under the safety of the bridge. "Do it again," I said. "Let me see you do it again." I held out my hand, and he positioned his arm directly above it.

Then he swung down.

My eyes boggled and jumped out of my skull as I watched his entire arm pass through mine. Then he brought it up and did it again.

I only felt the barest wisp of a tingle each time he passed through me.

"Enough," I gasped, bending over to put my hands on my head. It was throbbing, and that same explosion of feeling was happening at the base of my neck again.

"Now do you see, Abbey?" Caspian asked. "Do you understand why I had to stay away?"

My head exploded, sending a temporary dark spot over my left eyeball. When it cleared, I stumbled to my feet and backed out into the rain again. Holding both arms out in front of me, I used them as a shield to ward him off.

Then the pain to my heart came.

It was a brutal searing pain, so strong that it made me drop to my knees and wretch. Heaving again, and again, I vomited until there wasn't anything left, my body shuddering and convulsing. When the worst of it had passed, I crawled to the edge of the river. Paying no attention to my clothes, or the brackish taste in my mouth, I dipped into that cool, rushing water and gargled.

Soft noises behind me told me that Caspian had followed me out, but he hung back. I gathered my heavy sodden hair into one hand and twisted it to the side before getting to my feet. I was completely soaked, but I didn't pay any attention to it.

"Just tell me one thing," I whispered through a sore throat as I turned to face him. Tears spilled out, and I struggled to regain my composure. "That night in my room, and the next day at the library . . . were you—were you going to tell me that you love me?"

He shook his head, but didn't answer. I waited. And looked deeply into his eyes.

"At least give me the dignity of an answer, Caspian," I cried when several minutes had passed. "You owe me that much."

He looked away, and then back at me again. When he spoke, each word was heavy and full of agony, as if they were being pulled from the very depths of his soul. "Of course I don't love

503

you, Abbey. I don't have a soul. I don't know what this feeling is, but it's not love. It *can't* be."

"But I . . . love you," I said brokenly.

And with that confession I turned my back to him and walked away.

EPILOGUE

I walked calmly, slowly toward Nikolas and Katrina's house with only one thought it mind. I must have hit my knee on a rock when I'd fallen in the rain, because each step was agony. Shooting pain radiated up from my kneecap, and I started to favor it, adopting a limping gait.

Every breath that I took along the way felt like sandpaper sawing away at my lungs, and I couldn't stop myself from crying. After a while there simply weren't any more tears left, and my body just sort of shuddered every now and then. But still I limped on.

When their door finally came into view and I had made my way up to it, I banged for all I was worth. I didn't stop, but just kept on banging. Nikolas was the one to answer.

"Just tell me one thing," I said hoarsely while he stood in front of me. "Just one thing. How did you know about Caspian if he didn't know about you?"

Nikolas opened his mouth to speak, but Katrina stepped up next to him and put her hand on his arm.

"We saw the black streak in his hair, dear. It marks him as one of us—a Shade."

I put up my hands to cover my ears. I didn't want to hear their words. "So, what?" I cried. "He's a ghost, you're a ghost. . . . Is Kristen a ghost too? Is she hiding somewhere around here? Where is she? Tell me! I need to see her again."

Nikolas reached out for me, but I took a step back.

"I am very sorry to add to your pain, Abbey," he said, "but Kristen is not one of us. She truly is dead. I saw her, but I could not help her."

His words didn't make any sense, but I shook my head and turned away to go back to the path once more. I couldn't stay and ask them to explain it all. Nothing made sense anymore.

Inspiration hit while I was limping my way out of the forest, and I pulled out my cell phone to check the time. It was 5:11. I could still make it.

Forcing my weak knee to bear my weight, I picked up my pace to a slow jog. Eighteen minutes later, I found myself panting for breath on the library steps. After checking the time on my phone once again, I opened the door and headed straight for the front desk.

"I need to look up some White Plains newspapers. From two and a half years ago, right after Halloween." I blurted out.

Mrs. Walker was on duty, and she looked at me with concerned eyes. "Abbey, are you okay? Do you need to use the first aid kit or anything?"

I glanced down at myself. I was a total mess. "Oh, no, Mrs. Walker. I'm okay." The lie rolled off my tongue easily. "I just remembered a last-minute school project, so I ran to get here in time before you closed. I tripped on the way, and then it started to rain, and . . . Well, I just really need to see those newspapers."

She reluctantly agreed and led me to a smaller computer room in the back of the library.

"Every newspaper article from the surrounding five counties is archived online here," she told me before leaving. "Just put in your search perimeters and hit enter. And if you need anything, *anything at all*, you let me know."

She gave me a stern glare, and I nodded meekly. Once I heard

507

the door shut behind her, I took a seat and typed in "White Plains Ledger November 1 to November 3."

I found what I was looking for in the November 2 issue, on page C-17.

> **Evening Edition**
>
> **A local Sleepy Hollow boy was pronounced dead on the scene earlier today, in a fatal car crash. Caspian Vander, a recent graduate of White Plains High School . . .**

A loud buzzing sound filled my ears, and I stopped reading. In the November 3 edition, they had his obituary with a fuzzy black-and-white picture of him. I recognized the black streak right away. . . .

I was still staring at the screen an hour later when Mrs. Walker found me rocking myself back and forth. She called my parents and stayed with me, talking softly, until Dad came to pick me up. He didn't ask me what was wrong, or why I was acting like a complete nut job, but carefully helped me down the stairs and into the car.

Right before we made the final turn toward home, he paused at a stop sign for an extra minute and waited.

He didn't have to say anything. I knew what he wanted.

"I need help, Dad," I whispered, turning to him. "I can't deal with—" My voice broke. "I think I just need some help right now."

He nodded once and put an arm around my shoulder. "I'll take care of it."

I withdrew, curling myself up into a tiny ball huddled in the far corner of the seat, and rocked back and forth slightly until we arrived home. Dad helped me inside the house, and Mom led me straight up to my room. She tucked me into bed like she used to when I was younger, and I fell asleep quickly. It was a blissful relief to escape from the real world, even if it was only for a little while.

In my dream, the rain was falling all around me, but I stayed under the protection of a tall tree. As soon as each drop hit, tiny blue flowers immediately sprang up, and the ground was awash in a profusion of blossoms.

Kristen came gliding up the path, and the flowers parted for her, guiding the way. She was wearing a red cloak with a hood that

hid her face. When she knelt in front of the tombstone and laid her fingers upon it, the raindrops froze, turning to hard pellets of ice that struck with a harsh pinging sound.

The flowers withered, and browned, dying in front of my very eyes.

I wanted to say something to her, yet I didn't know what. I tried to take a step out from under that tree, but I couldn't. My feet were rooted to the ground.

It was only then that I could see the letters spelling out her name as she traced each one. Over and over again she followed those etched words on that stone. Over and over again I tried to speak.

But I was mute.

Suddenly . . . the ice stopped. The flowers bloomed again. And Kristen turned to me.

"Don't worry, Abbey," she said. "I'll still be here when you get back. I'll always be here."

Special arrangements were made over the next week for me to leave school early, and all of the teachers agreed to give me my assignments for the rest of the school year to take with me. It had been decided that I would go stay with Aunt Marjorie and spend some time away from Sleepy Hollow due to "health reasons."

I think Dad was relieved I'd finally asked him for help, and he went out of his way to make sure that I would be seeing the best psychiatrist in the tristate region. All it required on my part was a session twice a week for the next four months, and I'd be back in time for summer vacation with no one the wiser.

That part relieved Mom.

As far as I was concerned, I was willing to do whatever it took to fix what had gone wrong inside my brain. I didn't care if that involved a psychiatrist, a psychic healer, or a voodoo priestess. All I wanted was to be sane again.

When the morning that I was scheduled to leave home came, I found myself in a daze. I walked out to the car stiffly, and climbed in. Everything around me felt surreal, like I was disconnected.

I asked Dad to stop at the cemetery before we left town, and he agreed, keeping watch from the car when we got there. Pausing for a moment at the entrance gates, I let my hand rest on the cold metal and turned back. "I'll be right back. Thanks for waiting, Dad." He nodded once, and I turned toward my destination.

I walked solemnly most of the way there, but my determination gave in when I reached the stone steps, and I flung myself up them. After pushing through the gate, I dropped to my knees in front of Washington Irving's marker.

"I'm leaving." It was blunt, and to the point. The only way I knew how to get all the words out. "Things are just . . . too much for me to handle right now, and I have to leave for a while."

Reaching out a hand to touch the carved dates, I forced myself to go on. "I'll come back. It's not forever. But I need some time to get myself fixed." I laughed quietly. "You wouldn't believe the head trip I've been on the last couple of weeks."

I stood up. "You know," I said thoughtfully, "you're the one person in my life who's the most real to me . . . and you're dead. That's funny."

I left the graveyard behind me. I got back into the car, and Dad pulled away from Sleepy Hollow. I guess I *should* have been thinking about all I was leaving behind. Or the fact that I was possibly in the middle of a nervous breakdown. And how I was going to see a professional because my problems were so huge that I couldn't sort them out myself.

Yet all I could think of was that red hair-dyeing incident with Kristen. . . .

It was funny.

ACKNOWLEDGMENTS

First and foremost, special thanks goes to Washington Irving. Without "The Legend of Sleepy Hollow," this book wouldn't be here today. Thank you for your words.

To Rachel Vater, and everyone at Folio Lit: Thank you for all of your hard work.

To Michael Bourret: Thanks for being the adopted parent on this project. You have made such a difference.

To Anica Rissi, editor extraordinaire: Your enthusiasm, dedication, support, and sheer awesomeness make this journey fun. Thanks for "getting" my book, and for doing such an amazing editing job on it. (And thanks for all the smiley faces, too!)

To Bethany, Mara, Jen, the Pulse editorial team, marketing team, publicity team, sales team, design team, and production team: Thank you for all your support. You have made me feel so very welcome.

To L.J. Smith: Thank you for writing the Forbidden Game trilogy. I hope my words inspire someone the same way yours have inspired me.

To Leah "GG" Clifford and Scott "Lege" Tracey: Thanks for

sharing my good news, calming my Panic Face, and helping to keep me sane through the process. Can't wait for the BToA.

To Lee and Lucy Miller: Thank you for all of your love and support. You stepped in when my parents bowed out, and you accepted me unconditionally. I'll never be able to tell you how much that means to me.

To my high school English teacher, Mrs. Vincenty: You once told me to consider becoming a writer (I still have the short story you wrote those words on!), and I took your advice. Thank you for your encouragement.

Thanks also go to Patrick and the QT gang, Bill at the Sleepy Hollow Cemetery (thank you for the tour!), and to the many artists, musicians, actors, and authors who have inspired me with your words, music, pictures, and scenes. They say that it takes a village to raise a child, and I believe that writing a book is the same way. Thank you for inspiring the pictures in my head.

Last, but certainly not least, to Erin and Keith: I hope one day you get to hear my side of the story. I love you guys.

About the Author

Jessica Verday wrote the first draft of *The Hollow* by hand, using thirteen spiral-bound notebooks and fifteen black pens. She likes: things that smell nice, rainy nights, old books, cemeteries, Johnny Cash, zombie movies, L.J. Smith books, abandoned buildings, trains, and snow. She is currently hand-writing her second novel, the continuation of Abbey and Caspian's story, from her home in Goodlettsville, Tennessee. Find out more at jessicaverday.com.

Don't miss this special sneak peek at the
dramatic conclusion to

L.J. SMITH'S

bestselling Night World series:

STRANGE FATE

Vampires, werewolves, witches, shapeshifters—they live among us without our knowledge. Night World is their secret society, a secret society with very strict rules. But the apocalypse is drawing near. And the Night World and the human world are about to collide in a cataclysmic way. . . .

*W*ings—
"Easy. Easy, Sarah. You're coming out of it."

Sarah opened her eyes and blinked, images from her dream mixing with the images of an attractive green bedroom.

A gray sky fading into a bleak horizon.

A lamp throwing dim light over an old-fashioned maple desk.

A mound of stinking rubbish in a faraway place.

An open window and curtains billowing in the midmorning Virginia air.

A boy's soft voice was talking to her, pulling her away from the sight and smell of the boneyard, helping Sarah fight off the dream. Sarah felt dizzy and nauseated, and she was prickling all over with sweat.

"Easy, Sarah. It's just one of your migraines," Mal Harman's quiet voice was saying from beside her. "Wake up, come on. Wake up now, Sarah. Wake up."

Who's Sarah? I'm Crispy. . . .

Mal didn't try to touch her. Sarah was normally a gentle person, the sort who would nudge a spider out the door with a broom rather than kill it. But if disturbed in the aftermath of a migraine, Sarah became a slim vortex of violence that attacked everything in range. Once, she had broken her best friend Kierlan's nose when he had gently tried to shake her awake.

But with Mal's cool, calm, almost indifferent voice gentling her as if she were a frightened animal, Sarah gradually awoke. Her stiff fingers slowly unclenched, and her cowering body relaxed muscle by muscle. Sarah began to register the serene room around her.

Then she knew who she was: Sarah, not Crispy. She knew there was nothing to panic about, and there were no such things as werewolves. It was just the stupid blood vessels constricting in her stupid brain, just as they had been all week. . . .

"You've been having migraines more often," Mal said, still softly, as if he could tell exactly what she had been thinking. He pulled Sarah's desk chair alongside her bed and straddled it. "This morning's makes it every day for the past two weeks."

And he doesn't know about all of them, Sarah thought. But what she said was, "They're not always as bad as this morning's." Her voice was shaky. She put a hand up as if to brush back her hair and wiped her eyes furtively. Then she sat up and straightened her rumpled, sweaty school clothes. They were clammy and clung to her unpleasantly. She felt as grimy as Crispy had been in her dream.

She was Sarah Strange, but the only strange thing about her was her migraines. Sarah often wondered what people would say if they knew about the dreams she had. About the other world she saw, and about how time there seemed to keep pace with time in her real life. A year ago Crispy had been seven and a half. Now she was eight and a half.

Sarah shuddered. Her visions had begun the day her mother died.

"Thank you," Sarah said to Mal, at last. "Thank you for—finding me. But"—she put a shaky hand to her forehead, feeling a sudden chill—"but *how* did you find me?"

"My class got out early," Mal said easily. "And I was in that hall when somebody said you'd just stumbled into the girls' restroom. I figured that 'stumbled' meant you were having a migraine. And I was right."

There. It all had a simple, logical explanation. Things that seemed strange about Mal, like his impeccable timing, always did. "It didn't bother you to go into the girls' bathroom?" Sarah asked him.

"Should it have?" Mal said urbanely. "It's not like the guys' toilet where everything is, um, all hanging out."

Sarah had to smile, but she fought the urge to laugh because her head still ached dully. Usually Mal left lines like that for Kierlan.

"Well, anyway, thank you for—for bringing me home and for talking to me," she said.

Sarah didn't know why she couldn't bring herself to say "for comforting me." Mal *had* comforted her. They both knew it. But somehow Sarah knew acknowledging it would cross an invisible boundary that existed between them.

Though Sarah felt vulnerable, she made herself look at Mal. It wasn't really such an ordeal, since he was probably the best-looking senior at E. B. Turner High. Mal had dark, carelessly disheveled hair that fell into gray eyes—a pale, clear, jewel-like gray that almost wasn't a color at all. Eyes that were shadowed by more lashes than any boy should be allowed to have.

Sarah knew his face well. Mal had very high cheekbones, an angular chin, and an intriguing mouth. It was outright sensual. A mouth made for kissing. But the rest of Mal's cool face made *that* seem like an impossible dream. Most of the girls at Turner had made it their goal to kiss that mouth. But none of them had.

At the thought of kissing Mal, the blood rushed to Sarah's face. These days whenever she looked at him, her face seemed to flush and her heart seemed to beat faster. Mal had always been there for Sarah, ever since they'd met when she was twelve. Even if she was only a junior and *knew* she wasn't beautiful enough to merit the interest of a senior whom all the girls at school wanted, Mal seemed to like being around her. She couldn't explain it, but there it was.

Desperate to redirect the conversation, Sarah asked, "Was he—Alan—still here?" Even after two and a half years, Sarah wouldn't call her stepfather Dad. She just *wouldn't*.

Mal shrugged, his gaze focused on the pattern of her bed-skirt and not on her. "He was going out as I carried you in."

"Didn't he ask you a million questions?" Alan was always taking Sarah to new doctors who were fascinated by her migraines but never had any answers.

"I didn't seem to have any trouble with him," Mal said briefly. "I guess he had to run."

"Amazing," was all Sarah could manage. "Usually he tele-commutes." Maybe Mal's icy air was too much even for Alan.

Sarah also had two stepbrothers and a stepsister, all strong and healthy and good-looking in an athletic, freckled way. All three of them teased her, and Sarah usually thought of a stinging reply or some clever remark far too late. Stepfather Alan was too busy to interfere and, as a result, Mal and Kierlan weren't particularly fond of him. Kierlan had dubbed them all "Alan and the Alanettes."

"Well," Sarah said again finally, "thank you—for everything. And for staying with me."

"I couldn't just leave you all alone," he said. "Not with the nightmare you were having."

Dread surged through Sarah. "Did I say anything? Like, talk in my sleep?"

"No, but you seemed really upset."

Sarah thought of the wings in her dream. "Yes," she replied. "It was a bad one."

At last Mal nodded, but didn't look up. Mal knew she had dreams during the migraines, and anybody else would have pressed her to talk about this one, but Mal didn't.

That was another thing about Mal. He allowed you your privacy, but expected you to respect his privacy in return. And that was difficult when there were so many secrets.

Mal lived alone, and Sarah had never heard him mention any relatives. Nobody knew where his money came from, and nobody dared ask. He only hung out with her and Kierlan Drache—and sometimes, with his chilly attitude, Mal made even that seem like a royal favor. He certainly wasn't Sarah's boyfriend, and Mal'd never said or done anything that would make her feel he wanted to be.

But they'd used to be more, well, comfortable together. A few years ago she and Mal could lie together side by side in the park and just look up at the sky. The silence had never seemed oppressive. It had felt okay—more than okay—just being together. Sarah missed how his tall and lean athletic body felt near hers.

What had happened to change that?

The only thing Sarah could think of was that she'd grown up. She'd finally gotten a figure, even if it wasn't much of one. But she wasn't breakable—which was how Mal treated her these days; touching her only when he had to and then with great care and dispassion. Like today, holding out his arms for her to collapse into instead of just sweeping her up into them.

It wasn't as if he didn't like her or was frigid toward her, but as if Sarah had turned into some kind of unknown creature from the depths of the ocean that might disintegrate if handled out of its environment.

Now he would hardly even meet her eyes.

And yet Mal always seemed to appear just when Sarah was most distressed. Like when she had *needed* someone to save her as her migraine hit—there he was.

Mal was a mystery.

Even as she thought the words, Sarah realized that she had been staring at Mal. Just as she was going to turn away from him, embarrassed, Mal looked up and their gazes *tangled*. Mal's eyes, those eyes that looked like windows into another world, seemed to get caught up with hers. His gaze was not cold or sarcastic, but serious and earnest. His look seemed to suggest that inside him, somewhere, there was warmth and affection just waiting for someone to let them out.

"Are you sure you're feeling—?" Mal began, but couldn't seem to complete the question.

Those eyes were looking straight into Sarah's. Sarah realized that she couldn't look away. It was like being hypnotized—such a pleasurable way of being hypnotized. Of being drawn in. No, of rushing in, as fast as if she were flying. Flying toward something at the center of herself, and of Mal, and of both of them. Overcome by wonder, Sarah could feel the rhythm of her own heart in her ears and the rhythm of another heart: deeper, slower, with beats timed differently from her own. But then the two rhythms began to merge. Sarah felt an unbearable wave of tension as the beats came faster, closer together. Soon they would both beat at once. And then . . . And *then* . . .

Mal was leaning slightly closer to her now, not as if he wanted to, but as if he were being drawn to Sarah. Mal's gray eyes were misty and half shut, as if in protest.

"No," he said, and suddenly his whole face was dismayed—dismayed and alarmed. "I didn't mean *that*."

"What?" Sarah asked over the thundering in her chest. She hardly knew what she was saying. All she knew was that she didn't want this feeling to stop, and she didn't want Mal to want it to stop either.

Sarah's eyes filled with tears.

She didn't need to worry. By now the rhythms were too strong for him, and somehow Sarah sensed this as acutely as she sensed her own feelings.

"No—*wait*—," Mal said, holding out a hand as if to ward off Sarah. As if he was *afraid* of her. That was ridiculous. Mal was so strong and Sarah was so fragile. He could break her in half like a twig. But he *was* afraid. Sarah could feel his fear. She caught at Mal's hand to reassure him.

That was when terror exploded in Mal and the world exploded for Sarah.

Just the touch of their bare hands was enough. They were rushing together, and all Sarah could hear was the pounding of their pulses, beating almost exactly in time. Sarah's whole body was *buzzing*.

Sarah was weightless, tingling from her toes to the fine hairs on the back of her neck. The humming feeling engulfed her. It was the most amazing sensation she had ever known.

And Mal was feeling it too, or feeling something like it. Sarah could sense his feelings; she knew them as certainly as she knew her own. They were careering now, unstoppable, toward that final heartbeat that would join them, open their innermost selves to each other, answer all Sarah's frustrated questions about Mal.

Their defenses were draining away, as if the lightest touch would make them open like a flower, the petals falling, the center completely exposed.

I should be afraid, Sarah thought. But she wasn't afraid. Mal was her friend, her *trusted* friend, and she was on the verge of knowing him better than anyone else in the world.

She wasn't worthy of him, but she desperately wanted him to know her, Sarah. In that instant, she knew why she blushed when he looked at her. She felt as if she would *blossom* for him, if he wanted. She *was* blossoming for him. She was willing to let him know anything—everything. . . .

That was when she saw it.

Stretching between the two of them, Sarah could see the

dim, silvery outline of what looked like a thread or cord. It connected them, beating heart to beating heart. And Sarah knew, somehow, that it was because of the cord that they would reveal themselves completely to each other.

And she wanted it. She wanted it more than she could remember wanting anything before.

"No!" Mal threw himself backward, almost falling off the chair. Mal wrenched his hand away from hers. He looked as if he had warded off some kind of assault.

From *her*. From Sarah.

Sarah took in great gulps of air, breathing as if she'd been drowning. She was shaking, and her face—her whole body—flamed with a blush of humiliation.

"You—you—," she almost sobbed.

"I—what? I didn't do anything. I didn't do *anything*."

In her normal state Sarah would have heard the difference in Mal's voice, which was no longer chilly or impassive, but rather desperate for reassurance. But Sarah wasn't in any normal state.

"And I did?" she demanded. "Are you saying that this was somehow my fault?"

"It was . . . no." Mal had regained his balance and some of his self-possession. "You didn't do anything deliberate. It was just—an accident."

That rushing, flying adventure? An accident? To Sarah's astonishment Mal sounded as if he were on the verge of tears too. Normally, the more angry or exasperated Mal got, the softer his voice became, and the more expressionless his face. Kierlan liked to tease Mal when he got like that. But when Mal said "accident," his voice cracked with emotion.

Kierlan, jester that he was, wouldn't find this—whatever had just happened between her and Mal—funny in the least. Sarah somehow knew she would never tell Kierlan about it, and she knew Mal wouldn't either.

Sarah had never imagined Mal could look so vulnerable. "Mal?" she said, and her voice sounded strange in her own ears. "What was that? What happened to us?"

"Yes," a voice from the doorway said, causing Sarah to turn to see the figure leaning against the doorway. "What happened to you? Am I interrupting something?"

Mal didn't speak, and somehow Sarah knew he wasn't going to. It was up to her.

"Oh . . . Kierlan."

Look for STRANGE FATE, coming soon. . . .